# THE
# SPARROWS
## OF
# MONTENEGRO

## Also by BJ Mayo

*Alfie Carter*

# THE
# SPARROWS
## OF
# MONTENEGRO

## A NOVEL

# BJ MAYO

Skyhorse Publishing

Skyhorse Publishing books may be purchased in bulk at special discounts for sales promotion, corporate gifts, fund-raising, or educational purposes. Special editions can also be created to specifications. For details, contact the Special Sales Department, Skyhorse Publishing, 307 West 36th Street, 11th Floor, New York, NY 10018 or info@skyhorsepublishing.com.

Skyhorse® and Skyhorse Publishing® are registered trademarks of Skyhorse Publishing, Inc.®, a Delaware corporation.

Visit our website at www.skyhorsepublishing.com.

10 9 8 7 6 5 4 3 2 1

Library of Congress Cataloging-in-Publication Data is available on file.

Cover design by David Ter-Avanesyan
Cover painting by Tawanna Thames

Print ISBN: 978-1-5107-7066-9
Ebook ISBN: 978-1-5107-7073-7

Printed in the United States of America

*"En las malas se conocen a los amigos."*

# Part 1

PART

# CHAPTER 1

**Village of Montenegro: Northern Mexico, circa 1865**

THE BINOCULARS CAME INTO PRIETO'S possession when he and his friend, Pablo, were both but fifteen years old.

Prieto Guillermo came across them while riding his burro along the Mexican side of the Rio Grande. It was his daily journey for firewood with his leather bags draped across the back of his burro. The village leather-maker, Señor Trujillo, made them sturdy and sized for Chico's small back. The cowhide leather tote bags were double-stitched with rawhide. Mr. Trujillo's unique lacing pattern was handed down from his father. The weave was so tightly sewn, it was known to hold water. Prieto always rode Chico down to the river and then led him back to the village with a small load of wood and sticks for his madre. Prieto noticed the bright reflection from some distance as he guided his stunted burro along the river trail. It was highly possible that the shiny object was tied to a human being. The Rio Grande was a constant lure for northern gringo outlaws and others who were on the run from the law. Once across the shallow depths of the river, immunity from being pursued and caught was informally granted to those who could survive on the southern side. Generally, they laid low until their provisions began to run out. Only then did they venture into the sparse sprinkling of small towns and villages scattered up and down the river. The villagers never asked questions of their guests, and they rarely gave out information on how or why they came. Prieto had seen several of these types come into their village from time to time. He did not like the way they looked around with their roving eyes while sitting on their horses. It did not go without notice that they all seemed to have a holstered gun on their side or a rifle in a saddle scabbard. Some of their riggings appeared to be stolen and were of better quality than their clothing. They were always given water and something to eat but were never welcomed to stay. He noticed they never seemed to look people in the eye when they were talking and paid particular notice to any and all of the females that walked by. The guns in his village, or at least the ones he ever saw, were few and far between. He often wondered what would happen if one of these men ever pulled his gun out in the village.

Mexican bandits running from the Federales would generally stay fairly close to the border once they crossed the river to the Texas side. One of their biggest fears was being seen by some ranch cowboy riding fence line close to the river. Their clothing and even their saddles drew immediate attention from a fence rider on the Texas side of the river.

Prieto slipped off his burro and walked slowly toward the object in the distance, shining as the sun's rays bore down. He pulled his hat down further to dampen the sun. The much-worn old hat was given to him by his father, Emilio Guillermo. His father had finally earned a little extra money to purchase a new one from his seasonal work. Mr. Guillermo helped an old farmer from time to time across the river. His father's days were long and full of toil under the relentless sun and low wages. Mr. Deets farmed about forty acres of decent bottomland about a mile north of the river. He was too old and broken down to walk all day behind two mules pulling an old plow. He paid Mr. Guillermo twenty cents a day to work from sunup to sundown. That wage also included unhitching the team at the end of each workday, wiping them down, watering them, and putting out their feed for the day. He always made quite a presentation of giving Mr. Guillermo his twenty cents before he left to walk back home in the dark.

"Now, where did I put my money bag?" he would always say while reaching into his pocket. "I know that you like to get your cash money every day when you are done working. Well, I ain't never got no problem with that as long as you turn in a good day's work for me. How far did you get today with them mules?"

"I get about this many rows, señor," holding up all ten fingers.

"Why can't you just learn to speak English and count in English? How many rows did you get yesterday?"

"I get the same yesterday, señor. The ground is very hard. I do not want to hurt your mules. I try not to use all they have so they can work again tomorrow after they rest."

Then Mr. Deets would hand Mr. Guillermo his twenty cents. "Well, I suppose you earned your money today. Don't get snakebit going to your house in the dark or drowned in that river. I ain't got nobody else that will help me out here on this damn place in this wretched, forsaken land. Them planting rows don't get plowed by their self, and my corn and hay don't get planted by itself neither. Hay and corn, that is all I got to feed these mules so they will work. Without my hay and corn, I can't keep my four cows and bull a-going. If I don't make no corn and hay, there ain't going to be no calves to sell in Rosario come spring. You just keep on a-coming over here until I tell you different, Mr. Guillermo. As long as you keep on working hard and it rains, I will keep a-paying you your twenty cents. And when that sun starts to come up there in the east tomorrow, I want them mules already hitched."

"Sí, señor, I will be here."

Now, it had been one full year since Mr. Guillermo's death. Prieto thought about him every day, especially on his firewood runs to the river.

"If I do not come to our house from working the Señor Deet's land, send Santiago across the river to find me," his papa would always say. "Maybe I get bit by the dark snakes that swim in the river, or maybe the chupacabra come flying down and catch me and take me to its nest, yes?"

Then he would hug Prieto and laugh. "I am getting older, but I am much too fast for the chupacabra to ever catch me."

ONE DAY, MR. GUILLERMO DID not come home as the sun was going down. Prieto became very fearful as he stood looking from an outcrop, waiting to see when his father crossed the river. He always watched him come across and then would run to tell his madre so she could prepare him hot food. By the time he told his madre and Santiago was notified, it was dark. Santiago wrapped a long piece of cowhide stripping to a mesquite limb and rubbed it good with bear fat from a jar on Adelina's shelf. Prieto watched him light the cowhide on fire as he mounted and headed toward the river. When he did return, the moon was full. Prieto was pacing on the outcrop looking down toward the river when he saw the lighted torch moving along the river. Prieto's heart began to race as he watched Santiago approach. He could see the shape of a man draped across his saddle. Somehow, he knew it was his father.

Tears began to fill his eyes as Santiago approached slowly on his horse. Prieto turned and ran toward his house. Bursting through the old wooden door, he ran to his madre, sitting in her chair. "It is mi papa. I think maybe he is dead. Santiago has him on his horse," he blurted out in tears.

His madre wrapped him in her arms and cried tears into his hair as she held him. Slowly she walked to the door and held his hand, pulling him along. Santiago sat quietly on his horse as she opened the door. She could see Mr. Guillermo draped across the saddle. In the fading light of the torch, she could see drops of blood dripping from his head.

Santiago wiped tears away from his weathered face as he looked at Ms. Guillermo and young Prieto. "It was the steel plow. Maybe something make the mules afraid while he was checking the plow. Maybe it was the lion of the mountains. They pull the plow into him and run a long way. I find him a little while ago. I am sorry, and it makes me very sad."

PRIETO LOVED HIS FATHER'S OLD hat and liked to smell the hatband. He could still smell the pungent remnants of sweat from his papa. The holes allowed a little air to cool his head with his abundant head of black hair. He punched holes in both sides along the brim. Taking the longest strands of hair from his burro's tail and braiding them together, he laced them through the holes in the hat. He cut a small piece of hollow cane from the tall stands along the river. It was abundant in certain places along both sides of the river where it became flat and placid after dropping sharply down through the steep canyons with their enormously high rock walls. He tied ball knots on both ends of the braid and could slide the hollowed cane piece up and down to keep the hat snug on his head. He could also flip the hat onto his back before the sun got up or pull it down on his head and cinch it up tight when the wind whistled down through the canyons in the fall and winter.

Prieto paused and listened intently from about three hundred feet away from the object still glistening in the sun. Yet, except for the sound of his own heart beating and the steady breathing of his burro, he did not hear or see anything out of the ordinary. He always watched his Chico's ears. They were in constant motion, quick to pick up on the slightest sound. Sometimes, even a grasshopper or a yellow-headed lizard moving slowly would catch his attention. Never bucking or braying, he would simply focus his ears and eyes straight in toward the sound and stop. Prieto would sometimes quickly spot the movement and sometimes not. He would scratch his burro on the neck and purr to him.

"It is all right, Chico. It is only a bug. We can go now," he would say quietly.

With a gentle touch of both feet, the burro would begin to move forward.

The red-tailed hawk flying above did not betray any movement below. Slowly, Prieto began to move, leading his burro behind him. Quietly he purred to him in steady whirls of his tongue, calming the small animal whose kin were constantly on the lookout for predators, mostly the large mountain lions that traveled broad ranges in the area plus an occasional jaguar passing through.

When he was within one hundred feet of the object, he could easily make out the looking-glass binoculars. Maybe a soldier from the U.S. Cavalry had left them there. They had routinely patrolled the area in the past on the Texas side of the border. Prieto heard that some of them ventured to the Mexico side of the river in search of the Mexican blackbird whores in some of the villages south of Montenegro and maybe a little mezcal or corn beer.

Prieto slowly picked the binoculars up and looked through the big lenses first. The leather wrapping was sun weathered and cracked. Everything looked small and distorted as he peered through them. He turned them around and looked through the smaller lenses. Scanning the ridge above him, he could make out the seeds on top of the tall grasses on the cliff top. When he began to rotate the small wheel in the middle, the grasses became crisp and he could see things very clearly from long distance. He slipped the leather harness attached to them over his hat and onto his neck. Prieto could not believe his lucky find.

No one in the village had such a thing in their possession. Mostly just pretty rocks and Apache arrowheads they found. One was still attached to the arrow shaft and still firmly embedded between the shoulder blades of a sun-bleached skeleton on the banks of the river. The skull still had remnants of scraggly black hair. No one from the village had ever talked about moving the skeleton and rarely talked about it. Some in the village feared the person killed with the arrow was a fantasma, and anyone disturbing the remains would be haunted by his presence, especially during a full moon.

IT WAS IN THE VILLAGE of Montenegro by the old tree that Pablo de la Rosa, Prieto's friend, first saw the binoculars. He said nothing, only passingly glanced Prieto's way when he was showing them to the others who were sitting on the wooden benches in the evening. Pablo never said a word to anyone about the desire to own the binoculars. He simply knew he would take them by force if necessary, and no one in the village would challenge him. His fierce half-Mexican, half-Apache blood boiled in a moment with little to no encouragement. Even at fifteen, his equal hate for both the Mexicans and the Apaches was strong. Born of an Apache father and a Mexican mother, he was a half-breed and was openly despised and somewhat feared by the village elders. Taller and more muscular than all of the boys his age in the village, he showed no fear of anyone below him or above him in age. His high cheekbones and distinguished nose were not of the Mexican people.

The long-running warring and hostage taking between Mexico and the Apache rose up from time to time and had been going on for three hundred years.

Pablo's mother, along with six more women, were captured by the Apache while gathering firewood for the cooking in the village along the river. After two years in the Apache village, she was the only one who survived. As for the other five women, the constant beatings by the Apache women and mistreatment by the braves left them with no hope, self-respect, or will to live. Four opened their veins at the same time after taking a pact to end their misery. In their eyes, it was the only decision that was in their control.

While the village slept, the fifth slipped off into the night to the edge of the box canyon gorge a mile or so away. Crying and angry as she made her way along the steep trail upward, she swore at the world for being alive. She stood overlooking the deep gorge, fully lighted by the moon. She reflected long about her previous life and her husband.

*Why has he not come to my rescue? Perhaps he could not find his way*, she reasoned.

Now, after such a time that she had been held captive and the relentless nighttime visits by the spirited Apache braves, she felt even if she were to be set free and somehow found her way back to her home, her husband would turn his back on such a forever-tarnished woman. At dawn, she stepped off the steep cliff into the abyss below.

Pablo's madre was primarily left untouched by the village braves. She became the property of Two Wolves, the chief's son. Stronger and much taller than the rest, he took an early interest in her and took his pleasures with her whenever he desired. With a strong desire to stay alive at all costs, she kept her head down in an act of servitude when he came around. Never speaking, she only responded by moving when he motioned her to do so. She listened with disgust to his grunting and groaning on many daytime and nighttime visits. She always felt filthy and violated after he left. She wished secretly to cut off his man parts in his sleep if she had a knife and could summon the courage to do so. However, she stayed relatively free from harm other than a routine swat with a pleated rawhide quirt carried by most of the women in the village. She never understood their constant screeching but did get the basic intent with their finger-pointing and laughter. The toothless old women made her the angriest. Faces wrinkled and dark with serpent-like eyes, dark and venomous when it came to her. She did not ask or want to be here.

During two years of captivity, her escape plots never seemed to take root. When she began to show, Two Wolves noticed and would routinely pat her on the stomach and point to himself and spit out some Apache gibberish and smile. She was generally fed well as the time approached by orders of Two Wolves. Her appetite was ravenous, and she accepted anything that was brought to the cedar-covered wikiup. There were no attendants when it was her time to deliver. She pushed with all of her might through many hours of labor and tried not to make any type of sound that would draw unwanted attention from the women. The contractions were sometimes severe as the sweat poured. Two Wolves left her a skin bag of water hanging on the center pole, which she would occasionally drink from when the contractions receded. Her labor lasted most of the night. Her baby was born at sunup with a very slight breeze passing into the door and sides of the wikiup. It was comforting on her wet skin. Her breasts were full, and the baby readily began to suckle as she guided his mouth to her nipple. She cradled his body in her arms as he nursed. She knew that this child's life would not be that of a normal child in this village or in her village if she ever made it back. He would not be welcome at either one as a half-breed, especially being half-Apache and half-Mexican. The Apaches were sworn enemies of most if not all of the Mexican people on the border. Their fierce and relentless raids on the Mexican villages saw an untold number of hostages taken. Some were killed, but most were used by the Apaches to work.

She had no immediate attachment to him as her motherly instinct kicked in to feed him. If she left him there and escaped, they would probably kill him. The Mexicans would not kill him but might not fully accept him if they knew his origins. She had been gone long enough that her husband would know this child was not his. For now, she decided she would take care of the baby and try and make sure that he remained safe.

She knew she and her young son could only escape when most of the fighting-age braves were gone from the encampment for a period of time. There were always the ever-watchful eyes and ears of the village dogs and the handful of old men and young boys left with the village when the others left. She left quietly one day when all of the women and children left the village to gather firewood. She could hear the women laughing and some of the children singing as they walked. She listened carefully until she could hear no sounds in the village. They seemed to forget she was in the wikiup, or maybe they believed it would be better if she escaped and died on the trail with her baby. She grabbed a handful of dried venison and the water sack. Slipping out of the wikiup while the baby boy slept, she scoured two wikiups. Her double leather sandals were the ones she was captured in. They were well worn but still usable. She found the cedar cradle board in the second wikiup. She could secure her young son inside and then strap it to her back for better carrying than in her arms. She would have to climb in rocky, cactus-filled terrain. The water bag could be refilled along the river. Her health was relatively good after two years in the Apache village. She slowly opened the leather flap on Two Wolves's wikiup door and peered outside. There were no dogs, people, or horses to be seen. Even though it was mid-morning, it would be her only chance. If they caught her, they might kill her and the boy. If she made it out of the village, the terrain and elements might do the same thing. Thankfully, the baby slept as she eased out of the hut and disappeared. She knew that the group that captured her headed el oeste toward the setting sun for two days before arriving at this village. Her father had taught her how to tell directions at a very young age. Pointing her right arm toward the early morning sun, she knew that was el este, her left arm pointed straight out was el oeste, her nose would be pointing norte, and her back was toward the sur.

She headed due el este. If it took two days by horse, she figured it would take her four to five days by foot and carrying a child to get back in the vicinity of Montenegro. She thought she could tell the shape of the mountain from afar if she could ever see it. If she made it home with the child, the reaction of her husband and the village was far from certain.

# CHAPTER 2

PRIETO HEARD THE WHIR OF the rope much too late as it landed and pulled tightly over his arms. The braided cowhide rope, once thrown, pulled up tight on anything it landed on. He was yanked off his burro and pulled a few feet before he heard the unmistakable voice of Pablo de la Rosa.

"Como estas, Señor Prieto? I have been waiting for you for a while this morning. Maybe you have not been waiting for me, but I have been waiting for you."

Pablo threw the tail of the rope over a low-hanging juniper limb and slowly pulled him to his feet.

"Stand up, señor. Stand up. I want to see what you have there."

Prieto struggled to his feet and lunged at Pablo. Pablo began to laugh uncontrollably. *"Oh, so you want to make fight with me, yes? I want to make fight too. Let me take off this rope, señor, and see what happens when we make fight. I think you will not like what I do to you. Maybe you be mi puta, my little whore, no? Or maybe I just cut off your ears."*

Before he released the rope, he quickly picked up a handful of dirt and threw it into Prieto's eyes. Prieto began to flail about wildly as Pablo freed him from the rope. Pablo laughed heartily as Prieto swung wildly at the air.

"Señor, you look like you are swinging at a piñata."

Suddenly, Prieto felt a large blow to his head from behind. He fell instantly, and, barely conscious, felt the warm flow of blood oozing from his skull. Pablo leaned over him.

"You no like my fight, señor? I like my fight."

He pulled out his large hunting knife and pulled it across the hairs on his arm. "Oh, Señor Prieto, this knife, this knife, she is very sharp. I think she is very hungry for your ears."

He quickly sliced off each ear at the skull. Blood gushed as Prieto screamed in pain reaching up slowly to cover the holes.

"Now maybe, Señor Prieto, you remember your friend Pablo when you want to make fight, no? I take your looking glass, señor. I need them more than you do. Here, I leave your little ears with you on this rock. Maybe your madre can sew them back on again if you get to the village quick. Maybe they put a little mezcal on them and she sew them on with some horse tail. Oh . . . and, Prieto, I think this means we are no longer friends, yes? I was never really your friend. I think that maybe you no like me because I am half-Mexican and half-Apache. I never like you or that donkey you are riding. You are nearly as big as him, señor. If you ever come to make fight with me, I will not be so good next time."

Pablo grabbed Prieto by the hair and his head up to face him.

"Look at me, señor. I said, look at me, señor." Prieto, stunned and half-conscious, blinked his eyes toward Pablo.

"That is good, señor. Look at me to my eyes. The next time you try and make fight with me, I will cut off your head."

Turning Prieto's bleeding head toward the river, Pablo smiled.

"You see hombre, this river is just like me. It never stops. See how the water runs? It comes from a hole in the ground up in the mountains, yes? Nothing can stop it, señor, and nothing stops Pablo. Do not ever tell anyone in the village that it was me that cut off your ears, señor. I will be listening and I will know. Then, then it will not be good for you. First, I will kill your burro and hang his head at your door. Then, I kill your madre and then I kill you. If that stinking papa of yours was still alive, I would kill him too. You cried like a baby when he died. And why did he die early to his grave? He die early to his grave because he worked for that stupid man across the river for nothing. That is why he die early to his grave. He was a stupid man, your father. When they ask who cut off your ears, señor, you tell them it was a bandit. I never see this bandit you say. He . . . he was like the cat of the mountains that comes from behind. You tell them that it was Gato Montes, the cat of the mountain, that cut off your ears. You tell them you never see this Gato Montes because he hits from behind. Now, I want you to pick up your ears and get back on your donkey. Maybe he can carry you back to the village if he has no firewood in the bags today. Remember what I tell you. You must never tell anyone, señor. My knife will be hungry for you."

Pablo laughed as Prieto slowly managed to get on his feet. The flow of blood from his skull was starting to subside slowly, but he had lost quite a bit of blood. He located his ears and put them in his pocket as Pablo screeched with laugher. He laughed thinking about how Prieto's new ears would look when his madre sewed them back on. For now, he would have to beat Prieto back to the village and make sure that no one ever saw the binoculars and to hide them in a safe place. He left Prieto and his donkey all alone as he headed back up to the village.

A few of the children first saw Prieto as Chico carried him into the village. He was leaned over Chico's neck. There were bloodstains on both sides of the donkey's neck and on Prieto's face and clothes. The children ran to the old tree screaming.

"Prieto has lost his ears," one screamed. "He is bleeding badly. Go get his madre to come quickly. She must help him."

One of the village men ran up to the donkey.

"Oh, Señor Prieto. What have they done to you?"

He quickly grabbed him off the donkey and ran carrying him toward his mother's house. He could hear Prieto moaning and trying to speak as he ran.

"What is that you say, Prieto? Are you trying to say something?"

"My ears, they are in my wood bag. Don't lose my ears."

The man carrying Prieto got to his madre's door just as she opened it.

"What has happened to my Prieto? Has he been shot? There is so much blood on him."

"No, señora, he has no ears. Someone has cut off his ears. I don't know. He tells me his ears are in his wood bag. I will go back to get them."

"Quickly, get him inside quickly so we can stop the bleeding. You go back and find his ears. Maybe we can sew them back on, but we must hurry. Let me wrap his head and then lay him on the bed there."

"Mama, can you sew back on my ears?" Prieto moaned.

"Yes, we sew them back on. Who did this thing to you? Who would cut off your ears? Such a person should not be allowed to live. Who did this to you, Prieto?"

"I do not remember, Mama. I never see him."

"What do you mean, you never see him? Was he a fantasma? You have had to see something, Prieto. You must tell me."

"I do not know, maybe he was a bandit or something."

"Prieto, why would a bandit cut off your ears? Why would any man cut off your ears? Whoever did this is very evil. Did he say nothing at all?"

"He say, I am like the Cat of the Mountain or Gato Montes. Like the mountain lion that hits from behind. That is what he says."

"If your papa was still alive, he would go and kill him. May Dios rest his soul. He would hunt him down and kill him. I will do it myself if I have to. I swear I will. Right now, you must rest."

"My head, it is light. I do not think too well, Mama."

"There now, Prieto, you just rest. You have lost a little blood. That is all. The man is coming with your ears. I will stitch them back on where they will be as good as new, okay? I will clean the blood away from your eyes and face."

The man who had retrieved the ears knocked on her door. "Señora, I have his ears. Can I bring them in?"

"Yes, señor, you can bring them in."

"There are many people outside that want to see him. Do you want to let them in?"

"No, do not let them into my house. All they want to see is a young boy that got his ears cut off. He is my Prieto, and I will not have that. Just stay for a little while and help me get them cleaned, and I will sew them back on. My Prieto will be normal again. Please clean them with the mezcal there on the table."

The old man cleaned each ear with a cloth dipped in mezcal and laid them close to Prieto. Prieto slowly opened his eyes and turned to look at them. He immediately began to scream.

"Prieto, you must stay calm. Screaming is not going to help me sew your ears back on. I promise to make you look like you did before. I promise.

"Señor, please hand me one of his ears."

She carefully sutured them both on with horsehair and a saddle maker's needle. Prieto winced in pain as each stitch was pulled. It took her the better part of two hours to get both ears sewed back on.

"Well now, Prieto, look for yourself," she said as she handed him a small mirror. "Your ears look as good as new."

Prieto slowly took the mirror and brought it to his face.

"See Prieto, my angel, your ears. They look as good as new."

Prieto looked at each ear for a moment and could see the horsehair sutures tied in a little knot at the end of each stitch. "They do not look the same as before. Maybe the others will laugh at me."

"There will be a little scar, but it will not be bad to look at, Prieto. I will take out the stitches in a little while when your ears have grown back to your head. We must keep them clean and free from the infection every day. Do you understand? That means that you will stay in the house where it is clean. No going outside for a while."

After two weeks, the right ear appeared to be healing perfectly all the way around. The left ear developed an infection on the lower half after about two weeks as pus began to ooze out between the horsehair sutures.

Prieto cried when his madre told him that the bottom part of his left ear must be removed or the infection could spread to all of his ear and then to other parts of his body.

"Prieto, it is better that we cut the bad part away and not let it make the rest of your body bad. After all, it is just a little piece of flesh. You will never miss it. Just like Santiago, the keeper of the cattle. He takes a piece out of each of the calf ears on the left side when they are very little. That way we can tell that they belong to the village. Just like you."

Afterward, Pablo ridiculed him from time to time when he saw him outside and no one was around.

"Como estas uno y medio Prieto? How do you like your one and a half ears, amigo? Does it make your head heavier on one side? You like to make fight with me, señor? I do not think your madre can sew your head back on, señor. No, I do not." Pablo said quietly. He could hardly contain his laughter.

"Maybe when I cut off your head, she can sew it on backward and you can see me before the cat of the mountain ropes you again, yes? You make me laugh too much, señor."

# CHAPTER 3

## 4th Cavalry Regiment, Fort Concho (Texas) circa 1872
## 190 miles north of Montenegro, Mexico

Captain Vassar Golden eyed the five newly sworn-in recruits with a weary look. "Step forward when I call your name and stand before my desk. Pig Green?"

"Yes sir. I am Pig Green." The young man was squat in stature with very broad shoulders. His blond hair hung uncombed over his eyes beneath his large-brimmed hat. His boots came up to his knees. His trousers sagged outward at the waist, supported only by two strands of rope for suspenders.

"How did you get a name like Pig? Your hair certainly looks like a pigsty. I reckon it fits your name."

"My mama and daddy just took to calling me Pig since I was a youngin."

"Maybe properly so. Why did you sign up for service in the U.S. Cavalry?"

"Jobs been scarce back home in Tennessee since the end of the war, sir. I just been taking anything I can get to make a living."

"So, you rode all the way from Tennessee to get to this outpost in the middle of nowhere? Do you have any idea what you have signed up for, Mr. Pig?"

"Not really, sir. But I can ride a horse really good and use a rope. I can shoot a squirrel out of a tree from right smart a distance."

"Well, Mr. Pig. That kind of shooting might come in handy someday in our outfit. Might need a squirrel shooter some time to feed the group."

Captain Golden called the other four young men up to his desk.

"Raise your hand when I call out your name. Lester Archibald?"

"Here, sir."

"Tree Smith?"

"Yes, sir."

"Cedar Jones?"

"Yes, sir."

"Benjamin C. Harris?"

"Here, sir."

"What does the C in your name stand for, Benjamin?"

The young man looked nervously at the floor.

"I asked what the C stands for in your name son?"

"Well sir, it stands for Connie."

"Connie? Is that not a girl's name, Benjamin Harris? "

"No sir. Well, maybe it is. That is what they named me. I can't help that, sir."

"I ain't making fun of your name. It is just we got us a Pig, a Tree, and a Connie. Your names will not make you any more or less of fighting men. They are just names. My name is Captain Vassar Golden. I am afraid the engagement you signed up for is likely to be fraught with unpleasantries. You will spend most of your time aboard the back of a horse. Our motto is Prepared and Loyal, and that you will be, at all times. You will take great care of your mount at all times. That means your mount is fed twice per day, curried, and brushed. Inspect and clean all four hooves every morning before you saddle up and every evening when you take off your saddle. You will wipe down your mount before you saddle up and check the girth for burrs. I want your mount's manes and tails to be combed out daily respectable of a fighting military man. Do I make myself clear?"

"Yes sir, Captain," the recruits responded.

"Why do you need to show such respect and attention to your mounts, you might ask? You are now part of the United States' mounted cavalry. The main forces we will be engaging in the Llano Estacado region are the Comanche Indians. The land they occupy is the Comancheria. They are perhaps one of the greatest fighting forces known to man, especially on a horse. They can outride us, outlast us when there is no food or water. Why? Because they have horses. They have a lot of horses. Your horses, gentlemen, are the only thing between living and dying on the plains. At this moment, we have just over one hundred men besides you. Some of them are out on reconnaissance now, and they are damn sure not on foot. They are on U.S. Cavalry–issued horses.

"Each of you will be issued a uniform, knife, bedroll, canteen, revolver and carbine, shells, and a gun cleaning kit. Keep your weapons well-oiled and in a state of preparedness at all times. Your lives may very well depend on it. Beyond your compatriots, your mounts and your weapons are your best hope for survival out here on the plains. The war between the North and the South is over, gentlemen, for some time now. I don't want it brought up out here, no matter which side of the fence you or your family was on. I personally do not give a rat's tail about it. A lot of soldiers died on both sides of that damn war, and it will not carry over for one minute out here. Our objective is to stop the Comanches from marauding and killing anyone that comes into their territory. I am afraid we are tasked with the dreadful and dangerous task of hunting them down and moving them to a place our federal government has set aside for them, the federal government all of you are now employed by. It does not matter what I think or what you think about the sanity of that task. That is our task, and it will not be shirked. Based on our past confrontations, they will engage us heavily. We will lose men. We have already lost several over the course of the last year. I am sure they will lose more. That, gentlemen, is what you signed up for. Are there any questions?"

Captain Golden looked at each one of the men, perhaps to gauge their level of tenacity just by looking at their eyes. He never trusted men that kept just a slight wrinkle of a little smile on their face when he was speaking. His stern gaze froze on Lester Archibald.

"Is there something particularly funny, Private Archibald? You seem to be smiling about something. Why don't you share it with us?"

"I was just smiling a little bit because I can't wait to kill me an Indian. I been wanting to kill me one for a long time."

Captain Golden's complexion fermented to a bright red as he jumped out of his chair. He walked over and stood in front of the young recruit.

"Look at me in the eyes, Private." The veins in his forehead were bulging below his mighty eyebrows. "I do not know what you are made of or what you are capable of. If I see you smiling again like that, I swear I will slap it off of your damn little twit of a face. You got that?" Flecks of spit flew out of his mouth under his mustache.

"First of all, these folks we are engaging are indeed Plains Indians, and they are not the only tribe out there, you can rest assured. They are also people, just like you, Private. They hunt for food, make their own clothes, and live completely off of the land. They are the very worthiest of opponents. My greatest wish is that we did not have to fight them. Do they kill? Yes, indeed they kill, torture too. They are pretty much masters at torturing, you might say. They might cut your guts open and put them on a campfire while you are tied to a post and still alive. They might pull your guts out and let their dogs eat them up while you watch. They have been known to castrate men and cook their privates on the fire, just like you do bull calves at a roundup. Barbaric and savage, you might say so. They will defend their lands to the death, Private. It is not because they particularly want to kill you, it's because they want to dissuade others from coming into their Comancheria, by any means necessary. I have personally seen our kind do things to other people we don't need to particularly be proud of. If you have to kill, that person is never going to breathe air again. Always remember that. Ain't no glory in killing."

He looked at each of the other recruits. The tall one was called Tree Smith, and the smaller-in-stature, white-haired one was called Cedar Jones. Both stared straight ahead without emotion. The tall one was massive in frame and stood well over six feet five inches tall. He appeared to weigh well over 275 pounds with large hands and very large feet in particular. His flaming red hair hung to his collar. His beard was unkempt and hung to the base of his neck. He was definitely a man of impressive size and showed no outward signs of fear or any type of emotion for that matter.

The white-haired one called Cedar Jones stared straight ahead as the sergeant came and stood in front of him.

"I have never seen a man your age with white hair, Private."

Cedar Jones said nothing, just stared straight ahead.

"You come to kill an Indian, Private Jones?"

"I come to serve in the U.S. Cavalry, Captain."

"How old are you, Private Jones?"

"I am eighteen years old."

"What about you, Private Tree Bigfoot Smith? You come to kill you an Indian? With feet that big, you could probably just step on one. You aim to do a bunch of killing down here, Private?"

Tree Smith knew he had probably acquired a new nickname that would follow him without mercy for the rest of his days. He was always somewhat ashamed of his oversized feet and hands, but there was nothing he could do about it.

"I asked you a question, Bigfoot. You aim to do a bunch of killing? You're just itching to kill you one of them Indians like Private Archibald there wants to do?"

Tree stared down at the captain and looked deep into his eyes.

"I just joined the cavalry, Captain. That's all. I don't want to have to kill nobody."

"You ever kill anyone, Private? You ever seen a man die before?"

"Yes sir. I have."

The captain looked surprised by the response. "You are saying you really did kill someone?"

"Yes, sir."

"I am sorry, Private. When you take someone's life, men, it is gone forever. They are never to breathe God's breath of life again. Gone. They are gone. We will take no pleasure in killing if we are forced to do so. Our goal is to engage peacefully if possible. Of course, out here, that is rarely possible.

"We will be leaving Fort Concho very shortly. We will be following the Concho River north to its headwaters, continuing toward the big spring and then further northward toward Mushaway Mountain in Borden County in the Llano Estacado. The men currently on reconnaissance are expected to return in a day or so. When we leave, there will be thirty men in the patrol with us, and the remainder will stay to guard the fort and get some much-needed rest. There have been previous scouting reports of a large encampment of Quahadi Comanches at the base of Mushaway Mountain. That is about seven days' ride from here. We believe they are trading with the Comancheros who are coming to and from Santa Fe, New Mexico. We are liable to run into them at any point along the way. Plenty of places to ambush us. Those cutthroats are running guns and horses to the Comanche as well as any beeves they steal along the way.

"Now, get settled in the barracks, and you will be issued your mount and all of your equipment this afternoon. See the quartermaster at his office. We will see who can ride and who can shoot a gun tomorrow. I will be designating two more scouts that will ride ahead of the troop and report back with frequency. The scouts out now have been gone a while and are in need of rest. I am quite sure none of you are quite suitable for this task. If you would like to volunteer for this assignment, see me shortly in my quarters. Dismissed, gentlemen."

# CHAPTER 4

CAPTAIN GOLDEN HAD ONLY BEEN sitting at his desk in his quarters for a short period of time when he heard the tap on the door.

"Come in," he said.

He looked surprised to see Private Tree Smith and Private Cedar Jones enter the door. Private Smith had to duck his head to get under the door header board.

"Gentlemen, I assume you need to speak to me. Not wanting to get out of the cavalry this early, are you? You just joined."

Private Tree Smith looked at him from under his hat with piercing eyes.

"I want to sign up for the scouting duty you talked about."

"What about you, Private Jones? I am assuming you do too?"

"Yes sir, Captain. I do."

"Well now, whatever possessed both of you to sign up for such hazardous duty? You do know that you are required to go out in front of the troop and scout? To scout means just that. You scout the land ahead of us and bring back any and all information on existing threats, potential threats, location of good water for the stock and ourselves. It means you have to have good instincts and memory about landmarks. You have to pay attention to directions and the details of where you have been and where you are going back to. The Comanche do not particularly like the cavalry scouts, gentlemen. If you are caught, it is likely you will be the subject of some type of severe torture and then death. You still want to scout for the U.S. Cavalry, gentlemen?"

Private Tree Smith nodded his head.

"Yes sir, I do."

"And you too, Private Jones?"

"Yes, sir. Me too."

"All right, gentlemen. It does not pay any more money, I am afraid. But it should. For your assignments, you will both be issued two more boxes of ammunition for each of your weapons and an extra canteen due to the distance you will be traveling. Your binoculars will be your friend. Take care of them. Just like your mounts. Without them, you are in trouble of the worst kind. I will be giving you your orders shortly as we prepare to move out. Thanks, gentlemen. I wish you the best. You are both dismissed."

THE QUARTERMASTER SELECTED THE BIGGEST mount in the remuda for Tree Smith, mainly due to his enormous size. The big bay gelding stood nearly seventeen hands tall and about 1,250 pounds. The U.S. Cavalry tried to look for horses of uniform size, but, like the new recruits, they came in all shapes and sizes. Along with their mounts came a saddle pad and blanket, bedroll, rifle scabbard, halter, bridle and bit, lead rope, hoof pick, set of replacement shoes, a saddle, leather soap, a currycomb, and a brush.

Tree Smith and Cedar Jones were currying down their mounts outside the livery when the other three recruits led their horses up to the hitching rail.

Lester Archibald looked over at Pig Green.

"Well, looks like Old Killer there and the white-haired boy done beat us to the hitching rail, Mr. Pig. I saw both of them go into the captain's quarters a while ago. Wouldn't surprise me none if they don't want to get out right quickly in this man's cavalry. Killed somebody, my ass. That man ain't no killer. He is just a big lug of lead. Kind of like one of them Confederate cannonballs. That is why them boys got their asses tore up. They were just too big and slow, just like old Bigfoot Killer there. Bet his pappy was a damn Reb."

Pig Green never responded. He just tied his horse up and began to unsaddle him. Tree's hands began to tremble as he continued to brush his mount. He felt a firm hand on his shoulder. It was Cedar Jones. Cedar looked up at him for a moment and then patted his shoulder.

"You need not comment," he whispered. "That little loudmouthed twit is not worth getting kicked out of the cavalry. Let it lay."

Lester smirked and looked at Pig out of the corner of his eye. "Now, just take a look at them two. They are whispering to each other like little girls, Mr. Pig. This here cavalry don't need no whispering little girls. It needs real men."

Cedar Jones laid his horse brush on the ground and quietly walked over to Lester on the opposite side of his horse. He laid his hands on the saddle and looked toward ground for a moment before looking up. The south wind was just beginning to pick up. Cedar spoke just loud enough for Lester to hear.

"Why is it that there is one of you in every crowd? A loud, crowing rooster just itching to stir up more trouble than he can ever possibly get out of. My advice, just do your job and leave Tree Smith alone. Leave me alone for that matter."

"Or what, White Hair? What you going to do? You don't look much big enough to be telling folks what to do."

"Just be mindful of what I said, Lester. Just be mindful."

There were no more words spoken as the new recruits groomed their mounts, tended to their feet, and then put them in the livery stable for the night with feed and water.

Everyone left for supper but Tree. He remained alone in the livery. Cedar Jones poked his head back in the door.

"You going to eat, Private Smith? I bet they have some good vittles over there. Long time until morning."

"Believe I'll just pass this evening."

"You are not letting that little rooster get under your skin, are you, Tree? Hell, he is just trying to pick a fight. Probably been a bully all of his life. Some folks just can't resist getting in other folk's business. That's all. Besides, why do you look so glum? I ain't never seen a smile on your face since I met you a while ago. What's wrong?"

Tree looked at the wall and sat down on a wooden bench along the wall and sighed a long, drawn-out breath. He looked at the ground and clasped his large hands together.

"I am getting a little shaky. Just might need me a drink. Truth is, I been drunk the better part of two years. Up till now, I can't remember being sober since I was sixteen."

"Well, you are sober now. I am sure there must have been a reason of some sort. You are sure sober now."

"Had something eating on my gut for a long time now. Never told anyone."

"Well, you don't have to tell me anything. Some things are just better left alone."

"I come from Ohio. My father fought for the Union Army. He was a colonel and had a lot of men under him. Never saw him much for a few years. While he was away, my mother wanted me to be some kind of damn musician. She made me take violin and singing lessons from an old man in our town while the war was raging around us. He was way too old to fight. He taught me to play a harp too. It was a little hard to pay attention to an old man when there was rifle and cannon firing to be heard around. When my daddy returned home after the war, I had just turned fourteen years old. He was just bound and determined I was going to be a military man, just like him. He thought I would wind up a colonel in the next big war, just like him. Fighting for the Union. He enlisted me in Bremmer's Military Academy in Virginia. Packed my clothes and saluted me as he put me on the train. I endured the two years it took to get out of there. They held sports contests on the last day we were there. They had running, shooting, horsemanship, and the like. My commander insisted that I enter the bare-knuckle boxing matches, mainly just due to my size. The fellow I was matched up with was pretty big, just not as big as me. We mostly just squared off and circled as the other cadets hollered. They wanted to see action. Finally, after a minute or so, the commander stopped the fight."

"'You boys going to start swinging or stand there and blow sugar kisses at each other? Let's see what you got. This is your last day here. Show us what you got. Now, hit that bell and let's get this round going.'

"The young cadet I was paired with began swinging wildly and punching my ears. I just kept my face covered while he pounded. Then, he decides to kick me in my hangy-downs. It hurt really bad, and all of the other recruits started laughing. Next time he charged in toward me, I was kind of stooped over. I raised up and hit him one time in the face pretty hard and he went down. Everyone started hollering and clapping. When I hit him, it crushed his nose and pushed it plumb back into his skull. There was a lot of blood coming from where his nose was. He fell to the floor and died right there. I kilt him. I damn sure kilt him. I sure did not mean to, but I did." His eyes were watering. "I been a drunk ever since."

"You got to put that behind you, Tree. That was not any fault of yours. It just happened. Besides, he kicked you in your hangy-downs. That ain't fighting fair."

"No, sir. I know I am strong. I should not have hit him in the nose. Maybe the chest or something. But I hit him in the nose. A person as strong as me should never have done that."

"Were you just supposed to stand there and let him pound on you without fighting back?"

Tree took a deep breath with tears streaming down his face.

"They did not charge me with anything. My commander just told everyone to leave the area before they hauled him out of there on a gurney. They covered his body with a sheet. That sheet did not hide the blood coming out of his face. I packed my things and never went home. My father had given me one hundred dollars when I went in. I never spent a dime and kept it hidden in my waist pack. I took me a steamer on the Ohio until it tags up with the Mississippi. Rode it all the way to New Orleans. Stayed drunk most of the way. Stole and bought anything I could drink. I was so damn big, nobody ever thought about bothering me, much less that I was just sixteen years old. They probably thought I was close to twenty. Anyway, I stayed in New Orleans for a week or two and then took a railroad train to Texas. Bought me a horse and saddle from a man and started riding west. Wound up here."

"Why did you join the cavalry? There is likely to be killing, and you might be on the giving end of it in a fight."

"That is true. But I also might be on the receiving end of it too. That might not be a bad thing."

"Are you saying you want to be kilt?"

"I am just saying, that might not be a bad thing."

"So, you came in here with a death wish of some kind? I have not known you very long. But I would not have figured you for that."

"Private Jones, you have never killed no one I reckon. Now, let me be. I am fixing to go to my bunk. Don't go rattling off what I just told you, neither."

"You don't have to worry about me. You are your own worst enemy, it seems to me. You sure don't need another one. Your business is safe with me."

Before walking out, Cedar turned to look at Tree.

"You see, even if you had the wings of Pegasus, just flying around above the earth, you still got to light on the earth every now and again. When you do, you are just likely to step on a hot coal or two. There ain't nobody immune to life's troubles Tree, not even you. I have had my fair share. You might just remember that while you are nursing that sugar-tit you been hanging on to."

Cedar left Tree alone and was deeply bothered by their conversation. He made his way to chow and sat alone as conversations droned in all directions around him. He liked Tree immensely even though he had just made his acquaintance. He saw a man that was tormented much beyond the pale of what most folks could probably stand, maybe himself included.

Cedar finished his meal and made one last trek to the stable to check his mount before turning in. When he opened the door to the barracks, he could see Tree's massive frame on his bunk. The blanket covering him was barely big enough sideways and about two feet too short to cover his calves and feet. After listening to loud snoring in the barracks, Cedar was finally able to drift off to sleep.

The bugler sounded reveille at sunrise the next morning. Cedar awoke to find Tree's bed empty. He never heard him make a sound during the night, causing him to wonder how a man that big could get up, get dressed, leave, and never make a sound.

*Maybe he slipped out in his stocking feet without his boots on*, he thought.

Chow was at 6:00 a.m. The troop had just begun eating breakfast when Captain Golden entered the building. All of the new recruits noticed and quickly sprang to their feet at attention.

"Everyone, keep your seat and finish your breakfast," he said. "I want everyone on the firing range just south of your barracks at 8:00 a.m. sharp. We will find out who knows how to use your weapon. Hopefully, you oiled your weapons last night. You will each be issued one box of pistol and carbine ammunition for this exercise. I will see you there."

"You ready to do some shooting, Tree?" said Cedar. "I don't guess I ever heard you get up and about this morning. I figured you was anxious to get your gun oiled up and out on the line or something."

Tree kept nibbling his eggs and a strip of salt pork.

"I can shoot a pistol a little, up close I reckon. I have never shot a rifle."

"Well, there ain't nothing to it. Just put the butt up to your shoulder firmly and cock the lever. That will load a shell into your carbine. The hammer will be back and ready to fire. Be mighty careful of the trigger. Make damn sure somebody is not in front of you. Once you pull that trigger, it is too late. Then, just look down the barrel at the sights and line them up at your target. Take a deep breath and ease into that trigger slow. If you miss your target, might have to raise the sights one notch and try again until you hit it. Just do what I do. Course, having a good set of eyes don't hurt you none."

# CHAPTER 5

CAPTAIN GOLDEN WALKED UP AND down the line of five men.

"Gentlemen, there are three targets in front of each of you. One at fifteen steps, one at twenty-five steps, and one at fifty steps. There is a red circle drawn with a vertical line and a horizontal line painted on each of them. Shoot for the dead middle of each target when I tell you to load and shoot. Never shoot at a target if you do not know what the target is. Do not shoot at a sound, and, most of all, do not shoot me or someone else in the troop. Load your carbine with one shell. On my command, shoot at the closest target. I will go inspect each of the targets. If you hit anywhere outside the circle, you will have to shoot at that target again and will be indicated by a white flag. The flag of surrender. If you hit inside the circle of the target, I will raise a yellow flag and you will proceed to the second target at my command. If you hit the target dead center, I will hold up the red flag. We will see if there are any sharpshooters in this bunch. Each of these targets is the size of the main portion of a man, his waist to his head. You hit that area, he will not be having a good day on the frontier, folks. Cock your weapon and inject your shell. Once it is loaded, you may fire at your first target."

Each recruit fired their rifles nearly simultaneously.

"Put your weapons down and step back away from them," said Captain Golden. He walked to the first target with each recruit looking on nervously. He waved the yellow flag at each station except for Cedar Jones's. He squatted down and looked closely at the bullet hole before looking back at Cedar. He slowly raised the red flag. Coming back to the group, he quickly stepped behind the line.

"Load your weapons, gentlemen. Fire at the second target. Once the bullet has cleared your carbine, stand up and stand away from your weapon."

After each recruit had fired his weapon, he slowly made his way to the second target and began his inspection.

Pig Green watched him as he made his way toward his target. The captain slowly raised the yellow flag as Pig smiled to himself.

*Told you I could shoot a squirrel at a fair distance*, he thought.

The captain slowly made his way to each target. Tree, Lester, and Benjamin all received a yellow flag as well. As in the first target, he squatted down and took close notice of Cedar's target. He took out some type of measuring device and measured something on the target before standing up. He turned back toward the group and held the red flag up high. He never spoke a word as he came back to the group.

"All right, gentlemen, load your weapons for your final shot on the last target. That target is a pretty long way off for most folks. If you just hit the target, it will be somewhat of a success. Load your weapons and fire when ready. Step away from your weapon as soon as you have fired."

Captain Golden took his time in reaching the last set of targets. He approached Pig Green's target first. He turned around and looked in Pig's direction and slowly brought up the yellow flag. Pig raised his head and was clearly happy. Next came Benjamin C. Harris. The captain raised the white flag as he continued toward Lester Archibald's. As with Private Harris, the white flag came up.

"Hell, I coulda swore I hit that target in the circle. This gun must be off or something," Lester squalled.

Tree stared intently as the captain made his way to his target.

He stared expressionless as Captain Golden brought up the yellow flag.

Lester Archibald looked in disgust and spat on the ground.

"He probably gave you a better shooting gun just to make me look bad, Killer." Tree continued to stare straight ahead without comment. Captain Golden finally made his way to the last target on the field, Cedar's. He squatted down and looked at the target for a good bit and took out his measuring device again. He measured up and down and then across before standing up and looking back toward Cedar Jones. He slowly raised the red flag and waved it a couple of times slowly.

"Well now, ain't you just the fancy little shooter, Mr. White Hair!" said Lester.

"He probably gave you the best shooting gun."

Cedar put down his carbine and walked over to Lester.

"I done warned you once, leave me be."

"What you going to do, White Hair? Shoot me?"

"Only your lips, Private. That way you won't be flapping them."

Captain Golden made his way back to the recruits.

"All in all, that is not bad shooting. That far target is always a little stretch for everyday kind of shooters. Private Harris and Archibald, you will remain on the range until you hit within the circle," he said as he looked directly at Cedar Jones. "Private Jones, where did you learn how to shoot like that? We have never had anyone come into this fort that hit each target pretty much dead-on between the lines, never!"

"Just had a lot of practice, sir. Shooting deer, mostly. We did not have much ammunition at our place."

"Well, however you learned, you learned it well.

"Gentlemen, I will also inform you that Private Jones and Private Tree Smith have signed up and been accepted for the two cavalry scout positions I spoke about yesterday. No one else showed up."

Lester Archibald raised his hand.

"Yes, Private Archibald, what is it?"

"Well, I was just going to say that I might be interested in one of those positions, sir. I was just thinking on it a bit. Does it pay more money?"

Captain Golden's face turned scarlet. His dark hair was offset by the intense burning in his face.

"Private, did you not listen to anything I said yesterday? I said if you were interested, see me today. That was yesterday. This is today. That window has closed. Besides, you are not cavalry scout material. Must I remind you of the target you just missed? You do not have the temperament nor the eyes for the job. Now, do not ever ask me about it further. Do I make myself clear? Never again!"

"Yes, sir, Captain. You are clear."

"The troop out on patrol is expected back at the fort shortly. We will leave shortly after they arrive. Scouts Jones and Smith here will leave as soon as they arrive and work ahead of us at all times. We will leave from the fort and head due north following the Concho River to the big spring about four days' ride from here in normal weather. That big spring is a Comanche watering hole and a dangerous place. The scouts will see if there is any Comanche or Comanchero movement up ahead of us and report back with their findings. They will generally be scouting twenty or thirty miles ahead of us at all times. The Comanches' area is quite large, and they will continue to come all the way to where you are standing at this very moment. They tend to spend more time from the big spring and northward but do still go into Mexico from time to time.

"Once we leave the big spring, we will head north east toward Mushaway Mountain out toward the Caprock. We are fully in the Comancheria at that point, and if they see us, they will more than likely engage us, and it may not be in the daylight. If we see nothing, we will return with whatever information we can obtain in whichever way we can obtain it. And last, this is springtime in Texas, gentlemen. When you see a big thunderhead building up, pay attention. It can get ugly fast when the wind and lightning come whipping in. It can hit a man on horseback if he is the highest thing on a hill or in a flat for that matter.

"Private Jones and Private Smith, see me in my quarters. The rest of you are dismissed."

Captain Golden was smoking his pipe and reading in his quarters when Cedar and Tree arrived. Cedar quietly tapped on the door.

"Come in, gentlemen. Come in." Cedar walked in as Tree ducked under the door frame.

"You two can stand easy for a few minutes, and let's visit. Would either of you care for a brandy?"

Cedar looked at Tree and then back toward the captain.

"I believe I will pass."

"What about you, Private Smith?"

"No, sir. I will pass too."

"I want you two to look after each other. If you get shot at, you are probably going to have to shoot back. If either of you gets wounded, doctor up as best you can and head back to the troop as soon as you can safely do so. By the looks of things on the target range today, you can handle that quite well. One of you better than the other. However, you did not do bad at all, Private Smith. Keep your fires low when you are camped. I would advise always camping on a high spot you can easily defend with a patch of brush or trees in it. The trees will help filter a very small fire and I do mean small with very dry wood or twigs, nothing that gives off a bunch of smoke. They seem to be able to see a gnat moving on a blade of grass a mile away. Make sure you hide your horses out of sight. Graze them and water them only in the day as you travel. Keep those binoculars on your neck at all times until you hit your bedroll. My advice, one man sleeps for three hours or so while the other takes watch and then switch off. That might just keep you alive. This is certainly no kind of Sunday social, men. Prepare yourselves, your equipment, and your mounts to leave at first light two days from now. We will be right behind you a little way, following the exact same route. You will be doing exactly what your new and glorious title says, scouting. Best of luck gentlemen. You will need it. You are dismissed."

# CHAPTER 6

CEDAR AND TREE SADDLED THEIR mounts by the light of a lantern in the livery. Neither of them said much as they inspected their riggings.

"I think it's a good idea if we try and eat a good, hot breakfast before we head out, don't you? It ain't good to start out on an empty stomach. It may be the last one for a while."

Tree nodded his head in agreement.

They sat by themselves as the other recruits began to file in. There were many more men now that the main troop had arrived. They looked over the five new recruits and then turned their attention to the bacon, eggs, coffee, and stacks of biscuits piled up on a tin plate. Lester Archibald, Pig, and Benjamin Harris filed in quietly. They came to sit by Cedar and Tree as soon as they loaded their plates.

Pig Green stopped eating for a minute and looked over toward Cedar and Tree. "You boys be careful, you hear? I wished I was going on ahead with you. Sounds like you two will rendezvous back with us now and again. You can tell us some exciting stories then."

Lester Archibald never looked up or stopped eating.

Cedar and Tree finished their meal and got up from the table. Cedar turned back to the group of new recruits and waved.

"We will see you in a day or two. Adios, muchachos."

The Concho River was beautiful to follow as the sun rose to the east of them as they rode. They had ridden a good five miles north before a word was spoken.

"I already told you about me, Cedar. Where did you come from?"

"Well, I'll be. A question from Mr. Tree. I am honored. Well, I did not come from back east like you. I come from New Mexico, up in the Gila Bend country north of Silver City. Lots of Apaches up that way. They travel all over Arizona and New Mexico in their stretch of country. Mostly Jicarilla and Chiricahua Apache. Damn bunch of Comancheros up that way too. Comancheros killed both of my parents when I was five years old. They ain't fit for breathing air on this earth. Came onto the ranch at night when we were all asleep. Killed my father first. They threw a rock at the house and he went out with his gun to investigate. They roped him and drug him to death behind a horse. My mother got me up quick. She helped me get my clothes on and slip out the back window. I ran as fast as I could and hid in the hay in the top of the barn. I heard her screaming when they started in on her. I hid up there all night, afraid to death. They finally left about the break of day. I finally worked up the nerve to come down the ladder in the barn and go to looking for my folks. I figured they was both dead. My daddy was not recognizable. They beat his head in with the butts of their rifles, I reckon. My mama's throat was cut, and she did not have a stitch of clothes on her body. Seeing my mama laying there naked like that nearly done me in. I rode to the neighbor's place about five miles away. Otis Hankey was his name. He saw me riding in and ran to me. His face began to turn white when I told him what had happened. He helped me bury my folks on our place in a little grove of cottonwood trees down by the river. He and his wife Wilma took me in. They didn't have no kids, and she took to mothering me something fierce. We had over fifty mama cows and a bull on our place, which was mostly fenced pretty good with barbed wire. I lived with Mr. Otis and

Mrs. Wilma until I was about fifteen years old. He is the one who taught me how to shoot and ride well. I shot a lot of tree squirrels, turkey, and deer for food on the table. He always told me that bullets were short in supply and never to waste one of them. 'Take your aim, take a breath, shoot once and shoot straight. Don't never get rattled one little bit before you squeeze that trigger. Eyes on the target at all times, even after you shoot. Don't let nothing distract you.' So, that is what I learned to do.

"When I was nearly sixteen, I got a little restless and decided that I needed a change of scenery. Mr. Otis and I talked a little about it. He said, 'I am not your papa and cannot keep you here with me and Wilma. You are certainly welcome to stay and live with us, help me on our ranch, and I'll help you take care of your folks place, just like we been doing.'

"I told him he and Mrs. Wilma could have my folks' ranch, which wouldn't but about a few hundred acres and the cows that was on it. I wrote him a piece of paper saying so too, and told him the deed to the land was in a lockbox under Papa and Mama's bed. I told him, 'The land will be yours free and clear. Pa paid it off well before he and Ma were kilt.'

"He asked me, 'Where are you thinking about heading?'

"I told him I was going to join a cattle drive heading down to Texas because I heard him talking about the big cattle drives heading to New Mexico, Texas, and Kansas. Plus, there were always cowboys passing through and would stop in for breakfast and a cup of coffee. That was all they talked about. It sounded exciting to me. I said my goodbyes to the Hankeys and rode out one fall morning in early September when the leaves were just starting to turn yellow on the aspens in the high country and the cottonwoods along the river. The outfit was leaving Silver City on or about September 15th and then driving cattle all the way into Texas, somewhere near San Antonio. I got there and they let me hire on as a cook's helper. That is how I wound up in Texas. It was a good trail drive with no casualties and fairly good weather. We delivered our herd to market. I learned a lot about cooking in the process, and here I am."

Tree looked ahead, scanning the horizon and listening as the only sound was the clip-clopping of the horses' hooves. He always paid close attention to his horse's ears. They would see or hear things well before he ever noticed them.

"How did you end up at Fort Concho?"

"Rode a horse west. There was a fella at the stockyards that told me the cavalry was hiring young recruits. I figured it was worth looking into. Now, just look at us. We are both riding free cavalry mounts and scouting for Indians like we both had good sense. Now that we both know the nitty-gritty details about each other's lives, let's you and me make a deal. You won't hear me pissing and whining about mine, I don't want you pissing and whining about yours going forward. Is that a deal?"

Tree nodded in agreement.

"Good," said Cedar.

"That is a big step forward. I figure we can make the big spring in about three or four days of easy riding."

The scouts covered the next seventy miles with good skies and quiet nights. They rode the cedar-covered limestone rims above the river during the day with constant vigilance with their binoculars before easing their mounts to the river to graze and drink several times a day. In the late evening, they tried to pick the highest point or overlook with a brushy top on it, just like the captain said. Fires were kept very small, with meticulous care taken to only put small dead wood in it. Cedar even rode off a distance each evening when the sun went down to see if he could see the smoke from the campfire. It was just like the captain said. You could see a very little wisp filtering up through the trees, but not much. He was certain if he could see just a little smoke, so could the Comanches.

After three days' ride to the north, Cedar could begin to make out the slight escarpment just to the east of the big spring. He stopped his horse and eased out of the saddle.

"Private Tree, I reckon we are just a few miles from the big spring and we ain't seen a thing. See that little sharp ridge way up there to our right, that stands just east of the big spring about a mile or so. We better ride back and find the troop. There is a big cloud building up in the west, yonder. The one with the anvil-looking head on top of it. We better ride and see if we run into the troop back behind us."


CAPTAIN GOLDEN HAD JUST GOT the camp organized when Tree and Cedar came riding in.

"How far ahead of us were you, boys?"

"About ten miles or so, Captain. It took us about three hours of easy riding to get to you."

"See anything?"

"Just a few javelina hogs and a rattler or two. They are just starting to come out of their dens good. We did not see one Comanche of any kind and we done a fair amount of scanning with those binoculars."

"Good to hear. Might get your tents set up as soon as possible and get those horses unsaddled and under them pecan trees close to the river. Looks like a big storm is fixing to come whipping in by the looks of that big cloud to the west and the dirt on the horizon. That dirt cloud means it has strong winds with it. Maybe hail too. It is kind of lime-green looking below it. That is a bad sign. Be sure and light your lanterns in your tent when it is set up. May get dark quick. Get moving, gentlemen."

First came the howling gusts of wind and dust. The sky turned a dirty brown, and the temperature dropped over thirty degrees in fifteen minutes. All of the men ran to steady the horses on the picket line to keep them from breaking free. Most remained fairly calm, but several became wild-eyed and began to pull against their head stalls and picket line ropes. Then, the dark clouds came rolling in with the lime-green ones rolling in below them. Mighty booms of thunder began to rumble, sounding like mountains colliding. The lightning became strong and intensified. The only protection for the horses and the men was a grove of large pecan trees along the banks of the river, which was also the worst place to be when the lightning started. The troop watched as it hit a tree upriver with a loud pop.

Nobody was prepared when the hail began to come down on the men and horses. The noise of the large hail hitting the river water was so loud the men could not hear each other's voices well.

"We got to get these horses out of here now fore they get us all kilt," one man screamed.

His partner replied, "Just where do you suggest we take them? They ain't no place to go. Just keep your hands over their eyes best you can and hold your head up against their necks. We got to ride it out. Just don't look up."

The hail continued for at least half an hour before letting up. That is when the rain started. It started light and then over the course of ten minutes it began to come down in cold and heavy torrents. The men were able to leave the horses on the picket line when the hail stopped. The horses and the men were heavily bruised from the beating. The horses ducked their heads and turned their butts into the rain as it continued to fall. All of the saddles and gear were left exposed to the elements. The men ran to their two-man tents, hurriedly lit their kerosene lanterns for warmth, and began inspecting the large welts on each other's backs and shoulders. Their felt hats were beaten down and hanging flat on their heads dripping with rainwater.

The rain set in with a dreary and monotonous roar. The insides of the canvas tents would begin leaking immediately if they were touched with a finger. The men tried to settle in for a little sleep as the rain continued to pour down for most of the night. Tree and Cedar never slept through the night. In the wee hours of the morning, Tree stuck his hand under the door flap and over the entrance flap to feel of the ground.

"This here river bottom may not have been the best choice for us to set our camp," he said. "There is water starting to lap up against this tent, and it is starting to come in under the tent. I think this damn river is on the rise from all of the water run-off funneling down here from both sides of these hills. I am going out now and tell Captain Golden and the boys."

The river was starting to rise fast out of its banks. The men and the horses could sense the urgency as they could hear and feel the fast-approaching waters. Any man or animal caught in the current would be rapidly swept away.

Captain Golden was barking orders at a fast pace.

"Don't worry about those tents, men. Get your canteens, revolvers, and rifles. Save yourself and your mounts. Get them blankets on and them saddles, and I mean now. Get on your mounts, don't lead them. Head uphill and quick. Share a lantern if you have it, but don't go back into your tents to get one. Follow any man with a lantern and go uphill, away from the river. Get moving now. We will meet up about a half mile or so from here where we were riding on that ridge yesterday. Stop there."

Pig Green was one of the last two men that came in. Benjamin Harris was holding a lantern in one hand and leading Pig's horse with the other.

"Captain, I think Pig done looked up during the hailstorm and done lost one of his eyes. Help him off his horse, boys. Be careful, he is bleeding pretty bad from that left eye."

Pig was moaning slightly as they put him on the ground. The rain was finally starting to dissipate, and it was still bitterly chilly.

"Get a raincoat around this man," barked the captain. "All of the blankets are wet. We need to get him warmed up as quick as possible. Private Harris, rub his back and shoulders down with your hands when we get this coat on him. If we can't get him warmed up, strip off your clothes and his. Get up next to him and wrap up in this rain jacket. Now move."

Captain Golden gently pulled Pig's hand away from his left eye. He had been hit directly in the eyeball by a large hailstone. The eye was oozing and bleeding, looking milky and completely lifeless. He went to his saddlebag and came back with a dry bandage. He began wrapping the bandage tightly around Pig's head.

"Am I blind?" he moaned. "I can't see nothing out of it. It hurts really bad."

"Right now, you need to concentrate on getting warm. You men, see if you can come up with quite a bit of firewood. We will pour a little kerosene on it and see if we can get a fire going. Everyone has dry matches in a bottle in your saddlebags. Try to not waste them."

Toward morning, the soldiers finally had a fire going. The saturated wood was slow to take light, but with every little drop of kerosene, it began to grow. The men gathered around it for warmth and to dry out the clothes on their backs, saddle blankets, and bedrolls.

"Private Harris?"

"Yes, sir?"

"You are responsible for getting Private Green back to the fort and to the infirmary. He needs to get there as soon as possible for care of his condition. You are to leave immediately. You should not run into trouble, as we have just come from that direction. You still need to be watching behind you as you travel. Keep the river to your right and head south until you come to the fort."

The two men had been gone but a short time when Captain Golden called the rest of the men to the fire.

"Men, that is why you never look up during a hailstorm. That boy will never see again out of that eye, I fear. Get your saddle blankets dried out on a rope line next to the fire and your guns cleaned with the kits in your bag. Do it now before they rust. We will stay the day here and head north to the big spring in the morning."

# CHAPTER 7

---

CAPTAIN GOLDEN RODE WITH THE two scouts a few hundred yards ahead of the troop.

"We are getting mighty close to the big spring, gentlemen. We will exercise extreme caution from this point forward in our journey. The escarpment up there on the right will be our lookout point. We will follow that little ridgeback up the back side of it and ease up to the most western point. Once we are there and glass a while, both of you will ease down to the west into a little canyon area. There lies the big spring. Private Jones, keep that rifle of yours ready at all times. You too, Private Smith. Watch your horse's ears. They will pick up sound and movement long before you do."

The entire troop sat silently on their mounts with binoculars focused on the big spring in the valley below. After a full hour of glassing, the captain looked at Cedar and Tree.

"Just because we have not seen movement does not mean that there is nothing down there. They could have their horses tied up a mile away and be hiding behind the large rocks on the south side of the spring. It sits down in kind of a rocky hole. You two take your time and head on down there with your rifles out and ready. See or hear anything you don't like, stop immediately and raise your rifles in the air for a few seconds or so where we can see them. I will fire off a couple of shots, and we will come down this mountain fast and come to you. If you are engaged by hostile forces, engage back and shoot to kill. Once you get to the spring, one of you wave your hat a time or two in the air. We will begin heading down at that time. Now, head on down, gentlemen."

Cedar and Tree took their carbines out of their leather scabbards and checked the actions on each. They each loaded a shell on the rifle chamber and eased the hammer back down before pointing their horses down the mountain. It took the better part of an hour for them to reach the spring, stopping every so often to glass ahead with one hand while the other held the rifle butt firmly resting on the top of the saddle. Finally, they were within one hundred yards of the spring. They stopped their mounts and sat quietly as Tree's horse blew his nostrils. Nothing moved on the horizon around or above the spring in any direction. Cedar looked at Tree and nodded his head. They eased their horses ahead until the hole of the spring came into view. The tranquil pool of green water overflowed into a very small stream to the east. Birds dipped and darted through the abundant grasses and reeds on both sides of the small stream. Both horses picked up the water smell a long ways back and were quick to put their heads down for a drink. Cedar took his hat off and waved it before wiping his brow with his shirtsleeve.

"I reckon the captain will be heading the troop down the mountain now. Keep a good lookout. I would hate to get shot at a watering hole."

It was a full fifteen minutes before Cedar could see the column of soldiers making their way down the escarpment as they wove their mounts between the cedar and mesquite trees.

"Well, they are coming."

When the troop arrived, Captain Golden had all of the men water their horses well before having them mount back up.

"We will not camp here this evening, gentlemen. Our destination is back up on top of the escarpment we just came down from. We can see down from on top of that thing, which is to our advantage. Tomorrow, we will head back down and continue northeast toward Mushaway Mountain in Borden County. That is a day and a half ride from here. Let's move out."

The captain led the troop over the top of the escarpment and continued on the rim for approximately two miles east before stopping to make camp. "Gentlemen, dry twigs for fires. One fire only. Keep it small and absolutely no green wood. Green wood makes smoke. Smoke attracts attention."

Cedar looked down onto the vast prairie below for a few minutes. "Tree, it will be amazing if we see anything in that expanse. We are clearly at a disadvantage. They can see us coming from a long way off."

"Maybe you forgot, Private Jones. We are not exactly riding with the troop. We are riding out in front of them a few miles scouting. Maybe they can't see two as good as a whole herd of us."

"Maybe that is true, but I reckon they have scouts just like us out looking, don't you reckon?"


CAPTAIN GOLDEN THREW OUT THE dregs from his tin coffee cup while the rest of the men were finishing their evening meal.

"Like I said before, there have been reports of a large group of Quahadi Comanches gathered at Mushaway Mountain. Engagement can happen quick with no warning. The scouts will ride ahead of us and get as close to the encampment as possible. If they are engaged and hear any type of shooting, we will come in as a group and fast. You may have to shoot from the saddle. If they shoot your horse out from under you, use his body as a shield. Only shoot what you can hit. If you are taken prisoner, you can be guaranteed that torture will follow. At that point you would have to assess your situation. We do not know at this time if there are any Comancheros in the area. If there are, there could be a reasonably large fighting force we would encounter."

Lester Archibald listened to Captain Golden's words with great intensity. His desire to kill an Indian seemed far removed from his mind. He suddenly realized that his only chance of survival against these brutal warriors of the plains was his ability to shoot a rifle and hit something and the other men in the troop. He had to spend an extra hour on the gun range just trying to hit the farthest target. The captain finally let him quit when he hit the target about four inches outside of the circle.

"If that had been a real man you were shooting at, you might have hit him on his shirtsleeve. If he had one on, that is," snorted Captain Golden. "You are the worst shot of the entire group and are clearly at risk if we are engaged. We can't waste any more of our ammunition on seeing if you can hit anywhere in the circle on this target, Private."

Archibald decided then and there that he would do his best to stay behind the others and hope that nobody noticed. If they were engaged, maybe the men in front could end the battle quickly and then he would come on in at a run. Maybe there would not even be a battle.

*That would suit me just fine*, he thought. He could not bear the thought of one of them Comanches cutting his stomach open, especially while he was still alive.

Cedar and Tree curried their mounts and checked their feet. They had their horses saddled before breakfast the next morning.

Captain Golden walked over to them at the fire holding his morning cup of strong coffee.

"Best of luck, men. Same rules as before. You can see Mushaway a long way off. Gail Mountain is a big rimrocked mountain to the northwest of Mushaway Mountain. You can spot Mushaway very easily. It is a baldy-knobbed hill and is the tallest thing you will see out there excepting for Gail Mountain, which is long and runs north and south. Always look behind you. They may have seen you coming and send their scouts to get in behind you where you cannot turn around. I cannot help you there. If there is any type of shooting, we are coming in at a run if we hear it. They are armed with bows and arrows as well. I would rather get shot by a bullet than one of their arrows, so be careful of any type of ambush point. That may be a little gully or maybe a tree that stands off by itself. If you don't see anything about a mile and a half away from the mountain, come back to the troop, and we'll all ride in together."

THE SCOUTS RODE ALONG CAREFULLY and slowly. They decided that the night camp would be a dry camp with no fire, and they would only eat a can of beans and a cold biscuit from breakfast. There was an eerie feeling of being watched without ever being able to see any type of movement. Each time they stopped and looked through their binoculars, only the gentle movement of the long buffalo grass in the breeze could be seen. They did spot a large group of antelope grazing ahead of them a few hundred yards. The large male with his great black prong horns was busy chasing any straying female back to the main group. He would chase them down one at a time and poke them with his horns in their side. They quickly returned to the herd as he resumed his guarding forty or fifty yards away. He quickly raced away with the females in tow when he spotted the movement of the two scouts.

Both scouts had heard of hostiles crawling along with animal skins on their backs while stalking prey, like the antelope. Cedar turned to Tree. "Keep your eyes out for coyotes. They might just be hostiles dressed to look like a coyote. They are likely to have a bow and quiver or gun in one hand while they are crawling along."

They each took a three-hour guard that night. Neither slept well while the other was guarding. The night was filled with the howls of coyotes, owl hoots, and other night sounds. They could envision the Comanche giving signals to each other by simply howling like a coyote or maybe hooting like an owl. Both of them were extremely glad to see the sun start to come up the next morning.

Water from their canteen and dried beef jerky was breakfast. Cedar pulled out a hard biscuit from his saddlebag. "Here, you need a little more food than I do, Tree. Eat this. May be a while yet before we dine again."

Tree took the biscuit and smiled back at Cedar. "Thanks."

"Well damn, if all it takes to get a smile on that pretty face is a biscuit, I am going to start carrying a bag full. I was afraid you didn't have any teeth or something."

Cedar believed at their current pace they would be within striking distance of Mushaway by noon. They would proceed slowly and carefully. He figured the Comanche would have scouts watching their encampment from a distance. The country was starting to get a little rougher as the mountain came into view.

Just as the captain had said, they could easily see the escarpment to the northwest of Mushaway called Gail Mountain.

The mountain, at least from a distance, looked to be a good place to defend from if you were engaged and were actually on top of it. Mushaway Mountain was indeed a baldy-knob out in the middle of the plains. If you were on top of it, no adversary could get close without having to climb up it. However, without wood or a water source on top, attackers simply had to play a waiting game below over the people above that were defending it.

Cedar stopped his horse and stared straight ahead.

"Stop your horse real slow, Tree. I believe we have been seen. Do not make any sudden movements. There is a large group of men ahead of us about three hundred yards or so. I believe they just came out of a little canyon or something. They were not there a minute ago."

Tree slowly stopped his horse and did not move his head, only his eyes.

"Try not to look straight at them. Keep your head turned like you are looking toward Mushaway. I count about twenty, maybe twenty-five or so. Ease your hand into your bag and make sure you have more ammunition than your gun will hold. Get it ready now. They are coming toward us."

Cedar had three cartridges in his carbine. He immediately reached into his saddlebag and located a box of shells. Quickly removing five shells, he stuck them into his lips, hanging down like fangs.

Before Cedar could react, Tree dug his spurs into his mount and pulled his pistol out of its holster. He charged the group at a full run with his pistol in the air.

Cedar cocked his carbine and took off behind him at a dead run. With the bullets in his mouth, he could say nothing. He watched in horror as Tree closed the distance to the oncoming men. The closer he got to the approaching riders, the easier Cedar could recognize the gun belts across the chests of Comancheros. There were maybe two or three Comanches with them with no saddles. All of them had rifles.

Tree was closing in on the group with his pistol still in the air when the first shot rang out from the Comancheros. Cedar slammed his horse to a halt and bailed off quickly. He got his mount steadied enough to lay his rifle across the saddle horn.

The next minute was a complete blur. Tree charged through the surprised Comancheros at a dead run. Cedar emptied his carbine. One at a time, he took a shell from his lips. He injected the shells, loaded, and shot until he had shot eight times. The men in the group immediately turned their horses and over shouting from a commander, headed their horses in four different directions.

Cedar quickly reached into his saddlebag for more shells from the open box. By now, all of the men had retreated.

There were seven Comancheros and one Comanche lying on the ground. Their horses fled with the splintered groups as they retreated. Tree kept his back to Cedar with his head down and still holding his pistol in his right hand.

Cedar mounted his horse after reloading his carbine. Slowly, he rode by the dead men as he rode toward Tree.

"You going to tell me why you never fired your damn weapon, Private? You wanted them Comancheros to kill you, didn't you? Most likely over your damn guilt over accidentally killing that boy in military school. You are alive. *Alive.* Get over it. He is accidentally dead and in the grave. You are alive and breathing."

Tree turned slowly and put his gun back into his holster. The front of his shirt was covered in blood.

"You been hit below the left shoulder, Tree. Let's get you off of your horse.

"Looks like there are two bullet holes in you, man. We need to get pressure on them now," he said as he pulled off his neckerchief. "These both missed your vitals, Tree. You are really lucky. Both bullets went clean through you."

He looked into Tree's eyes as his anger mounted. "You never fired a shot. Not one bullet. Well, you are still alive, but I really don't know how with all of that lead flying your way. You ever pull a stunt like that again with me around, and I will just go ahead and shoot you myself. There ain't nobody holding that boy's death against you, Tree. Nobody excepting you. I would suggest you get on with your life instead of trying to take it."

Captain Golden and the troop came riding in from the south at a fast clip and formed a large cloud of dust that could be seen for a mile. Tree and Cedar sat quietly as they approached. The captain slowed the men down when they were about one hundred yards away and brought them to a walk as he assessed the situation. His two scouts were standing quietly looking at several bodies on the ground all around them.

"Looks like you boys were engaged, I'd say. Either of you hurt? "

"Yes, Captain," said Cedar. "Tree got shot twice in the left shoulder. Looks like the bullets went on through."

"You all right, Private Smith?"

"I am fine, Captain. Just shook up a little bit."

The captain carefully counted the dead men.

"Private Jones, it looks like you all got eight of them. How many do you think there were?"

"I reckon there was about fifteen or more that took off in all directions. There may have been a few more. Happened pretty fast."

"Private Tree, let's get that shirt off of you and take a look at those wounds and see what needs doing. The rest of you men set about getting these men buried. Even this type of varmint needs to be buried."

Lester Archibald sat on his horse with his eyes big as saucers. During the charge, he had failed to cock his gun all the way as the lever hung down. He quickly dismounted, ran a short distance from his horse, and began throwing up, not unnoticed by the rest of the men.

Cedar looked at Tree and smiled.

"Looks like that little crowing rooster might just be a hen, Tree."

Tree slowly turned and looked at Cedar. "I have to thank you for saving me from all of them bullets. I would have surely died. Maybe it took nearly dying to help me understand how much there is to live for. I am much obliged to you for what you done."

# Part 2

Part 2

# CHAPTER 8

**Rolling J Ranch, circa 1880**
**Texas Southern Border Country**

TREE "BIGFOOT" SMITH SAT ON his big gray gelding on top of Stone Ridge, eyeballing the deep river valley below. Tree, at Cedar's encouragement, had hired on to the Rolling J and had worked there for near on five years. He thought about their last week in the U.S. Cavalry, when Cedar first brought up the Rolling J Ranch down on the Mexico border.

"We spent nearly all our last five years on the back of a horse, Tree. When we are done here, I want to find me a camp cooking job somewhere where my knees don't hurt every evening. As much as you like being by yourself, I believe you might can get hired on as a cowboy on this Rolling J Ranch I heard about down south of here. You can spend your entire life horseback if you like and talk to nobody but the cows. They just might need a camp cook. Won't pay a lot of money, but it will be steady, and we will have a bed to sleep in and a roof over our head. We spent many a night out here in the woollies without a roof over our head. I do not know of anything else lest we head to New Mexico, that is, if you want to partner up with me."

The partner-upping part of it brought a smile to Tree's face. Five years had passed since the events of Mushaway. He still felt pain now and again in his left shoulder from the bullet wounds, but he never dwelt on the accidental killing at the military school again from that point. Cedar never spoke a word to a soul concerning the events of that day. He was questioned over and over again by others in the troop about how many Comancheros and Comanches he himself had killed that day at Mushaway and how many Tree had killed. His answer was always the same. "Mucho ruido y pocas nueces." His questioners would stand there dumbfounded as he walked away without ever bothering to explain what it meant.

Tree's fiery red hair hung clear to his shoulders now. His long beard hung down nearly to his ninnies. He brushed it out from time to time. It was scraggly, red, and dusty most of the time. He really liked riding alone most of the time and never complained when he pulled drag when moving a herd of cattle. He would just pull up his torn red kerchief over his nose and move along, keeping the cattle moving.

On Sundays, the point on Stone Ridge overlooking the Rio Grande was Tree's favorite spot to sit on Bonner and just reflect about the life he was living and look down toward the Mexican village below and just across the river.

He was thinking about Lester Archibald as he glassed the Mexican village down below. Lester ended up getting killed in a little brothel close to the fort one Saturday evening just one week after he finished his five-year enlistment and was free as a bird. No more orders and no more getting up early. Lester got plenty drunk and mouthy before trying to drag a girl back to one of the courtesy rooms in the back of the place. The owner of the establishment pulled a gun on him and told him to let her go. As soon as Lester dropped the girl, he started running his mouth and ran toward the owner with a knife. The owner shot him three times. One of the boys from Fort Concho was with him as he lay mortally wounded on the floor of the brothel.

"I would have killed me one of them Comanches if I would have had the chance. I just wanted to kill me one of 'em."

Tree heard someone riding up behind him and put his binoculars down to turn around.

"What are you looking at, Mr. Tree?" Roney McCallister asked.

Tree slowly took his eyes away from the binoculars and cast a sideways glance toward Roney, the youngest cowboy on the Rolling J. "Don't you have work to do at the ranch, Roney?"

"Well, it's Sunday, and we are off for the most part. I saw you saddle up and ride away south this morning. I just thought I would see where you were heading."

"If you got to know, I'm a looking at them Mexicans down there across the river there, all gathered up at a graveyard."

"A graveyard? Did somebody die or something?"

"There are a whole bunch of people that are sure enough dead down there all right. I think today is their Day of the Dead or something like that. The two vaqueros that work on the Rolling J live in that village. They call it something like Día de los Muertos. Those folks come into the graveyard and park their carcasses right up next to the grave and have dinner or supper. I mean right there with them dead folks. I been a watching it for three years now at the same day every year. It just looks like a big celebration of some kind. I can hear music sometimes at sundown and they have a big fire into the night."

"Can I look through them binoculars, Mr. Tree?"

"Quit calling me Mr. Tree. My name is just Tree."

"Yes, sir, I got it. It just does not even feel very respectful to me."

"I tell you what, Roney. If I think your tone is disrespectful, I guarantee I'll let you know. Now, focus in with these here and look right down there just to the left of the church steeple. You will see a little fenced graveyard. Get it yet?"

"Well, yes, yes I see it. Looks like there is about thirty or maybe forty people in there and a few dogs outside the gate to the graveyard."

"Yes, those dogs were there last two times I looked at em. Those damn dogs just hike their legs and piss on about anything they see. I reckon that is why they don't let them inside of the fenced area. I wouldn't either. That place is sacred to them. I don't like going in them graveyards none at all."

Roney stared for the longest time through the binoculars. Finally, he put them down and rested them on his saddle horn.

"Tree, it just doesn't make no sense to me about what they are a-doing."

Tree looked long and hard down below before talking. He slowly rolled his chew from the left side to the right and spit the juice out below, hitting the red plum on top of a cactus.

"Well, Roney, your life, my life for that matter, everybody's lives are like those old kerosene lamps on the walls of the bunkhouse. We fill them up with kerosene, and the wick burns when you strike a match to it. Now, you can turn it up a notch and get a brighter light, but when you run out of kerosene, well . . . the lamp just goes out, just like that. You just got so much kerosene in your lamp, and when it is used up, your lamp is out, understand?"

"I ain't never thought of myself as no kerosene lamp, Tree."

"What I am a saying is, turn up your wick, so to speak. Live your life like it is worth living, celebrate while you are alive, not like them folks down there do when you are dead. Don't be a-pissing and moaning about your upbringing or lack thereof. And I don't care what kind of bad place you come from. Ain't none of our faults where we come from, but it's surely our fault if we let it direct our paths. I damned sure learned that. You know where you came from, don't you? I know where you came from because you told me. But in spite of that, you are alive and well right out here on the Rolling J. After all, it is not where you start in this life, it is where you end up. Dead is a little too late to be celebrating then, don't you think? This much conversation is wearing me out, Roney. Have a good day," said Tree as he reached over and took the binoculars.

"And don't be following me. I don't want nobody a following me, you hear?"

"Tree, you know where I come from, cause I done told you. I ain't never told nobody else in this world, about my mama and daddy and all."

"I know you did Roney, you sure did. It was a shame what your mama and papa done to you. But here you are. Alive and well out here on the Rolling J."

"Well, If I told you about me, why don't you tell me about you? I don't know where you come from. What kind of circumstances and such did you arise from?"

Tree clicked his gray into a slow lope for a little ways and stopped.

"Maybe one day I will tell you a little about me. Where I come from is just not that important."

Tree always watched the big gray gelding's ears. He could usually pick up signs of trouble just by watching them as they moved independently toward sounds. Bonner picked up sounds that a human could not hear. Old Bonner certainly could hear about anything that moved or breathed. He could spot a mouse from thirty feet away or a little moth flying through the air. His specialty was rattlesnakes. Tree remembered how bad Bonner's head swelled up when he was bitten on the upper lip by a large prairie rattler, deftly concealed in a patch of cactus next to a little grass patch. His head swelled so bad, it closed up his nostrils and his throat. Bonner could barely eat for two weeks. He struggled to drink water from the trough but somehow made it through. He was never the same horse after that. After that, he always spotted a snake in the trail or around the barn well before Tree saw them. On the trail, he would put both ears clearly forward and blow. No rearing and bucking, he would just stop and blow. Deep snorts with both nostrils. Tree always reached down and rubbed his neck to calm him and would ease off the left side, taking extra care to dismount with just the toe of his boot in the stirrup in case Bonner spooked. There had been many a cowboy that tried to dismount on the right side of the saddle, leaving too much boot in the stirrup. If their horse ever shied away for any reason, they sometimes could not kick their boot free of the stirrup and got drug to death. Tree always remembered the young Cates boy from Montana that was helping in the fall gathering on the Rolling J two years prior. He threw a loop on a big heifer that needed doctoring, stepped off on the right side just about the time a big covey of quail flushed in front of his pony. The horse wheeled and took off at a dead run with the heifer tied to the saddle horn and the youngster hung in the stirrup on the right. When two cowboys finally got the horse ran down and roped, the young Cates boy was nearly torn in two, along with a dead, mangled heifer.

Tree pulled Bonner to a slow stop and turned him around. He pulled his binoculars up and scanned the point to see if Roney had followed him. He finally picked him up heading back toward the ranch headquarters at a slow walk. He headed Bonner back toward the point. Maybe he could see if some of those Mexicans was still in the graveyard by the village.

He eased up the slight incline to the point where the big rocks stood. When he reached the furthermost point of the outcrop, he trained the binoculars on the church steeple below and then located the graveyard. There did not seem to be any people left except for one woman in a blue dress. He watched her intently as she walked among the tombstones. She would stop and put her hand on one and then bow her head for a bit before moving on.

She stopped at two more graves before she turned slowly and walked toward the entrance. He watched her stop and turn slowly at the grave-yard gate. She gathered her dress and looked like she was wiping her eyes. She held her dress hem to her face for a while and finally let it drop. The evening sun was just starting to set and shadows to the east were start-ing to form behind the bigger trees. He quietly admired her statue-like silhouette against the beautiful evening sky.

Tree slowly turned his horse and started back to the ranch at a walk. He would easily be there in the short time available, while it was light enough to see the trail. There had been a full moon the last two nights, and it lit up the trail just fair enough to help Old Bonner spot any mouse-hunting rattlers as they moved along. The coyotes had just begun howling to take evening head count when Tree got off and opened the gate to the main pony corral. Bonner was glad to get unsaddled and wiped down before heading to the water trough. After taking a long drink, he followed Tree to his barn stall. The longer tenured cowboys got their choice of the six available barn stalls. All of the others had to let their ponies go in the big corral and catch them the next morning. Nobody ever dared to put their horse in Bonner's stall. Tree pulled him a small bucket of oats and three forks of hay before heading to the bunkhouse.

All of the cowboys knew not to ever question Tree about his comings and goings, especially on Sunday when chores were light. Tree always ventured off after breakfast on Sunday and usually did not return until after sundown when things were slow. Of course, the two Mexican vaqueros from the village of Montenegro that worked on the ranch never said much of anything to anyone. Both of them worked harder and longer than any of the gringo cowboys and mainly just kept to themselves. Their riggings were also different than the rest of the boys. They were always on the move and cast a prominent and unforgettable silhouette with their broad sombreros. Their backs were always straight up in their saddles as they rode. They were always in exact rhythm with their horses in a brisk walk or at a dead run. While some cowboys bounced along in their saddles, heads bobbing up and down and flailing their arms, the vaqueros rode smoothly in the saddle with reins perfectly in hand and virtually no arm movement, while perfectly centered in the saddle. Tree admired their immense riding skills. The seemingly perfect coordination of applied knee pressure and rein positioning was like watching an orchestrated dance between horse and rider. Neither man made many vocal signals to their horses, only a slight click with their mouths. Mostly, it was knees and reins, which both rider and horse were highly in tune. Their leather breast and butt straps kept their saddles from forward or backward movement when traveling the rough up-and-down mountainous terrain on the Rolling J and especially the ride from and back across the Rio Grande to their village. Their stirrups were framed with tapaderos to protect their boots from the abundant mesquite thorns. They never seem to worry about any other cowboy's business, especially Tree's. Neither man had ever seen the inside of the bunkhouse and always brought their own food with them, packed away in their leather saddlebags. Mostly just tortillas wrapped over beans with a little meat and a few habaneros or jalapeño peppers.

Their canteens were always filled at the river when they were coming to the Rolling J in the morning darkness and going back across the river at night. They could never be found mooching water off the other cowboys. When all the boys were finally saddled up and ready to go of a morning, the two vaqueros were already on point and ready. Their uphill ride from the river valley and downhill at dusk added an extra thirty minutes a day they did not get paid for. Both men were just happy to bring home the sixty dollars a month they were paid. Other than Cedar Jones, they were just about the only two men Tree talked to, albeit only in short sentences and in Spanish. None of the other boys at the ranch spoke it at all, much less good enough to follow along with folks that was talking it. Tree had picked it up rapidly once he went to work on the Rolling J, mostly from the two vaqueros. They would point at something and say the word in Spanish. He learned how to count cattle in Spanish. After a while, he was able to put a few words together and learned to roll his tongue with some words, much to the vaqueros' delight.

"You are starting to sound like a Mexican, Señor Tree. Not many gringos can roll their tongue like you."

DeWitt Murphy came to the Rolling J a short time after Tree and Cedar showed up. His specialty was listening in on other folk's conversations and trying to get in their business when he could.

"What was them vaqueros just saying, Tree? I don't know no Mexican words much."

Tree always gave a wry smile when Dewitt quizzed him.

"Well DeWitt, they said that your hangy-downs would go good with a jalapeño pepper and some beans, especially if they were just barely cooked on the branding iron fire. Nice and tender. If you cook them too long, they just explode."

"Well, damnation," DeWitt said. "Them dang Mexican boys must be some kind of cannibals or something. They are not getting my hangy-downs. They really say that, Tree?"

"They said as long as they salted them a little, they would be as good eating as some of that salt pork our cook puts in the beans. Better keep a lookout, DeWitt. You sure had better keep a close lookout."

DeWitt always kept a good distance from the two vaqueros on horseback. When they were working the fire together, castrating and branding, he never took his eye off them. They thought his mind was not clear and he might be deranged the way he was always looking at them.

Tree slowly opened the bunkhouse door hoping most of the boys had hit the sack. He always tired quickly of their never-ending stories about this working girl or that working girl at the saloon or how bad the food and pay was. But mostly, the talk was about the fancy girls in Rosario and their sweet-smelling perfumes and garter belts and mostly about some of their abundant accessories. It was idle chatter for the most part, with some of them just talking to be talking.

He glanced around the bunkhouse, and most of the boys were in their bunk trying to get enough sleep to make the 5:00 a.m. breakfast call. If you did not get up on time, you did not eat. If you slept in more than twice in one month, you were politely relieved of your cowboying on the ranch. Roney McCallister was standing in front of the big mantel that held the kerosene lanterns when Tree walked in. DeWitt Murphy was sitting in a chair smoking his pipe and reading with his little reading glasses on.

"Tree, that young boy has been turning that wick up and down for a little while, just a watching it get darker and then lighter," DeWitt whispered behind his hand. "He said something about . . . he ain't no kerosene lantern or something like that a minute ago. I think that boy may be off in some other part of the world right now. What do you make of it, Tree?"

"I don't guess I make nothing of it, DeWitt. Nothing at all. Let's go out on the porch a minute."

The moon had come up and completely lit up the brilliant night sky. Tree could count nearly every pony in the corral. He kept his eyes on the corral. The stars were beginning to twinkle just right. The full moon made him want to stay out all night and just look up at it.

"You know much about young Roney McCallister, DeWitt? Do you really know anything at all about the boy?"

DeWitt, never quick on his feet, looked at the porch floor.

"Well . . . I . . . I know he is young and I . . . maybe I don't know him too well. I think you is the only one he talks to very much. Damn good on his pony and can handle a rope right smart, especially roping and dragging calves to the branding fire. He has that sixty-footer braided leather lariat, you know, and he keeps it oiled up good. I do know that. Don't know how he come by it, though. Them things are good ropes and he would have to save a spell to get him one, I reckon." Dewitt paused and turned to look at Tree. "I guess you could say I don't right know much about him at all."

Tree turned slowly without giving DeWitt his full look.

"No sir, you probably don't. Roney McCallister come from up around Bozeman, Montana. His Pa ran out on his Ma one fall before a bitch of a winter hit. Roney was not much over twelve years old at the time. His Pa cowboyed on the Twin Nickel Ranch just out of Bozeman. Kind of a fair provider, until a bronc threw him and broke his back and one leg. That is where Roney learned about horses and such. It was mostly from the cowboys on the Twin Nickel that he got his horse and rope learning from, not his Pa. His Pa's leg right near healed up over a year or so, but never could quite mount up again and when he did, his mended leg and back started to hurt so bad one of the other cowboys had to help him get off his horse. He just plain could not work on a ranch no more after that and started feeling like less of a man, you might say. There was no work to be had or at least none that his Pa would do. He thought cowboying was like the Wild West stories he read about back east. Didn't want no other type of non-glorying work.

"He took what little money Roney's ma had saved from his wages and drank it up or whored it up in Bozeman. Roney even seen him walking with one of the whores down the street in Bozeman, drunk as a skunk and hugging all over her. Those whores did not laugh at his condition, at least to his face anyway I reckon, but they were sure enough glad to take his money. Then, before that winter hit, he lit out in a little livestock car on a train bound south and never looked back."

"Damnation," Dewitt said.

Tree stared toward the horse corral and continued.

"They barely made the winter and probably would not a-made it. A few of the neighbors got wind of it and gave them potatoes, a few sacks of dried beans, and a little dried venison to eat. That's all they had along with snow melted in a pot to drink. If they did not have a good supply of firewood they were given along with food from the neighbors, they probably would have starved.

"Come early spring, Roney's ma kind of reached her breaking point. Underweight and nervous to boot, she sat young Roney down at the kitchen table one morning and said, 'Your Pa has done left us, Roney, and he ain't a-comin back. I hate to do what I am fixing to do but ... well, I ain't got no choice. I may not be here much longer, Roney. I can feel it in my bones. I'm aching all the time ... and this cold, cannot never get no warming in my bones.

"'You ... you are going to have to strike out on your own somehow, just like them wolf pups when their mama done run out of her milk. I can't fetch for you none, and you are way better off on your own than counting on me every day. You probably need to hop a train out of this cold forsaken place that never gets warm. It was your Pa's dream to be a damn cowboy up here, not mine. The man never should have brought us here from Ohio like he did. He would not listen to me. He damn sure wasn't no cowboy, just a want to be. I imagine you are better on a horse and all than he ever was. So, here we are and he ain't nowhere to be had. It is probably a good thing to not be relying on his sorry whoring ass anyway. He always took his whoring and liquor over me anyway. Drank and whored up most of the cowboying money I stashed back. He always seemed to find it somehow. I hate to be talking to you like this, but that is just how life is. That is just how it is.

"'It would be best if you headed out, maybe today, when that Northern Pacific train pulls out around ten o'clock this morning. It will be heading toward warmer country somewhere. Bundle up and put something under your hat to keep your head warm. I just can't take care of you no more. And, don't be a fool like your daddy was. He wasn't nothing but a damn whoring fool.'

"So, Mr. DeWitt, those were the last words his mama ever spoke to him: 'Don't be no damn, whoring fool like your pa.' That is sure something to arm a young man with against the wolves of this world, ain't it? She just told him to hop a train and head out on his lonesome. She wasn't no better than his pa was.

"Roney got off a train somewhere in Texas and somehow got to this ranch all of the way from Bozeman. I imagine he saw a little hardship on the way down, don't you think? That has got to be close to fifteen hundred miles or better. Lot of time for a young boy like that holed up on a cow hauler trying to stay warm. He said he found a few potatoes on the boxcar and about half lived on them. Probably came from Idaho, I suppose. I don't think there was a lot to eat or drink on his train ride. He said he slipped off and back on at watering stops and stole any food he found just to stay alive."

"Dang gum, Tree. I ain't never heard you speak that many words before. Maybe in the whole time we been a-knowing each other. He told you all of that? That is a lot of remembering you just told me."

Tree finally turned and looked at DeWitt with the moonlight reflecting on his high cheekbones and thick beard.

"You probably won't ever hear that many again and don't you be a spreading nary a word of what I just told you, ever. You understand? Leave the boy alone. I better not see anyone abusing him or laughing at him neither."

"Yes, sir, Tree, yes sir, why I wouldn't even dream of saying . . ."

Tree walked away in mid-sentence and walked into the moonlight toward the corral, clearly done with talking.

"Damnation," DeWitt said. "Damnation."

Tree waited for the bunkhouse door to close behind DeWitt. He sniffed the night air with all the familiar smells. The smells of sweet horse sweat, manure, and a little cedar melded in his nostrils. The horses always seem to stay calm when he was close. He would click to them every little bit to get their attention. Ears pricked at attention, sometimes a slight nicker, they never ran when Tree was leaning on the top corral rail. Some nights he would stay out there for the better part of an hour. Mostly he was more comfortable with the horses and the night sounds than listening to the cowboys' meandering through fields of bloviated experiences that never mounted to as much as a tinker's damnation of a hill of beans. He generally waited until he saw the kerosene lamps turned down to nothing before he slipped in and hit his bunk. Sometimes when no one else knew, Tree would see old Muley Banks slip out the side bunkhouse door and head to the outhouse. Everyone that heard him thought he was tending to his necessaries but Tree knew he kept a bottle hid behind a loose board in the barn. Muley was a tenured hand, and a good one when sober, which was most of the time. He just always took a little detour to the inside stable to check on his pony a few times a month, always at night. He would skip out with his bottle tucked under his arm and head for the outhouse. Sometimes he would come out after a quick snort to calm his nerves. Other times it might be daylight when he stumbled out squinting his eyes, cussing and scratching his belly at the same time. He always let loose with a belly full of gas. Tree never understood how Muley stood the smell of the outhouse all night long. Even with the lime in the crap hole, it still never hid the smell completely. The yellow jacket nest in the summer time never seemed to scare Muley none like it did Tree. He would as soon take a beating as sit underneath a wasp nest while he tended to his necessaries. Many times, he just squatted behind a mesquite tree with a few old magazine pages for paper. At least he would not get stung.

No matter how inebriated Muley became, Tree never knew him to not saddle up in time to be ready to go with the rest of the boys. He had pulled on the bottle for so long now, the whiskey was part of his body makeup. He probably could not live without it in his system. Muley was never known to go into town to the drinking saloon like the rest. Somehow, he always managed to have a bottle hid in the barn.

# CHAPTER 9

TREE WAS LOATH TO STAND and admire himself in front of a mirror. In fact, he almost never took the time to do so. His tall muscular frame was a sight to behold for most men, and though he was highly regarded by the other cowboys, he never saw himself in that light.

On his rare trips into town, women often turned their head in admiration. When he did notice that they were staring at him, he assumed it was because he thought he looked like a freak of nature. His large frame and oversized feet firmly connected him to the ground. His large seven-inch set of knuckles looked like a grizzly bear paw.

The women who turned their heads were amazed at the sight of a male that big. Quite handsome, with his flowing dark auburn red hair along with his ninnie-length beard and weathered bandanna. His rugged, high cheekbones and square chin sat squarely on large broad shoulders that most shirts could barely contain. He especially drew stares when he was atop Bonner. Straight backed in the saddle, Bonner's ears straight forward taking in every sound, Tree was pretty shiny to everyone but himself.

He stood alone in the bunkhouse looking into the mirror on the east wall. He seemed to have as much hair coming out of his ears and nose as he did on his back and chest. All of it mostly red. Of course, the nose hair helped filter out the endless dust the cattle stirred up pulling drag, but it was sure unbecoming from the view in the mirror. The boys hung two fancy-girl pictures next to the mirror on each side. He rarely glanced at them or the mirror. He had never had much use for girls for the most part. They scared him. He certainly never understood the few he had been around back home when he was a young boy. He never talked to nobody about his parents or his mama in particular at any time anyone could remember except for Cedar Jones. DeWitt asked him about it one time, and Tree simply walked away and that was that. He knew that Cedar was like a bear trap that you could not open when it came to keeping things secret. Their friendship was long built on mutual trust.

He figured it was getting time to ride into town and see the barber if there was one there. Riding the fifteen miles or so into Rosario was pleasant enough, but he always enjoyed the ride coming back to the ranch more. His gut always knotted up in the saddle when was heading to town for some reason. He generally tried to go in at least twice a year and get trimmed up and especially get the hair on his neck, ears, and nose cleaned off. Once all of the trimming and cutting was done, he always paid the extra dollar to get a tub filled with hot water and scrub down with lye soap and soaking powders. Bonner always gave him a good smelling over when he came out of the barbering and bath house.

"You think I am a dandy, don't you, boy?" Tree would always say. "I may smell like one, but I am not one."

He would always rub Bonner under the chin. "These fancy powder smells will wear off in a day or two, so get that wrinkle out of your nose."

The scrub brush always felt good against his skin when he was using it. He could always smell himself when he got in a tub as the steam off the hot water rose to his nostrils. The hot bath was not like the baths he took in the river. The cold river baths were refreshing as he scrubbed away with his little bar of lye soap. Hot baths with good-smelling salts were relaxing to the point of nearly sleeping.

He decided he would ride in on Saturday morning after ranch chores and see if there was anyone at the barbering place in Rosario. As always, his stomach immediately began to knot up as he draped the saddle blanket on Bonner.

"Well, we are fixing to head into town, boy," he said as he scratched Bonner under his bottom lip.

"I don't care for them town people no more than you do for them fancy buggy-pulling horses. But I need a new set of shoes and nails for you, cause your damn feet are not the normal size, just like mine," he laughed.

"Yours is getting plumb wore down."

He gently lifted the saddle on him and reached under to check the girth strap for stickers before cinching it up and latching the breast strap and the tie-down leather. Tree always left Bonner haltered up when he saddled up and never put his double-reined bridle on until afterward. The bit and bridle were removed and halter put back on as soon as Tree got back to the corral. One cowboy draped his single reins over the saddle horn when he got off his horse at the corral. He slapped the horse on the rear to clear the gate. The reins hooked on a cedar post going in and pulled the bit down sharply on the horse's tongue, nearly severing it against his teeth. Tree never forgot the cowboy's guilt and the animal's pain over the incident. He took great pains not to replicate it.

He grabbed the saddle horn with his left hand and swung up into the saddle. Bonner never moved a muscle until Tree clicked at him. They eased off toward town at a light trot with Tree uneasy in the saddle. He patted Bonner on the neck, "I wished we was done and heading back."

CHARLES WHITTMIRE III BOUGHT THE only barbering house in Rosario at the turn of the new year in 1880 and was into his first year of ownership.

His father and his father before him were barbers back east. When he decided to make his way out west, his father told him:

"If you can cut hair on four of them cowboys per hour on their pay-days plus give their stinky, cow-smelling butts a place to take a bath before they hit the saloon, you can make a sizable amount of money in a year. At least enough to raise a family on and put the rest in the bank. Why, in a few years, you can buy another business in town and might even be the mayor one day. In fact, most of them do not know what to do with their pay other than spend it quickly on whiskey and the saloon girls. You might as well get in front of those activities and take a good cut up front instead of on the tail end when they got nothing left. Lots of money in something as simple as cutting a fellow's hair," he would say.

"Throw in a shave and a bath, and you just took in a dollar and fifty cents of their money. Get that stink off them, and them saloon girls might just think they're smarter than they are. Those girls and whiskey take a good portion of what is left after barbering. One month later, the cycle starts over again if they come in on payday, which is a good bet."

Tree saw a wooden barber pole painted red, white, and blue on the street corner when he rode into town. The town was readily flowing with a steady stream of horses and riders. There were folks going both ways walking on the boarded walkways. Some of the men had on little derby hats with pheasant feathers on them. He saw Logan's Hardware Store, with two men loading barbed-wire rolls off the loading ramp onto a horse-drawn wagon. He decided he would make his way over there after his barbering and bath and get Bonner's new shoes.

Tree dismounted Bonner in front of the barbering shop. He tied him to the hitching rail and loosened the latigo strap from the buckle.

The sign above the shop was large and very visible. "Barbering, shave, and hot bath (with powders) for $1.50."

*That is a lot of money for all of that. Well, I'm here and I am not coming back for a while, so I might as well get on with it.*

There were two other customers in the shop when Tree ducked through the door opening. With his broad hat on, he brushed against the top of the door frame when he entered. The men stopped their conversation when he walked in. They had not seen a man that large enter the shop.

"Can I help you, cowboy?" Mr. Whittmire said. "Looking for the hardware store?"

"Not just yet, just need a little barbering and maybe a hot bath."

"Well, I would certainly say you could use both of those," Mr. Whittmire said, not looking him in the eyes. "I reason you have not had neither in a while by the smell and looks of things. Might hang your hat on that hat rack over there, but put it on the end please away from these gentlemen's hats. Would not want the dust off of that thing getting on their fine beavers."

Tree pulled down the holder on his hat cinch and hung it on the end peg of the hat rack. The two gentlemen's hats were little black derby hats with a small pheasant feathers stuck in the broad band of each. *No, I sure would not want to get one of them high-rooster hats dirty.*

Mr. Whittmire and the man in the chair continued their conversation while the other gentleman in waiting kept a keen eye on Tree as he sat down a few chairs down from him.

"Yes, like I was saying, they said it was some kind of outlaw Mexican bandit that did the mutilating a good while back on that young boy across the border at that village. Montenegro, or something like that. Said that he cut off the boy's ears, and his mama sewed them back on with horse tail. Maybe he and his band are the ones been stealing, killing, and raping on the border. Hell, I thought that kind of thing was finally starting to slow down in these parts. I heard there is maybe twenty men in his band. They say he stabs folks in the back of the neck with some kind of spike or something and then cuts their ears off. Just leaves them stuck in their pockets if they have any or sticks them ears on the spike where it comes out the front of their neck. Sometimes he leaves their ears on their forehead. That wanted poster I saw at the sheriff's office says his name is

Gato Montes. All it shows is a Mexican man with a sombrero on with long hair that somebody drew up. He is wanted for murder and horse stealing it says. There is a $5,000 reward out for him and $1,000 apiece for any member of his band caught with him. They must want him really bad for that kind of reward. That is a hell of a name for a bandit, Gato Montes. They say after he cut the ears off of a Mexican boy, they went and kicked him out of the village. I hear he comes across the border at will and nobody can stop him. I heard they ain't nobody ever really got a good look at him other than he has long black hair plumb down below his shoulders. That is what I heard."

Mr. Whittmire listened intently as he clipped away at the balding man's hair. "Charley, just who told you that? You make it sound like this bandit is right at our door."

"Well, I heard that over at the saloon when I was having my evening 'tide me over until morning' drink. I heard them cowboys talking about it."

"Well, that certainly explains it!" said Mr. Whittmire. "Those dumb turds only know which end a cow poops out of and where the milk comes from. And most of them never take a bath until they finally make their way into town with their wild stories. And that is what they are Charley, wild stories. I'd bet that cowboy sitting over there half-asleep has some wild stories to tell. I would also bet that most of their stories are as big and tall as he is too. And they probably stink to high heavens, just like he does. I don't believe I would put too much stock in what you hear from those range cowboys. Most of them do good to read and write their own names. That will do it, Charley," said Mr. Whittmire as he untied the cloak. He brushed away the hair and splashed a little honeysuckle juice in his hands and wiped it on Charley's hair.

"Charley, don't you be fretting about that bandit now. With cowboys like that man sitting over there and the ones in the saloon, we are greatly protected from such a bandit and his compadres, all twenty of them," he laughed.

"You protect those ears now, would not want to see him come in and cut them off, you know," he laughed. "Lester, you are next."

Lester McCoy made his way to the barber chair.

"Lester, you were in here two weeks ago. Your hair really needs no trimming."

"Just trim it anyway, Mr. Whittmire, it gets me out of range of that terrible woman. I can't believe I married her. Course if she did not have all that money from her daddy, I would not have, I suppose."

"Well, I suppose I can take a little off the edges. I take it you are going to join Charley for a 'tide me over' later?"

"Well, I am going to get over that way later but it will be for more than a tide me over. It will be more like a 'keep me asleep for a month,' I guess. They can't serve me enough whiskey to keep me from hearing that screeching voice of hers. It is like listening to a squeaky wheel on a horse buggy."

"Well, Lester, that is the price you pay for success, I guess. At least you are not having to work for it.

"All right, that will be fifty cents. Don't get caught up in any of those high tales over at the saloon. See you next time, Lester."

Mr. Whittmire shook off the cloak and peered over at Tree.

"You are next, cowboy." Tree slowly opened his eyes. He stood up slowly and approached the barbering chair.

"Seems like you cowboys would learn to leave your chaps and spurs outside. There is absolutely no need for them in here."

"You want me to take them off?"

"No, I suppose not. Just try and not hook them things on my new chair. Shipped it all the way in from Virginia. I don't want some cowboy's spurs scratching it up. I will go ahead and cut your hair before your bath, but if you do ever come in here again, let's get you a bath first. I suspect you have not entertained one in a while. I guess they don't have the necessary facilities where you come from. You want that beard cut off or trimmed?"

Tree could feel his face flush under his beard. "Just trimmed, I guess."

"And your hair? It is very long."

"Cut it pretty short, I reckon."

There was no further conversation during the barbering. Even though Mr. Whittmire was long on the mouth, he had a rather gentle hand with the razor on the neck. Tree's skin tingled and pricked up with each pass of the straight razor across the lathered hair on his neck. When Mr. Whittmire was through, he did not extend any pleasurable talking, he just said:

"I will need all of the $1.50 now, then I will go and draw your bath and plenty of smelling powders."

Tree pulled the coins out of his pocket and handed them to Mr. Whittmire.

"Be around to the back in a few minutes, and I will have your bath poured up. I keep a full kettle on the coals all day, so it will be hot. It's going to have to be to get that stink off of you," he muttered.

The wooden floor in the barbering shop was smooth worn and squeaked when Tree walked across it to retrieve his hat from the rack. He went out the front door and slowly made his way to the alley door in the fence. The sign said "Bath Here," with an arrow pointed inside the fence. He slowly opened the gate and looked inside. Mr. Whittmire was pouring hot water into a large tub. He closed the gate and walked toward the tub.

"You can hang your clothes over on that rack there. Wiping-down towels are right there next to the tub. You can leave out the back, same way you came in."

Tree slowly undressed. His body was white excepting his face, forearms, and hands. All other parts never saw the light of day. He slowly put one foot into the hot water and let it adjust before putting the other in. Finally, after covering his hangy-downs with his cupped hands, he slowly sat down in the tub. The water was very hot and exhilarating, in a way. He did not start scrubbing down with the brush and bar of lye soap for a bit. He cleaned his entire body and washed his hair and beard. The water felt good over his body as he dipped jug after jug into the tub and over his head. Finally, he just lay there buckled up in the short tub and relaxed. The little sack of fresh clothes he brought on Bonner were sitting next to the tub when he dried off. He had previously washed the salt off them in the river and let them dry on a big rock. At least they did not stink. He dried off completely and combed out his hair with his pocket comb. Slowly he dressed and studied his next move. Stuffing the soiled clothes into the sack, he pulled his boots back on and then he buckled and tied his leggings back on. Finally, he tied his clean neckerchief and then put on his old hat.

TREE MADE HIS WAY OUT the back gate and around to the hitching post where Bonner was tied. Bonner's nicker was very low but audible. He was used to Tree slipping him one small sugar cube a day, usually in the late evening. He always smelled Tree's front right pocket to see if there was one there.

Tree tied the sack of clothes on the back of the saddle before turning to go back into the barbering shop. Mr. Whittmire looked surprised to see Tree when he slowly opened the front door and ducked his head as he stooped through.

"Can I help you, cowboy? That was not much time to get all of that stink off."

Tree did not say a word as he approached him.

"Can I help you?" Mr. Whittmire repeated in an agitated voice. "You cowboys . . ."

That was the last thing he said as Tree backhanded him hard, in the jaw. The force completely flipped Mr. Whittmire over the arms of the barbering chair. His glasses were half-cocked on his face, and most of his hair was hanging down on one side. It looked like he grew it longer on one side to comb over a bald spot. His nose bled slightly on his white fancy-collared shirt with a red garter on the right arm. His father always told him to wear a red garter on his arm while he was barbering.

"When those cowboys ask why, just tell them it came off one of them saloon girls' legs and that they like their cowboys shaved and cleaned up before they come in and try to cozy up close. That way you get them all worked up to spend their money in your establishment before they head over to see the fancy girls."

Clearly stunned and barely conscious, he thought at that moment he might die.

Tree slowly leaned over him and stared intently into his eyes. Tree's eyes were hard to see from under his hat. Mr. Whittmire was absolutely certain not to speak at this moment. Tree stared at him for a good long spell before saying a word.

"First of all," he said, "My name is not Cowboy. You will refer to me respectfully as Tree next time I see you. I stink because I work. Ain't nothing wrong with working, is there, Mr. Whittmire?" as he grabbed him by the chin. "Cutting hair is probably necessary work, you just don't have to sweat to do it, you see."

Mr. Whittmire slowly shook his head no.

"That beefsteak you eat at the parlor did not raise itself. Us that stink raised it, so you could eat it, while sipping red wine with your fancy friends in this here town. And, next time, don't let your alligator mouth outrun your little canary arse. At least not with me, understand?"

Mr. Whittmire blinked wildly and nodded his head yes.

"And I mean one little peep out of that squawker of a mouth the next time I run into you, well, you will not be eating steak with those pretty teeth you got there. They will be feeding you soup with a spoon."

Tree turned slowly and walked toward the door. He turned slowly around before stooping his massive frame out of the door.

"By the way, I can read and write my own name and am quite fluent in the social graces if I am a mind to do so. I can even do arithmetic and memorize and recite poetry. I just don't talk out loud about doing it. Just because I stink, don't mean I am stupid, señor. Adios."

Tree untied Bonner from the hitching rail and turned to walk over to Logan's Hardware across the street. There were all kinds of new noises and smells that Bonner was taking in. Tree cautiously led Bonner to the metal hitching rail on the south side of the street. This one had metal rings on it rather than the wooden rail in front of Mr. Whittmire's Barbering House.

TREE HAD JUST PICKED OUT the four large horseshoes and twenty-four horseshoe nails when Sheriff Leonard Brody approached him from behind. The sheriff was well into his late sixties and well-polished in his duties. Having been reelected eight times for the four-year term, he was well respected and had seen Rosario go from a rowdy border town to somewhat of a place where residents enjoyed a life relatively free of riff-raff and constant trouble. That was not to say that the area was totally cleaned out of Comanches, Apaches, and outlaws from both sides of the border. That was to say that it had improved a little over time. Sometimes, he struggled with who the bad folks really were. He always knew if he was in the Comanches' place, he would sure be fighting to keep the lands they had fought for and won.

His knees hurt more often than not from countless up and downs on horseback, tracking down every kind of cutthroat that was known to man. He had been stepped on, kicked, cut up, and shot at least twice in his years of being a sheriff. That don't count the times he was shot at over thirty years. Most of the shooters concentrated more on drawing fast and did not know how to aim their weapon. He had personally shot over twenty-two men during his tenure as sheriff of Rosario and had to kill four of them. Those four were high-stepping roosters bound and determined to fight. He always tried to shoot them in the leg if he could, but it sometimes just did not work out that way. The best way was to get them to simply drop their weapon. That too, did not always work out for the best. He never could keep an honest, nondrinking deputy for very long. Most of them were always grumbling about the low wages and the piss-poor attitude of the rowdy cowboys when they swung into town on payday. So, he had sworn off ever hiring one of those dandies again, preferring to work alone. Most of them would not stand tall and turned yellow in any kind of confrontation anyway.

He sized up the large man in front of him well before he spoke to him. He did not notice any threatening movements nor nothing other than someone focused on horseshoes. He appeared to tower above the sheriff by at least a foot at the top of his broad hat. He noticed his very large hands with long fingers and the broadness of his knuckles as he picked up a different-size horseshoe. This man was definitely a bone to be chewed if he were ever cornered, the sheriff surmised. Of course, he had seen some very large men that had the makeup of a five-hundred-pound bull calf that was still sucking on his mama's teat, when it came to getting riled. They would as soon lay down and take a nap as get in a tussle even if they were to be challenged hard by some rooster looking for a fight.

This man's worn outerwear and the calluses on his hands told a story of repetitive hard work. The sheriff figured this man was one who probably never said much, but when challenged, would certainly engage. Possibly once riled up, he might not easily un-rile.

"Howdy," Sheriff Brody said. "Finding what you are looking for?"

Tree turned slowly and eyed the sheriff and noticed the strapped-on pistol on his right side. He also noticed that the strap was unbuttoned on the holster.

"Yes, sir, just buying a few horseshoes for my horse outside."

"Yes, that I can see," said the sheriff.

"You been over to Whittmire's Barbershop this morning? Like maybe in the last little bit?"

Tree looked at his horseshoes and then at the sheriff.

"I just came from there."

"Well, a feller just came to my office all out of breath and said he saw a feller like you leave right before he walked in. Says he just found Mr. Whittmire, with his face bloodied up a bit and dazed. You and Mr. Whittmire have any trouble while you were there?"

Tree looked at Sheriff Brody a good minute before he answered.

"There was a pesky fly come by and needed swatting."

The sheriff looked the tall and muscular cowboy over, knowing there was probably more to the story and that it would never be known for sure exactly what happened. He did know Mr. Whittmire's propensity to let his dislike for some of his customers outrun what little sense he had. He thought that might be the case here. Mr. Whittmire always gave him the impression that as the proprietor of the barbering shop that he might just be a head above his clientele, especially if they come from beyond the town's borders. He especially did not seem to care for the infrequent Mexican cowboy that came in for a barbering with other trail cowboys. The sheriff had heard him make a statement or two while waiting on a haircut.

"I don't understand why they bring them boys in here. They just don't belong in my place of business."

Hearing tale of that kind of talk tended to make the sheriff's blood boil. Especially from a little bully the likes of Mr. Whittmire. Of course, loudmouthed talking from a man the likes of Mr. Whittmire was not against the law. He thought a minute as he stared at Tree, not even asking him his name.

"Well sir, I believe the next time you encounter a pesky fly like that, why don't you just resort to a flyswatter? They get the job done, I reckon. I'll be moving along now. Have a good visit to our quiet town while you are here. Good day, sir."

Tree stood there as the sheriff walked off. Slowly, he approached the counter to pay for his horseshoes and nails. He also picked up two small rolls of cured rawhide string for leather stitching. The man behind the counter looked surprised when Tree asked if he had any boxes of sugar cubes.

"Yes, sir, we got them. How many do you need? They are twenty cents a box."

"How many are in a box?" Tree asked.

"Why, I think there are about a dozen, sir."

"Let me have six boxes then."

"Yes, sir. That's a mighty sweet tooth to keep satisfied there."

Tree did not look up as he pulled out his leather sack of money.

"I like them in my coffee of a morning."

"Oh, yes, sir. Yes, sir. I like milk in mine. That will be ... Let's see, $1.00 for the horseshoes and another nickel for the nails. Your total comes to two dollars and twenty-five cents, sir. The sugar cubes amount to nearly half of your purchase. With that kind of sweet tooth, you interested in some good chocolate? We got some real good chocolate shipped in here all the way from Chicago."

"How much you get on those?"

"They run a nickel a bar, but they are really good. Most folks don't want to spend that kind of money on just sweet chocolate."

"Give me three of them."

"Very good, sir. I will wrap them up nice in paper, but you need to eat them pretty quick if it starts to get warm, or they will melt on you. Now that brings your total to two dollars and forty-five cents, sir. You work around here?"

Tree picked out the coins from his bag and handed them to the man at the counter.

"No sir, I work a-ways away from here," and took his purchases from the man.

"You come back now. We appreciate your business. Yes, sir, we do."

Several men were sitting outside of Logan's when Tree stooped through the door. Two of them briefly stopped their game of checkers and eyed him over from the rear.

"I would sure hate to make that fellow mad," one said. The other looked Tree up and down as he walked toward Bonner. Tree placed his purchases in his leather saddlebag. He walked up to Bonner's head, and the horse began sniffing his front pocket. Tree reached in and pulled out a sugar cube. He opened his hand flat as the pony eagerly scooped up the treat.

"The way I see it, Charley, any man that will feed his horse a sugar cube is some kind of dandy. He looks about as stupid as he is tall. Bigger they are, harder they fall, I always say. Your move!"

# CHAPTER 10

## Village of Montenegro, Northern Mexico

THE VILLAGE OF MONTENEGRO was slowly coming to life. The early fall morning was gently crisp. The sun was just beginning to come awake and spread its magnificent rays on the eastern horizon.

This was Julia de la Garza's favorite time of the day. The rich aromas adrift in the air in the small mountain village brought to memory everything that was good in her life. From the time she was a small girl in the village, she loved the morning smells. Villagers were putting sticks into their chimineas and bringing them to life to fight off the morning chill. The fragrant smell of burning mountain juniper sticks was wonderful at daybreak. Seeing the fresh smoke rising up from their small chimneys and curl upward was like watching fog lift off of the ground. Some families used the dried mesquite they picked up along the river as their preferred fuel source. It seemed to burn a little hotter and faster than the juniper, and it smelled every bit as good. The mesquite wood, when aged, was especially good for cooking all types of meat on their outdoor domed clay stoves. The bricks were fire cured and once used a time or two seemed to enhance the flavor of nearly any food that was prepared in them. She had watched her father build many of them for families in the village. He knew where the special clay mud was along the river and how to cure the bricks once they were taken out of the molds. She always liked to watch him take the clay and spread it over the domed bricks to make it bello.

"See Julia, the brick is now so bello, just like you with your lovely face."

She usually sat under the magnificent oak tree early in the morning. The tree dominated the central portion of the village of Montenegro. The village elders held that it was over three hundred years old, or maybe older. The tree, with its giant girth and extraordinary canopy, served as the playhouse for generations of village children. Climbing and laughing as they climbed upward and outward on the mighty outstretched limbs, the tree seemed to serve as a surrogate madre to the children. The children were warm and safe in its embrace, except when they encountered a mother bird who attacked unmercifully to protect a nest at the top of a branch. When this happened, the children screamed, often to no avail, until they began backing off the limb, holding on for dear life with arms, hands, legs, and bare feet until the mother bird stopped her attack and returned to the nest.

Julia loved to drink her morning fresh-ground coffee under the large oak. Arbol Viejo was the common name for the tree, which in the language of the villagers simply put was the old tree. Village woodworkers had long since built sitting benches of split pine that sat below the mighty tree. More benches were added through the years to accommodate additional people in the village, which now was home to twenty-six families. Bench tops, long and now very smooth from wear, accommodated children hopping from bench to bench followed by young kid goats and a seemingly endless supply of foraging hens anxious to scratch underneath the benches for food fragments.

Arbol Viejo was a major part of the social fabric of the village, only second to the family home and the village church with its high rock steeple enclosed in the magnificent arches facing each direction.

The cast-iron village bell sat squarely in the center of the steeple and only rung for moments of village importance. Church services,

quinceañeras, weddings, deaths, and other significant events were sig-
naled by the priest ringing the bell three times. The large group of mud
wrens that made their nests in the top of the bell tower flew en masse any
time the bell ringing occurred, often seeking refuge at the top of the old
tree until the ringing stopped.

The village was just one week separated from the Día de los Muertos
celebration. Julia sighed as she took a slow sip from her mug. Even at her
relatively young age of twenty-five, the yearly event was both nurturing to
her soul and yet somewhat heartbreaking in remembering and cherishing
the lives taken from the village families, her own family. Her madre died
of the high fever when she was just a young girl. Her papa slowly lost
his sight and his heart finally failed him when she was just twenty years
old. She always wore her flowing blue dress with the siete dark roses in
her beautiful black hair and meticulously painted on her Catrina on the
morning of Día de los Muertos. She loved the Dance of the Sparrows at
the church. She would always give her veil to her father because she had
no husband to give it to. The dance always started with the oldest woman
in the village out of respect. She began dancing to the guitarra songs
as the old man strummed it lightly with his velvety fingers. With their
bright, flowing dresses and beautiful flowers in their hair, it was a sight
to behold for the men and children in the village. Julia liked the dark red
roses while others liked the wild mountain caléndulas to meticulously
adorn their beautiful hair. Once the youngest woman of age joined the
other women, they all joined hands and began moving in a circle until
each woman had delivered her black veil to her husband, father, or grandfather. The oldest woman always removed her veil first and stepped out of
the circle. Once the veil was removed, her beautiful painted-on Catrina
was revealed. All of the women in the village relished the semblance and
the art of the dance of the veil. It was very dear and special to Julia. Her
father always smiled greatly when she took off the veil and handed it to
him. She always held his face and kissed him on both cheeks as tears
came down her face.

"I love you, mi papa. I have no children for you to squeeze." He always smiled gently and looked back at her.

"Maybe one day, my Julia. If Dios wills you to have the children, you will have the children. But first, there must be a husband!"

The excitement reverberated within the village like a wildfire weeks before the annual event. After the work of the day had ended, families fed, goats milked, and chickens fed, the women and young girls gathered under the old tree to stitch together new dresses for the girls or mend the old ones for themselves. The young children were content to climb the lower limbs of the old tree and would often be followed by two or three limb-climbing kid goats playing king of the mountain.

Then, after weeks of planning and the early chills of autumn began to set in, the days began to take on a fever pitch. There were sugar skulls and pastries to bake in the stone ovens, fresh tortillas, corn beer and mezcal, red chili peppers ready after weeks of drying. The great feast at the fenced yard of graves was an enjoyment to the entire village, never letting their loved ones that had passed be forgotten. Each family in the village was given the time to speak about their loved ones. Tears of joy and respect were always shed surrounding the celebration of past lives. A remarkable rejuvenation and joy of life seemed to flow through the veins of the participants after the event, knowing that when they too had passed, no one would ever forget them. It let them know, they were not just a little shooting star, passing the nighttime horizon, burning quickly bright and fading just as quickly. No matter your age, the village families never forgot your existence on this day. When all of the families were given ample time to talk about each of their loved ones, normally by their tombstone, then the food that the deceased loved the most was often laid on a flat stone in front of their grave marker with the anticipated return of their spirits for the event. Cano, one of the village elders, always closed out the celebration. He would stand when the last song had been sung and waited until all eyes and ears were turned toward his voice.

"Mi familia. What are we but Dios's little sunflowers? We all come from a seed in the spring of our life, no? Then we pop up from the earth and begin our climb upward toward Dios's beautiful sky. Then, with rain and sunshine, we sprout our beautiful petals with many seeds within the petals. Beautiful, for all to see. Then, we turn our face to the sun in the heat of the day and rest at night with our heads down. Look upon the field of sunflowers and tell me it is not true. Then, it is the autumn of our life when the cold wind and the freezing rains and snow come. Our beautiful petals fall, our leaves wither and then Dios sends his birds to eat our seeds." Then, after a long pause, he continued.

"Ah, but they do not eat all of the seeds, and many of them fall to the earth. Some may be covered by the birds scratching away at the ground. And next spring when the ground is tender, life is born and begins anew. Is it not wonderful? Yes, it is indeed wonderful, my children. Such is the essence and times of our lives. So, I say to all of you in your time of life. Be a beautiful sunflower during your time and climb toward the sky. Share your inside and your outside beauty with all of us while you are here. Unlike the sunflower that only moves with the wind, you are each free to crawl, walk, run, climb the old tree higher and higher like the young children and the goats, to eat and to sing, to receive love and to give love. Yes, it is most important to give love. Always give your love to everyone. Especially to the children and to our old ones. Wrap them in your arms. Pull them to your bosoms. Teach the children your good ways, and they will take care of you when your sunflower stalk begins to bend and your petals begin to fall. They will feed you and comfort you until the end that Dios has prepared for you. Children are our future and they are our past.

"Then, when you are gone, we shall enjoy, as we have today, speaking and singing about your radiance when you were born, your life, and then our grief at your passing."

Día de los Muertos always ended in the village at midnight. A big communal fire burned brightly. The children, full of wonderful food, often played under the old tree until they could no longer stay awake. Then after many handshakes and hugs between the adults, everyone would slowly walk away, hand in hand as a family, to retire to their adobe homes to begin another year.

Julia sipped her coffee and contemplated on all of the sunflowers she had celebrated at Dias de los Muertos over the years. Some were so very little, barely young sparrows trying to learn how to beat their wings fast enough to take flight. Some had just begun to explore the old tree at its exposed surface roots when they were taken by some type of sickness or maybe a snakebite. They were always looking up at the other children above them in the great canopy. It was said, the roots belowground were bigger and deeper than the great canopy above. She knew the great tree was firmly attached to the ground below by virtue of the storms it had weathered in her short lifetime and those before her.

So, life goes on. As one life comes to a stop, another is just beginning, just like the old man said of the sunflowers. Her father had been a mighty sunflower in her life before his life ended.

*It is surely true*, she thought.

Her love of children was great. She loved hearing them sing, without thought of someone listening. Their cheerful smiles while playing, and chasing the young kid goats or the chickens under the old tree.

She always wanted a child of her own or maybe many. Often looked at by the unmarried men of the village, none of them ever seemed to be someone she wanted to make a life with. Her father always told her,

"Julia, hopefully you will pick a man someday. That man does not have to come from this village. Be careful, my daughter, when you pick your man. Look at him from a long distance before you give him your heart. Will he work? Will he provide for you? Will he fight for you and even more, will he die for you? These are the questions I ask my daughter. You see, some men think more of themselves than they will of you. Those men, they take what they want and never give back. Men like that take the last cup of water when there is no rain for a long time and water supplies are low, while others are thirsty. They are the first to grab food from the table in front of other people to fill their own stomachs. Those men, they never look you in the eye when you ask them a question. You be sure to look at what I am telling you. You need the best, the strongest, and the most courageous of them all. Sometimes being courageous just means to not say anything and let your words speak through your actions. That is the kind of man I want you to have, my daughter. That man will make strong and courageous babies and will care for you when you are old."

Julia knew all of the young courters in the village. There were absolutely none that she cared for enough to take her hand in marriage or to have children with. Some did not bathe or clean their teeth daily, and their foul breath was offensive as the smell of their body when they came close by. Others drank more mezcal and corn beer than water. Often, they were drunk into the night, singing to each other by the old tree or singing to a horse in the pole corral. She thought of her father's words every time one of them talked to her.

*Men like that were men she would have to be a madre to, not a wife.*

# CHAPTER 11

Tree eased Bonner along back to the Rolling J. It was dusk, and he was heading due south with the sun barely above the horizon in the west. He figured he had about an hour to get back to the ranch without getting in a hurry. His body felt good after the scrubbing and the smelling powders. He studied on his reaction to Mr. Whittmire's needling at the barbering shop. Maybe he should not have backhanded him like that and kept his temper in check, he thought.

*No, sir! A loudmouth bully like that will just keep on bullying if you let him*, he thought.

He reached down and stroked Bonner on the neck.

"What do you think about that, Bonner? That is what I thought. I think you are agreeing with me. Maybe you are just trying to get another sugar cube."

The Rolling J ranch owner had called a meeting with all of the cowboys for Monday morning at seven o'clock sharp in the bunkhouse. Mr. Gillstrap never called a meeting unless he had something very specific he wanted to share that he considered of consequence. Like the time a couple of years back when he announced that his son, Lewis Gillstrap, was coming in on the train to Rosario in a week or so, and would be handling the ramrodding from that point forward, rather than himself.

"Of course, you boys are going to have to help show him how to cowboy, but all of you know your business and what to do and what not to do when it comes to horses and cattle. We run a cow-calf operation out here, and you all know it better than I do. But I make the decisions, and those decisions are always based on making a profit of some kind in this business." Lewis Gillstrap showed up with his brand-new cowboy hat and new leathers. He spent a day or two in the saddle with the boys and barely could get off his horse, he was so sore. He lasted about two full weeks before Mr. Gillstrap rode him back to Rosario and put him on a train back east where Mr. Gillstrap's wife was thought to live. Tree overheard Mr. Gillstrap telling a guest that his wife simply refused to live in barbaric conditions and around barbaric cowboys with cow dung on their boots.

"You make the money and wire it back. If that is the lifestyle you cherish, then go live it. I am not leaving the city. I refuse to live in filth."

Tree never heard what city that was.

Tree had no idea why this particular meeting was called. He would always translate in Spanish after any meeting to the two Mexican vaqueros from across the river. He generally would wait until all the cowboys were well out of earshot before he told them what was said and answered what few questions they might have. He had grown to admire both men, and they seemed to have great admiration for him. Maybe it was because he treated them both with respect and like men. Their horsemanship and cow sense were far higher than those of any of the other cowboys. The two of them together could handle the workload of at least three of the gringo cowboys on the ranch, not counting their coming and going traveling time across the river. Tree liked the fact that they looked into his eyes intently and without fear. They were quick to share food or maybe a laugh when something went wrong. Tree's command of their language had become fairly good, and they loved to hear the words quietly come off his tongue, especially when it required rolling his tongue to say a word. He never engaged in long conversations, nor did they. Franco Paz was the more talkative of the two if you could call it that. Pedro de Garza was very composed and reserved. He always thought before speaking and usually answered in one- or two-word sentences. Cedar Jones knew a little Spanish but never told many folks he understood it. He mostly would just listen when he did overhear Tree talking to the two vaqueros.

Some of the cowboys considered Cedar Jones to be one of the best camp cooks on the border.

"He is a dang gum good cook but that son buck has the temperament of a constipated grizzly bear," said DeWitt Murphy. "That feller don't laugh much at nothing."

The night riders at the Rolling J could smell his biscuits and bacon cooking from a long way off when the wind was right. He always served the night herd watchmen first, and anyone who tried to cut in line received an immediate tongue-lashing about manners.

"You been sleeping all night while these men been out tending the herd and you got the gumption to eat before they do? Get out of my sight. You can eat last."

It usually only took one shaming from Cedar and it was never desired or wanted again. Of course, no cowboy had ever heard a shaming that was not justified. Even though his cooking was always the best one could enjoy on the range, it was never a good idea to make a negative comment about the food and especially his coffee. DeWitt Murphy took a sip of coffee one morning at a fall gathering and spat it out.

"This coffee tastes like horse crap smells." Only problem was, Cedar overheard him.

"You didn't know I boil horse turds for your personal coffee, DeWitt? If you don't like the doings around here, get on your pony and head to another ranch. Just hush up that pissing and whining."

Cedar wore an old black hat that was severely stained around the brim. His white hair had not a stitch of gray in it and offset his sky-blue eyes. He washed his worn green bandanna at least once a month but was never seen without it. He always had on an old and well-worn blue cotton shirt and suspenders made out of a pair of old horse reins. His apron was made out of white flour sacks. You could still see the red writing on some of it, but that did not bother him. It was covered in grease stains from bacon popping from the frying pan. The cowboys consumed at least three pounds of bacon a day and more than three dozen eggs. He always cooked his sourdough biscuits in a large Dutch oven over mesquite coals. When the cowboys arrived around 5:00 a.m. for breakfast in the mess cabin off the bunkhouse, Cedar had already been up since 3:30 a.m. and was waiting on them.

When Monday morning's meeting with Mr. Gillstrap rolled around, the boys were long finished with breakfast and were sitting in the bunkhouse waiting when he suddenly walked in the door.

"Hello, boys," Mr. Gillstrap said as he scanned the room. "Anyone seen Mr. Tree?"

No one said a word until DeWitt Murphy finally answered him. "Mr. Gillstrap, I believe you might find him out to the corral with his pony. He generally likes to visit him early of a morning."

"Thank you, DeWitt. I will ease out there. Boys, we will meet at 7:30 this morning rather than 7:00 a.m. I will come back in here, just make sure everyone is here."

He quietly closed the bunkhouse door and left.

"Well, I guess he's got some important business to discuss with Mr. Tree," said DeWitt.

"Maybe he is a little more important than the rest of us, for sure."

Outside, the two Mexican vaqueros sat quietly on their horses as Mr. Gillstrap passed by. He briefly looked their way without acknowledging them.

Tree had already fed Bonner his ration of oats and forked over a little hay into his stall when Mr. Gillstrap walked in. Tree slowly turned and looked over Bonner's back at the door.

"Good morning to you, Tree. A fine morning, I would say. I always admire that horse of yours. Big in the front and solid."

"Yes, sir. He is a good pony. Something I can do for you this morning?"

"Well, actually there is, Tree, but I would like to talk to you about it at the main house if I could. There are way too many ears out and about. Okay if we go over there?"

"Yes, sir, you are the boss. We better get on over there if you are meeting with the boys at 7:00 this morning."

"Well, Tree, I done spoke to the boys and moved the meeting to 7:30 so you and me could visit a little before. Not a thing to worry about, just I think we need to visit before the meeting."

Tree hung the brush on a wooden peg on a stall corner post and patted Bonner on the back as he walked toward the barn door.

DeWitt had the bunkhouse door cracked as he saw Tree and Mr. Gillstrap walking toward the main house.

"Well, damnation," he said as he turned to the boys. "They are a-walking to the main ranch house. Whatever is going on, it must be important with Tree going with him and all."

Cedar Jones never spoke much at all.

"DeWitt, why don't you close the door and quit fiddling in other folk's business. I reckon we will know soon enough what is happening. Quit acting like some gossiping old widow woman."

There was a bay mare tied to the hitching post in front of the main house that Tree did not recognize. This one had a little split at the top of her left ear. Mr. Gillstrap's personal horse was a big red sorrel gelding with a scar on his left flank. Tree took notice of the mare but said nothing. Mr. Gillstrap opened the door in front of Tree.

"Come in, Tree. I have someone here that will be speaking to the boys after I do. Sheriff Leonard Brody, this is Tree Smith, otherwise known as Tree 'Bigfoot' Smith." Tree eyed the sheriff closely as he approached.

"Hello, Mr. Tree, I believe we met when you came to Rosario, as I recall."

Sheriff Brody stuck out his hand to Tree. Tree slowly reached out and shook his hand.

"Yes, sir, we did meet before."

"Well, I did not know you two fellas had met before, that is good. That is just really good," said Mr. Gillstrap.

"Tree, I know you are wondering why I called you in here and certainly why Sheriff Brody is here. I will be as brief as I can so we don't lose much time on the ranch today. The situation is, well, it is not easy for me to say something like this. I have a real problem that has come up. It's a problem that I can't fix from this ranch and quite possible for a long period of time."

Tree looked him in the eyes intently and then turned and looked at the sheriff.

"What kind of problem, Mr. Gillstrap?"

"Tree, what I got to say is the hardest thing I have ever had to say. I have to leave the ranch. I surely have to leave today." Tree said nothing as he listened.

"Sheriff Brody brought me word from the wire office in town this morning. You see, it is my wife back in Illinois. She did not have any desire to come out here to the ranch, never. Not one time. She wanted to stay up there with her friends and what she called the civilized part of society. Never wanted one piece of life on the ranch with me. Maybe it was better that way. And that boy of mine, he was never cut out to be a cowboy. That would get in the way of his political ambitions. You saw what he was like on a horse when he was here. Well, my wife has taken ill, really quite ill, you might say. I am all she's got besides the boy, and he's too fond of himself to ever think about taking care of another human being. So, I have to leave and go take care of her. It is my moral duty, you see. Tree, I want you to take over the ranch. You run everything already, or should I say the boys look to you for leadership on everything as far as I can tell. I don't know much about where you came from, but I know you make good decisions, and the men all respect you. You know my operation better than I do. I will pay you half again as much as you make, if you will take the reins. I must warn you though, I may not be back for a long time. Who knows what is in store when I get off the train back home? Who knows? My back is up against the wall. None of the other boys can even remotely come close to handling this operation. They are followers, not leaders. Now some of them think they are leaders, you know who they are, but they are not. They talk about what they would do or would have done after the fact but that is no leader."

Tree never took his eyes off Mr. Gillstrap while he was talking. "What is the sheriff here for, did I do something wrong?"

"No sir, Tree. Not at all. Sheriff Brody, can you explain why you are here to Mr. Tree?"

Sheriff Brody pushed his hat back a little on his head before he spoke.

"I am riding to all of the border ranches over the next two to three days to warn them of a big problem that has flared up a few times during the last few months and seems to be getting worse. This ranch could surely be affected. There is a very bad man coming in and out of Mexico with a small band of cutthroats that ride with him. Nobody knows where he is holed up, where he came from, and worst of all, where he is going next. They call him Gato Montes or Spanish for Cat of the Mountains. I guess he calls himself that because he always hits folks from behind, just like a mountain lion. I guess nobody ever sees him, at least not up close. Ropes them from behind if they are on a horse and pulls them right off. Then he stabs them in the back of the neck with a long, sharpened spike. They have found three folks so far killed in exactly the same way. All have that spike entering the back of the neck and sometimes it comes out the front as well. Then he cuts off their ears at the base of the skull. They have found the bodies rolled onto their backs, with the spike sticking out and the ears impaled on the spike. He is a bad one. Only thing we know, and quite honestly, we do not know for sure is, he has dark black hair down in the middle of his back. He wears an old dark sombrero, and maybe he does not wear a shirt, maybe he does. The accounts are all shaky, and the couple of ranch hands that saw the band leaving were simply scared out of their wits when they saw that spike. They could not tell what color horse he was riding or the men riding with him. Anyway, there is a $5,000 bounty on him if we catch him on the Texas side and $1,000 apiece for the three other folks he has riding with him, whoever they are.

If we get wind of where he is holed up, we might just slip across and see if we can find him. I don't think the Federales would say anything, but you never know. We are kind of hunting a ghost with a dark sombrero on his head. Point is, you have to be vigilant out here, especially. The town folks are worked up into somewhat of a frantic tizzy thinking he and his band are going to come ripping through town at any minute. I barely found a man to deputize and to look after things while I am away. The one I did find is a saddle maker with a family. He agreed to be deputized, but quite frankly, I think he would not stand up in a real fight if he had to. But I give him credit, he at least was willing. Anyway, that's it."

Tree walked to the window and pulled the curtain back to peer out as both men looked on. His giant frame was silhouetted in the window frame. He said, "I never hired on to be the boss, Mr. Gillstrap. I been here a good while now and really was not looking to leave and head somewhere else. Telling someone they are in full control of their ranching operation is not something I take too lightly. Is that what you are saying, Mr. Gillstrap? You want me to take over your ranch lock, stock, and barrel and run it for you?"

"Yes sir, Tree. That is exactly what I am saying. That is handling the money part as well. I have an account set up at the bank in Rosario where all cattle sales money is deposited. Also, we have an account down at the hardware store where you can take care of any and all of the ranch needs. I trust you, Tree. You are not going to steal from me. I have watched you around the men, more than you know. I saw you settle a fight one time just by walking between the two men and putting out your hands. They were ready to kill each other, and they just stopped. I think I heard you say three words which I will never forget. You said 'That's enough, boys.'

"You will be in charge of payroll, food, the gatherings, brandings, and all. I mean all of it. Tree, I would not ask you if I did not trust you. I really need you. There just is not anyone else that can handle this. Especially if that killer comes riding in. Those boys would scatter like a covey of those blue quail."

"I guess that is what you wanted to tell the boys this morning. You just wanted to make sure I would accept before you went over there and told them."

"The sheriff there," as he pointed to Sheriff Brody. "You wanted him to speak to the boys after you told them I was taking over, is that right?"

"You are very perceptive, Tree. That is right. They might just all walk out the door if they don't have a leader. One they can count on when the skies get a little dark and the storm clouds roll in. Somebody that can handle their pissing and whining too, as I have heard it called. Somebody that will listen with an objective ear, but solid enough to tell them the truth and stick to their guns. That person is you, Tree."

"Mr. Gillstrap, you make it sound like there is no one else that can handle what you are asking. I can assure you that is not true. But, being as there isn't no one else in here but me and the sheriff, I reckon I can help you out with your request until you get back."

Mr. Gillstrap was visibly relieved as he reached to shake Tree's hand. Tree reached to shake his hand without smiling, his bear's paw of a hand easily swallowing Mr. Gillstrap's.

"I thank you, Tree. I thank you. I have a considerable investment in this ranch and particularly in the cattle. I still have to have a return on that investment to pay wages and try and make a profit, you see. You can send a cowboy into Rosario weekly, and I will send you a wire. Maybe every Wednesday or so. We will stay in contact that way. Good with you?"

Tree slowly nodded his head yes as he turned to look at the sheriff. He slowly released Mr. Gillstrap's hand.

"I reckon I will be wearing a gun from this point on and carrying a saddle gun with me. I am going to have the boys do the same. You got any problem with that?"

"None at all," said Sheriff Brody. "In fact, that is what I would expect. Our town is tamed down a bit from when I started years ago. Tell them the rules before they come in to spend their money. I don't want to have to lock up one of your boys for a bad mistake with a gun."

Mr. Gillstrap looked at Tree.

"Here is the key to the lockbox in the corner of the bunkhouse. Inside, you will find at least twelve loaded pistols, gun belts, and holsters. All of them are Colt .44s, so all of the ammunition is the same. Probably twenty or thirty boxes in there. You can get more in town at the hardware store if you need it. I check it from time to time when the boys are out. Might oil up them guns. The ammunition is good and none of it is molded on the caps. I believe we need to ease over to the bunkhouse and tell the boys. Like you said, I will speak to the boys first, and then, sheriff, if you would, take over from there please."

The two Mexican vaqueros were sitting on their horses in front of the bunkhouse when the three men approached. Tree motioned for them to dismount, tie their horses, and come in to the bunkhouse. He said something in Spanish that was barely audible so neither the sheriff nor Mr. Gillstrap understood what he said.

All of the cowboys were sitting in the bunkhouse chairs when the group came through the door. Cedar Jones stood quietly in the corner with his back up against a large post. His large white mustache covered all of his mouth and extended beyond the corner of his lips. The two vaqueros made their way to the back of the room and stood fairly close to Cedar Jones.

Mr. Gillstrap slowly looked around the room at the group and cleared his throat before he began to speak.

"I know all of you are probably wondering what is going on this morning, especially with Tree and the sheriff being with me and all up at the main house. I won't keep you waiting any longer. The truth is, I will be leaving. Leaving today, for that matter. My wife has taken ill, and I have to head to back home now, to go up there and take care of her in our house in Chicago. The fact is, I do not know when or if I will be back. Mr. Tree here has agreed to take on the ramrodding of this ranch. That means all of it. All of you, the herd, the sales, the money. All of it."

The cowboys all exchanged looks with the exception of Cedar Jones, who stared straight ahead.

"And, boys, he has the power to hire and fire. His rules are the ranch rules and will be followed at all times. He does not have to go through me on anything, and I mean anything at all. He is now the ranch boss. Everyone in this room understand what I just said? If you did not, please speak up now, and you will get your question answered. Got a problem with any of it, draw your pay today, saddle up, and head out. If you leave, don't never come back."

Slowly one of the cowboys raised his hand.

"Yes, sir, you have a question?"

"Well, my question is: Do we still get to go into Rosario on occasion like on payday or do we have to stay on the ranch?"

Mr. Gillstrap turned to Tree and said, "Well, I will let your ranch boss answer that question. Tree?"

Tree took a slow deep breath before answering. He turned to the cowboy. "You will have your normal days off as they are now set up. What you do with them is your business, but the ranch comes first. No one heads to town if we have a storm coming in, same as before."

"Any more questions for Mr. Tree?" said Mr. Gillstrap. He waited for about a minute and looked around at the group. "I guess there are none. I will just say this, none of you are bound here. You are all free to leave, seek other employment. My advice is if you choose to stay, stay and be happy. Happy as you can be on a ranch. Just don't complain. That is like a rotten apple in an apple barrel. We don't need that. Sheriff Brody, if you will."

The sheriff looked over the group slowly canvassing each man's eyes and facial demeanor before he spoke. He was quite used to reading folks' faces and could usually tell a lot about their character just by looking at their faces. Of course, he had been wrong on more than one occasion about his assumptions. His gaze stopped briefly on young Roney McCallister. The young man did not look over sixteen years old and was wide-eyed. He was just starting to grow a little mustache and some chin hair. Sheriff Brody knew what he was going to say might not set well with the older cowboys, but especially this youngster.

"I am making visits to all of the border ranches from here to about one hundred miles or so downriver. Every one of them in the next week or two. I am sure you may have heard rumor of a man they call Gato Montes. There is a pretty big money reward poster down at my office in Rosario for him and for the folks who have been seen riding with him. There may be two, maybe three of them. That reward money is quite large, even for these killing scoundrels. Everybody is plumb scared. Some of the merchants kicked in two, maybe three hundred hard-earned dollars each to the reward pool money. Folks are so scared that the merchants are afraid they might just pack up and leave. Nobody knows for sure what he really looks like because they always see him from his back side when he is leaving. He wears a dark sombrero, may or may not wear a shirt, and has very dark hair that hangs down to the middle of his back. We are not sure about his horse or the horses the others ride. When they were seen leaving by a couple of folks, there was a dead body left behind. They steal any horses that are in the corral or staked on a picket line. Two of the folks had rope burns on their necks. All of them have a spike with a very sharp point stuck right through the back of their neck and the point coming out the front."

The cowboys in the room seemed visibly shaken and stared at each other and back toward Mr. Gillstrap.

Sheriff Brody continued. "That seems to be his calling card for three killings so far; that, and the fact that all of them have had their ears cut off at the skull. The ears are found impaled on the end of the sharp spike. Rolls them over on their backs and punches the ears on the spike. So, there it is. It isn't pretty, but I can't do nothing about that. Those are the facts as I know them. Mr. Tree here will be giving you further instructions on wearing firearms in town. That includes pistols and saddle guns. Just remember the rules in Rosario. If you go into the saloon, you will surrender them at the door. No exceptions. I would not be without one at all times, especially when you are on a horse. There are not many of you. Watch after one another. If this killer and his band come in, I would not expect it is to sip coffee with you. They will be after your horses and maybe food. They are stealing horses and may be trading them in Mexico for money or maybe guns. Stay alert. I am fixing to head out in the next few minutes. Best of luck."

Mr. Gillstrap looked over the boys. "Boys, stay together, and, most of all, listen to Mr. Tree. I will be leaving by noon today. I wish you all the best of luck."

Tree looked at the two vaqueros and motioned for them to follow him outside. He headed toward Bonner's pen as they followed. Once they were inside, he motioned for them to sit down on the pine bench on the west wall of the stall. He reached into his pocket and pulled out the chocolate bars, handing each of them one. He began to speak to them slowly and deliberately in Spanish, as they put the chocolate bars in their vest pockets for later.

"*Señors Franco and Pedro, Señor Gillstrap is leaving the ranch to take care of his wife. He asked me to be the patrón.*" Each of them nodded in agreement and smiled.

"Señor Tree, you have always been patrón. This is not different."

"Also, there is a bandit killer somewhere in this area. He and his band have killed at least three people in a short time. They steal horses and maybe sell them in Mexico. He uses a reata from behind when people are on their caballos. He kills with a stab to the back of the neck with a sharp espiga. He cuts off both orejas at the cràneo and puts them on the espiga."

Franco and Pedro looked at each other slowly and then down to the floor. Franco slowly looked back up at Tree.

"Señor Tree, this killer, does he have a name?"

"They call him Gato Montes or Cat of the Mountain. I suppose, because he hits from behind maybe."

"It is not easy for me to say, Señor Tree," said Franco. "This Gato Montes, he is from our village. His real name is Pablo de la Rosa. He is very bad man, señor. He is the half-blood. Apache father named Dos Lobos and a Mexican madre from our village. She and other women were captured by Apache long ago and only one day escape with baby. Came back to our village, Montenegro. When he was in our village, he cut off

Prieto's ears when they were young boys over a pair of prismaticas. His madre, she sews them back on with caballo tail hair and mezcal. No one know who did this terrible thing because Prieto never speak again and one day, he walks into the river and he never come back. Before Prieto leave and step into the river, we were close by and hear Pablo talking one day to Prieto when he thinks no one hears him. He laughed and make fun with Prieto while Prieto cry.

"He says, 'Remember what I told you on the river, señor, you tell them Gato Montes the bandit, cut off your ears. If you tell, I kill your burro Chico and cut his head off and hang it on your door, then I kill your madre, then I will find you and I will kill you. The looking glass I took from you, I need it more than you.'

"We hear this, me and Pedro. We never say nothing to now. Pablo leaves the village a long time ago. Maybe dos años. He is a very bad man, señor. Very bad, veneno del alma. He will try to kill us if he knows we hear him talk to Prieto."

The two vaqueros sat quietly as Tree went to the tack room and brought out his rigging and began to saddle Bonner.

"Take two horses and ride the north line. I will tell the sheriff what you have told me and come back. Go by the bunkhouse and pick up a pistol each. Adios."

Tree stopped by the bunkhouse on his way out. DeWitt was standing on the bunkhouse porch.

"Where are you heading to, Mr. Tree? I see you got your gun on your hip and a saddle gun. You going after them outlaws? That Gato Montes feller?"

"I am just going to ride far enough to find the sheriff. He has not been gone but a few minutes. Need to visit with him. You watch after things until I get back. It will not be but a little while. Tell Cedar Jones where I am heading. Make sure all of the boys are armed with a pistol, including both vaqueros. Here is the key to the pistol chest in the back of the bunkhouse. Make sure I get it back. Get a good count on the guns and ammunition. You and you only will hand out each gun and shells. One box each. I will talk to everyone when I get back. Be sure they keep their sidearm pointed down at all times, make sure they are all loaded with one missing bullet on the hammer so it does not just accidentally fire off if one of them drops it on the floor. Got it?"

DeWitt dropped his jaw. "Yes sir, Mr. Tree, I got it for sure. You are coming back, aren't you?"

Tree mounted Bonner and clicked him into a lope heading east downriver. "I'll be back."

Sheriff Brody's tracks were easy to follow. His bay mare was moving him along at a gentle lope when he heard a noise behind him. He pulled her to a stop and eased his gun out of the holster before he turned around. Tree waved his right hand and slowed Bonner to a walk.

"I have not been gone but a bit. That killer already come riding into your ranch?"

Tree brought Bonner to a halt and relaxed the reins.

"Well, you could say he has come in, maybe in those cowboys' heads, I'd say. The two vaqueros working at the ranch come from the Village of Montenegro just across the river and up the mountain a-ways. They been working here a while. Best we got. They know who this killer is. Maybe not the boys riding with him, but they know who he is. His real name is Pablo de la Rosa. He is an Apache half-breed from their village. The two vaqueros might come in handy in identifying him if we catch him. Thought you might want to know."

Sheriff Brody looked toward the river and put his hand over the brim of his hat.

"I kind of figured he was from around here close. He seems to know the area pretty well. He does not waste any time when he comes in, it sounds like. Ropes them from behind if he can, drags them off, spikes them in the neck, and then cuts their ears off. Runs off with any horses in the pens. One of the three that was killed was not on a horse. Last time they saw him he was feeding the horses in the corral. Gato Montes must have already been hiding in there when he walked by."

Sheriff Brody reached into his saddlebag and pulled out something wrapped in old blue cloth. Once he unwrapped it, Tree could see it was a long dark spike covered in dried blood.

"This here is what that animal uses. Don't know where he got them. Nearly looks like those long thick nails they sell over at the hardware store in Rosario. Looks like he sharpens it to a needle point somehow. Those folks don't have a chance when he stabs them in the neck with this thing. Probably paralyzes them right down the spine. I bet they are still alive when he cuts their ears off. He is one sadistic animal. He is killing for the sport of it. My bet is he won't stop, and it is likely to get worse before it gets better. He has several horses now. Hard to know what he is riding."

Tree looked at the spike carefully and turned back to the sheriff.

"The two vaqueros said his madre was Mexican and his father was an Apache. His father was the chief. Two Wolves, they called him. They took her and some other Mexican women in a raid on the village. She did not escape for a while, maybe two years or so. By that time, he was born. I guess maybe he did not fit in with the Mexicans or the Apache."

The sheriff began to roll up the bloodied spike in the cloth and carefully put it back into the saddlebag.

"I am going to head on. Just wanted you to know, had Mr. Gillstrap not asked you to take over the ranch, I was going to see if you would be my deputy. But that would mean you would have to move into Rosario, and I don't know that it would wear well on you. Too many flies in town, I reckon. Anyway, we have got to get them stopped quickly. The rumors are spreading in town like a prairie fire with each passing day. Keep a close eye. Adios, Mr. Tree. Keep a good eye out."

# CHAPTER 12

WHEN TREE RETURNED TO THE ranch, he could see Mr. Gillstrap's buggy horse hitched up to his riding buggy. Mr. Gillstrap was just closing the door on the main ranch house when Tree rode up to the buggy.

"I am really glad you rode up before I left, Tree, I was afraid you had trouble with the cow herd or something like that. Anyway, here is the keys to the main ranch house there. It is now your home. Take the big bed."

Tree reached out and slowly took the keys. "I don't reckon I need to be taking your house and your bed, Mr. Gillstrap. The bunkhouse will do me just fine."

"No sir, Tree. I won't have it. If you are running this operation, you need peace and quiet when you are working on the books, away from the boys. You will find the bed quite comfortable. More comfortable than the bunk bed you are sleeping on. I have everything laid out on my desk that you will need to operate. Inventory ledgers, monthly ranch bills, and payments. We need an accurate tally, as always, of our cow production rates and calf weights at market. Don't sell nothing below five weight, and if a cow does not produce one cycle, cull her and sell her while she is still walking and will bring good money. Those barren cows eat the same amount of grass as one with a calf inside her. Rotate your bulls as you think necessary. Of course, you already know all of that.

"I pulled everything out of my safe behind my desk. Here is the combination on this piece of paper. Keep hold of it. Put anything you deem important in there and lock it up. That thing weighs about eight hundred pounds, so I don't think no one will be coming in and stealing it. I can't tell you what to do if that killer comes riding in but I expect you will know how to handle it. Remember, every Wednesday, send a cowboy into the telegraph office, and I will have a wire there for you. Probably right after noon. Best of luck, Tree. I hope to be back, but who knows what is over the next hill."

Tree watched him leave. The Morgan buggy horse was a natural trotter and a beauty to watch as the buggy wheels stirred up small clouds of dust behind them. Her long dark mane was gently blowing in the wind and her ears were forward; she was always eager to meet the day.

"Best of luck to you too, Mr. Gillstrap. I imagine we are all going to need it before this is over."

Mr. Gillstrap's house was large and quiet. There was a tinge of the western sun filtering through the two triangular pieces of glass in the west apex of the roof. There were the same triangular pieces fitted on the east apex to catch the morning sun. There was plenty of light to see, with the rays of light coming in through the top and hitting the beautiful hardwood floor. Even though the place was swept clean, Tree could see the small flecks of dust floating in the rays of light. There were two kerosene lamps in the main room, with its large rock fireplace and offset cooking area and one lamp for the bedroom. Unlike the two outhouses north of the bunkhouse, he now had his own private privy. Most of the outhouses were set behind the houses to the north so the prevailing southern breeze did not carry the awful smell toward the bunkhouse. Of course, in winter when the north wind bore down from time to time, that was a different story. Mr. Gillstrap always had the boys pick up plenty of lime to drop in the bottom to keep things tolerable. They always went by the newspaper office in Rosario and picked any old unsold newspapers and placed a stack in all three outhouses for the purpose of cleaning one's posterior. Tree had heard DeWitt say, "Them old papers that been sitting outside in the sun are the best cause they are the softest. Don't like them new ones, none at all."

Tree picked up his small amount of clothing and personal effects at the bunkhouse. He returned to the main house and set about putting his clothes in the dresser drawers in Mr. Gillstrap's bedroom. He found four pairs of socks in one of the drawers and a pair of dungarees, but nothing that would come even close to fitting his large feet. The dungarees looked like something a young boy would wear compared to Tree's. He took his fiddle and placed it in the bottom drawer. As far as he knew, nobody even knew he had it except Cedar Jones. When he was done, he walked over to the large rocking chair sitting in the corner of the room. Carefully he sat down and immediately felt the craftsmanship of the curves that perfectly aligned with his back. His tips of his shoulders protruded past the edges of the chair a bit, but, all in all, it was very comfortable. His folks had a rocking chair when he was a little boy. He had vague memories of his mother rocking him in it before he became too big to hold.

He sat for a long while assessing the events of the day and certainly the unforeseen nature of what might lie ahead. Mr. Gillstrap had up and left to tend to his ailing wife up north. Who knew when or if he would ever be back to the Rolling J? There was a killer on the loose with a band of two or three cutthroats running with him. They were horse thieves to boot. Even though Tree could easily handle a pistol and a rifle, none of the boys knew much about handling firearms. The one thing standing up for any type of law and order from Rosario to the border was Sheriff Leonard Brody, and he was riding downriver to warn the rest of the ranches about the killings. Tree felt an immense obligation toward Mr. Gillstrap and the hands, all of them. The two vaqueros were more at risk than the rest because of the distance they had to ride to and from Montenegro to the Rolling J every day, mostly before the sun came up and after the sun was starting to set.

Tree took out his timepiece. It was four o'clock. He wanted to get over to the bunkhouse after the boys had come in and had time to eat and visit with them.

Cedar Jones had just finished picking up the last plates when Tree walked into the bunkhouse. The two vaqueros had already headed back to Montenegro and were now armed. The rest of the boys were sitting on the long pine benches next to the table. Tree slowly looked them over before walking up and setting down at the end of the table. Cedar walked through the doorway of the cookshack wiping his hands on his apron. Rarely if ever did he sit at the table with the boys, and this would be no exception. He quietly leaned against the bunkhouse wall.

Tree began to speak.

"Boys, I moved out of the bunkhouse this afternoon. I'll be living at Mr. Gillstrap's house. That is where the books are, and I will be tending to 'em. Our business is to raise cattle and get them to sale so we all keep a job. There just happens to be a few things get in the way sometimes. This Gato Montes and his band, whoever they may be, they are as bad as they come. Sheriff Brody showed me the nail spikes they stick in people's necks when they kill them. They are a bunch of cowards. Rope folks from behind and pull them off their horse before they poke them in the neck. Don't know where they are holed up, but they are on the run and most likely not holing up in one place long. Looks like they are hitting the ranches they may know something about. The two vaqueros told me that Gato Montes came from Montenegro. That is right across the river. That means he probably knows something about the Rolling J. I want everyone riding in pairs if you are sent to ride fence. There are but eight of you and the two vaqueros. If we are moving cattle, always take time to look behind at the point man. The point man needs to keep his eyes moving all the time, taking a look back now and again. If you are sent into town for supplies, there will be two of you. Cedar, I want you to teach these men how to use their weapons starting tomorrow afternoon. Teach them how to clean them and how to load and shoot at what they are aiming at and not some shadow behind a bush or a cow. Any questions?"

DeWitt looked at Cedar Jones and then back to Tree. "Tree, I was just wondering why you won't be teaching us about these here guns. I mean, Cedar is a pretty good grub cook, but I ain't too sure about the shooting part of it."

"There are things none of you know about. Some of them will never be told. Cedar knows more about shooting and guns than most people walking the earth, just leave it at that. We are moving cattle out of the north trap in the morning. Get a good's night sleep. Adios."

Cedar turned and went back through the door into the cookshack. Tully Snyder pulled out his tobacco sack and slowly began to roll a cigarette. He licked the paper up and down and plopped it in his lips. Dragging a match across his britches, he lit up and pulled hard. Slowly exhaling the smoke, he said:

"Hell, I could probably whip the whole damn bunch, guard the gate, and drag off the dead at the same time."

"That is mighty big talk there, Tully," said DeWitt. "Especially by someone that got whipped by a little old saloon girl in Rosario. What was she, five foot tall?"

"The only reason that happened, is because I was too drunk to fight back," said Tully. "Besides, she had that long hat pin stuck in her hair and pulled it out stuck me in the rear end with it. I thought I would never stop bleeding. Anyway, we got these here guns now and with old Cedar teaching us to shoot 'em, we probably won't have no trouble with them little outlaws. That is, if Cedar can really shoot a gun like Tree says he can."

Cedar walked back through the doorway and paused with his hand on the frame. He stared at Tully with his cold, ocean-blue eyes.

"If you can be taught to shoot as good as you talk and yammer, you might be able to hit something. I don't think you can talk outlaws to death, not this bunch. Like Tree and the sheriff said, he kills with a spike. I reckon he won't be using a hat pin if you just happen to meet up with him."

# CHAPTER 13

## Texas Side of the Border

GATO MONTES CLEANED THE GAP between his front teeth with a mesquite thorn. He was always meticulous when it came to picking the food remnants from between them. As a young child in Montenegro, he could still remember watching his mother clean her teeth every night before sleeping. She told him to always keep his teeth clean, especially after he ate, or his mouth would stink. "Your wretched father Two Wolves never cleaned his teeth. His mouth smelled like the skunk."

Meals were more consistent and good while he was in Montenegro. Now, he had to kill game and cook it or steal whatever he could find from unattended ranch houses across the border. He suspected that at least two of the men in the village might know who he was and may have heard him talking to Prieto. There were two of them for sure, because he saw them slip away and go toward the Old Tree.

He believed they were the two vaqueros that worked across the river with the gringos at the big ranch. He would kill both of them when the time was right.

His blood ran hot thinking about them. He had never seen them with pistols or a rifle. That did not mean they did not have a gun in their leather saddlebag. If they did, the only time they may have used them would be at the big ranch. He recalled hearing a gunshot long ago across the river. There was no way of knowing who fired it. Maybe a gringo cowboy shooting at a snake.

He hated the gringos more than he hated the Apaches or the Mexican people. He liked to watch the gringos writhe on the ground when he stabbed them in the neck with the long spikes. They looked like a slow-moving snapping turtle on the edge of the river. After they flailed about slowly with their arms and legs, he would flip them over where their wide-eyed stares tried to focus on his face, just like he used to flip the snapping turtles onto their backs and watch then writhe helplessly. Their eyes grew wide when they looked at his eyes. He like to brush the wet charcoal paste all around his eyes in big oblong circles. He liked to use the cactus and red flower paste to paint between his eyes and his nose a dark red color. You could only see the white portion of his eyes. The look in his victims' eyes was pure fear looking at pure evil with darkened circles around his eyes, long black hair, and a dark sombrero. He would slowly pull out his long knife and drag it slowly across the little hairs on his arms.

"Señor gringo, this knife, she is so very hungry, señor. I think maybe she is hungry for your ears. It does not look like you want to make fight with me, no?"

Gato laughed as he thought about the three gringos when he cut off their ears. The blood sometimes oozed out slowly at first. They tried to scream, but their mouths just came opened, and a gurgling sound came out with a blood bubble. One of them looked like the young bull that the cattle keeper of Montenegro dehorned one day. He cut the young animal's horns off at the base of the skull with a small old saw. The blood would shoot in the air in little streams every time the young bull's heart would beat. When the gringo started shooting streams of blood where his ears once were, Gato began laughing hysterically.

"Señor, please stop. You make me laugh too hard. You, you look like the young bull. But, señor, the young bull, he lives. You will not live."

Gato Montes looked with disgust at the two men and a boy he could see sitting by a fire. Two gringos and one Mexican. He watched them through his binoculars for a long while before deciding to ride up on them at their campfire on the Texas side of the border. The Mexican was quick on his feet when he finally saw Gato ride in from behind a group of trees. Gato never took his eyes off of him and already had his rifle butt sitting on his saddle and finger on the trigger. He walked his horse in slowly.

"I need something to eat."

One of the gringos stood up and began to howl like a coyote. He threw his head back and pointed his nose straight up. Gato stared at him.

"Is this one crazy in the brain maybe? Does he think he is a coyote or maybe a lobo? Tell him to close his mouth now before I shoot him!"

"Oh, don't mind him none," the other gringo said. "His name is Coyote. He howls like that when he gets plumb excited or maybe after he kills a snake or something like that. My name is Bill. My friends just call me Billy. What is your name? Oh, and this here Mexican, he ain't really ever told us his name. He can ride a horse better than any man I ever seen before. Slips off to either side with his leg hung on the saddle at a dead run. Holds on to the mane or the saddle horn. Why, you can't even see him none. So, we just call him Ghost. He kind of likes it and don't seem to mind none."

"You always talk this much, señor? I just want to know if you have some food."

"Why yes sir, we got a little rabbit left here on this stick if you want it."

Gato slowly dismounted, continuing to hold his rifle. He grabbed the stick and began to gnaw slowly on the little piece of rabbit.

"What do you boys do?"

Billy smiled. "Well sir, I guess you could say we was kind of like a gang or something. We ain't really done no gang jobs, but we been thinking about planning one maybe."

"And what is your gang called, Mr. Bill?"

"Well, I don't rightly know. I been a-thinking about maybe the Ghost Gang or something. We done got a ghost that's been riding with us and all. That sounds really good to me, the Ghost Gang. What do you think about that, Mr. Ghost? Damn if we ain't named a gang right after you."

Gato Montes finished the small piece of rabbit and walked slowly to his horse to get his canteen. He pulled the cork and sipped a small drink. "I am sure the ranches will be in fear of such a gang. A howling coyote, a Mexican that rides on the side of a horse, and Mr. Bill, who likes to talk. That is a fearsome gang, señor. What will your gang be known for, maybe stealing onions out of someone's garden? I go. You make me laugh too much."

"I'll tell you one thing, Mister," said Billy. "We are a meaner gang than that. If you want to join up with us, we'll show you, well, at least me and Ghost will. Coyote there, he ain't too bright in the head, but he is loyal like a little puppy dog. You say fetch and he will go get a stick."

Billy picked up a small stick and threw it as far as he could. "Coyote, go fetch that stick, boy, go fetch it for old Billy."

Coyote jumped up smiling and tore off running. He found the stick and held it high above his head and began howling.

"I told you so!" said Billy. "He is as loyal as a little puppy. You sure you don't want to join up with the Ghost Gang?"

"Why would I want to join up with you? I ride by myself. You, all of you, would just get in my way. Besides, I go where I want and take what I want. I don't think I need the likes of you hanging around getting in my way. All of your brains together are not bigger than a cactus pod. I, Mr. Bill, I am the whole cactus and the pod."

Billy and Ghost stared at the ground while Coyote smiled holding the stick he had retrieved.

"I might let you all ride with me though."

"Really?" said Billy. "With you being a little older than us, that might be all right. What do you say, Ghost? You okay with that?"

Ghost shrugged his shoulders.

"Looks like he is good with it, mister. I don't rightly remember you telling us your name."

"My name, it is Gato Montes."

Ghost slowly turned his eyes toward Gato. "You a mountain lion, señor?" Ghost laughed.

Gato stared at Ghost long and hard, narrowing his eyes. "Yes, I am, Señor Ghost. Except I can see and kill a ghost before they know I am there. Mind your tongue or I will show you. If you boys ride with me, including that stupid Coyote, he must be kept quiet, no howling. And you two, you will ride for me, not me for you. I do all of the planning and thinking. You understand? If not, ride by yourself and don't ever try to follow me. It will be your last trail."

"Well, Mr. Gato Montes, I'd say you got yourself a gang. The Ghost Gang. I always wanted to be part of a gang," said Billy. "Now, I am gonna be something. Maybe we can rob a bank or maybe one of them trains that come through."

"Right now, just go find us some firewood and something to eat, that rabbit was not near enough."

"Yes sir, Mr. Gato. Let's go Coyote. Remember, no howling."

Ghost watched Gato unsaddle his dark bay gelding. Carefully he pulled the saddle off and stood it up on the ground with the saddle horn down. He opened one of the cowhide saddlebags and pulled out something rolled in soft cowhide. He unrolled the cowhide, exposing the long sharpened spikes. Maybe twenty of them. Gato held one up to the fading sunlight and felt of the tip.

"So, you are him!" said Ghost. "We heard about a man they are calling the neck stabber. Nobody got to see your face really good, until now. I know who you are. The neck stabber is you."

Before he could move, Gato was on him. He jabbed the spike into his jugular area without penetrating the skin but enough to make it bleed. He pulled Ghost's hair back and continued to apply pressure with the spike.

"Yes, señor, it is me. How do you like someone you have never seen until now just like those dirty gringos? I will kill you just like I killed them, except yours will be in your front vein here. You will die quickly. Do you know what my name is, little Ghost who rides on the side of his horse? My name is Gato Montes. I am the cat of the mountains. Remember, Señor little Ghost, you usually will not see me, just like the mountain lion when he attacks the deer. I get you by your neck and you never see me. You also will not live after the cat of the mountains is on your neck." Ghost was wide-eyed with fear.

"Speak, Mr. Ghost, tell me what you have to say. You want to make fight with me, señor? I like to make fight."

"No, señor, I no want to make fight. I want to live. I no make fight never with you."

"This is good, Señor Ghost. If you do or those two friends of yours, you will all find a spike in your neck before you can think, comprendo?"

"Yes, comprendo. You are el jefe. I ride for you. No make any trouble. No trouble."

Gato let go of his hair and slowly removed the spike.

"Just remember, I like these spigas, but I am much quicker and better with a lazo and really much quicker with my pistol, or my rifle. I can kill you while you are sitting by the fire while I sit on the side of a mountain. You be a good Ghost, and I let you live. And just so you remember what I have told you, I give you something to remember me by when you are sleeping and when you are awake."

Gato pulled the two-inch mesquite thorn from the band on his sombrero. Before Ghost could move, he grabbed his right ear and plunged the thorn through his ear. Ghost screamed in pain. His eyes were wide with fear.

"You see, Señor Ghost, I do not like you. You are a little man with a very big mouth. Your ear, it bleeds a little, but you still have your ears. The others, well, they do not have their ears, amigo, because my knife was hungry for them. If my knife is hungry for your ears, it will mean that the spiga is probably already in your neck and you are squirming like the turtles on the river, very slowly and not moving along. Then, I turn you over and you can watch me while my knife eats your ears. Now go! Go and pull the thorn out of your ear, and when the howling Coyote and Señor Bill comes back with food, tell them what I have said."

Billy and Coyote returned to camp after a couple of hours.

"We done killed us a big old rattler, mister. He is a great big one. Coyote done spotted him and took to howling. I come walking up while he was looking at him."

"Just get it cleaned and get him cooked. I am walking to the river for a little while. My horse's front feet are tied. They better be that way when I get back. Mr. Ghost will make sure my horse stays tied."

Gato took his rifle and his pistol and walked toward the river.

"What does he mean, Ghost, about you making sure his horse stays tied? That feller shore likes to boss other folks I reckon."

"Shut your mouth, you fool. That man is the man that has been sticking people in the neck with spikes. He stuck one in my neck when I told him I knew who he was while you and a Coyote were hunting. He has the spikes in his saddlebag. Many of them. Look at my ear. He stuck a mesquite thorn through my ear and said he let me live and keep my ear. This man, his name is Gato Montes. He is very bad. I think if you cross him, he will stick the spike through your neck and then cut off your ears. He is the man that killed the ranch people."

"Ghost, he can't be that bad. He just came riding into our camp and all."

"Listen to me close, Billy. This man, he is a killer. I saw it in his eyes. He is very strong and very quick and moves much quicker than any of us. He came on me so fast I could not think. I believe he will kill us all if we do not do what he says. I think maybe he is not just Mexican. He has the bones in the face of the Apache. Maybe Comanche. But he is not all Mexicano. He may be Comanchero. This I know. He may kill us if he hears us talking about him. I think maybe we are at wrong place at wrong time. And you, Billy, you asked him to join up with the Ghost Gang. There is no Ghost Gang."

"Yes, señor, there is a Ghost Gang," said Gato Montes as he walked up to the fire.

"I thought you was a-going to the river. Me and Ghost here was just talking a little."

"I told you to cook that snake when I left. He is not cooked. Either get him cooked so we can eat or I'm going to cook you on the fire. It is cold out here."

"I'll get him skinned and cooked pronto, mister. There ain't no need in you getting all rankled up."

"If I was rankled, Bill, you would done be cooked and we would be picking the meat off your sorry bones. Now shut your mouth and get moving. Andale muchacho. Andale. All of you will need a good night's sleep. We are going to go visiting tomorrow."

# CHAPTER 14

Sheriff Brody eased his horse Sister along, paying close attention to the lay of the land on the south and north sides of the river. He always watched his bay mare's ears when on the trail. Her left ear was slightly torn. A dog got hold of it and ripped it about an inch while she was in her corral at the livery in Rosario. She had her ears laid flat back while he would run in and out of the cedar railings. When he did finally latch on to her ear, she pulled him into the corral and stomped him in the back and he turned loose. She grabbed him with her teeth in the stomach and pulled the skin nearly right off of his gut. When Sheriff Brody went to feed her that evening, she was bleeding from her ear, and he saw the dead dog. She was still worked up and staring hard at the mangled creature.

"You okay, old girl? Looks like you got a little cut, but that dog got the worst end of this thing."

He was able to clean and stitch the ear, but there was still a gap at the very top, and the hair did not grow right there.

"You are still the prettiest mare this side of the river," he would always say. "And the word must have gotten around to the rest of the dogs in town. They just don't come around no more, girl."

He figured Gato Montes and his band might be watching him from some rim or the side of one of the mountains. He was still a good fifteen miles from the Rolling J on his return trip. He traveled to all three big ranches down east of the Rolling J on the Texas side to give them fair warning. The Turtle Draw ranch foreman had not heard about the killings, but the word had spread like wildfire at the High Bridge and Cholla spreads. The cowboys took great interest as the sheriff rode in. Once they saw his badge, they came toward him and Sister. Almost before he could get off Sister, they began asking questions about the killer. Every one of them had some type of sidearm. Once he dismounted, Sheriff Brody would ask who was in charge and addressed him first.

"Is this all of your boys? If it's not, get the word to them as soon as practical. I know there is a lot of concern, out here on the river especially, about this killer. We don't know a lot about him, exactly what he looks like and what he rides. My advice is to ride in pairs, no matter what. Keep a close eye out at all times."

"You aren't riding with nobody," said one cowboy on the Cholla.

"Well, that's right. I don't have anybody to ride with, just old Sister here. She will do. Keep your ponies secured at night. I suspect they are stealing them to sell or trade to the Comancheros or the Apaches, maybe in Mexico. They may be swapping mounts, we don't know. I need to head back to Rosario and check on the man I left in charge. Best of luck."

THE SHERIFF PLANNED TO MAKE the Rolling J by noon and then ride on into Rosario. His knees were aching from getting up and down out of the saddle so many times over the last two weeks. Even though he was drinking plenty of water from his canteen, it seemed it took him forever to relieve himself. He was coming up on the little canyon with the natural spring in it. He had stopped at the spring coming in. The water hole was clear and cold with a little grass around the edges for Sister. He eyed the trail ahead carefully and paid close attention to Sister's ears. She made her way carefully down the little slide into the canyon. The water hole was still about two hundred yards ahead when he heard a horse nicker. Sister immediately threw up her head and nickered back. Sheriff Brody immediately pulled her up. He could see a small group, maybe ten or twelve horses inside a little roped-off area right up next to the canyon wall. Slowly he began to approach the small herd, scanning the area. He unlatched the strap on his gun and slowly removed it.

"Easy, boys and girls, ain't nobody going to hurt you. Easy now."

Sheriff Brody stayed on Sister and surveyed the ponies.

"How do you like my horses, señor?" said a voice from behind him. "No, señor, do not turn around, do not even move or you will live no more. Put your hands in the air with your gun now. Drop the gun on the right side of your horse. Then we can talk a little while."

The sheriff was extremely angry that he did not look behind him when he came into the canyon. He only focused on the horses. Slowly he raised his hands and then dropped the pistol.

"Very good, amigo. Now, you get off of your horse on the right side and never look back to me."

Once he was on the ground, a rope went around his neck quickly. He never heard the footsteps. He was yanked off of his feet and to the ground. He heard the man mount his horse and then he began dragging him. He quickly grabbed the rope to prevent being choked. The man stopped his horse and he could make out the sound of him throwing the rope over a limb. Once the rope was over the limb, he heard the man click to his horse, and he began to be pulled onto his feet. The man stopped when his feet were just touching the ground. He continued to hold the rope above his head and tried not to pass out. The man lowered him to stand flat-footed.

"Now, señor, put your hands down behind your back."

The man used a small rope to tie his hands. Finally, he walked in front of the sheriff.

Sheriff Brody slowly eyed the man standing in front of him. His eyes were circled with black, and his nose and face were painted dark red. His jet-black eyes were mean and fixed. He wore a dirty dark brown sombrero and had black hair down to the middle of his back.

"Buenos dias, amigo."

He had a large gap between his large white front teeth that was noticeable when he spoke.

"What is your name, señor? The man with the badge I see riding along my river. I hope you are not looking for me, señor, that would not be good. Now, what is your name? Can you speak, or is my rope too tight on your neck? Maybe I loosen it a little bit so you not choke and can speak to me, yes? I think your horse leave us. That is okay, señor. Maybe she lives, maybe she will die."

The man went to the tree and let a small amount of slack out of the rope. Sheriff Brody immediately began gasping for air.

"Now, what is your name?"

The sheriff slowly began to get his wind back. He eyed the strange man. "I am Sheriff Brody. Sheriff of Rosario."

The man turned his back on the sheriff and looked at the horses. He was very tall for an Apache if he was one. His arms were very developed and strong. He had on deer-hide moccasin shoes. He had no shirt on, and his pants were made of deerskin laced on the side with rawhide.

"Sheriff Brody of Rosario, you make a big mistake coming here. Maybe you will not be the Sheriff of Rosario anymore."

Gato Montes could hear the riders coming in. Billy, Coyote, and Ghost came into the east end of the canyon. He could hear Billy talking before he heard the horse's footsteps.

"What you got you there, mister? He's strung up like a pig for quartering," said Billy.

Sheriff Brody looked the three men over good and their horses. He had not seen the man's horse that had him tied up. Billy got off his horse and approached the sheriff.

"Well Mr. Gato Montes, this here feller looks like he might rather be somewhere else, don't he, Coyote?"

Coyote got off his horse and got on the ground on all fours and let out a little howl.

"I don't reckon he is taking a liking to you, mister. He does that when he is on the hunt. That there is Coyote, and that there is Mr. Ghost. Why, he can ride a horse on the side and all."

"Shut your mouth, you fool," said Gato. "I could hear you talking a mile off. I told you about that Coyote and his howling. He can't howl without his tongue."

Sheriff Brody took a good look at Coyote. He was short and stunted. His dirty brown derby seemed too small for his head. His green eyes belied a severe lack of intelligence and nearly looked like those of a coyote. His pants were patched and came up halfway to his knees. His shoes were badly worn and awkwardly leaned to the side while he was standing. His pony was a small gray Welsh, with a mane that stuck nearly straight up about eight inches or so. The one they called Ghost was very dark. He rode a tall buckskin horse. His dark hair was cut straight at his shoulders. He sat emotionless on his horse and did not dismount.

"Get off your horse, Señor Ghost. I have business for you with the sheriff," said Gato.

Gato turned and walked back to his horse. He untied him and led him to the rope where the horses were enclosed. He tied the reins to the rope and began to open his saddlebag. His horse was a beautiful Appaloosa gelding with some kind of cross blood. His butt was white with dark circles and his mane was dark as Gato's hair and about a foot long. Sheriff Brody watched the horse as Gato led him. His right front foot kicked out slightly with every step and he was shod. He could not tell anything special about the others' horses. The saddle on him was very old with a high horn and cantle. There was a rifle of some type in a leather scabbard and a leather-braided lariat tied on the saddle horn. He had never seen anyone carry two ropes before.

Gato pulled the bag of spikes out of his saddlebag and began to unroll the cloth. He pulled one out and held it up to the sun, testing the point with his finger.

"Señor Ghost, of the famous Ghost Gang, let us see how you do with the spiga, yes?"

Ghost slowly got off his horse and stood by him.

"Come, señor, the sheriff is waiting for his spiga, can you not see it in his eyes?"

"Why do you have to kill this man? He has done nothing to you. He just rides his horse by the river."

Gato ran to Ghost in a flash.

"I told you before, I will kill you. You are afraid."

"I ain't afraid," said Billy. "Give me that thing. Where do you want him stuck, mister? How about in the eye or maybe the ear?"

Billy walked over to Gato and stuck his hand out for the spike. Gato looked with contempt at Ghost and slowly released the spike.

"Stick him all the way through the neck, from behind." Billy marched to the sheriff and gleefully looked him in the eyes.

"We fixing to have us a pigstickin', Sheriff, and you are the pig."

He walked behind the sheriff. Sheriff Brody listened as Billy approached and tried to anticipate when the spike would come. He heard him lift his arm and quickly turned his head to the left and stood up on his feet. He screamed with pain as the Billy drove the spike into the top of his right shoulder and down into his chest.

"I didn't quite get him in the neck, mister, but he is shore stuck good though, probably clean down into his lungs. Moved his head on me."

Gato looked on with contempt and disgust. The sheriff was bleeding profusely and had his head hung down.

"He will die soon anyway. At least you are not scared like that Ghost over there. Take my rope off of him and leave his back hands tied. I need that rope. He will bleed quickly. We will leave his ears for the buzzards to eat. Señor Ghost, maybe you are better with the horses. Make sure they are all tied together. The sheriff's horse took off. If she is close, catch her and put her with the rest. We are heading north to a place called Mushaway. We will sell the horses there and then maybe go into Santa Fe."

SHERIFF BRODY LAPSED IN AND out of consciousness for the rest of the day. He had lost a lot of blood. The blood flow would stop for a while and then begin to ooze every time he moved. His tongue was parched, and the red ants had found him by the smell of the blood. They were beginning to crawl all over his face and neck. His face was baked from the relentless sun. He thought he was dead or maybe dreaming when he felt Sister gently nuzzle his face. His throat was too parched to talk. He slowly lifted his left hand and touched her muzzle.

"Good girl, Sister," he whispered. The pain in his shoulder and upper chest was nearly unbearable. He was coherent enough to know that the sharpened point might puncture his heart. He was still breathing fairly well, but it was a great struggle to take a deep breath. He rolled onto his back and laid for a good spell. The ants were biting him all around the bloody area. In one mighty heave, he forced himself to sit up. He could feel himself starting to lose consciousness and sat with his legs crossed and his head down. Sister continued to nuzzle him with her nose. "I'm trying, little girl." He was very light-headed even after nearly sitting perfectly still for about an hour. He figured his heart was pumping more out of him than staying in him. Slowly and with all of his might, he stood up. Immediately he leaned on Sister's saddle and closed his eyes. The world was disappearing before him. He could see nothing but darkness and a big ray of sunlight in the middle. Sister reached her head around and nickered low and pulled at his pants.

"Got to get my hands untied." He turned his back to Sister and tried to lift his hands. "Grab that knot, girl. Just like you do on your gate."

Sister sniffed of the small rope. She loved to nibble on ropes, especially on a tied gate. The sheriff had cussed her more than once when she got out of her pen and would come stand in front of the sheriff's office by the tie rail. Someone would always poke their head in the door. "Sheriff, Sister is a-standing outside, bare as a button with no head gear on. Reckon she's busted out again."

"Get the rope, girl, just like your old gate rope."

Sister played with the rope knot for a little while and began to bite and tug at the ball. He could feel the rope pressure began to release when she pulled the first loop out. His hands were numb from the pressure. He began to feel a little burning sensation back into his hands as he began to fade off again. Sister pulled the rope loose and stood there with it hanging in her teeth. Sheriff Brody began to come around and lifted his head off of the side of the saddle. He was able to move his left hand.

"You are a real good pony, Sis."

The right rein was still around her neck and draped over the other side. He slowly and deliberately took hold of the left rein and finally was able to ease it over her neck. It took all of his strength to grab the saddle horn with his left hand.

"Sister, if I can get on, you got to head to the Rolling J straight ahead. I am not too sure I can get on."

Sister nickered low two times and turned to look at him. Her senses told her he was hurt bad. She nipped him on the pants one more time. He slowly lifted his left foot and put the tip of his boot in the stirrup. With one mighty lurch, he pulled himself into the saddle. His head was swirling so that he nearly fell off the other side. Instinctively, he took the reins in his left hand and just sat leaned over in the saddle.

DeWitt Murphy was smoking his pipe out on the porch of the bunkhouse and looking at his pistol when he spotted the horse and rider coming in from the east. "Somebody, go get Mr. Tree at the main house. We got company coming in. Whoever it is, he is a-leaned way over in that saddle."

Tree ran out the door as soon as one of the cowboys hollered, "Rider coming in from the east, Mr. Tree. You might want to get out here."

Tree immediately recognized the sheriff's horse, Sister.

"DeWitt, that man is hurt bad. Ease out there and walk her in. Tully, get that buckboard hitched up now and put some blankets in back of it.

Maybe throw a little hay in it before you put the blankets in it. Move now."

Cedar Jones stuck his head out the bunkhouse door and saw the man on the horse. He moved quickly to Tree. "What in the world we got here? That's the sheriff."

Tree looked the situation over quickly seeing the spike stuck in his right shoulder with about four inches sticking out with a head.

"Look out for that spike on his right side, it's buried really deep. The way he is gurgling don't sound good. He's lost a lot of blood. We got to get him into Rosario quick, or he is going to die. Don't move him too much getting him off of his horse, Dewitt. Let's move slowly. Bring him up here by the porch where we can ease him off slow and together. Stay with us, sheriff, we will get you to town. Get them ants off of his neck there."

Slowly Tree, Cedar Jones, and DeWitt eased Sheriff Brody off Sister as she stood completely still. The saddle was covered in blood as well as the right side of the horse.

"This man cannot have much blood left in him, Tree," said Cedar.

"I reckon not. I'm going to take him in. DeWitt, saddle Bonner and tie both him and this mare behind the buckboard. We don't have a lot of time. Cedar, you are in charge of the ranch until I get back, whenever that is."

"Yes sir, I will handle it."

Tully came around with the buckboard hitched to the big strawberry roan gelding. He looked more like a big plow horse than anything else. Once you put his side blinders on, he pulled straight ahead nice and steady with no jerking and head throwing. He could trot all day and never lose his wind.

"All right, boys, let's get him in this thing without killing him."

"I put hay down like you told me, Boss," said Tully.

"Let's ease him in here and keep his head flat. That spike is sticking in his chest and may be next to his heart. Just slide him in. Tully, you get in back there and keep his head from moving. I mean don't let it move a bit."

DeWitt came trotting up with Bonner saddled. "I didn't tie his saddle on riding tight Tree, but it ain't falling off neither."

"Good. Tie both of them to the back rings on the buckboard and loosen that mare's saddle just the one on Bonner."

Tree climbed up into the buckboard seat and released the brake.

"Keep an eye on things, boys. That gang may not be far from here. Keep your guns ready."

He clicked the big gelding into a fast trot, hoping that Sheriff Brody did not bleed to death by the time he got him to town.

The trip in seemed like it would never be over. Tree looked back at Tully now and again. "You keeping his head straight, Tully? Don't let it move none at all."

"Yes sir, it ain't a wiggling none."

"Is he still breathing?"

"I can still hear a little air coming out his nose. Yea, he is still a-breathing, but it ain't so much."

Tree drew stares as soon as they entered Rosario with the big roan lathered up and two horses tied to the back.

"We need a doctor and fast. Where is the doctor's office? The sheriff is bad hurt."

One man yelled out: "It is up ahead on the corner." Folks began to gather quickly and started to run after the buckboard.

Tree never let the big gelding slow down until he saw the shingle on the doctor's office. He bailed off the wagon and slammed the door open. The doctor was sitting at his desk reading when Tree came through the door.

"Get out here quick, we got a dying man in the buckboard. It is Sheriff Brody. He has a spike in his right shoulder and is nearly bled to death. Got to move now." The doctor jumped up and ran outside. He crawled into the back of the wagon and began looking at Sheriff Brody and quickly assessed his vital signs. He grabbed his left wrist and checked his pulse.

"Is he breathing?"

"Well, he is barely breathing, but he is a-breathing," said Tully.

"He does not have much pulse. Let's slowly get him out of the wagon on a stretcher. I have one inside. I want to lay it beside him and then we will gently pull him onto it. It is inside behind the door on the wall."

Tree ran through the door and looked behind it. He grabbed the green stretcher off the wall. He ran to the buckboard and slid it alongside the sheriff on his left side.

"Okay," said the doctor, pointing at Tree, "You handle the front, and we will handle his feet."

Tree climbed onto the buckboard seat and gently stepped over. He put his massive hand under the sheriff's head and between his shoulders.

"Okay, men, gently, gently slide him over. Do not let his head move at all. Good. That will do it. Now let's ease him out of here and take him into my office and go through the right door once we are in there. Help keep his head secure while we are moving him inside. Do not let it turn at all. I have to get to work on him now if he is going to have a chance."

Tree had Tully stable Bonner and Sister before heading back to the ranch.

"Keep a close eye, Tully. Keep your pistol ready and keep your pace slow and steady going back. That gelding needs a little breather."

"You think that Gato Montes is close, Mr. Tree?"

"He is not far, Tully. He is not far. I can't ride with you, now go."

Dr. Clay had Tree heat a kettle of hot water on his wood-burning stove while he kept a slight pressure to the wound area with a clean cloth.

"Lucky this was not on the other side. He has still lost a lot of blood. He is breathing, but I will tell you, it will be hit-and-miss on him living. This spike has to come out. He may get blood poisoning anyway. Get me that bottle of chloroform and that bottle of whiskey there on the wall. I am going to try and pull this thing out of him and we will see what happens from there. It has surely torn some meat and ligaments and might have gone into a piece of his lung. Might be right next to his heart. We just do not have a choice."

Shortly after midnight, the exhausted Doctor Clay laid the long spike in a metal tray. It had taken over three long hours to slowly pull from the wound. He would pull a little bit and watch for bleeding, then repeat that step over and over a little bit at a time.

"That thing is over twelve inches long. Who in the world would do such a thing? I am going to stick a hot rod in there to cauterize the bleeding. He may never feel it. You have got to keep his shoulders and head from moving."

He held the small rod over the top of his metal stove until it was glowing red. "Are you ready, sir?"

Tree nodded his head yes. The sheriff moaned slightly as the doctor inserted the small steel rod as far in the wound as he could. Tree could smell the burning flesh and opened his mouth to breathe, trying not to gag. Then as fast as he had put it in, the doctor pulled the rod back out and touched the top of the wound with the still-hot rod. He laid it in the steel tray and wiped the sweat from his forehead.

"Okay, let's have that whiskey and put a little on this sterilized cloth."

Tree poured some on the cloth and the doctor dabbed the top of the wound. "Now, we are going to take this sterilized wrap and wrap this wound and also his right arm. Have to make sure he does not move that arm."

Tree slept in one of the chairs in the doctor's office for the remainder of the night. Dr. Clay stayed in a chair beside the sheriff. At sunup, Tree opened his eyes and stood up. Approaching the side door to the operating room, such as it was, he poked his head under the frame of the door. Doctor Clay had his stethoscope on the sheriff's chest and had his ear next to his nose. He heard Tree come in and raised up.

"How is he doing Doc? Still with us?"

"Well, he has lost an awful lot of blood. I doctored him before for two bullet wounds. He is a very tough old cod. Yes, he is still with us. His pulse rate is still lower than I want, but it is steady. His breathing is shallow but getting a little stronger. If he does not get blood poisoning, he might just pull through. There are no signs of infection or blood poisoning with red streaks and all. He is a firm and steady fixture around here. Folks look up to him. Have never seen him not handle any type of situation. I cannot fathom how someone was able to stick a spike in him like that. He usually knows what is going on a mile around him in all directions. You probably need to get something to eat over at the café and bring me something back as well. I need to stay with him just in case by some miracle he wakes up."

"I'll do that. Be back in a bit," said Tree.

Hardin's Boardinghouse had several rooms available when Tree came in. The woman at the desk looked him over from top to bottom when he came ducked his head through the door as he still had blood on his pants and shirt.

"Can I help you?" she said.

"Need a room if you got one. The sign outside says you have several available."

"We have plenty. They run a dollar a night. We serve hot breakfast and supper for another fifty cents a day."

"I'll take both."

"How long are your planning on staying?"

"I don't rightly know, I guess. Maybe a day or two."

"You're the man that brought in Sheriff Brody yesterday, aren't you?"

"Yes, I reckon I am. Can I just get my room key? It's been a while since I slept."

"Yes, why sure. Maybe you can change out of those bloody clothes. They do draw attention, you know. Room number twelve, just down the hall there. We serve breakfast at 7:00 in the morning and supper at 6:00 in the evening. Do you need me to help you bring your things to your room?"

"No, ma'am, what I have on is my things. Did not have much time for packing."

"I will see if I can find you a fresh shirt and pants. That may be hard to come by, due to your size. I'll look around through our clothes that folks left in their rooms. That sure was a bad thing that happened to the sheriff and all. I heard someone tried to nail him down to the timbers of a railroad track or something."

Tree walked away with the keys. "Something like that."

# CHAPTER 15

Dr. Clay was feeding some broth to Sheriff Brody when Tree came in. It had been five days since the spike was removed from his shoulder. Every day before that, Tree had found the sheriff asleep when he poked his head in the door.

"Good morning, Mr. Tree," the doctor said. "He is hungry as a bear and has a pulse."

Tree smiled when he looked at Sheriff Brody.

"You look a little better today than you did a few days ago."

Sheriff Brody slowly lifted his hand slightly and extended it to Tree. Tree could see the stains of blood coming through the bandages on his shoulder.

"Careful now, you don't want to go bleeding again."

The handshake was feeble but was heartfelt.

"I would not have made it had it not been for you. I am so weak I can barely take nourishment. I want to thank you for hauling me in. I do need to talk to you a little bit after I sleep a while. Can you stick around or maybe come back after lunch? I am just so weak, I can barely . . . stay awake."

"Tree, why don't you come by around 1:00 this afternoon? You can visit with him then, if he is awake. I would not count on it being very long. If he is asleep, we will let him sleep. He is very weak."

There were horses and riders going both directions and fancy horse-drawn buggies. *These folks all look like they are in a hurry to get somewhere*, Tree thought. He could walk from one end of town to the other in a minute or so. Seems like they just got gussied up to be seen or something. He sat down on a porch bench and watched the people all morning. A lot of the women that walked by on the boardwalk stole a glance at him. As always, he thought himself peculiar and large. Whenever they turned a glance toward him, he always looked away. The town made him nervous and fidgety. He liked the loneliness of the ranch country. It was really hard to dress up and impress a bunch of cows, and Bonner did not much take to town either. It seemed hard to tell what the women were thinking when they looked at him that way. He finally sat there with his arms crossed. He figured that they at least could not see most of the dried blood on his shirt if his arms were folded. Of course, there was still a lot of dried blood on his shirtsleeves too. The woman at the hotel never found any clothes big enough for him to wear.

Dr. Clay was in his office when Tree tapped on the door at 1:00 sharp and ducked through the door frame.

"He is awake. Does not want me in there. Says it's sheriff's business. Call me if you need anything."

Tree walked into the room and Sheriff Brody was laying down with his head slightly propped up.

"Please close the door, Tree. We need to visit a little. Sit down by the bed here. I get a little light-headed when I go to moving and talking, so listen to me as best you can. Get down here close, cause I do not have a lot of air, it seems. I got a good look up close at that killer, Gato Montes, and the boys that is riding with him. He was riding a big Appaloosa gelding. Big black spots on his rump all sizes. Black mane and speckled on the head." The sheriff closed his eyes and began to fade away for a minute or two before he slowly reopened them. "Where was I?"

"You were telling me about Gato's horse. Take your time, Sheriff. You are mighty weak. I can come back."

Sheriff Brody continued, barely above a whisper at times and very slow.

"The horse was shod. Right front foot twists a little out when he walks. Probably more when he is trotting and loping. There is a man about twenty-five called Ghost. He rides a big buckskin gelding about sixteen hands tall. Real long mane. Longer than most horses. He is very dark, maybe from South America or somewhere. He does not talk much. There's one named Billy. He talks all the time. Gato Montes ordered Ghost to stab me in the neck, but he wouldn't do it. Billy volunteered to do the job. I just moved my head at the right time and he stuck it into my shoulder. I guess it could have been worse. He rides a real dark palomino horse. Don't know about shoes on the other horses. Then the last one. He is a short little kid around fourteen or fifteen years old or so. Little derby on his head with big green eyes. They call him Coyote. He rides a gray Welsh pony about ten, maybe twelve hands tall. His pony's mane sticks straight up about eight inches, maybe. The boy is not all there and howls like a coyote. Got down on the ground like a dog and looked at me. They have about twelve horses or so, all stolen, I bet. Gato Montes said they was heading toward Mushaway Mountain out toward the Caprock. I've heard of that mountain. It is plumb out in the Llano Estacado past that big spring to the northeast a day or two's ride. Travelers use that spring to water their horses, including them Comanches and the Comancheros too. There is a big Quahadi camp up there, I am told. They trade with the Comancheros all the way up into Santa Fe. Gato Montes may be trying to sell the horses there and maybe go into New Mexico, or he may be trying to hide out for a while and lay low. He is taking a mighty big risk, I'd say, riding into their country like that. That is a really big risk."

"You have a good memory for a man who nearly died. Most folks would not have remembered those kinds of details, Sheriff."

"Tree, I may die right here. Dr. Clay said it was hit-and-miss on me for the first two days in here. The man I have taking care of this here town is barely capable of doing that with me gone. But with me here, even in this condition, it will keep him settled down until I at least get where I can get up and walk around, if I am able. I need you to go after this man. We don't have time to get a federal marshal in this territory at this time. If they get up into New Mexico, we may lose them for good. They only have one U.S. marshal for this region, and nobody knows where he is at or how we would even find him. I don't know where you came from or what you can do, but I somehow think you are up to the task. You ever been north of here toward Llano Estacado area?"

Tree stood up and looked toward the window. "I been north before, several times. Been to Mushaway. I was in the cavalry. Rode with Captain Vassar Golden on a patrol up that way. Our ranch cook, Cedar Jones, did too. He was a scout like me and a sharpshooter, probably one of the best in the country as far as I am concerned. He saved my life. Killed seven Comancheros and one Comanche when I was trying to get myself killed a few years ago."

"I knew it. There was something about you, Tree."

"Well, I am no longer in the cavalry, Sheriff. Those days are long behind me. I finally grew up. I am just helping take care of the Rolling J while Mr. Gillstrap is away tending to his ailing wife back east. I am nothing but a cow herder. I gave my word to Mr. Gillstrap that I would run his place while he is gone. Who knows how long that might be?"

"I don't have time to try and find somebody willing, Tree. I may die before the end of our conversation. You must go. Only you and me know where they are heading and what they are riding. If this bunch gets too far ahead, they are gone for good. You can carry my power and authority anywhere I tell you to go if you let me deputize you. That is unless you cross into Mexico or New Mexico, and then you can just claim you are lost. We have to stop that man if we can catch him. It's not just the horse stealing, it's the damn killing. He kills for the fun of it. Some kind of vendetta or something. I looked that man in the face. Eyes covered in black charcoal paste or something. Paints his nose and between his eyes dark red. He is the evilest kind of man I have ever seen, and I have seen a lot of bad folks in my time."

"Sheriff, if I agree to do this, it will take some time. Could be months. Mr. Gillstrap left me in charge of the Rolling J. I left Cedar Jones in charge when I hauled you in. He is really capable, but he is the ranch cook as well. That is hard on a man with both of those jobs. There is no quit in him, and he is as independent as they come. I am sure he can keep a lid on things."

"I will tell you what, Tree. I will send you a cook out there from the boardinghouse. They got at least two over there. They are both good cooks. As far as the Rolling J, it will have to wait a little as far as I am concerned. This killing bunch has got to be reckoned with now. Not a month from now."

"Cooking in a boardinghouse and cooking on a ranch next to the border with a killer running around are two completely different things, Sheriff."

"Well, he said he was heading north. Maybe the cook would be safe for a while out there. Besides, this one is pretty tough. Came into town after being on a 1,000-mile cattle drive. Only woman on the drive. Her name is Felicity Two-Feathers. She is a Lipan Apache Indian. Escaped a white man's boarding school when she was young. They gave her that name, Felicity, and tried to make her follow their ways. She ran off and walked into a cow camp one evening and they took her in. Probably was about seventeen, maybe eighteen years old or so. She nearly killed a cow-boy one night when he slipped into her wagon and tried to get affection-ate with her. She pinned him down with a hunting knife nobody knew she had. I reckon she will be all right on your ranch as long as the boys let her do her job and leave her be. Cooks really good too. Look, you can take my mare, Sister, as a packhorse if you need to. She is a good mare and honest as the day is long. Good ears too. Untied my hands with her teeth. I would have died without her coming back to where they left me to die. Just remember, use my rope on my saddle with the metal clip when you tie her and you can hobble her if need be, but she does not much like hobbling. She can't untie that rope with the clip on it."

"I feel like I am going back on my word to Mr. Gillstrap. Get to deputizing, Sheriff. I don't like the idea of wearing a badge for folks to see. Especially if he has a pair of looking glasses like they say. He could see me coming from a long way off."

"You are not going back on your word, Tree. You are just changing the timing a little, nothing more than that. Besides, nobody else may be able to handle this. He is likely to see you coming from a long way off whether you have a badge on or not. He probably has a pair of binoculars. Just put it on your shirt and keep your vest on. You will be paid deputy wages plus a little travel stipend. About $125 a month is the best we can do, but at least it is something. Tree, I need to do a little more sleeping. I have done way too much talking, hopefully you will remember all of it. The best of luck to you. Watch your back trail, side trails, and what is in front of you. There should be plenty of tracks to follow with the horses they will be taking along."

TREE STOPPED AT THE DOOR and looked at Sheriff Brody, now fast asleep on the bed. He looked at the badge in his hand and then to the street. He put it in his front pocket on the way to the boardinghouse to check out. It was not worth a wet horse turd outside of the boundaries of the town.

He made a stop by Logan's Hardware before he went to the livery to saddle up Bonner and Sister. The man behind the counter recognized him immediately.

"I did not figure you would be out of sugar cubes so soon, sir. Looks like you been in a fight with a mountain lion with all of that dried blood on your shirt. Trouble somewhere?"

"I need a little ammunition and a bottle of whiskey. Forty-four-caliber Colt. Six boxes and four boxes of 30-30 carbine."

"Certainly, you trying to start a war or something? That is a lot of bullets."

"Or something, I reckon. Just give me my ammunition and a bottle of that whiskey there and also give me eight cans of beans."

"I hope you don't plan on drinking that whole bottle with all of that ammunition sir, you know guns and liquor don't rightly go together."

"I ain't going to say it again. Give me what I asked for. The whiskey is for disinfectant if I need it or maybe the chills if I get wet. Now get moving."

He slowly pulled the badge out of his pocket.

"Put this on the sheriff's office account. I work for him now."

The little man behind the counter blinked fast behind his spectacles as he looked at the badge while sacking up the ammunition and the whiskey.

"Are you saying you are the new sheriff, sir?"

Tree grabbed the bag and walked out the door.

"I never said nothing of the sort. I just said I work for him."

Tree saddled both horses and headed back to the Rolling J. He knew when he started out, he would have to head north toward Fort Concho and the Concho River. If Gato was really heading toward Mushaway, he would have to follow the river a good portion of the way to keep the stolen horses watered and grazed along the way. The headwaters started about twenty miles south of the big spring. The foothills on both sides of the river provided plenty of cover to watch riders in the valley below, as he well remembered. He would try and cover twenty miles a day, swapping horses if he had to. The country was rigorous. The springtime lightning storms killed many a horse and rider traveling the trail. It was late fall with winter coming on, so that would not be a worry. Maybe the cold would not be too bad in the Llano Estacado. He had also heard tales of folks freezing to death in the flat plains when the blue northers came in. Especially when there was any kind of rain, sleet, or snow. He would be careful to pack a small tent, firewood axe, a lantern, and plenty of wax-covered matches.

# CHAPTER 16

THE TWO VAQUEROS HAD ALREADY returned to Montenegro after their day's work on the Rolling J when the priest rang the church bell three times. Slowly, folks began to come out of their homes with aprons still on having just fed their families supper. The priest was standing on the top step as the villagers began to assemble at the steps. The children ran to see who could sit first on the top steps.

Santiago made his way through the crowd and up the steps, taking a place next to the priest. The crowd spoke in low tones as babies were passed around, adoringly held and kissed. Julia de la Garza loved the babies.

"I will bring him back to you tomorrow, señora," she said as she picked the young baby boy out of his madre's arms.

"You can keep him, Julia. He is not sleeping too good at night and he eats like a caballo, maybe dos caballos. My milk needs a rest."

The priest tinkled a little bell to get everyone's attention.

"Hola, a good day to all. We are here to announce the Fiesta de Quinceañera coming up next Friday for Marie Abuello, the niece of Adelina and Santiago. As with all of our beautiful children that Dios sent us as blessings, we anxiously await the celebration of her quince años where she is no longer a child, but a young woman. Our celebration will begin at noon, when the bell rings three times that day."

Marie Abuello nervously smiled in the crowd as people began to touch her shoulder and some women hugged her and kissed her on the cheek.

One old woman shuffled up to her and grabbed her gently by the cheeks. With tears streaming down her face, she said, "You are the little baby girl that I rocked in my chair. I watch you see your first bird one day. You smile so beautiful and try to point at the bird. I love you so much. Now, look at you. Your beautiful face. Dios gave you long and bountiful hair and kind, dark eyes. You are lovely to look at. Your face is more beautiful than las caléndulas at the Día de los Muertos. May Dios shine his light on you always."

She kissed Marie on the left and the right cheeks and held her hands for a moment before letting go. Other women approached Marie and kissed her on both sides of the face.

The priest tinkled his bell again.

"I think maybe you want to start the celebration for Marie a little early, yes?" The crowd laughed as people continued to surround Marie.

"However, you will have time to prepare for the great celebration next Friday. We will have singing, the dance de quince with the oscura veil and of course, we shall eat what Dios has blessed us with, abundant food and those especially that know how to prepare it well. Now, Santiago has something to share with all of you. I pray that you will turn your ears to him."

Santiago smiled at Marie from the steps and kissed his fingers to his lips and then blew the kiss to her. She reached in the air and captured the kiss as was their tradition and placed it upon her lips. He turned to face the crowd and began to speak.

"Everyone, thank you for coming to the ringing of the bell and to talk about one of our beloved children, Marie Abuello. Dios smiles on this village with our children. I will ask you to send all of the children except the babies to the old tree to play while I speak. The older children," as he looked at Marie, "will take care of the younger children while I talk to everyone." Marie looked over the group.

"Come children, let us go to el arbol viejo. We will play the burra and burro hide game."

The children squealed in delight at the donkey hide game. The boys were the burros and the girls were the burras. The children loved this game of hide-and-seek. Finally, when all of the children were securely away from the crowd, Santiago began to speak. "This day I speak to Franco and Pedro. They tell me in our village, we have one that was brought here that maybe he is veneno de la sol. His name is Pablo de la Rosa."

There were audible gasps from the crowd.

"I do not like to ever say such a bad thing about someone, but I believe it to be true. You see, he left our village some time ago and has never returned. His madre, she was captured by the Apache with the other women and taken to their camp for dos, maybe tres años, like I remember. It was long ago. The other women never come back, and their husbands mourned them as most are still among us taking care of this salty wound every day in their hearts. Pablo's madre somehow escaped the cruelty of the Apache and made her way back. You remember the day she came back into the village and went into her home with the young boy. She felt shame that the father of the child came from the Apache. You saw the young boy as he became older and saw that he was different with the other boys and children. No one in the village turned their back on this young boy and his madre. Her husband, he left to look for her and he never returned to the village to this day. Maybe he died of the very lonely heart. He never come back. You will remember, our young Prieto was riding his burro Chico along the river to gather firewood and found the looking glasses and brought them back to the village for all to see under the old tree. A short time later, Prieto came back from the river covered in blood and his ears were cut off."

Some women in the crowd surrounded Prieto's madre as she began to weep.

"I do not tell you this to make you sad and to make you cry. I have to tell you the truth. Mr. Trujillo gave horse tail hair and mezcal to help his madre sew the ears back on to Prieto. One of them make the yellow pus and became rotten on the bottom and it have to be cut off. Prieto never speak much after he came into the village with his ears cut off. His beautiful smile and love of life disappeared. He would only tell his madre that a bandit named Gato Montes cut his ears off. She asked him, 'Who is this cat of the mountains? Did you see him?'

"But Prieto, he never would say if he knows Gato Montes. One day, Pedro and Franco, they hear Pablo taking to Prieto when Pablo does not think anyone can hear. They hear him laugh and call Prieto uno y medio. He was laughing and make much fun of Prieto's ears. Franco and Pedro still listen from behind the trees when Pablo asked Prieto if he tell anyone that that he is Gato Montes, the bandit."

A hush fell over the crowd as Prieto's mother continued to weep. Two women wrapped their arms around her.

"A short time later, our young Prieto, he stepped into the river and never return to us."

Prieto's madre began to wail loudly and had to be led away from the crowd.

Santiago continued: "It was not but a short time after Prieto stepped into the river that Pablo de la Rosa left the village on one of the horses from el corral for caballos that I take care of. He also stole a saddle and lazo trenzado. He takes the grande apalusa with the beautiful round marks on the back. This is a very fine caballo. His madre left her home in the night and she never return to the village.

"Franco and Pedro stand with you. They are both very good men and bring money to the village from their long day's work on the gringo rancho across the river. They tell me that they are the better of all of the men on the rancho with their caballos and their lazo de cuerdas. Pedro and Franco tell the large gringo patrón, Señor Tree, that it is Pablo that is Gato Montes. I ride to the gringo rancho this day and talk to the man they call Cedar Jones. He tell me what has happened.

"There have been tres killings along the gringo side of the river and many caballos stolen. They say the killer is Pablo, now calling himself Gato Montes. They say he ropes the people from behind like a coward and pulls them down off of their horse. He may have done this to young Prieto along the river. There were burns on his neck from a lazo when he rode Chico back into the village that day. They say, he then takes a long and sharp spiga and sticks it through the back of the people's neck in the bone. This way, they no move and fall to the ground. Then he cuts off their ears and sticks them on the sharp end of the spiga. He cuts their ears off just like he cut off Prieto's ears. So now, there are tres people that no longer breathe Dios's air because of Pablo, this Gato Montes. Our people, all of us, we turn our back on evil and we will turn our back on this Gato Montes. He does not stand for our village. Our village is one of love and patience, not the maiming and killing of the innocents. Do not blame Pedro and Franco for saying nothing about what they heard. These men ride daily on their caballos to the gringo rancho and work all day and return before the sun is setting and sometimes after that as you all know. They risk their lives, yes? They risk their lives every day, especially to know that this terrible man, Gato Montes, is still somewhere and killing the people. And for what reason? Why does he hate the people? We do not know the answer to the question. We only know what I said earlier. Dios sends the rain on the good and the bad. So, we will let Dios deal with this Gato Montes in the way that he sees fit. It is not ours to judge.

"And the last thing I want to say. There is a Sheriff Brody from Rosario. Cedar Jones tell me he followed the river a long way to warn the other gringo ranchos going este for many miles, about Gato Montes. They say he now has tres banditos, maybe even Comancheros, riding with him. Two of them are gringos and one is maybe from south of Mexico to the ocean. He is very dark. He is called El Fantasma."

"Gato Montez and his banda, they steal horses and hide them in the arroyo where the agua is good to drink and the grass is good. The sheriff rode into the arroyo looking at the horses and Gato Montes catch him and rope him from behind. The sheriff nearly die from la spiga. They leave him to die with his hands tied behind his back and the ants on his face. He lost much sangre from his body where the spiga is in his shoulder. Somehow, he got on his caballo and rides to the gringo rancho across the river. I think maybe Dios was looking down on him while he rides. The big gringo, Señor Tree, is now el jefe of the rancho. He is a very good man with a very large body and a very big heart.

"So now, I have told you all of the truth that I know. Some of it is very painful to hear. Let us pray for each other and let us pray for this man, Sheriff Brody."

# CHAPTER 17

Tree turned Bonner toward the Rolling J. Bonner didn't pay Sister much mind as they loped along, periodically slowing to a trot and then back to a walk. He wanted to visit with Cedar Jones in private and then the boys if he could. He also wanted to provision up and trade Sister's riding saddle for a packsaddle. There were several smell teepee tents in the barn just big enough for one man and his bedroll that would at least keep the wind and rain off of his back and keep him warm.

Cedar Jones saw Tree ride up to the main ranch house and tie the horses.

"I see you are leading Sheriff Brody's horse. Did he make it?"

"Well, he is kind of alive and talking. The doctor got that spike out of him. I helped him a little. Didn't want to pull out. He had to cauterize it with a hot rod to stop the bleeding. Going to be a while getting on his feet."

Tree took out the badge from his front pocket.

"Sheriff Brody wants me to go after Gato Montes and his band. Says he heard him say they was heading to Mushaway right before one of them put a spike in him."

"He put a badge on you? What about the ranch and Mr. Gillstrap? Mushaway is a damn pretty good piece from Rosario, as I recall. That badge does not mean piss up that way, Tree. You know that. Especially to them Comancheros we ran into. We whipped that bunch, but we had numbers on our side. Seven of them, as I recall. I reckon they are still there trading with that band of Comanche Quahadis. Not a real good spot for a gringo with a red beard to go riding off into. You certainly are not the person you were on that day. You have become a true leader. Even I look up to you. But I can still outshoot you, and you know it. You need me along."

"Well, all things considered, I didn't have much of a choice, I reckon. Him, laying there nearly dead and all. Said he didn't have no one else, and I was just postponing my promise to Mr. Gillstrap for a little while. That's all."

"No choice? You always got a choice, Tree. Some choices are just better than others. I reckon you are probably even wanting a scrap with that killer and that band of his. If you get kilt, how are you going to keep your promise to Mr. Gillstrap? Ever thought of that? I would end up having to keep a promise you made if you get killed by this bunch or maybe the Comanches.

"I know you better than anyone on this here ranch knows you. The boys don't even know we served together for five years in the cavalry because we have never even told them we knew each other in the past. I know what happens when that damn red-haired temper comes out when you really get riled. You don't back down now. Dead people are not exactly heroes, they are just dead, my friend. And that is what you are likely to be, buzzard stinking dead with a spike stuck through your neck or something.

"Besides, if you wait around long enough, he'll come to you, and you won't have to do all of that riding and can sleep in your nice warm bed right here. Winter is coming on and I don't recall you ever having lived on the open plains during a winter. It can get really bad out there. Did you tell the sheriff about me? Being able to shoot and all?"

"I don't reckon I'm inviting a scrap with him and his band none at all. They are liable to get clean away with the head start they got. That man is a bad killer, he just does not use a gun that we know about. That spike that came out of the sheriff's shoulder was over a foot long and real sharp. Nearly like he turned it on a sharpening stone. Yes, I did tell him about you and that we served together in the cavalry. I told him I left you in charge at the place until I got back. That's it."

"That, is it? That's it? The sheriff don't know how valuable I would be to you because you did not tell him. That bandit and his gang are nothing but a bunch of cowards, Tree. Let one of them Comancheros or the Quahadis kill them. They might even hang them upside down above an ant bed. They don't take to them Apache half-breeds anyway. They don't want anybody coming through the Comancheria."

"I don't believe you have ever saw him, Cedar. You don't know how big he is. I don't reckon he is any bigger than me."

"He may be smaller than you, but he damn well may be quicker too. Have you ever thought of that? If you are bent on going, I don't guess there is any talking you out of it. Your head is harder than that pile of rocks over there. What do you need me to do? I suppose you might be gone more than a week or two. Hell, that's near three hundred miles, Tree, one way as I recall. That is a six-hundred-mile round trip, and you are not exactly going picnicking on the river. If Gato Montes and his band did go that way, why is he going that a-way? You ever thought about that?"

"I don't know why. Maybe to sell them stolen horses to the Comancheros or maybe getting to Mushaway and turning west toward Santa Fe to hide out. That is a lot of country between Mushaway and Santa Fe. That would probably take about twenty days just to get to Santa Fe from Mushaway. I suspect if he is going to all that trouble, he may not be coming back this way for a while. I think he may be trying to dump them horses where nobody knows what they look like and can identify them. He is riding a big Appaloosa with black splotches on his rump that he stole from the Mexican village across the river, Montenegro. Those two vaqueros know exactly what he looks like. If he stays on him, I got a chance of finding him or maybe somebody has seen him and that horse passing through. And that little gray Welsh that the one the call Coyote is riding, his mane sticks straight up a little, kind of straight. That kid wears a little dark brown derby on his head and patched pants. Has great big green eyes, just like a coyote. Between that horse and the Appaloosa, I reckon they might stick out a bit in a crowd. Just going by what the sheriff told me, nothing more than that."

"Cedar, what I got to say don't go no further. You know the country I will be traveling through. I don't rightly know when I'll be coming back or if I will be coming back, for that matter. You got to keep these boys fed and paid. Sheriff Brody is sending a cook out here next week to take that burden off your hands. You can't be cooking for this bunch and bossing too. She's a Lipan Apache woman. Name's Felicity Two-Feathers. She ran away from a boarding school and joined a cattle drive when she was young, maybe eighteen or so. Good cook, he says and can hold her own when the wolves come howling at the door vying for her affections. Put a knife to a man's throat that got into her wagon on a cattle drive. Sheriff says she is a good person who just wants to work and be left alone. You can put her up in my room here and pay her the same amount we pay the boys. Not a penny less. There are the ranch books opened up there on the table. I do not have the time to walk you through them. I reckon they will not be a problem for you. The ranch safe is behind that cabinet there, and I will give you the key to get into it. It has enough money for a year's worth of payroll. Be sure and pull a blanket over it when you lock it and pile them blankets on top of it.

"We don't have any gatherings going on now. Next one is in the spring when we gather, castrate, and brand. Keep a watchful eye on our calves and tell the boys to keep the varmints and them Spanish eagles off them. If a mountain lion comes in, get that man with the dogs in Rosario out here quick or he's likely to keep killing until you get him stopped or run off.

"We got a line of credit at the hardware store in Rosario. Send a cowboy in every Wednesday to get a wire at the telegraph office from Mr.

Gillstrap. Tell him where I'm a heading and especially why and not to worry about things. I will keep my promise."

"Tree, this ain't no fairy-tale ride you are a-going on. I need to ride with you. I know the trail as good or better than you do and four eyes are better than two. And besides, I'm a-might better with a long-range shooter than you are as I recall. You don't know nothing at all about the trail west from Mushaway to Santa Fe. I do. New Mexico is my country I grew up in. I know it like the back of my hand."

"Appreciate that, Cedar. I just need you here on this ranch worse. These boys can't even suck on a sugar tit by themselves, much less run a ranch. They are like a bunch of smooth-mouthed old men just looking for something to gossip or complain or worry about. Especially DeWitt Murphy. He is plumb eaten up with the gossiping and likes to keep the fires stoked when he gets him a listener. He is a fair cowboy and we need him, just keep a handle on him. Keep them from bothering Roney McCallister too. He is not but a youngster. Besides, they might get a little bit better cooking than they been getting around here with Felicity Two-Feathers coming in. She probably does not boil her coffee with horse turds like some folks do."

"I reckon so," said Cedar. "Watch out for them winter storms that come blowing in. Don't never fall asleep outside of your tent in a snow-storm without a fire and a blanket. You might not be seeing the morning sun when it comes up."

Tree finished packing and took the horses to the barn to swap Sister's saddle and load the small tent.

He remembered to grab the lead rope with the metal clip off Sheriff Brody's saddle. He could not afford to have Sister untie herself and won-der away. He had enough dried venison, canned beans, and biscuits to last a couple of weeks or so, but would have to hunt along the way for food. There were plenty of turkeys roosting at night along the Concho in the tall pecan trees. If you didn't want to make any noise, you could always throw out a fishing line if you had a hook. He took two rolls of string rawhide and two leather stitching hooks out of the tack room and packed them in his leather saddlebags along with his binoculars and sugar cubes for Bonner. He checked the front and rear girths again on both horses' saddles for tightness and checked the buckles on their breast and butt straps. He wanted to start the uphill climb out of the Rolling J and get at least ten miles in before sundown.

He pulled himself up into the saddle and secured Sister's lead rope with a little dally around the saddle horn.

He rode by the bunkhouse, where Cedar stood watching on the wooden porch.

"Keep your rifle and them pistols oiled up and ready. Here is my leather lariat. It will spool out at sixty feet. It might come in handy if you fall off a cliff or something. Got your firewood ax and waxed matches?"

"Got both of them. Obliged. Keep plenty of socks and sugar handy, Cedar. Adios."

Cedar watched Tree ride off south until he could not see him anymore. The boy he met when joining the cavalry at Fort Concho years ago was long gone. It his place was a strong, self-assured, hardheaded grizzly bear. Unafraid of biting a rattlesnake's head off and skinning him with his teeth, he reckoned. Now, off he rides to go after a ruthless bunch of outlaws into the same Comancheria he was bound for and determined to get himself killed in before. A place full of Comanches that did not play by the same rules of engagement that the cavalry did. They are warriors of the plains. The best in the world, it is said. They have absolutely no fear and do not fear death. That alone gives them a tremendous advantage. The Comancheros, all ruthless killers.

He did not know if he would ever see Tree again. He did know that the cards were stacked against him returning to the Rolling J.

Heading north out of Rolling J and toward Rosario, Tree planned to camp on the north side of town just a little way away from the people and the sounds of the town. Sister nickered loudly as they passed the far edges of town.

Tree decided to ride around the outskirts of Rosario to not draw attention, especially leading Sister with a packsaddle on her back. The townsfolk would surely recognize the sheriff's horse, and the gossip hounds' lips would soon enough be salivating to spin yet another story until something else of interest came along. He did not know if Sheriff Brody had told a soul that he had been deputized and then loaned him Sister. Someone from Rosario that saw him leading her might just think he was a horse thief and try and bring him in.

He had always despised folks who flapped their jaws at other's expense, but maybe not near as bad as someone bullying an innocent. That got his blood up in his face. His face would begin to flush hot and turn about as red as his great beard. Once he got riled up, it took hours to get settled back down to normal. He just never could understand someone finding pleasure in hurting a defenseless person or an animal.

He smiled, remembering what Cedar had said. "You going after Gato Montes like some type of righteous crusader for humanity or something? You're liable to get yourself killed for your efforts, and them buzzards don't give a tinker's damn about your noble intentions."

"I'm just a cow herder that was asked by the sheriff to go after a killer and his band. Nothing more than that. Don't go acting like I am acting holier than thou. I don't take kindly to that kind of talk, even if we are friends. Don't never tell me how to run my business."

"Get down off your high horse, Tree. There is nobody trying to tell you no such thing and you know it. Besides, you know I can hold my own and you don't rattle me none at all. I just don't want to lose my good friend to some low-life coward killer and a damn band of mis-fits intent on killing, that's all."

Down deep, Tree wished that a man as capable as Cedar was riding along beside him. He was an expert marksman with that carbine of his and those peep sights. He could shoot the eyeball out of a turkey at a hundred yards. More than that, he stayed engaged in a battle and never showed a moment's worth of fear.

TREE MADE HIS FIRST NIGHT camp ten miles to the north of Rosario. He was a good seven or eight days away from Fort Concho, and would follow the river north from there. He made sure Bonner and Sister were secure for the night before settling in. He made a rope corral with Cedar's sixty-foot braided lariat and then latched Sister with Sheriff Brody's metal clip lead rope.

"You get out of that, Sister, and you may be mountain lion bait for sure. I don't believe you can open that clip with those teeth of yours."

It took a while to find a place to camp where he could see all around him. The hill he camped on was brushy with a few trees on the top third and nothing below that all the way to the bottom. It was not too big on top and flat enough to set up his tent and a little place for the horses. He had already stopped earlier and grazed them good at a water hole surrounded by green grass. The trees and brush on top provided good cover and would help dissipate smoke well from a very small campfire.

Tree made a little fire ring with rocks and dug it down a little until he hit solid rock. Then he gathered enough small sticks to form a little teepee shaped just like his cow tender tent.

He gathered a small handful of dried grass left over from the previous winter and wadded it up in a little ball, placing it under the teepee. He struck a wax-coated match on a rock, and the little fire came to life as soon as he lit the grass on fire. There was no need in building a big fire. Just big enough to make a cup of coffee in his tin cup and heat a can of beans.

He placed Bonner's riding saddle on the ground, horn down, with the packsaddle next to it, just in case he had to take cover behind it. The horses had a much better sense of smell and hearing than he did. Especially that Sister. She took a lot of notice of things and paid attention to her surroundings. Much more than Bonner ever let on. Sister moved her head from side to side slowly while they were moving and twitched her ears continuously, picking up the slightest movement or sound. She never bolted or shied but never missed a thing, just kind of extended her top lip a little with her ears pointed toward the movement.

Between the two of them, Tree believed nothing or anyone could get up the hill undetected and without some type of snort or blow from the horses. He would keep his carbine at his side at all times during the night with all of his ammunition stores. Both Colts were loaded and now had bullets in the firing chamber ready to go. Normally he would not keep a live bullet in the firing position in case the gun was dropped on a hard floor or a big rock. That might just cause the gun to fire and hurt someone. No such precaution would be taken on this journey, where a split second of indecision or the availability of a weapon might cost him his life.

Tree set out a biscuit on a rock next to the fire with his open can of beans and a piece of venison jerky. Cedar made a lot of it and kept it in the smokehouse with the salt-cured hams he served with pinto beans. The beans smelled good as they began to heat up and bubble up. The meal was not enough to fill him up but just like the grass he grazed the horses on at the waterhole, it was enough.

THE NEXT DAY, SISTER AND Bonner noticed the herd of javelina hogs before Tree saw them. Both horses' ears pricked to attention, and Bonner gave a couple of quick snorts as the hogs began clicking their teeth and trotting toward them through the brush. The hair on their backs was raised, and they were ready to fight. Some of the boars were squealing and making a barking sound.

"I think them things are going to make a run at us. Time to move."

Tree whirled Bonner around with Sister in tow. The javelinas charged full speed as the horses sped away. Tree had gone a full quarter mile before he felt safe in stopping the animals.

"There must have been thirty, maybe forty of them things," he said as he patted Bonner on the neck. "I never figured we would be run off by a bunch of pigs."

Tree rode the edge of the valleys during the day and then upward to a hill of choice in the late evening. He let the horses drink at every water hole they came to and graze for a little while before moving on. He kept both canteens full at all times and was sure to filter it coming into the canteens with his bandanna.

He did not plan to stop by Fort Concho and did not really want anyone to know why and where he was headed. The Concho River would keep his horses watered and well grazed for a good while. There would be cavalry scouts about and possibly even a full patrol out. The cavalry may have been alerted to the news about the killings and already headed out to find him, but he doubted it. He didn't think the news about Sheriff Brody had a chance to spread to the territories just yet. But with the telegraph service and all, the news had probably already hit the sheriffs' offices in some of the towns. That didn't mean they would be sending men out to find this bunch. The big bounties on the band, especially Gato Montes, might draw in some bounty hunters, but it might take a week or two for them to start looking. Besides, other than Sheriff Brody and Cedar, he was the only one that knew which way they might be heading.

TREE HAD BEEN RIDING FOR eight days when he saw the twin buttes close to the trading post on the river settlement called Santa Angela. He could easily make out the familiar large trees along the river bottom without his binoculars. He could see smoke coming from the trading post and toward the fort. The scouting patrols he and Cedar rode in covered a lot of ground in every direction out of the fort. As before, they were mostly looking for Comanches bent on attacking and raiding little settlements along the river north and eastward from the trading post.

As soon as he intersected the Concho River, he watered and grazed the horses well. Then, he rode a mile or so east away from the river to ensure that anyone looking at him from the river had to look into the bright eastern sun. He intended to find a low place and cross in the late afternoon when the sun was heavy in the west. The great glare of the western sun gave him an advantage if someone was trying to watch his movements in the evening from the river.

He once watched a red-tailed hawk fly in from the west into a tree full of roosting doves. They simply could not see the hawk as it flew into the branches of the tree. It quickly had a dove in its great talons and flew to the ground to begin picking the feathers off before eating. Tree never forgot the hawk's sun-hunting trick. He had heard many tales of the great Comanche warriors attacking their opponents or a settlement from the west in the setting sun. They would hit the settlement just as the sun was starting to set in the west. Charging in from the west, just like the red-tailed hawk, they could not be easily seen.

TEN MILES NORTH OF FORT Concho, Tree spotted the large group of buzzards circling close to the river. He quickly pulled out his binoculars and began to scan the tree line at the river. Whatever it was, their sense of smell brought them to it. Might be a dead goat or cow. Slowly he made his way with the horses toward the circling buzzards. He could see some of them dipping and diving in closer to the large pecan trees on the east bank of the river. Nights were beginning to get chilly, but there had not been a killing frost thus far and the leaves were still on all of the trees. He stopped to pull his carbine out of the scabbard and checked the action, then slowly closed the hammer with his thumb.

At two hundred yards, he could see buzzards on the ground pecking at a dead animal.

Looking through his binoculars, he saw a dead dog or coyote lying on the ground. Then he saw what appeared to be a small man tied to a tree. He eased Bonner and Sister upwind of the area and stepped down from the saddle. The buzzards were working heavily on the coyote. The animal's tail was missing. He secured both horses before walking slowly toward the person tied to the tree.

He was but a young boy. The coyote's tail was sticking out of his throat somehow. Tree pinched his nose as he came close. Flies were all over the young man's face, and a little dirty brown derby, cocked awkwardly, sat on his head. Tree could tell by looking at his dull and lifeless eyes that this might just be the one that Sheriff Brody described as Coyote. Tree gently pulled on the coyote tail sticking out of his neck and tossed it to the ground. The sharp steel spike looked foreign to its surroundings. It looked odd protruding out of the young man's neck. He may have angered Gato Montes somehow or became more of a burden to him than he wanted to deal with. Maybe he was just in the mood to kill and thought it fun to cut off a coyote's tail and slide it over the spike. One thing for sure, Tree knew the sheriff was at least right about the direction in which this bunch was traveling.

He heard the buzzards' wings higher in the next tree heading upriver. Then, he saw the gray Welsh pony hanging upside down from a large branch on the west side of the tree. His back feet were tied together with a lariat and he had been pulled up into the tree. His belly was cut wide open, and his entire gut sack hung close to his head. His eyes bulged as blood and mucus drained from his nose and open mouth. Tree could barely see that the pony's throat was slashed, nearly severing his head.

Tree cradled his rifle as he turned to walk back to the horses. Slowly, he wiped away tears on his sleeve. He started to convulse and then began vomiting profusely. He pulled his canteen off Sister's packsaddle and washed out his mouth before trying to swallow. He had often heard stories of the cruel treatment of captives by the Comanche and the Apache. Gato Montes was a vicious and sadistic killer. Maybe the band helped him do it, or he forced them to help. He liked to torture and kill people, and now, it looked like, animals as well.

Tree studied the corpses while his stomach settled. The stench was overwhelming. Slowly, he pulled his bandanna up and over his mouth and nose, thinking that breathing through his mouth was the only way he might get the boy buried.

He pulled his pointed spade off the packsaddle and walked toward the body of the boy. Slowly he dug a shallow grave and then rested a few minutes before cutting Coyote loose from the tree. He dragged him by his still-tied feet toward the grave and gently drug him into it. His hands were tied behind his back, just like the killers had left Sheriff Brody. Tree cut both ropes and then pulled the spike out of his neck and laid it beside him after he rolled him faceup.

"That is about the best I can do for you, Mr. Coyote, or whatever your real name was. I'm sorry your life ended this way, and that of your pony there. I'll cut him down, but I am not going to bury him or this coyote. Don't have the time."

Tree tried to make the boy's eyelids stay shut.

*Maybe the buzzards didn't peck his eyes out because they were busy on the coyote and the insides of the pony in the tree*, he thought.

He finally placed two flat rocks on them to hold them shut.

"Nobody ought to be buried with their eyes open," he muttered out loud.

The dark, clumpy clouds of dirt literally bounced off Coyote's bloated gut as Tree scooped one shovel at a time. Finally, he finished the task and was grateful to not have to look at the lifeless body of a young boy.

He cut the rope holding the pony, and six hundred pounds of horse-flesh crashed to the ground.

Tree retrieved his hand ax and cut two pieces of one-inch cedar from a tree and skinned it clean. He took out a string rawhide in his saddlebag and lashed them together.

"Best I can do is maybe mark your name on this with my knife and the day and year. I don't know your real name, but I bet it is not Coyote. Dust to dust."

Bonner and Sister needed to be watered and grazed. His best bet to find tracks was to immediately follow them north from the spot where they had killed Coyote and his pony. The fetid smell of the dead was still deeply implanted in his nostrils and was still causing the compulsion to vomit. He turned to take one last look at the pile of horseflesh beneath the large tree, now completely engulfed in the great flesh eaters of the plains. While some had their ugly heads in the pony's gut cavity, others hopped around with their large wings spread, waiting their turn impatiently.

Tree decided to ride crosswind heading east for a mile or so before turning north and riding parallel with the river again. The horses could graze there while he gathered his thoughts.

This killing looked like it may have taken place a couple of days before he rode up on it, three at the most. The boy's gut was swelled up, and that takes a day or so. That makes four killings in less than a month or so. Tree figured the other two in the band either helped him do the killing or were too scared to try and stop him. There was no turning back now. Not for Gato Montes and his band or for Tree.

He figured if the band was two or three days ahead of him and stayed due north along the river, they would be heading toward the big spring. He vividly remembered the tall mountain close to the big spring about a mile to the east. The cavalry troop had ridden to the top of it to look down toward the area where Captain Golden said the big spring was to the west, down in the valley. This time, there would be no backup. Gato Montes and his gang might decide to stay there a few days. He did not believe they knew he was after them but would take no chances.

# CHAPTER 18

SHERIFF BRODY SAW TO IT that Felicity Two-Feathers came by Dr. Clay's office shortly after Tree left heading north toward Mushaway.

She could not imagine why the sheriff would want to speak with her. She had never been in trouble with the law in her life.

Sheriff Brody was sitting up in his bed with his spectacles on reading a book when she tapped on his door.

"Come in," he said.

She quietly opened the door and poked her head in. The sheriff had never really looked closely at the woman before him. She was strikingly beautiful. She had on dark pants and a beautiful red shirt that complemented her long black hair. The cowboy boots caught Sheriff Brody's eyes.

"Come in, come in. I am Sheriff Brody. I sent a man over to the boardinghouse to see if you would come talk to me. I am glad that you did. I was just admiring those boots you got on. Don't see them on females much. Please sit down."

Felicity sat down on a chair next to the bed.

"Is there some reason you wanted to see me, Sheriff?"

"Why, yes. Yes, there is. But first, I would like to get to know you a little. There is no trouble, rest assured. I need a little favor, that's all. We'll talk about that in a little bit. They tell me you came into town on a cattle drive a few years ago. That must have been quite an experience."

"Sheriff, can you tell me what you need? I really need to get back to the boardinghouse to cook for people."

"Well, I certainly am not trying to pry, ma'am, I was just curious."

"Sheriff, I am a Lipan Apache from New Mexico. I was sent on a train with the others to a boarding school long ago. I stayed there for ten years until I was nearly eighteen. My real name is Two-Feathers, but they named me Felicity and they made me answer to that name. So, I am Felicity Two-Feathers. I stayed until I was eighteen years old before I left in the night with the clothes on my back and a little food in my pillow-case. I walked a few days and some nights until I saw men moving a big herd of cattle down in a valley. I walked into their camp where there were many cowboys. The boss man decided to let me stay. He made me a helper to the cook and he let me sleep in the wagon. I learned to ride horses very well and to help move the cattle as good as the cowboys."

"So that is where you learned to cook?"

"Yes, that is where I learned to cook."

"So, how did you wind up here in Rosario?"

"When we took the cattle to market in Texas, the boss man felt a little sorry for me I guess, and gave me a horse. One of the older cowboys was going to ride to the border ranches looking for work. I rode with him. He brought me to Rosario and told me it would be much safer here than on the border, so I never left. They gave me a job and a place to live at the boardinghouse where I cook for people. I keep to myself. The good women of Rosario do not take kindly to an Apache woman in their midst, you might say."

"Well, that is quite a story, and I really appreciate you telling it to a stranger like me. May I ask why you did not go back to your people in New Mexico?"

"What possible reason would I go back to my village, Sheriff? Or what remains of it. There is no good reason. I have spent much of my life away from my village and my people. I speak better English now than I do Apache. The village might not accept me back. Now, what is this favor, Sheriff?"

"Well, there has been some killing down on the border a little piece from here. There is a ranch just south of here called the Rolling J. It is owned by a man named Mr. Gillstrap. He had to leave in a hurry to take care of his ailing wife up in the East.

"He left a man named Tree Smith to look after things while he was gone. I got hurt warning the border ranchers about the killing, and Tree brought me here. Pretty much saved my life. Well, not just pretty near saved my life. If he had not hauled me in to the good doctor here in Rosario, I would have been covered with dirt. I deputized him and sent him after the killers. He used to be in the U.S. Cavalry over to Fort Concho by Santa Angela. His cook, Cedar Jones, is running the ranch and cooking to boot. He served in the U.S. Cavalry as well. That is not sustainable. Cedar Jones cannot cook and run the ranch at the same time. At least not effectively. I was wondering, if I guaranteed you won't lose your boardinghouse room or job, if you would consider cooking for that bunch out there until Mr. Tree gets back? Now, that might be a couple of months, maybe longer. Cedar Jones is a good man, and he won't let nobody bother you or anything like that. They will let you bunk in the big house and not with the cowboys. More than likely have the whole house to yourself. Sound reasonable? Pays cowboy wages to boot. We will make up what you lose at the boardinghouse."

"Sheriff, my job is all I have. It pays for my room and board. I am Lipan Apache. A Lipan Apache woman. I don't think there are many folks begging me to come work for them."

"Ma'am, I will guarantee you will not lose your job and I will give you a signed letter stating that. I just know that Cedar Jones could probably really use a little help out there for a little while. He would never ask for it. He is too stubbornly independent. But rest assured, that Rolling J is a big operation, and cooking twice a day takes up time he does not have to spare. If you agree to go, I can arrange for someone to carry you out there in a buggy or furnish you a horse to ride out there. If you ride horseback, I'll send a man to escort you all the way to the front door of the main house. How about that?"

"Sounds to me like you are expecting me to say yes, Sheriff. That is a little presumptuous, don't you think? I will go and help this Cedar Jones for a while, but I do not need anyone to carry me out there or an escort. I have a gun, and I know how to use it as good as any man, if I have to. I will take you up on the horse, because I gave mine to the old cowboy when he brought me here. There is not enough money in my pocket to pay for a horse or a saddle."

"Well, Miss Felicity Two-Feathers, you let me worry about your pony and saddle. Come by here in the morning at 8:00, and he'll be standing outside at the hitching rail. I'll have a signed letter from me to give to your boss at the boardinghouse and indicating full ownership of the horse, saddle, and riggings. I will tell you how to get to the Rolling J, which is not hard to find. I am certain your cooking will be much better than Cedar's. You might just brighten up the place a little."

TRUE TO THE SHERIFF'S WORD, there was a horse saddled and waiting when she arrived at Dr. Clay's office the next morning. She sat down her leather bags and walked around the big sorrel gelding and gently stroked his mane.

"Looks like you and I are going to be partners, boy. Maybe the sheriff will tell me if you have a name."

Dr. Clay was busy at his desk when she opened the door.

"Good morning, ma'am. I believe the sheriff is waiting for you. He may be tolerable to deal with this morning, because I just brought him a cup of coffee. Would you like one as well?"

"Yes, sir. I would and thank you. That would be wonderful."

The sheriff was reading a newspaper when Felicity opened the door.

"Good morning, ma'am. Please come in. I see you have coffee. Sit down over here and let's visit. Here, I drew you up a little map to get to the Rolling J. There is a signed letter from your boss at the boardinghouse that you will have your job when you return from helping out at the Rolling J. Signed, sealed, and delivered, ma'am, as promised."

"Why, thank you, Sheriff. Was there any problem at the boardinghouse about me leaving?"

"None at all. I sent for your boss to come over here. We had a cup of coffee and a nice little chat. All is well."

"Good, I certainly can't afford any hard feelings over this. I have to keep that job. The horse out front is beautiful. I am assuming he is the one I will be riding. Does he have a name?"

"Yes, ma'am. That is the horse you will be riding. He belongs to Curly Jenkins right outside of town on a little spread called the D-4. He hand-picked him for you. He is well mannered and loves to please. They call him Hawk. Curly tells me he is easy to rein, won't spook, and he gets on well with other horses. I am sure Cedar Jones will see to it that he is well fed and exercised on the Rolling J. He does not need to just stand in the corral looking over the fence."

"I will be sure and ride him as often as I can, Sheriff. It is probably time for me to start that way. Thanks for the coffee and the beautiful mount you have provided."

She stood up and gently shook the sheriff's hand.

"You bet, ma'am. Take care of yourself on the way out there. Most men will take notice of that sidearm you have in that holster. I don't believe anyone will bother you. Keep a good eye out, even when you get out there."

Hawk stood easy as Felicity lifted her two leather bags one at a time and tied them on both sides of the saddle before double-checking the latigo strap for tightness. Still standing on the ground, she took the envelope out of her shirt pocket and unfolded the little map to the Rolling J the sheriff had drawn for her. It looked like there was only one road south leading to the ranch out of Rosario.

Hawk did not move as she swung into the saddle. "Okay, Mr. Hawk, let's head to the Rolling J."

SHE ARRIVED AT THE ROLLING J about an hour after leaving Rosario. DeWitt Murphy was standing on the bunkhouse steps when she rode past the main ranch house. "Well damnation, if it ain't a dern woman comes a-riding in here."

Felicity rode up to the bunkhouse looking at DeWitt from beneath her dark felt hat.

"I am looking for Mr. Cedar Jones. Is he here?"

"Why yes, ma'am, he is here. I reckon he is up to the main ranch house you just rode past."

He noticed the pistol on her right hip. "Does Cedar know you are coming to see him?"

"No, I do not believe he does."

She turned her horse and headed toward the main house. DeWitt ran in the bunkhouse door where two other cowboys were sitting at the table.

"There is a woman, looks like she is maybe an Apache or maybe a Cherokee. She has a gun and is wearing a hat. Sitting up on a big sorrel gelding and heading over to see Cedar. She may be out to put a bullet hole in him. We might ought to get our pistols on and go take us a look. Get them pistols on, boys."

FELICITY DISMOUNTED AND TIED HAWK to the cedar hitching rail out in front. The boards creaked as she walked up the steps and onto the large wooden porch. Before she could knock, Cedar opened the door and stood flabbergasted as he looked at her. She stuck out her hand.

"I am Felicity Two-Feathers. I am assuming you are Mr. Jones?"

He looked at the gun strapped on her right hip. "Why, yes, ma'am, I am him. Can I help you?"

"Sheriff Brody told me you needed a little help cooking out here for a little while."

"Cooking? Oh, yes. Cooking. I was just taking care of the ranch books there. Here, come on in and sit down. I forgot my manners. We are not, well we are not quite used to being around any women and all out here, that's all. I am sorry. I was just taken aback a little. Let's just start plumb over."

He removed his hat and extended his right hand.

"Miss Felicity Two-Feathers, I am Cedar Jones. I am pleased to make your acquaintance, ma'am."

"And me likewise," she said as she gently shook his hand.

"Well now, that's much better," said Cedar. "I am not really good at making small talk but yes, I could very much use some help doing the cooking around here. It seems there are not enough hours in a day to get everything done that needs doing. I was told you might be coming but I really did not expect . . .well, someone as . . ."

"As what Mr. Jones? As Indian?"

"Oh no, ma'am. Not at all. It's just, you are such a beautiful lady, and this is a pretty rough bunch out here."

"I can hold my own, Mr. Jones."

"Well, I can see that with that pistol on your side."

"I can use it if I have to, rifle as well. I thought it wise to have it on coming out here, just in case. Of course, I don't normally keep it strapped on."

"You can bunk down right here in this house. Got the whole thing to yourself excepting when I have to do the books and all. Nice bed in there and a real comfortable private outhouse out back. You can draw your water from that little well you see out front with the rock ring."

"Are you not staying here now, Cedar? I do not want to take your bed."

"No, ma'am. I mean I have slept up here a little since Tree took off. I'll just bunk with the boys like I always have down at the bunkhouse. You go right ahead and set up right here. I can unload your things and put your horse in the corral while you get settled in. Just make yourself at home. I will be back directly."

Cedar walked out on the porch, and DeWitt Murphy was standing at the corner of the house with two of the boys. All had their pistols drawn.

"You okay, Cedar? We thought you might be in a little trouble or something. I saw that she was toting a gun on her hip."

"Put them guns away, boys. What in the world are you doing?"

"Well, she had that gun strapped on and all. We thought she might be up to something no good."

"You boys need to get to work. Sometimes your thinking plumb scares me, DeWitt. That woman is Miss Felicity Two-Feathers. She is going to help cook around here until Tree gets back, that's all. And she is not to be dallied with in any form or fashion. She will be treated with respect at all times. You boys got that?"

"Why sure, Cedar," said DeWitt.

"I mean it, boys. Anybody disrespects her or causes her any little bit of trouble, and you will get on your pony and head down the road. You won't be working here no more. She gets paid, same as you. Anybody got a problem with that, just go ahead and saddle up and head yonder, now. I am not going to put up with nothing of any kind. Now, you boys just git on to your jobs I laid out for you this morning. You done burned half a morning standing here."


FELICITY HEARD THE ENTIRE CONVERSATION through the front window that Cedar left cracked. With the exception of the trail boss on the cattle drive and the cook, no man had ever stood up for her. No man had ever said the things she just heard Cedar say. She looked out the window as Cedar put her bags on the porch and then mounted her horse to head for the barn at a slow trot. His white hair and sky-blue eyes were a combination she had not seen on a young man before. His face was rugged, yet showed compassion as his blue eyes sparkled when he spoke, along with his clean, white teeth. His large white mustache hung well below his top lip and off the corners of his mouth and slightly curled on the ends. She figured he was a man of character and wisdom in their brief encounter. Listening to his conversation with the boys when he did not know she could hear, she figured he was not a man to trifle with, especially if you got him riled up. She watched him round the corner of the bunkhouse heading to the barn. He sat straight in the saddle and didn't slouch. She hated to see men slouch in the saddle as much as she detested seeing them bounce in the saddle at a trot, not that they would care or that her opinion on things like that mattered. The trail boss told her one time that a man that slouches in the saddle and bounces at a trot, well, he might not belong on the back of a horse.

Cedar put Hawk in the barn in one of the single pens and forked over a little hay before checking the watering trough.

He walked back to the main house and tapped on the door. Felicity was putting her things away when he cracked the door.

"Okay if I come in for a minute?"

"Why, certainly, Mr. Jones. I was just putting my things away. What can I do for you?"

"You are quite well-spoken, ma'am."

"What you actually mean, Mr. Jones, is I am well-spoken for a Lipan Apache woman. Well, that is most certainly true. Ten years at a boarding school will do that for you. I can even read and write too."

"Ma'am, I meant no offense. It is just good to hear you talk. I am used to these cowboys, that's all. Their conversations are not the most mentally stimulating thing you will hear. Listening to them is like watching a game of checkers. Hop, hop, hop and it's over. No thinking required. Listening to you is like a game of chess. I have to think before I answer someone that speaks in intelligent and meaningful sentences. And don't be calling me Mr. Jones. Just plain old Cedar will do. Just like them old cedar trees you see around."

"I will take that into consideration, Cedar, and I certainly took no offense. Now, just what did you need to see me about?"

"Well, I probably need to take you to the cooking shack off the bunkhouse. It has its own door you can come in through. Be sure and light a lamp and carry it with you of a morning. Lots of rattlers out and about. Maybe not so much before winter, but they sure crawl to den up about now. I have all of the food sorted out. There is plenty of everything from coffee, salt-cured bacon, a few hams, a fresh side of beef, potatoes and onions, and flour, and we have a couple of milk cows at the barn. We raise our own chickens and have plenty of eggs for breakfast. There are plenty of cans of store-bought beans and probably about fifty pounds bagged up."

"Thank you for the invitation. I will make my way down there later and take a look around. I will start by cooking breakfast in the morning. Tell your men to be completely dressed and ready to eat at 5:00 a.m. sharp. If you have men working at night, they are fed first. No exceptions."

"Yes, ma'am, I'll tell them. Any other instructions before I leave?"

"No, but it was very nice to make your acquaintance, Cedar. Maybe we can visit a little more over a cup of coffee sometime before your man comes back and I have to head back to Rosario. Also, I am a very good chess player, if you have a board and an hour. There are not a lot of women in town that like to play chess. I like it very much. Do you play?"

"I'd like that, ma'am, a lot. I make a pretty strong cup of coffee, you know. Chess? Yes, I play a little chess. Sure do. I don't believe I have ever been beat by a woman. No disrespect meant, ma'am."

"Well Mr. Cedar. I certainly would not want to ruin your chess record with women. I guess we will see how that turns out, won't we?"

CEDAR COULD SMELL THE BACON frying and the strong aroma of stout coffee when he first began to stir in his bed. Everyone was bright-eyed when they began to assemble at the table.

"You boys are sure quiet this morning. Cat got your tongue?" said Cedar as he sat down.

Felicity walked into the room with a hot pot of coffee and four tin cups rung through her fingers. She had on a bright red apron and her dark black hair pulled up into a tall bun with a little red bow tied up in the top. The men sat in complete silence as she walked in.

"Good morning, gentlemen. I hope all of you washed your hands. It is time to eat. The night riders will be fed first if they are any."

She sat cups down in front of each man and began to pour the steaming hot coffee. She went back to the cookshack and retrieved four more cups and began filling them.

"We have fresh cow's milk for your coffee if you want to lighten it up a little."

She returned to the cookshack and retrieved eight warmed tin plates she had left on the stove. She did not like serving hot food on cold plates. The coldness just pulled the warmth right off of the food.

The boy's eyes lit up when she sat down the big plate full of bacon, scrambled eggs and biscuits with grease and flour gravy.

"Maybe this will stick to your ribs while you are out working," she said. "I packed up a little dried venison, a biscuit, and an apple for your lunches."

DeWitt Murphy looked up at her, still chewing his food. "You packed us a lunch, ma'am?"

"Why, yes, is that a problem?"

"No ma'am, no ma'am. It ain't a problem for sure. We just ain't never had nobody pack us a lunch before."

"Well, I am just filling in and helping Mr. Jones, and, as long as I am here, I will pack you a lunch. That sound okay to you?"

"Oh yes, ma'am. That really sounds okay. Don't it, boys?"

Cedar sat saying nothing as he ate the lovely breakfast. It was especially good because it was just good tasting and fresh, but more than anything, he didn't have to make it. This woman had a quiet way with the men. They would normally have been grumbling and complaining about having to do this or do that, the eggs were cold, the coffee was too strong. But not this morning. It was all manners and respect. They shook their heads as they scarfed down the hot food and chased it with coffee or fresh cow's milk.

Felicity seemed to be a natural when it came to handling a bunch of cowboys. Maybe she picked it up on the trail drive from New Mexico to Texas.

# CHAPTER 19

## Llano Estacado—Comanche Lands

TOCHE CAME BACK TO THE others that were camped on the foothills west of the Concho River.

"The Red Beard rides big kleh-pai horse. He leads other horse with supplies. Riders that kill boy and little kleh-pai horse not know he follow them. They ride to Mushaway with many horses. Maybe to trade with Comancheros. The riders call the leader, Gato Montes, lion of the mountain. He wears Mexican sombrero and ride big appalusa horse. Marks eyes like ghost. Maybe he is spiga killer from Mexico the Comancheros tell us about. Stick spike in young boy here from behind and tie to tree while he still lives. Then he put tail of coyote on spiga. Kill boy's horse and hang in tree for birds to eat. Red Beard put boy in earth and take down horse. Now Red Beard follows. Maybe to kill."

Lonely Horse sat on his horse, stoically looking off in the distance. "How many days ride to where is Red Beard?"

"He is two days' ride behind us. Red Beard is one who ride scout for cavalry soldiers at fight at Mushaway long ago. The white hair that rides with him kill seven Comancheros with his gun and one Comanche, Little Bear. The white hair has a warrior spirit and no fear. Red Beard is very strong and has a warrior spirit and no fear. He will kill you like a bear with his mighty paws if he gets them around you. He rode his horse, running into Comancheros. His face burn red like his chin hair. White Hair kill them with his rifle. This Red Beard will be strong in fight."

"Toche, I will take Running Dog with me, and we will go fast to Mushaway on the tops of the mountains and not by the river. We need to join others soon to fight the soldier warrior named Mackenzie where the river is red. He has been sent to kill us or move us to a land they want us to live on. There is small time to ride there to fight. You will take Tuwikáa with you and catch Red Beard at the big spring and bring him to me. If this Gato Montes comes to Mushaway, I will kill him and take his horse to fight Mackenzie and his army. No one will take Comancheria while Quahadi live to fight. We will live in no land but Comanche land. Make sure Red Beard does not get his great paws around you. Bring him alive. I will take his long red chin hair for my lance for luck. We will see how strong he is. Now go."

TREE MADE HIS WAY PARALLEL to the Concho all the way to its headwaters. It was one day's ride to the big spring. He continuously watched both horses' ears and eyes for any sign of trouble from any direction. Leading Sister slowed him down a little bit, and two horses were more noticeable than one. Bonner's gray dapple color stood out against the dark green cedar trees on the ridges if he rode at the base of them. He tried to stay well within the cedars and mesquites to remain as hidden as possible. The mesquites still had their leaves on before the first frost. They would provide a little cover for him and the animals.

It was said that the Comanches knew you were in their country long before you ever saw them, even if you saw them at all. Their ferocity and fighting skills were legendary. Tree had heard of them drinking the blood or the stomach contents of their horses if it was required to stay alive. They feared no other tribes and certainly no white men encroaching on the country they occupied. Captives were viciously tortured, and some would try to kill themselves before they were captured knowing the horrors that they would endure. Tuwikáa and Lonely Horse of the Quahadi were both considered masters of torture by the cavalry, and the officers gave frequent warnings to avoid being captured by either. Troops on patrol found settlers tied to poles with fires burning in front of them. Their stomachs had been cut open and intestines pulled out and laid to burn on the hot coals of the fire while they watched and could feel the intense pain as their insides burned. Other captives' waists were tied with long ropes tied high on two horse's tails. As soon as a gun was fired multiple times, the horses bolted in opposite directions, tearing the victim in two. Tree vividly remembered an entire family of settlers the Troop found tied to corral posts next to their cabin. Each person had been shot and killed with arrows. The father and the boy had arrows shot through an eye with the head of the arrow exiting the back of the skull. The mother and the little girl had arrows penetrating their chests and were scalped. Burial detail was never pleasant, and particularly not when children were involved.

Tree could envision the Comanche riders running by on their horses and giving a blood-curdling scream as they shot their arrows into the body of the victim. The head shot seemed to be revered, especially if it was in the eyes of the victim. Those without eyes were surely not able to see in the spirit world and would drift aimlessly.

The ride to the big spring was uneventful as Tree kept his senses on high alert. He would need to get his horses to water as soon as he took a good look from the mountaintop east of the spring. Slowly he made his way to the east and then turned on the ridgeback leading to the west to look down upon the big spring as he did once before on cavalry patrol. He took off his bandanna and wrapped it around the bright shiny rings at the end of his binoculars to keep sunlight from reflecting off them. He stayed behind a large group of cedars as he glassed the valley below. After one hour of looking, there was no sign of any type of movement in the valley or what he could see of the spring. Bonner and Sister grazed and periodically raised their heads.

"Well, boys and girls, I guess we will head on down and get you a little water. We can drink there and then at the Colorado on our way to Mushaway."

Slowly he turned back east and rode a short distance and then turned south down the gentle slope to the valley. The horses could smell the water, and Tree gave Bonner his head. "You can smell it, can't you boy? Let's see if you can find it. It is not far away." Bonner quickened his pace as they approached the spring. Tree stopped about two hundred yards away and sat quietly for a while before approaching. Birds called back and forth as they darted down toward the water. He slowly dismounted and led the horses in the last little way. The water was good smelling, pure, and clean. Both horses lowered their heads to drink. Tree took both canteens off of the packsaddle and lowered them into the water to fill, cautiously scanning the great rocks surrounding three banks of the spring. He watched the small covey of quail dodge and dart up to the edge of the water for a drink a short distance from where the horses were. Suddenly, they flushed and spooked both horses.

"You and your horses will come with us, Red Beard. If you move, we will kill you. Lonely Horse wants you alive."

Tree slowly stood up and put his hand on his Colt.

"I said, if you move, we will kill you. Move your hand from your gun and turn to look at me."

Tree took his hand off his gun and slowly turned around. Toche had his rifle pointed with the hammer back. He had his longbow strapped to his back with a full leather quiver of arrows. Tuwikáa slowly approached Tree. His fierce countenance showed disdain and loathing.

"I am Tuwikáa. Give me your hands."

He quickly tied both of Tree's extended hands and then tied the rope around his waist, taking both pistols and his hunting knife and his rifle scabbard off of Bonner and placing them on Sister's packsaddle.

"Toche will get puuku so we can begin our journey to Mushaway to meet Lonely Horse."

Tuwikáa pulled Tree's beard hard.

"Lonely Horse wants your chin hair for his lance for good spirit luck when we ride to fight Mackenzie. This time, you not have White Hair to shoot for you and help you. I might want to cook your stomach over the hot coals or let you meet my snakes."

Toche disappeared for a little while before returning with two ponies from just west of the spring. Tree watched him quietly as he brought the horses in.

Tuwikáa pointed his finger at Sister's ear and turned to Tree.

"I see this puuku on way to raid in Mexico. The lawman from Rosario village rides this horse."

He grabbed Tree by the beard.

"How you get this puuku, Red Beard? We make you wish you die," he said as he slapped Tree in the chest with his other hand. He got within one inch of Tree's nose and glared directly into his eyes. He slowly pulled the badge out of Tree's pocket. "He killed the lawman and take his star," holding up the badge for Toche to see. "Help him on his puuku. We must ride to Mushaway."

# CHAPTER 20

TREE TRIED NOT TO SHOW his anger as Toche led Bonner with Sister's lead rope tied to his saddle horn. Tuwikáa rode his horse ahead, never casting a glance backward, seemingly miles away in thought. Perhaps he was wishing he was already with the other Quahadi fighting Mackenzie and his army. Tree had heard that an Army man named Mackenzie was sent to wipe out the Comanche strongholds in all of the Comancheria. Tree thought Tuwikáa might be planning what he was going to do to him when they arrived at Mushaway. There were two hawk feathers tied straight up in his long black hair. There were two crow feathers hanging sideways on each side of his head. Each was wrapped on the ends with yellow string, perfectly wound around the tips and gently blowing in the breeze as he rode. His longbow and deerskin arrow quiver were on this back. A richly painted leather fighting shield hung from his saddle horn with two human scalps tied to the top with rawhide. The shield had many rows of red circles, possibly representing battle kills.

Tree realized the severity of the situation. Even if he was able to get his hands free and somehow break Bonner free from Toche, making a run for it would probably cost him his life. He knew they would quickly run him down and probably shoot him off his horse with their arrows or with their rifles. If he allowed them to lead him to Mushaway, it was a good bet he would be tortured to death in some form. He had no gun or knife to end his life if they burned him to death. Even if he did have either weapon, the Comanches would always have his hands tied. He knew they rarely made mistakes and would take every precaution to keep him alive as long as possible when the torture began. If there were Comancheros in the Mushaway encampment, some of them might recognize him with his large red beard from their first encounter. The Comanches might just let them have at him. He decided to try and stay alive and wait for any opportunity that might tilt the odds a little more in his favor.

THE RIDE FROM THE BIG spring to Mushaway was only a day and a half of normal riding. Tree figured that Lonely Horse and Running Dog were probably heading northeast to Mushaway and traveling day and night on the high ridgetops to ensure they beat Gato Montes and his boys without being seen. The full moon had just come on, and night visibility would be good. Lonely Horse and his band, like all of the Quahadi, knew every inch of the Comancheria territory. Traveling at night was not an obstacle.

Tuwikáa stopped the first night on a high ridge overlooking the broad valley below. He and Toche each took a drink from Tree's canteens but offered him nothing. They did let Bonner and Sister drink at a small watering hole full of rainwater. Tree thought they probably valued the horses much more than him. His throat was parched. Even with his hat on, the sun was hard on his face without the ability to adjust it on occasion. Both Comanches ate something out of a leather pull sack tied to their saddle horns without offering anything to Tree. They pulled him down off Bonner and allowed him to stand on his feet for a couple of minutes before telling him to sit. Toche tied a rawhide rope around his neck and looped it around his already-tied hands. He pulled the rope taut and secured the end to a limb in a mesquite tree.

Both of them looked at Tree with contempt and disgust. Bonner was tied to a mesquite and Sister was left tied to his saddle horn.

"You should not come to Comancheria again, Red Beard," said Tuwikáa. "I think maybe you not come again. Remember, the cuhtz is big and strong, is much bigger than the tseena. But the tseenas runs with the cuhtz until he can no longer run, then he is killed when they catch him. Do not try to run away. The tseenas will find you quickly."

Darkness was tempered to a mild twilight with the full moon. Normally, Tree would have enjoyed the beautiful low-hanging full moon that looked as if you could reach out and touch it. He reasoned that unless something changed, this might be the last full moon he saw. Exhaustion finally overtook him in the wee hours of the morning. He had not been asleep long when he heard movement of the horses.

"Get him on his puuku. We go now," said Tuwikáa.

Toche untied the rope from the mesquite and took it off Tree's neck.

"Stand up, Red Beard." He took Tree toward Bonner and then checked the latigo strap.

"Bend leg," said Toche. Tree bent his left leg as Toche put both of his hands under Tree's ankle.

"Pusha leg." Tree instantly sprang up and threw his right leg over and into the saddle. Toche secured Sister's lead rope to the saddle horn.

Tree knew the ride to Mushaway would only take half the day, and they would arrive when the sun was straight up. About mid-morning, they passed a burned-out cabin with a sod roof. There was an old burned wagon sitting next to the side of the cabin. He did not remember this being there before when the troop rode this way. Neither of the Comanches gave notice to the cabin or the four rock grave markers a hundred yards or so just east of the place as they rode past. The grave markers were surrounded by a little cedar-limb fence that was barely standing as they stood stoically, rising out of the dirt. The bare remnants of a rag doll were tied to the cedar fence. The doll was ragged and tattered from the elements. Her hair was made of black horse tail and blew slightly in the wind. The dark button eyes were still hanging by threads from the tattered head. Who knows who might have found the settlers and buried them.

It was hard for Tree to fathom a man toting his family all the way out here from somewhere far away and somehow deciding to set up a grub-stake right out here, right in the middle of the Comanche stronghold. More than likely, the Comanches were off raiding in Mexico and were not around when these folks first showed up. It might have been right blissful getting away from some city with their life savings and think-ing this is a good place to set up a little cattle operation right close to a stream. Their dreams probably lasted until the Comanches found them. Now, there they lay. Cold in the ground, right under those rock mark-ers. No ranch, no cattle, and, most of all, just plain dead. Tree envisioned the settlers' fear at the sight of these fierce warriors of the plains charg-ing toward their cabin whooping and hollering their blood-curdling war cries. There were not any city buildings to go running to, just a sod-roof cabin.

Mushaway stood alone to the east of Gail Mountain. Tree could eas-ily recognize the baldy-rock knob on top as they approached.

He could see smoke wisping upward from a fire close to the bottom of the western slope.

It was not until they got within a quarter of a mile away that he could make out horses tied to a picket line set up between two large mesquite trees. There looked to be at least seventy-five horses tied there. When they were within one hundred yards, he could clearly see a big Appaloosa with black spots on his rump tied with two other horses by themselves.

Toche stopped and got off his horse as Tuwikáa rode toward the Appaloosa. Tree could see Lonely Horse and several other Comanches looking at the horse and not particularly concerned with their arrival.

Toche pulled Tree down and made him sit on the ground. He led Bonner and Sister to the picket line and tied them both before returning to Tree. Toche left Tree's pistols in their holsters hanging by the gun belt on the packsaddle on Sister. The carbine was tied in its scabbard to the side of the saddle.

"Come," he said.

There were six large cedar posts buried in the ground in a row and two more that were spaced slightly apart. There were two men tied to single posts. Their foreheads and feet were bound with rawhide to the posts with their hands tied behind the post. The other man was tied with his nose pointing between the two cedar posts standing a few inches apart. The sombrero he wore was sitting on top of one of the posts. His long black hair was stained with blood on both sides by his ears. Tree could see a spike driven through each ear into a post, pinning him to both of them. There was a rawhide band pulled through his mouth and tied behind his head. This surely must be Gato Montes and the two boys riding with him. One of the men tied to a single post was a gringo and the other was very dark. He reckoned him to be the one they called Ghost and the gringo was the one called Billy.

Toche led Tree to one of the posts and pulled out a strand of rawhide and tied his waist to the post. Tree's head stood over a foot and a half above the top of the cedar post. He untied Tree's hands and pulled them behind the post and tied them. His throat was very dry after his having had no water for nearly two days. He doubted he would be offered any this close to his death. He was at least allowed to keep his hat on.

Lonely Horse slowly made his way to the captives and walked by each one slowly.

He stopped at Billy first and glared contemptuously at him.

"You reckon I might get a drink of water, mister?" Billy said.

Lonely Horse turned and looked at the Comanches behind him. "You can have water. Close your eyes and stick out tongue."

"Sure," said Billy. "I been powerful thirsty while we been riding and all." As soon as he closed his eyes and stuck out his tongue, Lonely Horse quickly grabbed it, pulling it out as far as he could, and sliced it off with his knife. Billy gurgled out a scream as blood poured from his mouth.

"Tie a band in Talks Too Much's mouth."

He threw the tongue in the fire, where it popped and sizzled as the other Comanches laughed heartily. Next, he stopped by Ghost. Ghost's eyes were full of fear as Lonely Horse stood in front of him.

"You no see? If no see you, maybe you no feel pain. Lonely Horse will see if this is true, soon."

Next, he came to Tree.

"The Comancheros still talk of the Red Beard and the White Hair from battle with Comancheros before. They say Red Beard is man of great courage. Run puuku into battle. They also say, he not ever shoots his gun. Maybe he wanted to die. White Hair is not with you this time. You very brave to ride into Comancheria alone."

He reached up and grabbed Tree's beard in his hand a little below the chin a few inches.

"I need your red chin hairs for my fighting lance. It will bring me great luck in battle with Mackenzie." He took out his bloody knife and cut it off. The beard was nearly a foot long.

"This looks like the tail of the little tseena," he said.

Finally, he made his way to Gato Montes.

"And you, this one they call Gato Montes, the pia wa'óo. We do not look on the face of such a coward. You are the man that kills with spiga from behind. You are the man that kills boy that howls like tseena with no mind. You also kill good puuku and hang him in tree and empty his stomach to the ground."

Looking toward Tree, he said, "This one called Red Beard, he charges his enemies in battle like the great Comanche warriors and looks them in the eyes with no fear of death. The Comanche is not afraid of death or the enemy. It is great to make war, die in battle with your enemy. You, are not a warrior and lower than sarii and kwasinabóo that crawls on the earth to its hole. Maybe the pia wa'óo good name for you. It kills arūka always from behind from a tree or a rock. The arūka has no chance to run from something it cannot see. That takes no courage."

Lonely Horse spat on Gato Montes.

"Lonely Horse will visit you tomorrow. The Comanche see where courage is, man that kills with spiga."

The sun was heavy on the captives faces except for Gato Montes. Tree was starting to get delusional as lack of water and food were beginning to take its toll on his strong body. His mouth was so dry he could not make spit and did not sweat. His strong legs still held him, but he did not know for how much longer.

THE LONG DAY STRETCHED INTO the evening. Toche was left to watch the captives through the night.

Late into the night, Tree could hear him talking softly to Ghost.

"You will die tomorrow. You are not too much a ghost. Maybe you are just a coward like the Gato Montes."

Toche slowly walked to Tree and looked to the side and behind. Grabbing Tree by the hair, he pulled his head back and stuck a canteen to his lips. Tree tried to drink a little as the warrior spoke low.

"Red Beard, you will die tomorrow."

He kept giving Tree sips of water from the canteen while he looked around him. "Red Beard, you should not come Comancheria."

He let Tree drink over half of the canteen before stopping. He pulled a small piece of dried meat out of his leather pouch and stuck it in Tree's mouth.

"If you make noise before sun rises, I will cut out your tongue like the other one." Then, he quietly disappeared.

Tree immediately felt the effects of the water in his body. He just needed more of it. Slowly he began to chew on the little piece of dried meat and suck the juice. He muffled a cough as the acidic juice went down his parched throat. He found it amusing that Toche gave him water and a piece of food only to kill him in the morning.

His whole body ached as he watched the sun just starting to spread its rays from the east. He felt much better and a little stronger from the small piece of meat. There had been no loud sounds from Gato Montes or

Ghost throughout the night other than a cough or two and a slight moan from standing all day and all night. Billy made the most noise with warbled moans and coughing as he tried to cough out the blood oozing from his mouth. In between coughing fits, he would whimper and moan loudly and try to talk, even with the rawhide band strapped through his mouth. His shirt was covered with blood to his waist. He would have been better off not to have spoken in the first place. Tree looked out toward the horses. He hoped they would be taken care of by the Comanche once he was dead.

He could not see Sister tied next to Bonner. She had been there at sundown. His heart sank. Even though he might not live to see the end of the day, he could never return the mare to Sheriff Brody. Neither horse had been grazed as far as he could tell other than the few minutes the Comanches allowed both of them to drink at the last watering hole before getting to Mushaway. Maybe they would not abuse Bonner as much, because they prized their horses. Tree was nearly overcome with emotion as he remembered all of the times Bonner would sniff his pocket for his nightly sugar cube. The Comanches surely did not believe in such luxuries or pampering of their mounts. He turned his head slowly as far as he could and still could see no sign of Sister. Maybe someone took her when he dozed off.

Running Horse was putting his saddle on his horse when Tuwikáa approached the captives, leading Ghost's horse behind him. He walked up to Ghost and cut all of the rawhide that bound him.

"Go to puuku."

Ghost looked at him wearily nearly unable to move. Tuwikáa slapped him in the face and pointed to his own chest.

"I say, go to puuku."

Slowly Ghost began to limp on his weak legs toward his horse.

"Make saddle to ride," said Tuwikáa. Ghost unbuckled the latigo strap and cinched it up and re-buckled. Tuwikáa could see the long, braided loop in the horse's mane hanging on the right side.

"Leg."

Ghost obeyed and bent his left knee as Tuwikáa clasped his hand under it. "Pusha." Ghost pushed and sprang up into the saddle.

"Toche take puuku. You, ride on side like ghost so Lonely Horse can see you."

Tuwikáa tied the reins together on Ghost's horse and laid them over the saddle horn. He tied a long rope to the shank ring of the bit in the horse's mouth. Toche rode up on his horse as Tuwikáa handed him the long lead rope. He held up four fingers.

"Ghost man run this many times by Lonely Horse."

Lonely Horse sat quietly on his horse with his bow in hand and an arrow nocked. Toche led Ghost out a-ways.

"Time to be ghost man. Get side of puuku."

Ghost looked at him wearily as he reached and ran his right hand through the loop in his horse's mane. He held the saddle horn with his left hand as he slid off the saddle hooking his left leg behind the saddle. Toche goosed his horse immediately and began to run with Ghost hanging on the side facing the Comanches. Lonely Horse drew his bow as Toche led him by and let the arrow fly. It hit Ghost in the left shoulder as the Comanches cheered. Toche immediately circled back and ran by Lonely Horse again. The next arrow hit Ghost in the top of the left knee. He grimaced in pain, desperately trying to hang on as Toche circled again. The third arrow hit Ghost squarely in the buttocks. Toche stopped before making the final pass.

"This time puuku walk with Ghost man."

He walked the horses by as Lonely Horse slowly pulled the arrow back. The final arrow hit Ghost in the back of the head. The other Comanches began whooping. Ghost's left leg came off the horse as he fell to the ground, his right hand still clinging to the braided mane loop. Lonely Horse walked out to him and cut the braided loop. "You not ghost today. Lonely Horse see you. Take his puuku to the others. He now Comanche puuku."

Lonely Horse stepped off thirty steps from where Billy was strapped to the post.

"He no talk. Now, he not see."

He nocked another arrow and drew it back. He waited a full five seconds before releasing it. The arrow found its mark in Billy's left eye, instantly pinning his head to the post. Billy let out a gurgled gasp through the rawhide band, and his body began to convulse. Lonely Horse turned to look at Tuwikáa as he nocked his second arrow. He quickly drew back his bow and moved the arrow tip slightly left to right before stopping. The flint arrow head ripped through Billy's right eye. Tree stared straight ahead as Lonely Horse carefully retrieved all of his arrows and rubbed them in the dirt to remove the blood. The other Comanches whooped loudly at the two eye shots.

Lonely Horse went to the tall Appaloosa and opened up the leather saddlebag hanging on the side. He found the roll of spigas wrapped in cloth and took one and threw the rest on the ground. Slowly he walked toward Gato Montes. He motioned Running Horse, Toche, and Tuwikáa to come to him.

"This man not belong to Mexicans or Comanches. He brings no honor."

He raised the spike and buried it in Gato Montez's neck. Tree could hear the sickening sound of the spike as it penetrated bone. Lonely Horse spat in Gato's hair, as did the rest of the Comanches as they walked by. He could hear Gato Montes gasping for breath and trying to scream.

"Men not fight with honor, die no honor."

He pulled out his knife and quickly cut off each of Gato's ears and left them dangling and bloody from the spikes in the post. He cut the strap holding his hands and his head. Gato Montes quickly fell to the ground moaning and bleeding profusely from each side of his head.

Lonely Horse pushed him over with his foot where he was looking faceup. The glare of the autumn sun caused Gato Montes to squint. The blood from his ears now covered his face. The sharpened end of the spike was protruding out of the front of his neck, dripping dark red blood. His bloody mouth was gaping open with his tongue sticking out.

"Take him fire." Gato Montes tried to scream as they pulled him toward the burning campfire.

"Hold feet and arms." Tree could see Toche removing his little shovel from his pack and walking toward the fire.

"Fire on head and face now." Gato began to scream loud as Toche scooped a shovel full of red-hot coals and dumped them on his face and into his mouth. Tree could see the steam coming out of his mouth as the coals melted his tongue, eyes, and nose. The spike sticking out of his neck was smoldering.

"He no eyes to see again, nose smell, or mouth eat in the spirit world. Now, put here," he said as he pointed to his stomach.

Gato could scream no more as Toche placed two scoops of hot coals on his stomach and privates.

"Leave this one here for tseena. Drag others away from here. Go wait below Mushaway for me."

Lonely Horse made his way to the post where Tree was tied. He cut him loose and allowed him to move his arms and hands.

"Red Beard, go to your puuku. Puuku you lead go in night. Maybe go back to Rosario lawman."

Tree slowly began walking on his weak legs and trying to move his arms and hands.

"Make saddle, ride," said Lonely Horse. Tree slowly lifted his sore arms and unlatched the latigo strap and pulled the cinch tight before re-buckling it.

"Ride puuku," Lonely Horse ordered.

Lonely Horse grabbed Bonner's reins and went to his horse. He quickly mounted and began to lead Bonner toward Mushaway. Tree had no idea what could possibly lay in store.

Were they going to kill him at the base of Mushaway with arrows like they did the rest? There was not a fire up there as far as he could tell. He had nothing to end his life with.

Lonely Horse rode completely around the base of Mushaway and to the east slope where he began heading up a small trail. He worked his way up the side and through the small outcrop of rocks to the top of the mountain. Slowly he made his way across the baldy top-knob of Mushaway and stopped to look toward the camp back to the west. Tree could see the dust as the Comanches dragged Billy and Ghost by ropes behind their horses. Lonely Horse watched in complete silence without speaking. Finally, Tree saw them loping back toward Mushaway. When they stopped at the base of the mountain, Lonely Horse looked at the sheer drop-off below where they stood. It looked to be at least fifteen or twenty feet straight down.

"Red Beard. This land Comanche. Comancheria. You came to our land before as warrior and now, to follow these that kill with spiga. You have chance to live. Puuku go down mountain. You, ride."

He got off of his horse and took a small rope off of his saddle horn.

"Hands, here." Tree carefully looked over the landscape below as he put his hands behind him. He still had on his spurs but it would be difficult to stay on Bonner without his hands unless he gripped the back of the saddle. Tree fumbled with his fingers and found one little latigo tie-down ring to stick one finger in as he gripped the back of the saddle cantle. Lonely Horse finished tying his hands and pulled out his rifle.

"If live, no come again Comanche lands. You come, big birds that eat dead will see you."

He pulled out his knife and grabbed the hair on the left side of Tree's head and pulled it toward him. He quickly cut the right side of his face from the cheekbone to his chin.

"Not come back Comancheria. Tell them, from Lonely Horse."

Bonner bolted over the edge as soon as Lonely Horse fired the rifle in the air behind him. Tree had already grabbed the back of the saddle as best he could and hooked his spurs into Bonner's sides. He still had one finger stuck inside of a saddle tie-down ring. Bonner hit the rocky slope below the drop-off and crashed to the ground with his haunches. Tree struggled to stay on as the horse tried to gain his footing.

"Stay on your feet, boy. Don't go down."

He desperately tried to remain balanced in the middle of the saddle as Bonner slipped and fell numerous times due to the downhill slope. He was not able to slow down until they got to the bottom. Bonner was blowing hard and shaking when he finally came to a stop. Tree slowly turned around and tried to look at his back legs. He could see blood covering both back hooves. The finger he stuck in the tie-down ring below the saddle cantle was cut and bleeding as he slowly pulled it out.

He pulled his finger out slowly and turned as far as he could in the saddle to look at it.

"Good thing I stuck my finger in there. It may have saved me from coming off," he thought.

"Steady boy. If they don't kill us now, we might just make it. I can't get off right yet until I know what they are going to do."

Bonner was trembling and took weight off each back foot every so often as Tree sat on top of him. "Steady now, boy. Just a little bit longer now."

Lonely Horse made his way down the east slope and back around to the others. He came by Tree and Bonner without looking and heading his horse northeast. The others fell in line behind him leading the large group of horses, with Tuwikáa being last. Tree watched them ride away, riding single file with each man leading a string of horses. Maybe they were going to fight Mackenzie. He watched them for a long while until they became invisible before swinging his right leg over the saddle horn and sliding off to the ground. Bonner nickered low as Tree walked behind him and looked at his legs. He had scraped the hide off of each leg, a good foot or so. Fortunately, he had not broken any bones that Tree could tell. He could see the spur marks in his side.

"I am sure sorry about that, boy. If it hadn't been for you, I probably would not be alive."

He turned to look back up at Mushaway.

"That is one heck of a drop-off you cleared there. Most horses would not have made it. We'll figure out how to get you doctored with some mud to keep the flies off."

Bonner turned his head to the south with his ears pointed forward. He let out a loud whinny. Another horse whinnied back. Tree could see a horse running toward them. Bonner continued to whinny as Tree could make out Sister running fast toward them with the lead rope hanging. He began laughing.

"Those boys didn't know to run the rope through the clip and just tied it."

She came to a screeching halt and slowly walked in to sniff noses with Bonner. "Good girl, Sister. Looks like you still got everything on your packsaddle including my guns. I am starting to think you are part human or something."

Remembering what Sheriff Brody told him about her untying his hands when Gato left him for dead, he turned his back to Sister. Tree threw his right leg over the saddle horn and slipped off the saddle on the left side of Bonner.

"Get this rope off of me, Sister. You untied yourself last night, now get me untied."

Sister sniffed the rope binding his hands and began to gently nibble it with her lips.

"Get them teeth on it, girl, he snugged it up tight. You are going to have to get rough with it."

Tree could feel her tugging at the rope with her teeth until she got the top knot loose. He began to wiggle his hands and got the bottom knot to finally loosen. He immediately put his hands on Sister's face and kissed her on the nose. Then he did the same thing with Bonner.

"Boys and girls, let's get these saddles changed. I don't believe Bonner needs to be carrying me for a while. We are heading home. It's chilly but the sun is shining, and we are alive, children, we are alive."

# Part 3

# CHAPTER 21

## Return to the Rolling J

THE COMANCHES LEFT BOTH CANTEENS on the packsaddle on Sister. Tree checked both of them. The one Toche let him drink from was half full and the other was nearly full. He decided to stop and water both horses at the water hole they passed between Mushaway and the big spring. That had been their last drink of water and a little grass before coming to Mushaway. He knew they were very hungry and thirsty.

He pulled off his hat and emptied the full canteen into it. Bonner was allowed to drink half before turning the hat to Sister. She licked the bottom clean. Tree went into the pack and pulled out two sugar cubes each.

"That will have to do for a little while until we get to water and grass. We will stay there for a day, and you can fill your bellies."

Both horses gobbled up the sweet cubes while bobbing their heads up and down as they crunched them up. Bonner sniffed Tree's pocket for more.

"That's it for now, feller." Bonner put his nose up and smelled the cut on Tree's face. Bonner put his head down and there was a little fresh blood on his top lip. The cut left by Lonely Horse's knife was nearly four inches long starting at the top of his cheekbone and running nearly to his chin. Tree reached up and touched the still-tender open wound. Some of it was crusting over, but he brought back bright red blood on his finger. Luckily or purposefully, Running Horse did not cut deep enough to penetrate the inside of his mouth. His wound would still have to be cleaned well and stitched somehow.

His thirst and hunger were great, but he resisted the urge to drink the half-canteen full of water. He pulled out two dried biscuits and crumbled up one in his hand and gave each pony a nibble. Slowly he took a little bite off of the crusty biscuit and sipped a little water before going about the task of swapping the saddle to Sister and packsaddle to Bonner. Digging out the bottle of whiskey he had purchased at the hardware store, he poured a little on his bandanna and gently pressed the stinging liquid on the cut on his face. The smell nearly made him sick to his stomach, because he had not had a drink of any type of alcohol since right before he joined the cavalry at Fort Concho. Right now, it would prevent an infection on him and Bonner. He gently tried to clean Bonner's rear leg wounds with the bandanna before dabbing them with whiskey. Bonner lifted each foot as Tree applied the whiskey.

"I know that burns, feller, but maybe it will keep the flies away until we get to that water hole. We will put a little mud on it there."


SISTER BORE TREE'S WEIGHT WELL even though she was a smaller-framed horse than Bonner. Tree always tried to keep his large body centered in the saddle to keep the weight load evenly distributed.

His ride down the west side of Mushaway with his hands tied behind him kept flashing into his brain. Bonner's sure-footedness saved them both. The Comanches said nothing as the pair careened down the treacherous slope but stood in silent appreciation of the skill of both man and animal when the horse and rider were still connected at the bottom of the slope.

THE RIDE TO THE WATER hole proved uneventful. Both horses could smell the water well before they arrived. Bonner came along easy but slow. His lacerations and tears were accompanied by deep bruising caused by the impact with the ground after barely clearing the rocks on the first jump from the mountain ledge.

Tree was vigilant and cautious but believed all of the Comanches were headed northeast to join the fight with Mackenzie. There could be more coming from Mexico and following the Concho, but he doubted it with cavalry patrols in the area. Still, he had strapped on both pistols, and his rifle was in its normal place on his saddle.

The horses slaked their thirst as Tree refilled both canteens and drank slowly and heartily. Both ponies began to graze on the rain-fed, tender grass shoots. It would not be long before the killing frost came. He could see the dark blue storm clouds in the north. Hopefully, they would be back to the Rolling J before it hit. He set up his teepee tent and set about building a small fire. The salt-cured bacon slices and can of beans smelled and tasted better than Tree ever remembered in his life, savoring each bite, fat and all. He could feel renewed energy as the food hit his stomach.

He mixed a handful of salt into the bacon grease and stirred it slowly while letting it cool.

Bonner did not look up while Tree applied the now-cooled mixture to all of his open wounds.

"That will make the hair grow back, and you will look pretty for the buggy-horses in town, when we go through Rosario," he said as he patted Bonner on the rump.

The gritty dripping mixture burned Tree's cut as he softly applied it up and down the cut. He then went to the pond's edge and dug up a few handfuls of dark mud to pack onto Bonner's wounds and his own face as well.

"This will keep the flies off of you and me. Maybe keep out the infection too."

Tree sat peacefully by the fire and reflected on the past three days with the Comanches. Never had he felt more appreciative of just breathing the air, smelling the watering hole smells and watching the jackrabbits chase each other around the little pockets of shinnery brush here and there. Everything looked better and brighter than before. He saw firsthand the Comanches' ability to mete out frontier justice in their own unique way. Considered cruel by others, they neither waited on a frontier lawyer or traveling circuit judge to render a long-winded assessment and judgment in front of a bunch of local town gossips in the jury pool. Somehow, he reckoned, they saw or heard what Gato Montes did to the young boy and his pony. In their eyes, it squared exactly with the punishment they delivered, which was death. In his own case, Tree believed they gave him a chance at living, even if it was not guaranteed, because he buried the boy and cut down the horse from the tree. It was probably not because he charged into the Comancheros, like a fool. Most of the city folks did not think the Comanche ever exhibited any mercy at all when attacking or with their captives. They did, but it was on their terms. He assumed that Lonely Horse would somehow get word to the others in the Quahadi band, that he was allowed to live as long as he never returned to the Comancheria. He never planned to come here again.

There was no need to try and rush back to Rosario and report to the sheriff with a lot of miles in front of him. He figured it would be about fourteen days of normal riding but with Bonner's wounds, he would slow it down and try to make it back in twenty days or so. He glanced back to the north and took a long look at the dark blue horizon. It had all the markings of a blue norther. The north wind was just starting to pick up a little. He might just leave in the morning and head toward the big spring where there were at least rocks to protect from the north wind.

Tree could see the tracks of the stolen horses Gato Montes was leading toward Mushaway, all the way from the watering hole to the big spring.

He dismounted and let both horses drink their fill and graze at length. Looking to the mountain to the east where he had studied the spring before his capture, he was amazed that the Comanches remained unseen not just by himself but particularly by the horses. There was not a breath of warning other than the covey of quail flushing and by then it was too late. Maybe they hid behind the massive slabs of rock on the east and west sides of the spring and left their horses tied well out of sight and smelling range of his two horses. Toche led them in from the west when they captured him. It was as if they knew every rock on the land, every arroyo and depression in the soil from Mexico north to the tip of Texas.

It was too late for second-guessing his capture and more about celebrating his freedom. He knew he could not possibly look at life the same as the day he left here heading to Mushaway with his hands tied. Just savoring a can of store-bought beans and frying up a little salt-cured bacon sent his spirit soaring.

Feeding both ponies a sugar cube and watching them crunch it up and beg for more made him laugh. He did not stay long at the big spring and slowly headed south to hit the headwaters of the Concho River. The winds were starting to be more sustained and chilled coming from the north. The large blue horizon seemed to be choking out the sun. His plan for a relaxing trip back was now taking on an urgency. He would look for protection for the horses. He had his tent.

Tree was starting to get chilled and brought the horses to a stop. After dismounting Sister and checking on Bonner's wounds, he dug through his pack for another shirt, leather gloves, and his wool vest. Both horses had to sniff them over before he put them on. Tree looked back to the north at the foreboding blue horizon. He rubbed his arms to get the chill bumps off them. When he turned back around, both horses were at rigid attention looking south.

"What is it? What do you two see?" Tree could make out at least the rear half of a horse moving into the cedar toward the river about one hundred yards in front of them. The horse looked to be carrying a rider.

He pulled his rifle out of its scabbard and slowly began to work his way toward where the rider disappeared into the high cedar. He took off his leather gloves and laid them behind the saddle horn and began to blow his warm breath on his numbing fingers just in case he had to use his gun. Pulling out his binoculars, he quickly scanned the area. He clicked to Sister as they slowly moved forward. When they were close, Tree called out. He had no way of knowing who might be on the horse or if he was fixing to be shot.

"Don't mean any harm. I know you are on a horse. Come out where I can see you." He paused a bit and watched his horse's ears. There was surely another horse close by as both horses nickered and another horse nickered back.

"Again, I mean no harm but I do have a rifle and will use it if you fire on me. Now come out and let me see you."

"If you want no trouble, why you have your rifle out, señor? I have a rifle too, but I want no trouble, just taking care of my goats."

"I will lay my rifle down on my saddle, and you can come out. I am not going to hurt you. Why don't you do the same?"

Slowly a man appeared out of the brush riding a buckskin horse. He wore a dark brown sombrero and a weathered old serape. His face was very dark with a large mustache. He had one pistol on his left hip.

"Here I am, señor. I am just a simple goat herder and want no trouble with you."

"And I am just a simple cow herder and want no trouble with you."

"Señor, there is only one problem, I have my goats here with me, but you have no cows. I see you when you pass this way before and you have no cows with you. I think maybe you are the man that bury the boy that was killed by the horse bandits on the river. They kill his horse too. I think maybe you were looking for them, yes? You have long, red beard when you come and now it is no longer. You have cut on your face that bleeds, and your packhorse has hurt legs. I tell by the way he walks. I do not think you are a simple cow-herding man. Maybe a bounty hunter, but you are not a herder of cows, señor."

"How did you know about the boy and the horse? That is a very long way from here."

"I have good ears, and I hear the bandits when they pass through here with the horses. They talk at night by the fire, and I come in close on my feet where they cannot see or hear me. Their bandit leader is a very bad man, señor. He laughed talking about killing the young boy with no brain and his little horse. He say he will not listen to the young boy howl like a coyote again. The two others did not speak much. I think they were very afraid. They leave going north the next morning with the horses."

"You sure know how to size up a man just by looking, I'd say. What is your name?"

"Mi nombre es Marco Martenez. Mi madre gives me that name from La Santa Biblia. The Comancheros, they take my madre away. They kill my little brother and my papa a long time ago. They not find me to kill, I hide. What is your name, señor?"

"Name's Tree Smith."

"I never hear this name like Tree. Maybe you are very tall like a Tree. I think this name you have, señor, it may not come from La Santa Biblia like mine. Where are you going, señor? Santa Angela?"

"No, I am heading to Rosario down by the border and then to a ranch called the Rolling J, where I work herding cows."

"Then why you come this far, señor? Did you chase the bandits?"

"I did, but the Comanches got to them before I could."

"Maybe you come with me to my camp house and stay for a night or maybe longer. The blue sky tells me it is going to get very much colder and very soon. I feed you good and your horses can stay in my little barn." Pointing to the north, he said, "That is a bad storm that comes tonight. Maybe I clean your cut on your face and sew it up with hair off of the horse's tail so it no make too ugly scar. Yes? Your cut and your horse legs, I have the aloe vera. Much good to heal, but we must close with the hair first. You come?"

"I reckon so, Señor Marco Martenez. I don't see this goat herd you are talking about. Where are they?"

"They are hiding in the cedar trees over there for protection. I call them with my goat call that sounds like them. They hear me and talk back to me in the goat language. Just like you and me talk the people language, yes? They follow us to the house and stay close in the cedar arroyo and it protects them from the wind and cold. They can come to the river to drink. As long as I am with them, they know they are safe. Let us ride. We are not too far to the cabin."

Marco put both hands by his mouth and began to make his goat call. Even with the wind starting to steadily blow, Tree could make out numerous goats answering back.

"See, I tell you I can talk the goat language. See them coming now out of the trees? I tell my goats to be very quiet when the bandits come by. My goats never made any goat talk while the bandits were here."

Tree followed Marco nearly one mile at a slow pace with his goats following and stopping to browse on the brush. He saw a chaparral take flight for a very short distance ahead of the goats. Once on the ground, he would pause, flare his head crest, and run along in front of them.

"That bird is a roadrunner, Marco. Does he stay with your herd?"

"El Correcaminos? His nombre is Culebra. Sí, señor, he stays with the goats all of the time."

"I don't reckon I have ever seen one take to being around animals."

"Culebra, his name means snake. He kills the snakes all around the herd. He kills the scorpions too. But he like to kill the snakes so the snakes will not bite my goats or their babies. I like Culebra too much. He loves to eat the snakes with the rattles and is much quicker than them. He stays on the window ledge at night at my cabin. You will see. Then, in the morning when I take the goats to eat, he goes in front of them. He is a very good bird, Señor Tree."


THE LITTLE CABIN WAS MADE of adobe bricks and slicked up with mud. There were four windows. Two on the front of the house and two on the back. The roof timbers appeared to be large pecan branches from the river packed with sod on top. The barn was made of pecan logs with cedar limbs layered on top over a foot thick. The corral was made entirely of cedar staves, completely sheared of their bark.

"Señor Tree, you can take off your saddle and pack by the cabin and they will stay dry inside. Then, we take the horses to the pen. They will not fight, I think. I draw water from the well for them to drink and we clean your big horse's wounds on his legs. Then I put the aloe vera from my plants I keep in the root cellar of my cabin. Take some hair off of the other horse's tail for your wound. The horses will be safe from the wind in my little barn. I have a much straw grass I pick close to the river. That is all they have to eat unless we take them out of the pen."

Tree watched closely as Marco dabbed water from a bucket on Bonner's rear legs. "You have done a good job on your horse. The wounds do not make the yellow pus. Maybe the salt grease and the mud you put on him." He pulled a piece of aloe vera plant out of his pocket and squeezed it up and down Bonner's wounds on both legs.

"I rub this in a little and then we leave alone. It will make the wounds heal faster. We check again tomorrow in the morning."

Marco lit two small kerosene lanterns. The inside of the cabin was remarkably clean. There was a small cooking stove and a bed with two small wooden chairs. He set his rifle in the corner.

"Welcome to mi casa. Mi casa es su casa tonight and until the storm is passed by. We stay warm and dry when the storm comes in."

Tree slowly sat down and thought about the day and the days ahead as Marco sliced up two potatoes and a yellow onion and started the stove fire with dried mesquite pieces stacked by the stove. He went outside for a few minutes and returned with a couple of pieces of red meat.

"I have a little room outside where I keep a little goat meat. You ever eat goat, Señor Tree? It is very good. I take a little piece of fat to cook the soft potatoes and the onions together. Very good."

"I can't say I ever ate any goat meat," said Tree.

"Goat meat will make you strong like me."

The smell of the potatoes and onions in the old skillet Marco was cooking them in wafted through the cabin. The blended smell of the onions and potatoes was overwhelming and wonderful to Tree. He watched as Marco slowly turned them with a wooden spoon, then placed a tin plate on top of the skillet.

"I keep them moving and keep them soft to eat. Very good. The plate on top, it helps to make the potatoes soft."

When he finished slow cooking them, he pulled down two tin plates that were hanging above the stove and sat them on top of the stove. Then he put both pieces of goat meat in the skillet, and they immediately began sizzling.

"This meat not take too long. Cook on each side a little."

He cut into the meat. It was slightly brown on the outside and still a little red on the inside. "This is just right, amigo." He forked the pieces into the plates. "All I have to drink is water from the well. I have two cups."

Tree stood up and went to his pack.

"I can do a little better than that." He pulled out the bottle of whiskey still about two-thirds full. "I bought this for doctoring, but it is also for drinking. Give me your cup. I will just drink the water."

"It has been a long time since I drink the whiskey. I take the whiskey one time in my life when a man come through with a wagon and stop. He has the whiskey and ask me if I drink a little bit with him. I only take a small sip. It makes my mouth on fire. I think I will just drink the water. We save the whiskey for your cut on your face. Let us eat."

Tree had never tasted food so good.

"That is mighty good cooking there, Marco. I'm obliged to you for putting me and the horses up and feeding me like this."

Marco took the plates and utensils outside and cleaned them with water from the well before coming back in.

"Señor Tree, you sit in this chair while I clean your face. This whiskey will burn like the scorpion's sting. Do you need a stick to bite on, amigo?"

"I don't reckon I do."

He did not move as Marco dabbed the whiskey on the long cut.

"You put the grease and salt on this wound. There is none of the yellow pus. This is good. Old trick. Now we must clean horsehair with whiskey and the leather needle."

He pulled off his hat and pulled the inside hatband down. A little paper fell out. He picked it up and unfolded it. Inside was a small circular leather sewing needle. "I keep it in my hat so I can find it. It is too small."

Tree watched as he cleaned a horsehair strand and the needle with whiskey.

"Your face is softer than the leather, señor, but not too much," Marco said, laughing.

"The needle must be clean so you do not get the red streaks on your pretty face." Marco carefully pulled the strand of horsehair through the eye of the curved needle.

"Your wound still bleeds. It will maybe drain a little from the bottom. It will be like a small raindrop and not the mighty river."

Tree winced when Marco pulled and tied the first stitch. The next nine stitches just felt numb. Marco cut off each stitch after he tied them and then cut them off with his skinning knife. He dabbed the wound clean with his bandanna and took out a small piece of aloe vera stem from his pocket.

"This plant makes your horse's wound be better too. Now, I use on your face to make you pretty again."

Marco slowly moved the gooey clear substance up and down the wound.

"This makes your wound heal quickly. It will make the skin soft. You must take some and put on every morning and night. The sewing, it must be pulled out after maybe ten days when you get back to your rancho."

Tree's stomach was fuller than it had been since he left the Rolling J.

"Señor Tree. It is only me and my goats here. The man I work for, he died a long time ago. No one come to take the land, so I stay here and tend to the goats. I hide when people ride by on the river. I see Comanche looking for soldiers, soldiers looking for the Comanche, people with wagons wanting to live on the land and sometime the Comancheros going to Mexico to raid and steal horses. Still, I stay. I have no familia left after they kill my people. Maybe you let me leave this lonely place and come with you when the blue-sky storm is passed, yes?"

Tree looked at Marco in amazement. "You want to come to the ranch with me? What about your goat herd? There must be a hundred of them. You can't go off and leave them. They will turn wild, and the varmints will get at them a lot easier if you are not here to guard them."

"I promise they will bring you no trouble. My goats are good goats. They will follow me and eat along the way. They will not slow you down. Two men are better than one on the trail, Señor Tree."

"You bet, I can just see the folks of Rosario and on the ranch, a cattle ranch at that, when a hundred head of goats come traipsing into a sophisticated town like that. Them things will be dropping pellets all over town."

"Yes, they will, amigo, but their pellets are small, not like the cows or the horses, only very little pellets."

Tree broke out laughing.

"I will tell you what. You fix breakfast before we leave. Whatever day that is. I will saddle the ponies, and we will head yonder with one hundred head of goats."

"Señor, six of those goats are very good milk goats with the long ears and the smiling face of the milk goat. Their milk is very good for the stomach and makes the good cheese. My goats will make you very happy. You will not be sorry. Gracias."

"I am sure they will."

"If we have to cross the river for some reason. I hope those goats can swim."

There was a pecking noise on one of the front windows. Marco went to look out the old burlap curtains.

"See, Señor, it is Culebra. He is pecking at the window to let me know he is there. He does this every night and then sticks his tail straight in the air while he sleeps there. He is on the side of the cabin where the north wind will not make him cold."

Tree walked to the window and there set the roadrunner.

"Well, I'll be. That bird is nearly just like people. He really likes to be around you and your goats. You reckon he will go with us when we leave?"

"Oh, sí, sí, señor. He will stay in front of the goats, just like you see today. The only thing, he will not have his window to sleep anymore. I think, as long as he sees me and the goats, he will be very happy, this Culebra."

# CHAPTER 22

THE WINDS FROM THE NORTH picked up their pace to a gale force as the blue norther came roaring across the plains. "This looks like it is going to set in for a spell, Marco."

Tree peered out the window toward the north. He could feel the cold air coming in through a little crack in the mud pack wall.

"Sí, señor. I am afraid it is with us for a while. I have plenty of wood stacked by the wall and we have a good and warm fire. There is plenty of drinking water in the little root cellar, and I have lots of goat meat, onions, and potatoes."

"The wind is blowing very hard, and it is tremendously cold. I can see little small pieces of sleet coming down. You think the goats and the horses are all right?"

"Sí. The horses are warm and dry in the adobe barn. Just like us. The goats? They are together in a little arroyo to the west of my house a short distance away. It is like a little canyon and is full of the árbole de cedros. The wind just blows over the top of it. If it rains, they will go to higher ground. A little bit of frozen rain or snow will not hurt them. My goats, they are very strong. They will be just fine, señor."

"I don't see your Culebra on the front windowsill. Where does he go?"

"Culebra, that bird is in the barn with the horses. He goes to stay with my horse all the time when the weather is mucho bad. I think he is companion to all of the horses now. He will make a little noise he makes and keep them from being scared. Sometimes, I see him on my horse's back just sitting there. My horse Josie, she just stands there like Culebra is scratching her back. She likes it. Maybe he will scratch on the backs of both of your horses."

Marco came and stood by Tree with the lantern.

"Let me look at your face wound."

Tree sat down in a chair for him to get a better look.

"You are very big, señor. You make two of me. This wound, it looks good. It drains out the bottom just a little, but it is not a river. Let us put the aloe vera on it again. It is magic plant."

The storm lasted a full four days before the nonstop high winds settled down and the sun finally began to show itself. Tree and Marco awoke to the sound of goats bleating in front of the cabin.

"Señor Tree, it has finally come. We can leave to your country. The sun is showing its beautiful face. Just look at my goats out the window. They are talking to me telling me it is time to leave."

Tree walked out of the house and looked at the clear blue sky with the bright sunshine raining down with its brilliant radiance. "Feels good on your face, don't it? I reckon we can tend to Bonner and get saddled up to get out of here. You just going to leave everything here that you own, Marco?"

"I will only take the clothes and food I can carry in my bags on Josie. I do not want to make my load too heavy for her back. The rest, I leave to whoever comes after me and needs it more than I do. The cabin is just mud and trees."

Bonner stood completely still as Marco checked his wounds and applied the aloe vera gel on the raw spots on his legs.

"They are starting to make scab. This is good. There is none of the yellow pus on his wounds. He is going to heal well. Just like your face because of my plant."

Bonner sniffed Tree's front pocket to see if there was a sugar cube behind the material. Tree laughed and reached into his saddlebag and pulled out three cubes. "Josie ever had a sugar cube?"

"What is this sugar cube? Let me taste it, señor." Marco licked it and smiled.

"I think maybe Josie will like this sugar cube. Yes, she can have it."

All three horses eagerly took the sugar cube they were given when Tree held his hand out flat.

"I have never seen a horse turn one down, Marco. Not ever. Let's get saddled and packed. Time for us to ride south. It is a little warmer down that way maybe."

It was noon before they pulled out as Marco sat on his horse and looked one last time at the cabin.

"I want to ride by the graves of my little brother and my father by the river on our way out. I do not know where my mother may have been buried when the Comancheros took her."

They moved out slowly with one hundred head of Spanish goats, a few milkers, one roadrunner, and three horses.

Tree looked at the mixed bag of creatures and smiled to himself.

*This may be a long trip back*, he thought.


"MARCO, THAT OLD GRAY NANNY up in the front of the herd, I've noticed she is the one that seems to be the leader of the bunch. They all follow her right along, even those males with the big horns."

"She is la cabra. She knows which way is better to go and where the best eating will be. The billies, all they do is fight the other billies over the nanny goats. The nanny leading the herd, she does not let any other goat take the lead as long as she lives. If they try, she will butt the head with her big horns until they turn away. She never loses battle. Many times, I watch. Las cabras, they are very smart. Much smarter than el macho cabrio. When they have the little babies, sometime one nanny, she stays with all of them and does not go to eat with the herd. I do not know how the others tell this la cabra to do this thing. Sometime the crows and the big buzzards come and follow the herd when the babies are coming. They try to make her leave the little goats long enough to peck out the eyes. Then, when they cannot see, they wait for the nanny to leave and they kill the little goat. Sometimes when I was a little boy, a man in our village tells me the chupacabra come and drink the blood of the goats. You think there is such a thing as this chupacabra, Señor Tree?"

"I don't reckon I have ever heard of one of them. I know that bats drink the blood of animals at night, mainly on their legs above their hooves."

"Do you have a woman at the rancho?"

"Do I have a woman? No, I reckon not. I don't figure there is one out there in this world that I might take a liking to. At least I have not seen one yet. They scare me a little, I guess. I can't never tell what they are thinking when they look at me. It is like a big spider watching something they are fixing to kill and eat. Besides, I am not exactly a woman's prize catch. I just always steered plumb clear of them. What about you?"

"I have no woman either. I once loved a girl in our village in Mexico a long time ago. Her name is Carmella. We live in Ojinaga before we come to Texas looking for work on the ranch where I lived. She was very pretty and she like me to go with her to pick the flowers. It made me very sad when we leave. She cried and I cry, together. We had no money, and mi padre wanted to come across the river to maybe find work. We were very young. I never think of no one else but her."

"You ever thought of crossing the river and heading back in Ojinaga? Maybe try and look her up?"

"Oh, no. I am sure she is married and may have little children now. She was very beautiful. I would not want to go and try to find her and see her married to someone. This would make my heart break. No, I will never look for her. I just smile to remember when we pick the caléndulas together for Día de los Muertos and give to her madre. You know this Día de los Muertos?"

"I saw it from a distance in the village down across the river. It does not make any sense to me at all."

"Maybe you do not understand because you are a gringo. It is a very special time for the Mexican people. Maybe one day you see a little closer than a long distance and maybe you understand."

"Yeah, maybe so, but I doubt it. I don't think I would care too much about going to one of them graveyards where folks are buried. That's plumb scary to me."

"A man as big as you, Señor Tree, afraid? You make me laugh so much. I think if you are not afraid of the Comanche, you should not be afraid of a place where the stones mark the graves of the dead. Día de los Muertos honors them. I have not been to Día de los Muertos since I was in Ojinaga. I miss it very much."

THE GOAT HERD BROWSED PEACEFULLY a short distance from the river as Tree and Marco watched them from a little ridge. Sister's ears perked up and pointed straight ahead, as did the ears of the other two horses.

"Something is out there in front of us. Get your pistol out of your holster and just keep looking straight ahead like normal. I am going to ease my binoculars out of my saddlebag without looking down. Just tell me when your gun is in your hand. Don't do anything real sudden like. The sun out of the east may reflect off the binoculars."

"Okay, it is in my hand. I look straight ahead like you say."

"There are two men on horseback up ahead a-ways. They have gun belts on their chests and sombreros on their heads. It looks like they are heading our way slow and easy. Just sit tight, we are not moving. I will get my rifle out of the scabbard. Don't know if they are up to no good."

"Maybe they are Comancheros, I think. Maybe from New Mexico here to steal horses for the Comanches. Like I say before, the Comancheros, they kill my madre and papa and my little brother when we first come to Texas. I run away and hide."

"Just sit tight. Ain't going to be no killing today. Unless they decide they want to get killed."

Tree watched as the two men approached. Both had their rifle butts planted on top of their saddles.

"Hello, amigos. It looks like you have a big herd of goats here. Where are you going with such a herd?"

Tree looked at both of them from underneath his large-brimmed hat.

"Where we are going is none of your business."

"Oh, but it is. It is our business because I make it our business. We like to make business with you and your friend. My business, I think maybe you pay us for each goat to pass through this land. Maybe if you pay us, we let you through to take your goats. They are eating on our land.

"It is easy to do, señor. Do this and you and your friend can go. Just like that. I will take a little smoke while you make up your mind, yes? I think maybe you pay us one hundred of your dollars and we let you go free. If you no pay, I think it will not be good for you and your friend there."

As soon as the man pulled out his bag and started to roll his smoke, Tree dug his spurs into Sister and ran her broadside into his horse. He reached and grabbed the rifle tip of the other men and yanked it out of his hand. In an instant he dismounted and dove on top of the man and his horse. He grabbed his rifle and grabbed him by the throat.

"Keep your gun on the other one, if he moves, shoot him in the gut."

The man's horse finally got to his feet and stumbled away. Tree held on to the man's throat as he yanked him to his feet. The man's eyes were now wide with fear as Tree towered above him over a foot and a half. He released his grip on his neck and drew his pistol.

"I don't reckon we are going to be paying to move our goats through here. Your land? You don't have any land. You two are roaming wolves, looking for something to kill. Tell your friend to get off of his horse now before I shoot him off of it. Marco, keep your pistol on that man and come get the leather lariat off my saddle. Get me two of them calf-tying ropes tied to my saddle straps. Let's get these boys tied while we decide what we are going to do with them. One thing for sure, we aren't going to turn these robbing and probably murdering pieces of scum a-loose."

Marco tied both of the men's hands behind their backs.

"Take them over to that big mesquite over there and tie them up good with that lariat. Get them gun belts and knives off them too."

Marco secured the two men and walked back to Tree.

"I never see someone move so quick, Tree. You scare these men when you run your horse and knock his horse down. I never see this before. What we do with these men? If you let them go, we will be looking behind us. These Comancheros are not good men. They just rob and kill the people like they kill my family."

Tree looked straight ahead for a bit before speaking.

"I reckon we'll take them with us into Rosario. Turn them over to Sheriff Brody. Maybe he will know what to do with them. They sure are not worth wasting a bullet on, and we will not be taking the law into our own hands out here in the woollies."

# CHAPTER 23

## Azul de Norte, Village of Montenegro

IT WAS TO BE ONE of the coldest times during the winter that anyone could remember in Montenegro, even the oldest living villager. The bitter cold came in from the north across the river, starting with the sweeping cold winds and the dreaded darkest of blue skies. The village vaqueros said the gringo cowboys at the Rolling J rancho across the river called it Azul de Norte. The nights seemed to be especially cold. The congenial mood of the village turned bleak and wearisome when the early fall brought caterpillars with long spiny hair, and the animals' coats seemed to come in thicker. Both of these were seen as a harbinger of bad things to come. The village elders talked in low tones under the old tree about the signs of the coming colder winter. They tried not to speak loudly as not to worry the children.

*Maybe it will just be cold for a very short time and no icy sleet or the unforgiving cold snow. Our country was not made for the cold, and we are never ready with our clothes.*

Most of the grownups had some type of leather coat made out of deerskin or thick cowhide. Some did not. The children had no such outerwear when the cold came.

"Azul de Norte never tells us for sure she is coming and how long she will stay here with us," the oldest villager, Moses Camarillo, would say. "We only know that when she arrives, she brings much pain and agony with her, and we are never sorry to see her leave."

The adobe brick homes in the village were tightly sealed against the weather. Each large mud brick was carefully made with sand, mud, straw, and pine needles to bind it together. Every brick was carefully prepared in its own form and left to bake in the summer heat for five days before removing it. Each summer, the young men of the village were put to work gathering the materials for the bricks and hauling them to the make site. The oxen yoke carriers were smooth to the neck and shoulders but not padded. The wooden buckets on each side were heavy but forgotten in the laughter and constant chatter of the boys making their round trips from the village to the river. Their boundless energy was usually spent after a long day of hauling mud.

Several men generally did the mixing and placing the mud into the forms and smoothing the excess off of the top. Nearly all capable men of the village participated in the laying of the rock foundation and laying of the bricks for a home. The small pine forest close to Montenegro offered trees of the right size to be felled and split for doors and window frames or for the poled roofs. Poles were set in the ground in the four corners of the dwelling to lay cross timbers pole to pole for a stable support for the roof. The smaller roof logs were hoisted, laid, and anchored with a wooden peg side by side the width of the building. The ends of each roof log extended a few feet on each end to carry off rainwater. The larger pine logs were split thin into planks that were nailed onto the pine logs on top. Starting at the bottom of the slightly pitched roof, each plank was nailed down tightly overlapping the one below it to carry off rain. Once complete, all cracks were carefully packed with pine tar and smoothed.

Most village firewood supplies were sufficient for the normal chilly nights of winter that gave way to beautiful days of sunshine, certainly not sustained periods of cold. To remain warm and continue to cook, firewood still had to be gathered in the bitter elements.

After two days of cold, it seemed as though the beautiful stars in the night sky would never reappear from the gloom, and the sun was not destined to show its bright face and warm the hearts and souls of the people.

Santiago Paz finished checking the village cow herd, carefully tucked into a small box canyon one ridge south of a Montenegro. He knew he would find them there, shielded by the bitter wind underneath the rock outcrop. There was usually an ample supply of winter weeds mixed with the grasses in the bottom. The small spring kept the little rock pool full in the worst of summer's heat. The cattle were not the only animals aware of the small watering hole. Most were willing to live and let live and just satisfy their thirst discreetly and then disappear. Others used it as a place of ambush, hiding in the high thorn-filled brush just off the trail.

Santiago's pace quickened as he headed back to the village. His cow skin jacket was not lined, the hair was left on the outside and the inside had been scraped and dried, then scraped again until it was supple. It broke the wind well, but never seemed to keep it from coming in from the bottom or whistling up the ill-fitting cuffs on the sleeves. He had forgotten to cinch down the cuffs with rawhide before he left the cabin. Now, he was paying the price. His rawhide-sewn cowhide mitts kept the wind off but had no inside lining. In weather like this, his fingers were frozen to the bone and burning numb. The piece of burlap he had wrapped around his neck came off a feed sack and did not keep the bitter wind from coming inside his coat.

Santiago had just stopped to catch his breath on the last leg down into Montenegro. He began rubbing his arms up and down and patting his hands together. The steam poured out of his mouth into the air. Looking down the mountain into the village, he knew his Adelina would have his supper hot and would greet him when he tapped the wooden door of their adobe home. The warm fire within and the aroma of her cooking would be all he needed to ward off the chill. He smiled at the thought.

His eyes were sharp for a man of forty. He was used to looking for anything that might hurt the cows or the horses. He had scared off several

mountain lions and even two or three black bears that ventured too close
to the herd. He was one of only a few men in the village who had a rifle,
and sparsely used any of his precious bullets from the few boxes of shells
he had. He never hesitated to shoot into the air to scare off a predator.
He would only shoot to kill if he was forced. Carefully surveying the village below, his eyes picked up a slight movement in front of his home.
Even though there was no sun, something did not look like it belonged.
Maybe it was a small bear trying to get into his home. The shape of the
creature looked similar to a bear. Santiago sidestepped the final descent,
partially sliding due to the steep slope and partially falling. He quickly
pulled off one leather mitt and grasped it with his teeth. His fingers were
cold and nearly frozen from lack of blood flow. He tried to make them
work in case he had to shoot this bear. They were so numb he could barely
feel them. The old rifle was barely in his clutch as he slowed his pace to
get his wind and hopefully stop shaking long enough to get off a shot.
He brought the gun to his right shoulder as he made his way toward his
home. The bear did not move. Maybe it was asleep. He closed the last
fifty yards quickly to get a clean shot. Pulling back the hammer, he aimed
at the bear as best he could see it for a body shot hopefully high up and
close to the heart. He heard the bear speak something in a woman's voice.

*Maybe it is a "spirit bear,"* he thought.

The bear turned its head, but there were no ears. The creature did
not move as he stepped close, keeping the butt of the rifle firm on his
shoulder.

It moaned a little as he touched it with the rifle barrel. Santiago slowly
put down his gun as he began to realize the bear was a woman wrapped
in some type of dark blanket including her head. He spoke to her with
no response, only a little wail. He tapped on the door. "Adelina, it is me,
Santiago. Open the door. We have trouble." The warmth of the candles
and small fire immediately greeted Santiago as the door was opened.

"What Santiago, what trouble?" He reached down and helped the
woman to stand. She was shaking and barely able to stand. He steadied
her as she rose to her feet. She was very short in stature and frail. He

helped her through the doorway and immediately shut the door against the howling wind. Santiago held the woman while Adelina stared in disbelief. The woman looked out from under the blanket.

"Please, señora, come to the fire," said Santiago, motioning to the flames. Slowly, she began to shuffle her way the few steps to the fire. Adelina reached for her hand to help her sit on the old cowhide stool by the fire. Slowly, she reached her hand to pull the blanket from her head. Her fingers were slow to move and grasp the garment. Adelina reached over and slowly pulled the blanket off her head and to her shoulders. Her hair had probably been very black at one time. Now, it was full of gray. Uncombed, it hung unwashed and untamed to her waist. The creases around her dark and hollowed eyes were furrowed and deep like little arroyos. Still, her dark eyes smiled as she sat.

"I think maybe she is hungry, Adelina. Something smells good to eat. Maybe she wants to eat."

Santiago looked down at her feet. Her leather sandals were coming apart and barely held together by old strings of rawhide. She glanced at him as he slowly reached his hand to touch her foot. She had not the strength to pull it away. Her skin was as cold as the river. Santiago motioned her to put her feet closer to the fire. She seemed to understand but could not move them. Santiago slowly placed his hands under her feet and turned them gently toward the warm fire.

"Adelina, I think maybe she needs some mezcal with some food to warm up her insides."

"I am coming, señor," she said. "I am coming." She carried in a plate steaming with corn tortillas, beans, onions, and potatoes with some meat. The old woman was too weak to raise her hands and hold the plate. "Santiago, get her a cup of mezcal, and I will feed her." The old woman slowly opened her mouth when Adelina touched her lips with the wooden spoon with a little food on it.

"Oh my," Adelina said, "she still has the teeth of a horse. All pretty and straight." The woman chewed each small bite slowly and seemed to begin to come back to life with each bite. Santiago brought the cup filled with mezcal to her lips every few bites for a tiny sip. As strong as the mezcal was, the old woman never acknowledged the burning in her throat. Adelina fed her the last bite.

"I don't think she has eaten any food in a long while, Santiago. I think maybe she has not slept by a fire like ours. She does not smell of smoke. We put blankets here by the fire for her to rest on this night, yes?"

Adelina and Santiago quietly ate their meal as they listened the old woman snore quietly under the cover of blankets.

"I wonder where she came from. And, what is her name? She does not talk. I think maybe she can hear."

"Maybe she is was too tired and hungry to talk. She came to our home, Santiago. She came in the cold. Maybe she has no family and lived in the mountains. I cannot tell you where she came from, only maybe Dios sent her to us."

"Maybe you are right. I just wished Dios let me know she was not a bear before I nearly shoot her with my gun," he said as he smiled.

"I am talking to the man that will not kill an animal unless it is a cow for meat for the village or maybe a deer. I think maybe you never shoot this woman, no? Your mouth is not as tender as your heart," she said as she patted his chest.

"Señora, your tongue, it cuts me like a knife," he said smiling.

Adelina kissed her finger and put it on Santiago's lips. "I do not think you will bleed too much, señor. Besides, my cuts are very little and not very deep."

"That is true, Adelina, but there are many of them. I bleed. I bleed. "

The next morning was still bitter cold outside when Santiago opened the door. The cold air chilled his lungs as he inhaled his first breath outside the house. Adelina fed him so he would have something hot in his stomach before he left to check the horses and cattle. The old woman lay asleep in front of the warm embers of the fire as Santiago ate.

Adelina found a jar of bear grease high on her shelf. Santiago had found a dead female bear one day while checking the cattle. Both bear cubs lay close by viciously slaughtered, most likely by a large male bear, and she had died trying to protect them.

She had only been dead a short time, possibly from the night before. Santiago set about skinning her and carved off any fat that did not come off with the hide. He laid the fat inside the hide and rolled it up. His horse was spooked by the smell of the dead animals. He was finally able to lay the hide behind the back of the saddle and tie it down. The inside of the hide was scraped many times to remove all meat and fat until it was smooth and pliable. The fat was boiled up and stored in jars for future use. The bear hide now lay in front of the fireplace in their home.

The old woman was beginning to stir by the fire at daybreak. Adelina slowly walked over and sat down in the cowhide chair. She gently placed her hands on the old woman's shoulder. The old woman turned to look at Adelina, who was holding the jar in one hand.

"Buenos dias." The old woman smiled vaguely and did not respond. Adelina slowly opened the jar, and the putrid aroma flooded the room. She stood up and went to the old woman's feet and gently began untying the rawhide straps holding on the decaying sandals. Her feet were very dry and cracked but warm this morning. Adelina picked up the jar, eased two fingers inside, and scooped up a little of the oil. She picked up one foot and gently began to work the oil onto the surface. Even though the smell was very bad, the effect was nearly immediate as she worked the oil over the complete foot and between each toe. The old woman watched emotionless as Adelina massaged the tendon in the arch of her foot very slowly. She started on the second foot. When she was done, she put both feet on a piece of cloth and went to wash her hands with soap. Adelina brought back a pair of wool socks from her room and gently pulled a sock on each foot, somewhat dampening the putrid smell. She gently patted the old woman on the foot and looked into her eyes. The old woman slowly lifted her right hand and laid it on top of Adelina's hand and looked into her eyes. Adelina could see her old eyes water up but she never began to cry. She patted Adelina's hand and looked at her feet.

# CHAPTER 24

FINALLY, AFTER NEARLY A WEEK, Azul de Norte began to release its chilling grip upon the land. The bitter winds subsided, and the village of Montenegro slowly began to come alive again. It was still a few weeks until spring really arrived with its abundance of fresh life in the south country. The beautiful jasmine plants behind Adelina and Santiago's home would start to peek through the soil to meet the sun when the time was right. Adelina always loved to spend time in her garden, especially to smell the delicate fragrance of the purple jasmine plants. She was always careful to cover them with dirt to keep the stems warm through the mild winters. Maybe they did not die because of Azul de Norte. They never liked the cold weather. Hopefully, the beautiful and fragrant flowers were not lost. The bloodsucking mosquitos did not seem to hang around when the plants were in full bloom, nearly all summer and into the fall.

While Santiago continued his daily tending of the cow herd and the horses, Adelina took diligent care of the old woman. After several rubbings with the bear oil, the old woman's feet began to soften, and the cracks began to heal. She never spoke a word and always gently patted Adelina's hand with hers when she finished applying the oil. When the oil was applied, Adelina always brushed the old woman's long gray hair with her brush. She worked all of the many tangles out and washed it with soap and water twice per week. Then, she would braid her hair into one long braid down her back, winding and tying a fine string of cowhide about two inches from the bottom. She heated water on the grate of her stove so she could help her wash her body with the lye soap. Even though she did not speak, her eyes said "thank you." "I wish you could speak, señora. We do not know your name. Maybe you could tell us where you came from and maybe we could take you back to your people. And maybe, you do not have any people. I just wished you could tell us something."

The old woman had gained enough strength to walk across the small room and outside to the outhouse without help. Adelina always waited nervously at the door until she returned to the front door of the house. She would always open the door all of the way and hold her hand out to the old woman. If there were clouds in the sky, sometimes the old woman would stop and begin to look and point at different clouds in the sky before she came in the house. One day, Adelina watched her sit on the ground and begin to draw in the dirt with her finger. She sat there for a while and finally got up and slowly shuffled to the door. Adelina helped her through the door and helped her sit down. Adelina pointed to the door.

"I will go outside for a little while," she said. She pointed to herself. Then, she pointed toward the old woman. "Señora, you stay by the fire, and I will be back."

Adelina turned and smiled at the old woman as she opened the door. She stepped out into the beautiful, but still chilly day. She made her way to the place where the old woman had been sitting in the dirt. Adelina stood looking at the dirt in amazement. There were several creatures that looked like birds flying. Also, there was a drawing of a bearded man with long hair flowing behind him as the cloud vapors and wind painted a beautiful portrait in the sky for a short time for all to imagine and see. She stared into the sky. She could still see the remnants in the nubes of what looked like a bearded man with a long mane of hair behind him. Only now, it was starting to look like something else. Maybe now, it looked like a large dog lying down for a nap. She looked at all of the nubes she could see and remembered her grandfather showing her the nube people and all of the nube animals in the sky as they floated past in the spring and summer and fall. She remembered the time at Día de los Muertos when her grandfather cried when the nube people came by. "Look, Adelina, there is your grandmama. See her in the nubes? She has come to say hello to me and to you. She is so beautiful."

Then, when the nubes moved on, he sat down and began to cry. "Adelina, now she is gone. She is gone. We have so much love while she was on the ground for many años, but now she goes with the nube people."

"Grandpapa, it is but a nube, just a nube."

"No, Adelina, I see her, and you see her. Maybe it is a sign from Dios to let me see her again uno more time. Oh, how she loved to see the nube people and nube animals when she was here with me. We used to walk hand in hand and look into the sky. She was much quicker than me and always saw the animal nubes first. I see the people nubes first before she sees them."

Adelina began to take notice every time the old woman went outside, particularly when the big white nubes were drifting past. Sometimes when it was warm, she would sit in the dirt for an hour. It always took her a while to get up and then shuffle along to the front door. Adelina would gently grab her hand and lead her through the front door. "Señora, you like to draw las nubes?" The old woman would just pat her hand and head to the cowhide chair to sit and rest.

Santiago came in from his cow tending and found Adelina sitting on the front step of their home. "Are you okay, Adelina?"

"Santiago, I think the old woman has no familia. She does not speak, but her heart is warm. She looks at las nubes when they come by and she draws the nube people and the nube animals with her finger in the dirt. They are very pretty. I do not like that she has to draw in the dirt. I think I will call her Nube. She cannot speak. Maybe she chooses not to speak, so she cannot tell us her name. Maybe her mind is in some other place than ours. I like Nube. I do not think it will be bad to call her this, señor, do you?"

"No Adelina. I do not. Maybe she does not understand, and her mind is gone except for the drawing of the people and the animals. I like this name, Nube. But the dirt, the dirt will blow and be washed away when the winds and rains come. Who will see her nube people and her nube animals when it does this? No one will see what you tell me is so beautiful. Maybe I find Nube something to make her nube marks on where they will not wash away, yes?"

"But what would you find, Santiago?"

"You let me worry about what to find, I will find something, you wait and see."

Santiago made his way down to Mr. Trujillo's house. It had three walls of adobe and a roof attached to it that served as his leather shop. Santiago brought him all of the skinned-out cowhides when he butchered a yearling calf or the skins of older cattle that died. The village hunters always brought him the fresh and beautiful deerskins and sometimes elk skins when they roamed to far eastward from their normal range.

Mr. Trujillo was a self-taught leather worker and made all of the leather goods for the village people of Montenegro, from the leg-protecting chicos the two vaqueros wore to the deer and cowhide jackets most of the adults and some children wore in the usually mild winters. Mr. Trujillo's shop was usually a beehive of activity. Someone was always getting measured for a belt, gloves, chicos, or maybe a saddle. The saddle tree was carefully carved out of pine trees and smoothed down. Mr. Trujillo could easily build pack racks to pack out deer meat for the horses that were perfectly balanced on their backs. The saddle tree took extra time and effort to sit exactly right on a particular horse. Once he had it exactly like he wanted, he began the laborious process of fitting and stitching the cowhide leather to the tree. Sometimes it would take him two months or more to build a saddle. As always, he liked to etch in his beautiful roses on the front of the swell and the back of the cantle. His beautiful rawhide stitching pattern would have sold well in the cities north of the border, but no one knew of his work but the villagers of Montenegro who owned horses. He made the saddles for both vaqueros working on the Rolling J, across the river. No one ever asked about the saddles but Tree. "La silla de montar. Muy bueno, señors," he said to the two vaqueros one day as he looked at the saddles. One of them turned to him and said, "Trujillo, la silla de montar."

He could even make a beautiful leather sombrero with the brim rolled exactly right, especially in the back with his unique upward bend. With his little metal punches, he would punch out the most delicate chain of roses on a belt or a small running horse and once, a charging toro. Sometimes, the village men wanted a name of a departed loved one on the back of their belt or on their pair of suspenders. Everyone in the village wanted something distinctly different on their piece of apparel, no matter what it was. Each piece of apparel was usually paid for in labor, chickens, eggs, cow meat, pottery, or onions and potatoes.

Santiago tapped on the door frame when he reached the little leather shop. He saw Señor Trujillo tapping a little metal punch with his leather hammer.

"Como esta usted, Señor Trujillo? Una mañana hermosa, sí?"

"Muy bueno, Señor. Muy bueno. Sí, una mañana hermosa. What brings you to me, Santiago, mi amigo? Maybe time for a new belt or maybe new chicos? I see yours, and they are getting to not be so good. You do not want a thorn in your leg."

"No, mi amigo. I need something much different. I am sure you know we took in the old woman during the Azul de Norte. She came to us when it was very cold on our doorstep. I think she may be a bear and had my gun ready to shoot, but she was no bear. Now she is better and eats well. Adelina rubs the bear oil on her feet that look like the arroyos by the river. They are much better now. This woman, she does not speak. Maybe she can no speak or maybe she can. But, she does not. When the day is warm, she goes outside and looks at the animals and the people in las nubes. She draws what she sees in las nubes in the dirt with her finger.

Adelina says the pictures are very beautiful. The wind and the rain blow and wash her beautiful pictures away. I think maybe you have something maybe she can make her marks on like the ready skin of a deer or a cow skin that is much thicker, no? Sometimes you make the pretty lines with the dark tinta and your little pluma. Do you have more of this dark tinta or maybe more plumas?"

Mr. Trujillo smiled as he listened to Santiago.

"Santiago, you and Adelina are my close friends. I think Dios will look on you well for taking care of this old woman who cannot take care of herself in her old age. That is the great custom of our people. The ones that gave us life. It is good to take care of them when they cannot take care of themselves so Dios in Heaven will smile on us. You come back to see me en dos dias. I make something for her so she makes beautiful the nube animals and people as they float through our sky over Montenegro."

Two days had passed as Adelina and Santiago walked slowly toward Mr. Trujillo's leather shop. They each held a hand of the old woman as she slowly shuffled along. The normal short walk turned longer as the old woman needed to stop and rest. Santiago tapped on the door frame when they arrived. "We are here, Señor Trujillo."

"Bienvenido mi casa, señoras," he said as he gently took the old woman's hand. "I make something for you. Please, please come see."

He led her to a cowhide chair and gently helped her sit down. He had something under a deerskin that was nearly as tall as he was. Slowly he removed the deerskin. There stood a small framed cabalette de arte. The small wooden easel was framed like a teepee. He had pegged it together and had leather thongs lashing hiding the pegs. Laying in the small flat tray were six small bottles of different colored tintas and two plumas. The plumas came from different birds. Sometimes children would bring them to him when they found one while playing outside. One was from a turkey and the other looked like it might have come from a beautiful red-tailed hawk. It had a very fine point, and the turkey pluma was fatter and broader on the tip.

The old woman's gaze was intent as Mr. Trujillo picked up the small hawk's pluma. He had tacked a square piece of clean and finished dried cow leather to the easel. Carefully he opened one of the little jars of tinta. "This one is rojo, just like the apple." He pointed to the sky.

"You now can mark tinta on piel de vaca when you see the animal nubes and the people nubes, yes?" The old woman took the quill from Mr. Trujillo.

"Yes, señora. This is yours. I give it all to you. You now make beautiful pictures. Santiago, I give her cinco piel de vaca to put her marks on. I am making many more ready to use for belts and gloves. I make her some more if she needs them, yes?"

Santiago and Adelina could barely contain their excitement and joy. Nube could not speak, but she could share her feelings with her beautiful drawings. They both hugged Mr. Trujillo in a great clasp of friendship.

"You are a good man, señor," said Adelina.

"May Dios give you and your family great happiness. We take Nube now and go home with what you have made with your hands, and now have given to her. Who knows what we will see in the piel de vacas with her tinta and pluma? Who knows? We will go now."

# CHAPTER 25

THE WARMING SPRING WEATHER WAS good for the villagers of Montenegro. Adelina helped Nube to set up her easel every day that it did not look like rain. Mr. Trujillo made her a new cowhide chair with a cowhide back framed out of strong pine limbs. Nube surveyed the chair when he brought it to her. Waving his hand for her to sit down, she cautiously approached, not seeming to understand what purpose the leather in back served. She slowly sat down and kept her back straight without touching the leather back. Adelina smiled and walked behind her and gently touched her shoulders and eased her back up against the leather. The leather back immediately took the stress off of her old back. She smiled and held her hand out to Mr. Trujillo. She clasped Mr. Trujillo's hands with hers.

"Adelina, where is her cabalette de arte? She must see what the chair is for."

Adelina went to Nube's room and retrieved the stand. Standing it up in front of Nube, Adelina smiled.

"Mr. Trujillo, you are a wonderful man, just like my Santiago. Gracias. Gracias."

"I make sure she has plenty cueros to paint her beautiful people and animals of the nube tribe when they come by to visit. She must have the beautiful tintas from the plants. I know where to find all of them, even the pretty azul, like the sky."

Nube loved her new chair, because it allowed her to lean back a little while she surveyed the clouds. When there were no clouds, she would paint the children in the tree or maybe Santiago when he rode his horse by. There were always little children close to her side and feet, watching with wide eyes as her paintings came to life. They would gleefully point and smile at the animal nubes and learned to look into the sky and point out their own nubes. With the constant motion of the clouds, the animal nubes usually did not hold their shape for long and what once was a magnificent bird might now be a horse. The little girls loved to stand behind her and sing quietly while they played with her long braid. Nube always continued painting in deep concentration. The children loved for Nube to paint the mustacho above their lips to look like Señor Santiago.

She was her happiest when the children surrounded her while she painted. Sometimes, a child would fall asleep with their head on her leg. They seemed to sense great comfort around Nube. She was someone that never spoke, but communicated quite well with her slow and subtle body language. Anytime she put her pluma down to rest her right arm, there was a little child's hand ready to grab hers. Often times, two children's hands. She would let them hold her hand and pull at the wrinkled rolls as she surveyed the painting. Finally, she would gently remove her hand, gently pat the child's hand, and reach for a pluma.

All of the children came by to sit with Nube. The younger ones that were not good at climbing would spend most of the day with her if she was painting. Julia de la Garza watched Nube from a distance. She wiped the tears from her eyes as she watched the little children play with Nube's long braid and quietly sing. She longed for her own children or maybe just one child.

She took her Santa Biblia and went to the church when no one was there. Quietly, she entered the doors and closed them behind her. The warm sunlight gently swathed the building in its glow through the glass window panes as she sat down on a wooden bench. She clutched her little silver cross on her chest and held her Biblia as she began to pray.

"Dios, this is Julia. I come to pray in your church when nobody else can hear but you. I believe in you and trust what you have for me in this life. Maybe it is selfish of me to ask for a man that I can love and that will love me. My papa always wanted me to have a good man, and I want a good man. One that says what he means and means what he says. Maybe a man that likes to make a meal for me, or bring me flowers. Is there a man like that that you might have for me? There are none in this village that I see for me. Maybe there is no one.

"I love the little children that you have sent us. I love the little bambinos when they are little and learning about the new things. Maybe the first time they smell the flowers or see the caballos when Santiago comes by. I have also cried before their little graves when you take them back to you. I cannot hardly bear to see them go and the pain is deep and long. But you know what is best for them. Even though I have cried at their graves, I am not afraid if you decide to ever let me have the child or maybe many children. I will love one or love all of them. I will try to never complain if you do not give me the husband or the little child because I will know that you never meant for me to have them. If that is true, then I will pour my love out like I do now for all of the children from our village, even though I do not take them home with me at night. I can only hold and kiss them for a little while.

"Gracias for letting me be alive.

"In el nombre de nuestro Señor Jesucristo, Amen."

# CHAPTER 26

FELICITY HAD BEEN AT THE Rolling J for nearly a month when Cedar tapped on her door on Sunday afternoon. She came to the door in a bright yellow shirt with her hair hanging down on her shoulders. She had on a little set of spectacles and was holding a book under her arm when she answered the door.

"Supper is not until six this evening, Mr. Jones," she laughed. "What, may I ask, brings you here?"

"Well, it is Sunday, and we try to not do only the necessaries around this place. I brought my chessboard, thought we might just have us a little game."

"That sounds wonderful, Cedar. I did not think we would ever have a chance to play. Come in, and let's set it up over at your bookkeeping table. This is very exciting."

Once the board was set up, the entire game was over in checkmate in about ten minutes.

"Where in the world did you learn to play chess like that? I have never seen those kinds of moves early on in a game. You hemmed me up, quick like."

"I guess, I learned them at the boarding school from one of the old man teachers. He was the only one I liked. He taught me how to play. I got where I could beat him, but it took me a couple of years."

"I'll tell you what, Miss Felicity, I don't like being beat. But if I was going to be beat by a woman, I am glad it was you that did the whipping. You tore me up pretty good. How about we go down to the cookshack and let me brew you up a hot cup of coffee?"

"Mr. Cedar Jones, I think that is a lovely idea, and I will take you up on it. Coffee sounds really good, just about now. Especially if someone else is bringing it to me."

Cedar poured up the fresh-brewed coffee and walked in with two hot pieces of apple pie.

"It is a pleasure to cook a pie for a woman. They might appreciate it more than these old cowboys."

"I have never had a man prepare me an apple pie, Cedar. It smells delicious."

"It is not bad, I reckon. It is my mama's recipe. Got that thin crust made with just the right amount of cinnamon and sugar on top. Don't like them too thick between the top and bottom crusts."

"It is so delicious. Your mama knew what she was doing."

"I was just wondering, while I was making up this here pie."

"Wondering what, Cedar?"

"I was just a-wondering if, maybe you might think about, maybe staying on out here. I mean . . . you don't have to say yes . . . but you sure have brightened up the place, a lot."

"Brightened up the place?"

"Yes indeed, a lot. In fact, you have put a smile on my face that has not been there in a long time, and the boys' faces to boot, I reckon. Just seeing you come walking in with your pretty shirt on and your hair pulled up on your head like that, it just kind of makes me smile, you know. You have done plumb spoiled the boys by making them those lunches every day. They have downright taken a fancy to you."

She took Cedar's rugged hand in hers and looked him in the eyes.

"The window was cracked in the main house when I first arrived, and you were talking to those cowboys outside. I guess they thought I was coming to shoot you or something. No man has ever stood up for me like that. From the time I was in the boarding school up until now, I have never really trusted a man. That is, until I met you. I have really never met a man quite like you in my life."

"Well, I have always shied away from the girls. I never felt comfortable even talking to one. I can't believe I am talking this way to one . . . I mean to you, right now. But it isn't scaring me like it usually does when a woman speaks to me. You give me great comfort for some reason. I don't really know how to explain it."

Felicity held onto his hand as she stood up. She dropped his hand and gently put her hands on each side of his face. "I am Lipan Apache, Cedar."

"I know that, ma'am. I am Irish with a little German, I am told."

She tenderly kissed him for a long time and then looked deep into his eyes. "I have never kissed a man until now, Mr. Jones. Never in my life."

"Believe it or not, I have never kissed a woman on the mouth before either."

"I will have to think about staying out here, Cedar. I feel comfortable and safe out here, I really do. But this ranch is owned by a man from back east, you said, and when Mr. Tree gets back, it will be business as usual. There may not be room for me in your operation."

"I'll tell you what, Missy, you let me handle that. I think Mr. Tree will think you are the greatest thing since baked apples with cinnamon and sugar on top."

"I did not say yes, Cedar, I will think about it. I have a lot of mixed emotions that I did not have when I first arrived that I need to sort out. Women are kind of like that. We have to think things through. We will see what happens. How about that?"

"I'd say that is better than a no, ma'am. Better than a no. And, I think that between now and the time he gets back, we need to have our Sunday-afternoon game of chess followed by coffee and pie."

# Part 4

# CHAPTER 27

TREE AND MARCO STOPPED RIGHT outside Rosario.

"I have a little business with the sheriff in this town other than taking these two men to him. I am riding his horse."

"This horse is not your horse? You did not steal this horse?"

"No, she ain't stolen. I will tell you about it someday, maybe. Right now, you got to keep them goats bunched up somewhere until I get through with the sheriff. Maybe right outside the first little road going in. Maybe they will stay calm with your bird close to them."

"I will wait for you there, Señor Tree."

SHERIFF BRODY LOOKED UP FROM his desk at the office when Tree ducked through the door with the two Comancheros at gunpoint.

"What in the world? What have you got there? How are you doing Tree? Damn, you lost weight. And your beard. What happened to your face there?"

"It is good to see you in your office, Sheriff. Getting around good?"

"No, I am not. I am slow, unsteady on my feet when I do walk, and I am walking with that cane there. The alternative to all of that is not so good. I am coming along real slow but coming along. Breathing much better than I was. Tell me what you have here. Who are these two?"

"These two boys tried to make us pay them money out on the Concho just to pass through with a goat herd we brought with us. They are thieves and who knows what else."

"A goat herd?"

"It's a long story. There is a man attached to the herd that is riding to the Rolling J with me, name is Marco Martenez. Anyway, these two need to be locked up until you figure out what to do with them. We just hauled them in to you."

Sheriff Brody pulled himself up slow and took his cane in his left hand. "I still am not too strong in my right arm. There is a little nerve damage somehow. If you will take these keys and open the cell door, we will get these two locked up so we can visit. We will lock them up in this first cell back in the back there. We got a circuit judge coming through in a couple of weeks. Attempted robbery sounds like it might be a charge the judge would believe."

"They did try to get a hundred dollars off of us to let us pass. I guess that is attempted robbery."

"You bet it is," said Sheriff Brody as he locked the cell door. He slowly made his way back to his chair and sat down, exhausted.

"Now, tell me what happened, Tree."

"Not before I give you this here badge, Sheriff. I am officially un-deputized."

"Well, I was kind of expecting that. Now, tell me about your trip. I ain't waiting all day."

"Gato Montes and his boys killed the young boy they called Coyote just little ways north of Fort Concho. I rode up on him and buried him. They drove a spike clean through his neck and stuck a coyote tail on the end of the spike. Killed his pony too and then strung him up in a tree close by where the boy was. Cut his pony's gut open. Hard thing, burying that boy.

"The Comanches kind of slipped up on me at the big spring while I was watering the horses. Two of them stayed back with me while the other two rode the ridgetops back to Mushaway. They knew that Gato Montes was heading there with a bunch of horses. Their leader is a man named Lonely Horse.

"He did not take kindly to what Gato Montes and his boys did to that boy and his horse. He and another Comanche caught them and the horses they stole as they rode toward Mushaway or maybe when they came into Mushaway. I am not sure which. They Comanches tortured Gato Montes the same way he been killing folks, with a spike in the neck. Had him tied between two posts with spikes drove through his ears. Had his face pointed toward the posts. They would not even not look at his face and called him a coward like he was. They cut his ears off and then heaped burning coals on his face and in his mouth before dumping them on his stomach and his hangy-downs. They did it so his spirit would not be able to see, eat, or hear.

"The other two, they cut out one's tongue and then shot both of them with arrows. That Lonely Horse shot that one called Billy with one arrow in each eye. They left me tied to a post while the killing was going on. I sure saw them kill Gato and his boys. The killings were not too good to look at, for sure.

"I was given a chance to live after Lonely Horse cut me on the face. He told me I had not better ever come back into the Comancheria. He tied my hands behind me and shot his gun. Old Bonner and me went off the bluff at Mushaway and somehow managed to get to the bottom in one piece. Busted up his legs pretty good. Your mare, Sister, well, those Comanches didn't tie her very well, and she busted loose during the night. Hid out somewhere, but I don't know for sure exactly where she was hiding. When the Comanches rode off, she came a-running in just like she came to you at that water hole. Then, she pulled that knot apart on the rope that they tied me up with. She sure likes to pull on ropes. Saved my life, I reckon. Anyway, I met up with a Mexican man on the Concho River to the north. Good man. Rode out the blue norther in his cabin for a few days. He doctored my horse and me. Stitched my face up using a piece of your mare's tail. He is riding with me back to the Rolling J. I don't know what will happen after that. He's got his entire goat herd with him. They follow him, no matter which trail he takes. I have never seen anything like it. Got a roadrunner bird running ahead of the herd killing snakes."

Sheriff Brody stood up slowly and shook Tree's hand. "I cannot believe you are still alive. I have to say thank you in a big way. I don't know what else to say.

"The main thing is you are safe and them murdering killers are dead and gone. I never thought I would be grateful to a band of Comanches. Who would have thought? I will be a long time healing, Tree. That damn spike took a lot out of me. I lost a whole lot of blood before you hauled me in. Just can't seem to get my normal strength back. It damaged some nerves in my shoulder, I suspect, because I can't rightly feel my arm all the way down. The doctor has me doing a little stretching and things, but it is pretty slow going. Damaged my lungs a little as well. Regardless of all of that, I am alive. I am obliged for you going off like you did. Even though you didn't rightly kill Gato Montes and his boys, their rewards are yours as far as I am concerned, including your deputy salary you earned. I'll get over to the bank as the reward is set up in an escrow account. That's about eight thousand dollars for the rewards plus your deputy salary. Nobody will question it just being rid of that murdering bunch, and I won't let you leave here without it. Be a nice little grubstake for you if you want to buy a little ranch or something. Those boys were responsible for five killings, if you count the boy from the village across the river that drowned himself. It would have been six killings if you had not got me in to the doctor in time.

"Now, about my Sister, she is a good one. If you will take her, I am giving her to you. I will probably never be able to ride again, at least not like I used to. I'm stove up in my knees these days. A hard day of riding just puts me to aching. I'm just here as kind of support for the deputy I have looking after things. I been doing this longer than I can count. It is about time to let someone else take the reins. They would make you sheriff if you wanted it. Of course, you would have to move up here, and I reckon that is not happening. You done right good, Tree. The town and the area are better off for it. Meet me back here in an hour, and I will have your money rounded up."

"I appreciate the horse, Sheriff. She is a good girl and smarter than a horse ought to be. She is already spoiled to a sugar cube at dark now. I am going to round up Marco, and we are going to get a haircut over at Whittmire's Barbering, if he is still open?"

"Oh, he is open, all right. I would like to be a fly on the wall when you two enter his door. He may just turn and run out the back door. I know one thing for sure, he has been somewhat of a different man they say since you were last in there. And Tree, don't be swatting any pesky flies today. See you in an hour."

MR. WHITTMIRE THOUGHT HE HEARD the bleating of goats on the street in front of his shop. He stopped with his customer and went to the door. He looked astonished to see the goat herd up on the boardwalk and in the street. His pulse quickened when he first saw Tree and Marco as they approached his door from the hitching rail. He stood to the side as Tree stooped through the door, followed by Marco. He quietly closed the door behind them and turned to look at them as they sat down in the chairs next to two more customers. The two men looked at Tree and immediately got up and hurried out the front door.

"I will be with you two fellas in a few minutes," said Mr. Whittmire, hesitantly. He nervously began clipping his customer's hair.

He cast nervous and fleeting glances at Tree and Marco over the top of his glasses. When he finished cutting his customer's hair, he removed his cape and brushed him off.

"Feel free to stay a while and visit when I am through with this fella over here," said Mr. Whittmire. The customer paid and abruptly left after he grabbed his hat. "What will you be having today sir? Just a haircut?"

"Well, both of us will be having a haircut today. You can start with my friend, Mr. Marco Martenez here. He needs your finest haircut and maybe a shave with some of that smooth soap you have there. Then, I need the same, except, no shave."

"Yes sir, yes sir. Just come up to my chair, and I will get started."

"You do a good job, and we might just come back. There are two vaqueros that work for me that sure might enjoy a haircut and a hot bath with them fancy-smelling salts you put in there."

"Yes sir, Mr. Tree. Anything we can do to accommodate. Yes, sir. You just feel free to bring them in anytime."

Mr. Whittmire cut both men's hair without saying a word.

"That will be one dollar, Mr. Tree."

Tree paid the money, and he and Marco walked out the door. There were goats and pellets all over the boardwalk in front of the barbershop. There were at least thirty townsfolk gawking at the goat herd.

"Well Mr. Marco Martenez, I'd say it's time to ease these goats on toward the Rolling J. They done paid their respect to Mr. Whittmire, I see."

"Señor Tree, this is the first time I have this done to me by someone. I cut my hair with my knife. Why does the man look at me the way he looks?"

"That's because he thinks you have a pretty little face there, amigo. I just need to stop by the sheriff's office on the way out. Call them goats up. I see a few of them have climbed on top of the sitting chairs along the boarded walkway. Let's ride."

# CHAPTER 28

Cedar found it hard to concentrate for very long on just about anything. He worried night and day about Tree. He could not bring himself to believe he was dead. Word traveled pretty fast with visiting riders to the Rolling J. There was not a stitch of information coming in.

*If the Comanches did not get him, maybe Bonner broke a leg or maybe he is afoot*, he thought.

He never let on to the boys how he felt when they asked about Tree. "Boys, I told you he will be back. He is as tough as they come."

Roney McCallister came by one afternoon and asked about Tree.

"You reckon he is gonna make it back, Mr. Cedar? He has been gone a spell and with that blue norther and all . . . I really like Mr. Tree, Cedar. He is kind of like my father in a way, excepting he is better than my father was, I reckon. I just wish he would come back."

"He will be back, Roney. He will be back. Let's just hope he is in one piece."

Never in his life had Cedar ever remembered thinking about a woman more than one minute. That is until Felicity Two-Feathers came riding into the Rolling J. Now, he found himself looking forward to being around her when she was serving up her breakfasts and suppers to the boys. Not only was the food better than anything he ever prepared himself, she just kind of lit up the whole room. Of course, all of the boys all wanted to help bring their dishes back into the cookshack.

"Them was the finest vittles I ever ate, Miss Felicity," said DeWitt Murphy.

"They were right better than what my mama used to fix us kids."

"Why thank you, Mr. Murphy," she replied. "That is very kind of you."

Roney McCallister never said much at the eating table when Cedar was doing the cooking. Felicity would come by and offer him more cow milk, and his face would flush red.

"Roney, would you care for more milk? Maybe another biscuit?"

"I, ah, yes, ma'am. A biscuit would be fine, ma'am."

Then he would quickly look down at his plate. As soon as she returned to the cookshack, the cowboys would start in.

"Dang gum boy, Miss Felicity ain't going to bite you. Look straight up at her and give her a big smile," said DeWitt.

"I believe I see them goose bumps popping out on your arm there too."

Cedar stood up to go get another cup of coffee.

"That will be enough of that kind of talk, DeWitt. That boy can have all of the goose bumps he wants. They are his and his alone. You tend to your own. You hear?"

"Sure, Cedar. I was just funning a little with the boy. I didn't realize he was such a tender-skinned young-in."

"Don't have nothing to do with having tender skin. I reckon his skin is a lot thicker than you might think. You just let him be."

Cedar let all of the boys clear the bunkhouse as he sipped on his cup of coffee. "Well Mr. Jones, did you get enough food in your stomach to get you through until supper?"

"You bet. You bet, ma'am. I like the way you fry up those eggs, keeping the yolk all pretty like that without busting it up."

"I am glad you like my egg frying, Cedar. That certainly is a small thing, but, if it makes you smile, that is good."

"Felicity, I was thinking about this tomorrow, it being Sunday and all. I don't know how many more Sundays we will have to play chess, drink a little coffee, and eat a piece of pie. Tree may come riding in at any time. I just don't know when. You never told me if you planned on staying on out here. I was thinking we might take a little pony ride to a favorite little spot of mine on the side of a mountain. We can take a blanket to sit on. I can make us up a little food and we can eat and talk a little. I might even build us a little fire for some coffee. What do you say, sound all right with you?"

"Cedar, I really do not know where this is heading. My heart goes to pumping when I see you. I do not know why. You make me smile. I guess I am afraid that all of this is some kind of dream. I came out here to help with the cooking and the next thing you know, I am kissing you, and I have not hardly even known you very long at all. That is not something I have never contemplated doing to any man, much less doing it without thinking about it. It just kind of came natural for some reason. Then, when I put my lips on your lips, it just kind of drained me, like I lost control of myself. Now, my emotions are stirred up pretty good. I find myself watching you through the window when you ride off in the morning on your horse and then when you are coming back in at supper time. What in the world would you do with a Lipan Apache woman, Cedar? What would you do? We come from two completely different worlds."

Cedar stood up slowly and took her hands in his.

"The question is not what I would do with you, it is what would you do with a grizzled cod like me? That is the question. I don't know that I have a good answer and I don't really care about trying to find one. I do know this. I have never met nobody quite like you. A woman who makes me look forward to getting out of bed of a morning. Someone who makes me smile when she walks into the room with her hair all pulled up in a bun with a little bow in it. You should not have ever kissed me, woman. Now it is my turn to return the favor."

He took off his cowboy hat and warmly embraced her.

"You see, I have never favored any type of woman, never. I mean, none of them except my mama when she was alive. Now, you come along, and I can't rightly get you off of my mind, day or night. I'm having trouble counting cows and calves, saddling my horse and getting on him on the right side. I lose my cow and calf count right in the middle and have to start over. That has never happened to me. What does all of that mean? It means that two people that came from far different places met at exactly the right place and exactly the right time in their travels in life. Those two folks are standing here holding each other's hands like they didn't know any better and staring into each other's eyes. They both can't help it because they like being around each other. That is what it means. Do you believe that being a Lipan Apache means you can't live your life any way you choose to live it? You are a free and independent woman. I am a free and independent man. Can't nobody make you or me do anything we don't rightly cater to doing."

He took her into his arms and kissed her warmly. They stood holding each other for a good while as he looked into her dark eyes.

"Them is the prettiest and most tender eyes I ever seen on a woman. Pity the man that gets you riled up. I could see a mighty fire coming out in them too."

"Your blue eyes look like the sky on a beautiful day, Cedar. I see life and joy coming from them. I see warmth and kindness as well. I can also see them turning into a dark and dangerous storm, where there is lightning and thunder rolling out of them, if someone ever tried you. That is what I see."

"Well, you just might be right about that. Now, about that horse ride tomorrow. How about I get the horses and come by about ten o'clock?"

"I will have my riding boots on, Mr. Jones."

"I will have something to eat and am packing my chessboard along. I have never been whipped by a woman when I was sitting on the side of my mountain where I could think straight. Maybe your fingers will be too cold to move the chess pieces."

Felicity was standing on the main house porch at 10:00 sharp. She had on her red shirt and her straw hat with a dark bandanna wrapped around her neck and a little coat. She already had her gloves on and riding spurs strapped on her boots when Cedar rode up leading her horse.

"You look prettier than mountain wildflowers in springtime, ma'am."

"I am sure you say that to all of the girls out here, Mr. Jones."

"Indeed, I do not. Only girls out here are the cows. They are pretty, but they are not nearly as pretty as you are."

"Now, that is a compliment for sure, Mr. Jones."

Cedar turned his horse east toward the sun. "That little spot up on the side of that ridge is where we are headed. You can see that little patch of trees behind it. When the wind lays, you can listen to the quiet until it puts you to sleep up there."

# CHAPTER 29

"Señor Tree, how long will it be to get to your ranch from Rosario."

"You talking about with or without those goats of yours?"

"My goats, they have to eat. They eat things the cows will not eat. It is good for the land, what my goats eat. They will not slow us down too much, I think."

"Well, I'd say without them goats and Old Culebra dragging us down, maybe less than an hour, just poking along and smelling the roses. Now with them, I'd say about three hours, if you keep them moving along. Speak a little of that goat talk of yours, and tell that head nanny we need to get there before dark."

"She moves as fast as she can, amigo. She likes to smell the wildflowers as we travel. She like the yellow ones in the spring. She is hunting for them now."

"I'm really sorry about all that happened to you and your family, Marco. You are alive, you know. And that is a little better than the alternative, like being dead. We are riding along smelling the good air with your precious herd of goats. You can't ask for much more than that."

"I never ask for more than that, señor. I am happy to be alive. My heart, it still grieves for my familia and sometimes, Carmella. I think that will never go away."

DeWitt Murphy spotted the little cloud of dust to the north with the two riders on horseback, leading a packhorse. He ran into the bunkhouse

"Mr. Cedar, there are two riders coming in and a cloud of dust. It might be that gang a-coming in with some stolen horses."

Cedar immediately turned to the boys.

"Strap them guns on now. Wait inside. If it is the gang and they try to come through that door, shoot to kill. But don't do no shooting until you know exactly what you are shooting at. I'm heading up to the main house to be with Ms. Felicity. Get ready."

Cedar strapped on his gun belt while he ran, opening up the pistol to check his shells without ever slowing down. He opened the front door to the main house.

"If you are not decent, get that way mighty quick. We have riders coming in. Get that pistol of yours and stay over there by the wall."

Felicity grabbed her gun and checked the bullets. She immediately ran to the wall and knelt down on one knee.

"Now, I don't rightly know who these folks are. Could be that Gato Montes band with a bunch of stolen horses. They may aim to kill us all and steal our horses to boot. You stay crouched down like that. If they somehow get through this door and kill me, have that hammer pulled back and shoot for the biggest part of their body. Don't waste every bullet you got on one man. They ought to be getting close now, get ready."

Felicity heard a horse blow and then heard the sounds of goats.

"Cedar, I hear goats. Do you hear them?"

"I do now. What in the thunder are goats doing a way out here?"

He peaked out the window and saw Tree riding the sheriff's horse and leading Bonner. There was a Mexican riding a big buckskin horse.

"Well, I'll be. It's Tree. He's on the sheriff's mare leading old Bonner. Got some Mexican man with him. Those goats are following them."

Cedar opened the door and called out to Tree.

"You a goat herder now?"

Tree stooped the mare and handed Marco the reins. He slid off and approached Cedar. "Good to see you, Cedar."

"What happened to your face there, mesquite tree or bear?"

"Something like that. How have you been, Cedar?"

Felicity stuck her head around the door and walked out onto the board porch.

"Excuse my manners. Tree, this here is Miss Felicity Two-Feathers. Finest cook in the territory. Miss Felicity, this here is Mr. Tree Bigfoot Smith. Only I can call him Bigfoot without no trouble."

Tree immediately took off his hat and approached the porch, extending his right hand.

"Howdy, ma'am. I am glad you came to help old Cedar. He might have buckled under by now."

"Who do you have holding your horse there, Tree?"

"He needs some introducing."

Tree let Felicity's hand go and walked out to Marco.

"Why don't you step off, amigo? This here is Mr. Marco Martenez. Found him living along the Concho a way back. Saved me and Bonner from infection and sewed my face up with horse tail hair. Fed us during that cold snap. He decided he and his goats wanted to come out this way. He says he may want to go on to the village of Montenegro across the river. He comes from Ojinaga a long time ago."

"Young fella, thanks for taking care of old Tree. He is a handful, even when he ain't got a cut on his face. I'm Cedar Jones, and this here is Felicity. You are quite welcome here. Graze them goats and get them watered too. There is no need to rush off. I believe I'll go down to the bunkhouse and tell the boys. They thought you was old Gato Montes and his band, a-riding in with a bunch of stolen horses. I did too. I'll be back shortly and help you with your horses. I am sure you have a story to tell."

Tree and Cedar left the supper table with the boys. DeWitt had been firing off his normal round of questions.

"Tree, when did you cut off your big old beard? How did you get that big cut on your face there? Some doctor did that stitching?"

"DeWitt, I am sure Tree will enlighten all of us on his journey when he's had time to rest a bit," said Cedar. "Can't you see he's tired? We are heading out to check the horses. And don't nobody come following us."

Roney McCallister was standing outside just around the corner of the bunkhouse when Cedar and Tree walked by. "Well, I'll be. How are you doing, Roney? I been thinking about you."

Roney grabbed Tree and hugged him with tears rolling down his face. "I been thinking about you a lot too, Tree. Thought you was dead or something."

"Now, now Roney. I sure ain't dead. We will pick up right where we left off. There is no need to cry, now." He patted Roney on the head with his big bear paw. "Dang boy, you done grew a foot since I set out. Ms. Felicity must be feeding you better than Old Cedar here. You wipe them eyes off and put a smile on your face. We will catch up shortly."

After Roney walked away, Cedar said, "That young man has sure been pining for you since you been gone. He kind of looks at you as his father, you know. He has looked plumb miserable since you rode off. Well, it sure looks like Bonner is glad to be back in his pen there, Tree."

"Just as long as that mare is next to him. Those two are inseparable now, I guess."

Cedar picked up a piece of straw from the hay before looking over at Tree.

"You going to tell me what happened or do I have to wait a month?"

"I ain't ever going to tell this again so listen close. I done had to rehash all of it to Sheriff Brody when we rode into Rosario. It was a long ride, both ways. The Comanches, there was only four of them. They caught me at the big spring watering while I was off my horse. Seemed like a small army. I sat on the ridge east of the spring, just like we did before and never saw a thing move before I went down there. Already had a gun on me, I reckon. They remembered me from the first time we went riding into that camp at Mushaway. Remembered my beard. They remembered you most of all. The White Hair that shot all of those men while I charged in with my gun uncocked. Their leader, Lonely Horse, he is the one that cut my beard off for his lance. He said it looked like the tail of a fox. He cut it off for good luck in their fight with a Mackenzie up northeast of Mushaway on the Red.

"Gato Montes and his boys killed that young boy riding with them named Coyote. Maybe it was just Gato that kilt him. I came upon him on the Concho heading north out of Santa Angela past Fort Concho a few miles. They kilt him and his little Welsh pony. Pulled that pony upside down in a big pecan tree and cut his gut open. Put a spike through the boy's neck. Decorated it with the tail of a coyote.

"The Comanches didn't much take to what they did. Two of them split off and got in front of Gato's bunch and caught them when they come into the Mushaway camp somehow. Anyway, all three were tied to posts when they rode in with me. They killed all three of them. I saw all of it. Gato Montes surely did get the worst of it. He screamed until no screams were coming out of his mouth when they stuck a spike in his neck, cut his ears off and then dumped hot coals down his mouth and on his belly."

"You sure it was Gato Montes, Tree?"

"It was him. Had his sombrero hanging on the posts above him. They had his face pointed in so they would not look at him. Spikes drove through both ears. Long black hair. It was him. He was a wretched-looking son buck just looking at him from behind.

"Lonely Horse rode off on that big Appaloosa he was riding. He was for dang sure shod like Sheriff Brody said. Saw that with my own eyes. He stole that horse off some rancher. The Comanches took it away from him.

"The other two were killed with arrows. The one called Billy, they cut out his tongue. They gagged him afterward and let him bleed on himself all night before they killed him. Ghost, they shot him with arrows while he was hanging off the side of his horse, four times. Never seen a better shot with a bow that Lonely Horse, the man that did the killing. He put an arrow, dead on, into each eye of the one called Billy."

"What about you, Tree? How did you come out alive? You would have figured they would have tortured you to death."

"Me? Lonely Horse took me up to the top of Mushaway Mountain and tied my hands behind me. Reached up and cut my face. Told me if I lived, to never come back to Comanche lands. Shot his rifle right behind Bonner. He bolted right off of that steep ledge, and I had to try and stay on him all the way to the bottom. I never would have made it without my spurs dug into his sides and him staying mostly on his feet. All I could hold on to was the saddle cantle and a little brass ring on the back of the saddle. I was barely able to stay straight up. Bonner cleared the rocks when he jumped off, but tore up his back legs pretty bad when he hit the ground. He has not mended from it yet, but the wounds are dry. If he would have rolled, neither one of us would be here right now. Soon as we got to the bottom, the Comanches left, just like that, riding northeast. Never even looked at me. They were moving about seventy horses or so.

"The sheriff's horse, Sister, got loose during the night and took off. Those Comanches did not tie her well with that lead rope with the metal cinch on it. She just pulled it apart, just like she does if it is not clipped right. She just came loping in after they left. That mare, right there, she untied the rope on my hands with her dang teeth. Saved me and old Bonner, just like she did Sheriff Brody when Gato first caught him. That's about the size of it. Sheriff Brody gave me $8,000 reward money, even though I didn't bring those boys in. Gave me $250 deputy wages to go with it.

"Marco Martenez, he is a mighty good man. Comancheros killed his little baby brother and his daddy. His mama fought them while he hid in the root cellar below their little smokehouse. Took his mama off somewhere to be traded. He never saw her again. That is the size of it.

"Now, enough talking about me. Please don't ask me about it again. It wears me out to have to tell it. How did you and Felicity Two-Feathers get on? She beat your cooking?"

"Before I go telling you about the goings-on around here, I am glad you are alive and survived. I just wish I would have been with you. You might not be dealing with that scar you brought back on your face. And then again, if I had gone with you and them Comanche recognized me, they might have just killed us both.

"I don't really quite know how to tell you what I got to say. You know I have never been around no women folks except maybe my mama, while she was alive. You ain't neither. Well, Felicity is different than any woman I ever been around. She kissed me, Tree. I done kissed her back, right on the lips both times. We been spending some Sunday afternoons together playing chess, drinking coffee, and eating apple pie. We even took a little picnic up on the flat spot up on east ridge last Sunday."

"That sounds pretty serious. What does she say about all this?"

"Well, she told me I am the only man she has ever kissed. She is the only woman I ever kissed except my mama. I can't rightly think of nothing else or nobody else. I even lost track of my cow-calf count the other day. I just cannot think straight at all.

"Truth is, I asked her to move out here. I know I overstepped my bounds, and I'll leave if you want me to. She said she would yesterday. But that all depends on you, I reckon."

Tree took out Bonner's brush and began to gently brush his back. Finally, he leaned over Bonner's back.

"Nobody has a right to dictate somebody else's happiness, Cedar. Besides, she is probably a better cook than you are. She is as welcome here as the rest of us. You two going to get married?"

"I want her to be my wife, Tree. There are no ifs, ands, or buts on that issue. She done said she would marry me. It happened like a tornado or something. I can't rightly explain it. I am thinking we need to wait and think this through. Then, I cannot stand to think about a day without her."

"Well, I'd say it's settled. Soon as you two get married, you and her can just take up residence at the main house. I'll come back to the bunkhouse with the boys."

"But Tree . . ."

"Don't but Tree me. It is settled. There is no going back. Let's go get a cup of your future bride's coffee. Maybe she has something sweet whipped up. I just don't know what such a fine-looking woman ever saw in a stubborn coot like you. She could have married up with one of them cleaner-cut fellas from town and been a lot better off."

"Yeah, they are clean cut all right. I wouldn't give you a fresh horse turd for a one of them, neither."

"You might not, but Miss Felicity just might. You are just jealous because those town boys have more than one changing of clothes and can speak a sentence without saying ain't or caint. The proper enunciation is are not and cannot."

"I have noticed you have a little language problem too, Tree. Miss Felicity can probably teach us both how to speak the English language better than we do. She makes it sound pretty and shiny when she talks."

# CHAPTER 30

"YOU THINK THE PEOPLE OF the village across the river will like me, Señor Tree?"

"I reckon they will like you well enough. I am not sure about a hundred head of goats and that bird of yours. Of course, we still have to get this herd across the low spot in the river down there. I have never been to the village, but I know where the two vaqueros cross. Rode down here a few times with them. It won't be over the knees of the goats. But from what I can tell, those goats hate the water except maybe for drinking."

"They will cross the river if I lead them across, señor. Take me to the low spot in the river."

"And the bird? How's he going to cross? Maybe he will ride across on a goat's back."

"He flies low but not far. I think maybe he fly across the river where it is not too wide."

SANTIAGO WAS ON HIS HORSE when he first saw the two riders and the goats coming across the river. He immediately turned him toward the river. He stopped and stood in the trail leading down to the river and watched them approach.

"Buenos dias, señors. What brings you to Montenegro with your goats?"

Tree looked over at Marco and then back to Santiago.

"I am Tree Smith from over at the Rolling J right there across the river. Two of your vaqueros work over there for me."

"Yes, señor. They speak of the patrón with the red hair. The one that go to find Gato Montez, the killer. And the killers that ride with him. You are very brave. Did you find them, these killers?"

"Well, the Comanches found them. I was there when they killed Gato Montes and his bandits. They are no longer."

"This here is Marco Martenez. He is from born in Ojinaga. His father brought the family to Texas looking for ranch work. Comancheros killed his father and little brother a long time ago on the Concho River in Texas. They took his mother and he has never seen her since. She might be in Mexico or maybe up by Santa Fe, or she might be dead. Been a long time ago.

"He helped me on my way back from hunting the killers. He is looking for a place to call home again. Maybe a place to keep his goat herd. He has a few milking goats in there. Make good milk. He says that milk makes good cheese. Said he wanted to come here. He just does not know nobody."

Santiago got off his horse and walked over to Marco.

"Señor Marco, my name is Santiago. We turn no one away at our village. It is our custom. You and your goats are welcome. The village needs goat milk and the cheese maybe. We have plenty for your goats to eat, but you must take them to it. We have the mountain lion and the bears on this side of the river that hide in the mountains. We have one little empty house you can stay in. You keep your horse with all the other horses. I show you where to take him."

Marco dabbed his eyes on his shirtsleeve. He got off of his horse and put his hand out to shake.

"You are a very good man to let me come into your village. I never make any trouble. I work hard. Gracias for letting me stay. I have no familia, alive. Maybe the people of the village can be my new familia."

Santiago mounted his horse.

"Come, Señor Marco Martenez and Señor Tree. We go to meet Adelina, my wife."

Marco turned and looked at Tree.

"Gracias, Tree, for the words you speak to him about me."

"I did not tell him how good a cook you are. If you are not really careful, I will. Then you will be cooking for the whole village. Let's go get you settled in so I can get back across the river before it gets too late, amigo."

ALL OF THE CHILDREN PLAYING by the old tree immediately ran to see the big goat herd. Many of the villagers came out of their homes and stood in front of their homes. The children surrounding Nube stayed close to her while the goats and riders approached. Santiago stopped in front of his house.

"Adelina, Adelina, come, we have friends from across the river. They bring the goat herd with them."

Adelina quickly opened the door and put her hands to her mouth. She began smiling.

"This is a lot of goats. We only have a few. Who brings the goats to our village?"

"It is Marco Martenez. He is from Ojinaga, a long time ago. Now he come back to Mexico. He has no familia. We will be his familia now."

Adelina walked up to Marco's horse.

"Welcome, Señor Marco. I am Adelina. We never see this many goats in Montenegro. Are there any of the goats that make the milk?"

"Sí, señora. I have the milk goats with the long ears and the smiling faces. They make the good milk that make the good cheese. "

"This is very good, Marco. We like the milk for the children that cannot drink the cow's milk. What is the bird that rides on top of the goat?"

"He is Culebra. He finds the snakes and the scorpions. He is a good bird."

Nobody noticed Nube get up from her chair in front of her easel. She slowly made her way to Santiago and then past him toward Marco. There was complete silence as she stared at Marco's face. She put her hand over her eyes to get a better look at him.

Marco never took his eyes off her as he stepped down off his horse. He slowly walked up to her. He reached out and took her left hand. He looked down at her hand and then back to her eyes. Nube's eyes welled up with tears as she tried to mouth the name "Marco" with no sound coming out.

"Mi madre. This is mi madre. She has the scar on her hand. The scar from the Comancheros. She knows it is me."

He grabbed her in his arms. Nube reached up and took his face in her hands and slowly shook her head back and forth. She pulled his face down to kiss him on each cheek.

"Señor Tree, it is mi madre. Her name is Ana. Ana Martenez. I am her son, Marco Martenez. She is alive. Look at her scar, señor. I never think I see her again or that she is alive. How did she come to this village, Señor Santiago? Did the Comancheros bring her here? Did you trade for her?" He glared at Santiago.

"No, señor. She come to the village when the Azul de Norte come to our village in the winter. She come to this house, and I find her right there at our door. We take care of her. Adelina takes care of her and make her feet well again. She does not speak. She makes the beautiful el dibujos of the animal and people nubes when they come by in the sky. She never speaks and tell us how she came to the village."

"It does not matter, Señor Santiago. All that matters is mi madre is alive, and I hold her again and she holds me. I will never let anything happen to her again as long as I live. I was just a little boy the last time I see her. Mi beautiful mama."

Tree stood by and watched the joyous reunion. It seemed very odd to him that if he not seen the rear end of Marco's horse quickly disappear into the brush that day, he would have just ridden right on by. How was it that his mother made her way to this particular village and they got paired up again after all of these years? She had not seen Marco since he was a little boy. That did not sound like pure coincidence to him.

Adelina wept tears of joy as she clasped her hands.

"Santiago, this one we called Nube. She is not Nube. She is Ana. Ana Martenez. This is her son, Marco. Dios has been good to us. He sent her boy back to her. We will tell the priest and have a celebration. This makes me so very happy. I cannot stop the crying."

Adelina walked up to Tree with tears in her eyes.

"Señor, we would be honored if you will stay tonight for a celebration. We will celebrate Nube's son, I mean Ana Martenez's Marco, finding her after all of those years. You are the reason that he is here."

"Look, ma'am, all I did was see him close to the river, and he came with me with his goats. I had no way of knowing what was going to happen."

"Yes, señor, but Dios did. Will you please stay? We will prepare food and eat under the old tree. We would be very honored if you will stay and eat, maybe sleep tonight at our home. Go to your rancho tomorrow. You are safe with us."

"Well, I reckon it wouldn't hurt."

"Good, then it is settled. Santiago, please take Mr. Tree to see your horses and your cows while we get ready. We have lots of work to do. I need to go tell the priest what just happened."

"Adelina, Señor Tree go after Gato Montes and his banda. He told me that the Comanche catch them, and now they are no longer. The killing has stopped."

Santiago and Tree had been gone for several hours when they heard the church bell ring three times.

"Come, señor, it is time for our celebration. We will go to the church first. The priest will want to speak to us before we eat the food that has been prepared."

Most of the villagers were gathered up close to the stone steps of the church when Santiago and Tree strode into the village. The priest waited for them to approach before he tinkled his little bell.

"Good evening to everyone," he began.

"This day brings us a joyous occasion that calls for much celebration. Our friend 'Nube' came into our village before dark one night when it was very, very cold. The Azul de Norte had just taken our land prisoner with her bitter and relentless cold and blowing winds. We know not of where she came from. Santiago found her on his steps. He and Adelina took her in and warmed her, fed her, and helped to heal her feet with bear oil. To this day, they continue to care for her. Nube makes the beautiful paintings on the cow skins that by now, each of you have seen. Still, she cannot tell us where or how she got here to Montenegro. Señora Adelina tells me about Marco. It was Dios's plan that she should come to our village, where one day he would bring the only living person in her family here. That is her son, Marco."

All of the villagers clapped their hands as Marco stood and kept his arm around Ana.

"We found out that her name is not the name Adelina and Santiago gave her. It is Ana. Ana Martenez.

"The one other thing, it is not so much a thing we should celebrate." He gestured toward Tree. "This man, his name is Señor Tree Smith. He is big and probably very strong, just like el arbol viejo in our village. This man, he may not want me to speak about what happened, but I must tell you the truth. Marco Martenez tells me just a little while ago.

"The Comanches found Gato Montes and his banda first and killed all of them at Mushaway. They also capture Señor Tree and cut off his beard and cut him on his face. The Comanche are not without honor. They give him the chance to live. That chance was to ride off a cliff on Mushaway. He lived, but his horse was injured badly. Then he began the ride back to his rancho and he finds Marco Martenez. This same Marco wants to bring his goats and come with Señor Tree to his rancho. Then Marco decided he wanted to come to Montenegro to be with his people.

"So, we thank Dios, our Creator, that he makes the circle of life for each of us to be in wonder of. Surely, he guided Ana's footsteps to Montenegro on the coldest of nights, Señor Tree's footsteps to Marco, and then both of their footsteps all the way here, to Montenegro.

"So, we shall celebrate with food and wine, the most joyous of occasions under el arbol viejo. Much food has been prepared with great love. Let us go to enjoy it."

# CHAPTER 31

---

Tree was the only gringo at the celebration. He could feel the warmth of the villagers as they passed by him and gently patted him on the arm or his back. Several of the little children came up and grabbed his hands. He watched as men, women, and children came by and warmly hugged Ana and Marco. There was a strong sense of family in this village. Everyone in the entire village was made to feel important, it seemed.

Tree thought about his own mother and father. He had not seen nor heard from either one of them since he left the military school and head out like he did, forever leaving their dreams for him behind. His mother, fervent in her desire to see him take up the violin and piano at a very early age. His father was equally fervent in his desire that Tree should have no part of such foolery and be placed into a military school for young boys. He could still hear his father's words like they were yesterday.

"We will get his ass firmed up for a position of leadership. He can't be a tough leader playing the damn piano and violin. Military men don't play a harp. The boy is going to be big. He is already big. By everything that I have in me, he is going to be a leader of men. A big and important leader of men, just like I was in the military. It is about honor and tradition, wife, not some damn piano-playing fancy boy. No sir, he will be a military man, that is a-certain. There is always going to be conflict somewhere in this world. The world needs their military leaders, always will."

As always, his father had won out. He was not apt to allow his mother to ever win out on any disagreement. It simply was not in him. So, military school it was for two years, now seeming like an eternity ago. The lonely nights of drunkenness that awaited him. The stench of lying in his own vomit could still be conjured up in his nostrils if he dwelled on it long enough. The warmth of the villagers engulfed his senses.

Adelina gently touched him on the arm.

"Señor Tree, you must come and eat. We did not make all of this food for you to stand by yourself. Come, let us eat."

Julia de la Garza smiled as Adelina brought Tree to the food line.

"Señor Tree Smith, this is Julia de la Garza. There are many families with de la in their names, so please do not be confused. Julia is a very good cook and her mole de panza is the best in Mexico. Why don't you try a bowl and have some corn beer, yes?"

Tree watched while Julia dished up a bowl of the soup and three steaming corn tortillas on the side.

"Here is a mug of the corn beer. Maybe you will like it with your food. I hope you enjoy the food Señor. It is Señor Tree, yes?"

"Yes, ma'am. It is. Thank you for the food and the corn beer. I will just go sit down on one of those benches and kind of stay out of the way."

Julia and Adelina watched him as he walked toward the benches under the old tree.

"That is the biggest man I have come to see in my life. He is as big as the old tree," said Julia.

"Yes, he is," said Adelina.

"I think he is as strong as this old tree, and I think maybe his heart is very big. I see the little children run up to him and grab his hands and he does not pull away. Little children are not afraid of him. We are not his people, but he eats with us and celebrates tonight. He honors us by staying in our home tonight before he goes back to his rancho. I think this gringo is a very good man. Maybe he will continue to be our friend and come across the river to eat and celebrate with us. I will take your place for a while. Why don't you go and sit with Señor Tree so he will not be lonely while he is in our village? There is some sadness in his eyes."

Julia quietly approached Tree as he sat one of the benches by himself.

"How is the mole and the corn beer, Señor Tree?"

"Oh, it is right tasty, ma'am. Actually, it is very good. I don't know exactly what you put in this, but it is really good. Especially when you add those corn tortillas and beer with it. I have not had any beer in a very long time."

"I am glad you like it. Some of the young men in our village drink too much corn beer and sing to their horses."

"Well, you certainly don't have to worry about me, ma'am. I will just drink enough to wash this good food down."

"I know you must feel out of place in our village. We are very glad you are here. I want to thank you for going after Gato Montes like you did. I do not know many men with that kind of courage. Most of our men would never go after a bandit like that, only Santiago maybe."

"Well, I suppose everyplace has folks like that. I don't consider myself any braver than the next man. I just went after him and his boys because Sheriff Brody asked me to."

"I understand, but you did not have to go. Some, maybe most, men, would not have done such a thing. It is very far to Mushaway. I have heard much about the Comanche warriors and what they do to their captives. It looks like your cut on your face is healing where they cut you. We hear Marco Martenez telling the priest about your cut. He told the priest that he sewed it up with tail from a horse and the magic plant medicine."

"That? That's just a little scratch. Yes, he done a little horsehair stitching. Doctored it with a little aloe vera stem."

"Yes, we use the aloe vera too for many things. It is very good for the burn on your hands or your face. Do you have a familia, señor?"

"Well, I have a mother and father if that is what you mean. They live in Ohio. That is a very long ways northeast of here as the crow flies. That is about all I have if they are still alive. I have not seen them since I left home to come out this way. What about you, do you have any family here in Montenegro?"

"Mi papa died some time ago. He could no longer see and his heart failed him. Mi madre died when I was very young. I have an aunt and uncle here. My brother works on your rancho. His name is Pedro de la Garza. He says you are a good patrón."

Tree looked at Julia in complete disbelief.

"Pedro is your brother?"

"Sí. He is my brother."

"Pedro and Franco are the two best vaqueros I have ever seen ride a horse. They do the work of several men on the ranch. The very best we have got."

"Can I ask you a question?"

"Yes, señor. It is nice to get to talk like this. Ask anything you want."

"Every year for the last three years, I have set up on that point right across the river there and watched some kind of celebration that takes place in your graveyard. Can you tell me what it is exactly that your village is doing? I mean, I may not need to be asking at all, it's just that, I have been wondering for a while."

Julia smiled at him.

"Señor, it is not a problem for you to ask me this question. This is our celebration. It is called Día de los Muertos. In your language, that means Day of the Dead. It is very simple, we celebrate the lives of all that have gone before us, just like they will celebrate my life when I die. In our celebration, you are never forgotten. Now, let me ask you a question, señor."

"Well, you answered mine, it is only right that you get to ask me one back, go right ahead."

"Why did you not come across the river and see for yourself when you saw us in the graveyard? We do not bite."

"To tell you the truth, I never once considered it. I would not have wanted to intrude on your village. I do not live here. It was just something I been wanting to know, that's all."

"I will tell you what, señor. If you are not afraid, I want to invite you as my guest this dos Novembre. This way you will see with your own eyes and heart what the celebration is like and you will not be sitting up on that hill wondering. What do you say?"

"What do I say? I am wondering what will your people say. I am a gringo, Ms. Julia. A red-haired gringo cowboy from across the river. Your folks might take a little offense to that."

"Señor Tree. Listen to me, please. The man and his banda that you chase into the Comancheria, he is responsible for our little angel, Prieto, stepping off into the river to never return. Pedro and Franco tell me that Gato Montes killed the young boy that he makes to ride with him, the one they call Coyote. This story travels fast, even across the river. They tell me that you find him, señor, and you make his grave. If your heart was not big, you would not have done this for a stranger. So, I think my people will love you for coming to Día de los Muertos. Not because you are not a Mexican, señor, but because you are a gringo who cares about all people. That is a good man. Besides, I think you will look handsome painted up in your Catrina. I will help you with that."

"I don't quite know what a Catrina is, Julia."

"You will, señor. You will. In a little while, they are going to make a big fire and the guitarra will play, some of our people will dance under the old tree. They dance to celebrate just to be living life. To breathe the air and to hold each other. Would you like to walk with me to the river while they make the fire, señor?"

"You need to get some water to bring back to the village? I can bring my horse along to help carry it if that is what you need."

Julia could not hide her laughter.

"No, I am not going to gather water. I just go to sit on a big rock and watch the water as it runs by. I like to hear the sound of the river as it comes by and smell the night smells."

"Are you sure you want me coming with you, ma'am? Sounds like you like being by yourself when you are doing this. I do the same thing at the ranch late of an evening."

"Señor Tree. I have just sat down a little while ago to visit with you. It makes me smile to hear you talk. I do not like to hear most men talk. Only my papa. He did not make the little talk. I like the men who do not make the little talk or that talk the big talk about themselves. No, it will make me happy if you walk with me to the river. If you do not want to go, no one can make you go with me."

"All right, Ms. Julia. I will be happy to walk with you to the river. You might need me to fight off a big snake or something."

TREE FELT COMPLETELY AT PEACE as he walked in the moonlight with Julia, slightly downhill toward the river. The beautiful moon was just starting its ascent from the east and was so close you could fairly reach out and touch it. She reached for his huge hand with her very small one. He did not quite know what to think as she grasped it and held onto it. She did not let it go as she led him to the big flat rock and sat down on it.

"The moon, it is very beautiful tonight, don't you think? It looks like we could walk right up to it. I think Dios lets us see the heavens when he brings the moon by this close for us to touch."

She sat as close to him as she could and laid her head against his shoulder.

"Señor Tree. I see a man sitting on a horse on the mountain when we have our celebration. I see him tres times. I did not know it was you, because I could not see too good. I wonder, who is this man and why does he watch from the mountain? Does he want to make trouble for us in our village? Now, I know that it was you.

"My heart, it has been very empty for a very long time. There has been no man that I let get near my heart. My papa spoke of men like you. I did not know if I would ever meet one. I pray in the church about this a little while ago. Now, I believe I have met the man like my papa told me about."

"What kind of man did your papa tell you about?"

"He told me that some men will take the last drink of water from a well when there is a drought and the village needs water. Those same men will drink the corn beer at night and sleep all day. They are the men that will not fight for you or fight at all."

"Julia, I appreciate the words you are saying. You are a beautiful woman that has a lot to offer a man. Me, I am just a cowboy, nothing else. I am nothing special to look at and I stand a lot taller than most men. Most women would find that somewhat peculiar if not flat-out annoying. My feet, well let's just say they are not your normal size. They are big. That is why they call me Tree Bigfoot Smith. At least one of them does. But he's my best friend. There is a lot about me you do not know."

Julia began laughing.

"Then you can be called Señor Tree Pies Grandes Smith. That means big feet in Spanish."

"I will tell you what Ms. Julia, I speak pretty good Spanish myself."

She stood up and pulled Tree's hand to stand up with her on the rock. She pulled his head down and gently kissed him. She held his hand as she stared at him.

"You, señor, you are like the arbol viejo in our village. They say it has roots as deep as the mighty branches above the ground. Your pies grandes, they are what keeps you tied to the ground. The old tree is tied to the ground where a big storm does not push it down. I think when a storm comes, you will still be standing and tied to the ground. Your face, it is like the rugged mountain. That is all right with me. It is a face that has seen trouble and pain. Maybe I can help you see joy and peace."

"Julia . . . We just met a little while ago. I am a gringo from across the river. Why in the world would you want someone like me?"

"My papa told me I would know when I have found this man. I pray in the church to Dios for this man. Now, Dios send me this man and he sits with me at the river. This man, he just did not know that Dios sent him to me."

"So, just like that, you know it's me? What kind of say do I have in the matter?"

Julia pulled his head down again and kissed him for a very long time. "I cannot force you, Señor Tree."

"I mean, I can't come over here and live. I have a ranch to run on the other side of the river. I have folks depending on me. And Mr. Gillstrap, he may never be coming back."

"I like you too much. Maybe you like me too much as well. That would make me very happy. If you like me too much, maybe we could get married. If we get married, I will go with you to your rancho and help you be the patrón of your rancho."

"Are you saying you are asking me . . . a woman is asking me to marry her?"

"If that is what you heard, yes, I am asking you to marry me. Is this a problem for the big red-haired gringo? A Mexican woman asking you to marry her when we have only known each other for a little while? I do know that you are the one I have been looking for and did not know it was you. That is all I can say."

She released his hand and turned and faced the moon. Tears began to flow.

"Maybe I should not have asked you to come to the river. You think maybe, that I make you come. I am sorry.

"But, señor, just like your ride to find Gato Montes. You could easily have not lived to see another day because of the Comanche, is this true? The sheriff, is it true that he nearly lost all of his life's blood but somehow was allowed to live?

"I have waited a long time for someone to come into my life such as you, even if it has only been for a short time, here you are and here am I. You did not come here looking for me and I did not go looking for you. Maybe our lives have come together at exactly the right time, just like when you found Marco. Maybe just by one blink of your eyes, and Marco and his madre Ana would never be together, and then I would maybe never meet you. Your looks, they are much prettier to other people than they are to yourself. Other men are also pretty on the outside, but their heart, it is not pretty. I see your heart with the little children and with Marco. I do not think you would be the man that would drink the last cup of water in the village when there is no more water. It is your heart I love, señor, even if you walk away and never come across the river again."

Julia pulled her dress hem to her eyes and wiped her tears.

Tree gently touched her shoulders and turned her around. Her eyes were still wet with tears, and her nose had begun to run.

"Here, take my bandanna. I don't quite know how to say this, but I just never felt really comfortable around girls or women at all in my life. I would not have even thought about touching you on the shoulder and was not trying to be forward. Women, well excepting you, they just scare me. I can't never tell what they are thinking. Maybe I should not even be trying. But for the most part, I just stayed away from them.

"Julia, I was in a military academy that my father made me join. I kilt a young man there."

Julia gasped and put her hands to her face. "You killed a man."

"Yes, I told you there were things about me you did not know. The commanders forced us to fight, or box as they call it. I did not want to fight, not at all. They forced both of us. When I finally fought back, I hit him only once in the face, and it crushed his nose. Pushed it into his skull."

Tree turned and looked up at the moon as he began to drag his shirt-sleeve across his eyes.

"It killed him right there. They did not charge me with anything. I was only sixteen years old. So, I left right then and headed out on a steamer boat to New Orleans. I stayed drunk for nearly two years trying to drown out what happened that day. Now, do you really want to marry someone like that? A fella that killed a person?"

Slowly she pulled him around and dabbed the tears from his face with her dress and then kissed him gently on the cheek. Then she pulled his wet face down to hers and kissed him on the lips.

"Señor Tree. We all have pain in our life we wish would have never come along. Now I know why your eyes are sad. Yes, it is true you may have killed someone. Killing someone for fun and killing someone by an accidente, the difference is as far as this river is long. Besides, Dios knows your true heart. Your heart is very big, but your eyes are very sad. Maybe if I kiss you again, your eyes will no longer be sad."

"I afraid I am not even a very good kisser, ma'am. I don't really know how to kiss, except Old Bonner, my horse and it is usually on his nose."

Julia reached down and took his right hand, which instantly dwarfed hers.

"Spread out your fingers, Señor Tree."

He spread them out and looked down oddly at her. Slowly she brought his large bear paw of a hand toward her bosom and placed it over her heart.

"Hold it there and do not be afraid," she said. Then she took her right hand and placed it over his heart.

"Do you feel our hearts beat? Mi La Santa Biblia says that Dios know me when I was in mi madre's womb. It is wonderful to know that Dios made the world and everything in it and to know our heart beats in our madre's womb before we were born on this earth. Since the time he makes the world, until right now at this time in his world, here we stand. Just you and me, señor. We are standing in Mexico, on a flat rock, in the moonlight, and we feel each other's heartbeat. I think maybe if you blink your eye, you miss Marco's horse when he tried to hide in the trees Maybe if we blink our eyes, Señor Tree, we miss the beatings of our hearts together. I think maybe Dios wants us to feel our hearts beat together, yes?"

Tree felt Julia's heart beating under his outstretched hand. He could feel his own heartbeat through her hand as it slowly pumped in his chest. His eyes filled with tears as he looked at her, weeping unashamed for the first time in his life.

"That is maybe the most profound thing I have ever heard anyone ever say in my entire life, Julia. Really, one of the most profound things when you put it like that with time and all.

"The real funny thing is, my good friend Cedar Jones across the river was left to tend things while I was gone. When I got back, he tells me the woman that came out to help with the cooking, they are getting married.

He just fell flat, head over heels for her. Now, I think they had a little while to get to know each other, but it wasn't very long. He told me he can't rightly think of anyone else since they met and even lost count during his cow-calf counting because of her. He even got off his horse on the wrong side a while back. I reckon he is in it for the long haul, if I know Cedar. He does not ever back up on his word. Not even for a minute."

"And what about you, Señor Tree?"

"No, ma'am, I don't never back up on my word. None at all. Yes, I will marry you. I cannot even believe I am here and we are doing this.

"I just have a feeling that after this night, I will probably be worse than Old Cedar when it comes to keeping my mind on my business because of you. I just hope I can keep my cow counts right and get off on the proper side of my horse, that's all."

Julia pulled Tree's head down and kissed him.

"I want to marry you, Señor Tree. I want to marry you after the Dance of the Sparrows before we go to the Día de los Muertos in Novembre to eat and to dance. This is my favorite day of the year, this Día de los Muertos. It is a little while from now. That is the day I want our hearts to be joined together forever until we die. On that day, I will remember all of my familia that has gone before me. I will also remember that day when I marry the man of my dreams that I meet just today and he feels my heart beat and I feel his big heart beat under my hand."

# CHAPTER 32

## The Dance of the Sparrows of Montenegro
## Día de los Muertos, November 2

THE WEATHER WAS TURNING MUCH cooler. There were no obvious signs that Azul de Norte would return to embrace Montenegro in the winter, with its unwanted effect on both men and beasts. The caterpillar's silky hairs were normal. The coats of the horses and cattle shined in the sunlight with their normal luster, not besieged with the stiff and dull mass of excessive hair brought on by a cold winter.

The spirits of the villagers were high, especially the women and young girls. Día de los Muertos was but days away. The news of Julia and Tree's marriage on Día de los Muertos had the whole village in a frenzy and consumed all of Julia's waking moments and most of her nighttime dreams. The women were spending hours in the afternoon under the great shaded canopy of el viejo arbol while the children played above and below. Some played king of the mountain on the pine benches with the young goats and then raced up the lowest limbs of the tree.

"I wished I had a little of their energy," said Adelina.

"The only ones who are sitting still are the two little girls in Ana Martenez's lap. See them playing with her braided hair and laying it over their heads. She loves the children and they love her."

Their hearts and spirits were light as they planned their dress for the wonderful celebration of life and rejuvenation and the great marriage ceremony. As usual, there were two children in Ana's lap at all times. She loved the children but still never spoke. Her cowhide paintings now adorned every door of every home in the village. Some were nube people and others were nube animals. Her beautiful picture of a woman dancing the Dance of the Sparrows now hung on the east wall of the inside of the church. Many stopped by to admire it every time they were in the church. Both women and men marveled at the beautiful dark roses painted to perfection in the woman's hair and her flowing blue dress as she twirled.

One of the women was secretly making Ana a red dress for the Dance of the Sparrows. Maybe she would be able to share her whole story through the dance. At least she would have a new dress to wear to Día de los Muertos if she did not dance. Ana's feet were completely healed because of the bear oil that Angelina continuously applied to them when she first arrived. She no longer shuffled along slowly, but was able to lift her feet and walk normally. Santiago and Adelina built a small adobe addition to their home. It had a cooking stove, beds, two cowhide chairs and a little fireplace. Marco now drew up Ana's water and left her clay jugs sitting by her door every two days. She used to take all of her meals with Santiago and Adelina. Now, she and Marco shared the little addition, and she was able to completely feed herself. She was very content to sit outside with her easel and paint from the pictures the sky gave her as the cloud people and animals came by on their way to the place where the land meets the sky. Sometimes, Adelina would see her with large stains of the tears as she stared at the clouds sitting on her cowhide chair in front of her easel. It hurt Adelina so to see her quietly weep without knowledge or a real way to find out why. Her son, Marco, was now here. At least they knew she came from Ojinaga and was captured by the Comancheros. Now, she had found her son. Adelina wanted desperately to know her pain so she might know how to ease it. But, Ana could not or would not speak. Her hearing was very keen, and she often smiled with her beautiful eyes and spoke with the touch of her hand when Adelina washed and combed her hair. Even though Marco did the cooking for he and Ana, Adelina still brought them food on occasion. When Ana lived with her and Santiago, she always ate very slowly and chewed each bite with meticulous concentration. It appeared that she was trying to squeeze every drop of flavor out of the delicious food that came from Adelina's stove. Santiago always told Adelina:

"This Nube, she takes days to eat a meal. Her food will get cold."

"Santiago, quiet! She chews her food like a lady, not like a wolf. She does not swallow it until it is chewed up." She tapped him on the chest.

"You, Santiago, should learn from Nube. Maybe your stomach will thank you. You should never tell a woman how to eat her food, especially if she prepares it for you. Now, go tend to your cows and your horses. You are getting in my way."

The women and the young ladies of age paid particular attention to the making of their veils for the Dance of the Sparrows. Each veil was made with intricate weaving of the dark laces. Some of the woven patterns looked like beautiful spider webs with perfectly spun octagons. All patterns were made to discreetly cover the eyes and mouth of the dancer, so as to not reveal their painted Catrina until after the dance. The dance restored the women and encouraged the young women of age, while the girls younger than fifteen eagerly awaited their time to join the beloved yearly ritual.

All of the village men quietly reflected on the coming dance and festival. It was only one of two occasions they dressed up in their dark pants, vests, white shirts with a little tie, and a dress sombrero. Sometimes there were more than one quinceañeras in a year, but there was only one Dance of the Sparrows before Día de los Muertos.

It was wonderful to see the women and their passion for the dance of their children.

Tree accepted the invitation from Julia to attend the celebration back on the river, the night they met and she proposed. Now, he was getting jittery.

He had made many trips across the river to meet with her during the months leading up to Día de los Muertos. The passion of the visits nearly overwhelmed both of them as they truly grew to know each other. It was all each could do to not be totally consumed in the desire for one another.

"Señor, we must wait. We must wait until the priest performs the marriage ceremony. Then, we will let the heat of our bodies come together as man and wife. I will be totally yours and you will be mine."

"Julia, these are your people. I just don't know. Can't we just get married now and not have to do it at your celebration?"

She would always put her fingers on his lips.

"Señor Tree, my people are now your people, and yours are mine. Even if they are just gringo vaqueros at your rancho. Besides, it will be much fun to help you paint on your Catrina. That is something I will do for you." She gently touched his face around the still-tender scar. "We will have to be very careful around your hurt places and not make it bleed. I have something very special in mind. Even when I go to live across the river at your rancho, we will still come to Montenegro for quinceañeras and Día de los Muertos. Maybe, you will understand why it is very special to me and our people. There is nothing to fear. I will hold your hand. Do not be afraid to walk with me among the stones. Besides, after the Dance of the Sparrows, you and I will be married by the priest in front of the village. After, when we walk among the stones of the dead, I will hold your hand as your wife. You will no longer be afraid."

THE CHURCH STEEPLE BELL RANG out three times at 10:00 a.m. on Novembre Dos, the day of the Dance of the Sparrows and the long-awaited Día de los Muertos.

Santiago, Tree, and all of the village men and boys of age had already lined up on each side of the steps of the church before the priest began to ring the bell. The priest was the only one allowed to look up at the women as they walked hand in hand in single file toward the church. Tree and Marco stood beside Santiago.

"Señors, as is our custom, when I tell you, remove your sombrero and hold it over your heart with your head down. Please do not look up until I tinkle this little bell."

He then walked out on the top step of the church and tinkled his little bell.

"Please remove your sombreros and place them over your heart and please close your eyes with your heads down upon your chest. As the Lord Jesus Christ creates life, we will now honor the bearers of that life and will witness The Dance of the Sparrows inside of our church."

The men could feel the breeze change as the procession of women passed silently by. They could hear the slight tapping of their sandals on the stone steps and the rustle of their dresses as they passed. The men and boys could smell the fragrant perfumes of the women and girls as the procession passed. The village wives had earlier painted all of the Catrinas for boys of age and for the men before they gave them their good clothes and told them to leave. Most of the men put on their dress clothes at Mr. Trujillo's leather shop and sipped a little mezcal he kept hidden there.

"This little drink will help to settle your stomachs and minds before we see the dance of the bearers of life."

Suddenly the priest tinkled his bell again.

"Señors, you may now enter the church and please line the walls of the church, as is our custom."

The men and boys kept their hats off and slowly filed into the church and formed a line around the walls. The young children were already sitting on the floor with some of the older children that were not yet of age holding the babies.

The men saw the women, all beautifully adorned in their dresses and veils. It was difficult to tell them apart without seeing their faces. They were in a circle with their faces pointing inward. The old white-haired guitarra player made his way through the circle of women. He carried a cowhide stool with him as he walked to the center of the circle. He sat down and properly settled his instrument on his leg. Slowly he began to play the Dance of the Sparrows on the low bass strings in constant movement and rhythm. One of the women slowly began to place her hands together like wings of a dove and bent over to the floor and fluttered her hands from the floor to her waist. Then she repeated the same move and this time she started at the floor fluttering her hands like birds' wings and slowly brought them over her head, fluttered them rapidly, and then released them. Slowly she brought them down to her side and stepped back into the circle with her face pointed inward. The guitarra player continued the slow methodic melody as each woman took her turn. There was muffled crying from some of the men and onlookers but none from within the circle of women. All of the young ladies of age held their hands to their side through the complete dance with their palms turned upward.

Some of the women would place their hands together like wings and never flutter them, just bring them to the floor and leave them there for a few seconds and then step back into the circle. Others would start at the floor fluttering their hands and then bring them over their heads and then separate them several times. Tree looked on, amazed at the pageantry and beauty of the dance, but he did not understand at all what the women were doing.

The last dancer was a very short woman in a dark red dress. She had a long braided pigtail behind her back. Slowly she walked to the center of the circle and stood close to the guitarra player. Her beautiful dark veil covered her facial features. The men and boys lining the wall and the women within the circle, knew it was Ana, the one they called Nube before her son came. Nube, who never speaks. Slowly, she placed her hands together like dove's wings and began to flutter them at the floor. She then brought them off the floor to her knees and then stopped. Then, she brought her hands to the floor again and gently began to flutter them like the dove. Slowly she raised her hands above her head and took them apart. She stared at the ceiling and then put her hands together again above her head and began to flutter them like the dove. Then she brought them to her heart. The she collapsed on the floor and placed her head in her hands and began to weep. The women and girls quickly surrounded her. Marco quickly started toward her. Santiago grabbed his arm.

"No, señor. You are not to go to the women in the circle. The women will take care of her. It is all right."

Quietly, the women wept with her and gently helped her to her feet while the guitarra player continued to play. Finally, the small woman returned to the circle with the women, all holding hands. The guitarra began to play a much brighter song as the women began to sway and move in a circular clockwise motion. Suddenly the column stopped. One of the women let go of the other women's hands. She walked straight to a man and slowly removed her dark veil. She gently placed it around his neck and tied it. Then, she kissed him on each cheek before returning to the circle. The circular motion continued until each woman stopped and removed her veil and placed it around her husband or any male relative who was still alive. Some that had no men alive in their family gave their veil to a close male friend in another family. There were but two women left and young girls of age with veils on. The procession stopped when Julia turned to face the men. Many of her former suitors looked on as she approached the large red-haired gringo in the room. He towered above her small frame by nearly one and a half feet. His frame was massively muscular and his face gentle. She stared at him as she slowly removed her dark veil, showing her beautifully painted Catrina. Tree looked into her eyes carefully hidden in the darkness of the painted black circles. She motioned him to bend his head over as she placed the veil around his neck and tied it. She looked deep into his eyes as she clasped his face in both of her hands. Great tears streamed down her face as she kissed him on each side of his face. She took his right hand and placed it over her heart. Then she placed her own right hand over his heart. Both of them, completely lost in the moment. She smiled as they felt each other's heartbeat. Taking her hand off of his heart, she placed her finger on his lips and then back to her lips. Slowly, she turned and walked back to the circle. The small woman in the dark red dress slowly turned and began to walk toward Santiago. Adelina had already placed her own veil around his neck. She watched from the circle as Ana approached Santiago. Large tears welled up in his eyes as she stopped in front of him. She looked at him deeply with her dark eyes hidden by her beautiful Catrina, painted on earlier by Adelina. She reached her hands to hold his face and looked back at Adelina. Adelina shook her head yes and clasped her hands to her heart. Ana slowly pulled her veil up and kissed each of Santiago's cheeks and then untied an object from around her neck. She motioned him to bend over as she tied it around his neck. He looked at it and smiled. It was a little hand-carved bear strung on a piece of rawhide. Santiago smiled at her as he looked at the bear. She was making fun of him for thinking she was a bear when he poked her with his gun the night she arrived. He hugged her mightily over the humor of her gift.

Then she walked to Marco. She pulled her veil off and motioned for him to bend his head down. She patiently put the veil around his neck and buttoned it before kissing him on each side of the face. Slowly she put her hands down and returned to the circle and was immediately embraced by Adelina.

The priest tinkled his bell and silence fell on the crowd with the exception of a crying child.

"We all love to hear the crying as well as the laughing of the children, yes? It is as if Dios is speaking to us out loud. All of the women will please file out of the church and take your places outside on both sides of the stone steps. I will now speak to the men and young men before they return to you."

As SOON AS ALL OF the women were gone, the priest closed the doors to the church and walked to the front to address the men and boys.

"It always makes my heart cry out to Dios when I see this dance. This Dance of the Sparrows. We are much more than sparrows. Dios teaches us from the sparrows. The Sparrows of Montenegro. How does he do this you ask?

"These women, they are not made like you and I. I think maybe that is a good thing. Like the mother sparrow, they take care of their baby sparrows. Ah, but some of the young sparrows, they never hatch from the egg. Others, they hatch from the egg but fall out of the nest, never to return. Then, some learn to beat their wings mightily and fly from branch to branch but injure a wing and must live in the tree until the winter comes and the mother bird can no longer feed it and it dies. Finally, there is the sparrow that beats their wings mightily and flies to the top branch of the old tree and then, señors, they fly. The Sparrows of Montenegro, they finally fly. You see, that is her greatest desire, this mother bird. To see the baby sparrows that fly from her nest. These women that Dios sends to help us. They bring us into this world. Some of us fly high into the air and never return to the nest. She smiles because her job is finally done. Others, she could not help. And for this, she weeps, as Dios in Heaven weeps with her to sustain her and takes the young sparrow into his warm embrace. Each of the women that have the young sparrows, they each tell their story through this dance. Some you see, the little bird falls out of the nest never to return while others see the jubilation of the free and flying sparrow. The madres, they want all of their sparrows of Montenegro to fly.

"So, go and see your mother bird. Tell her that she is more important to you than anything in this world that Dios has allowed you to live in. Go now to the front steps of the church where the women are lined on either side as is our tradition. It is time for Día de los Muertos. Time for eating and dancing. Before we walk to the celebration, I have a joyous occasion to celebrate on the steps of the church."

All of the men and young boys of age filed out of the church to the clapping of all of the women and girls outside. Each man donned his sombrero and made his way to his loved one. There were many hugs and tears as the women and men embraced. Finally, after a while, the priest tinkled his little bell and the crowd turned to look at him.

"I have been your priest for a very long time. Never, on Día de los Muertos, have I been so happy after such a long and very hard year starting with the Azul de Norte that nearly froze our village in the winter.

"Our Julia de la Garza has decided to marry on this day. Her madre and papa would be proud as they are watching down on her. I am sure that this secret was kept very quiet until this moment. Am I right?" He chuckled. "Julia, please bring Señor Tree to the top of the steps."

The villagers patted Julia and Tree on the arms and backs as they slowly made their way up the steps, his towering frame completely overshadowing hers. Two little girls grabbed Tree's hands as they walked up the steps.

"To the Village of Montenegro, this is Julia and Tree. I believe he looks very handsome in his painted Catrina, don't you? He is from the rancho across the river. You all know about him. It is not important that you know about him, it is important that Julia knows about him, because with this man, she will live until she is dead or he is dead.

"Who will give the ring to Julia on this blessed day?"

"I will give the ring," said Adelina. "The ring of mi abuela."

She walked up to Julia and kissed her on each cheek. She presented the beautiful old ring to Tree.

"And who will give the ring to Señor Tree?"

Mr. Trujillo stepped forward.

"I will give the ring. Señor Tree's finger, it is big as a bear. I have to specially make this ring."

All of the village roared in laughter as he held up the beautiful silver ring. He walked up to Julia and presented her the ring.

"My little Julia, I know you since you were a bambino. It makes me smile too much when I make this ring for your man here, this Tree that stands before us."

He placed the ring in her hand and folded her fingers over it. Then, he brought her hand to his lips and gently kissed the top of it.

The priest stood before them.

"Please take each other's hands and look into each other's eyes. I will ask you to each repeat what I say and then place the ring on the fingers that I show you.

First, to Julia, "With this ring, I become your wife. I will always honor you and love you forever."

Julia placed the ring on Tree's massive ring finger on his left hand.

"With this ring, Tree, I become your wife and will always love and honor you forever."

"Now, to Señor Tree. With this ring, I will become your husband. I will always love and honor you forever."

Tree looked down at the tiny ring in his great palm. He slowly picked up Julia's left hand and placed the ring on her fourth finger. He held her hands as he looked into her beautiful black eyes.

"Julia, with this ring, I become your husband. I will always love and honor you forever."

"To the Village of Montenegro, I announce this to you today, the day of Día de los Muertos. This is Señor Tree Pie Grande and Señora Julia de la Garza Smith. Let's welcome them in their marriage this day. They will stay here through celebration and tonight. Tomorrow, Julia goes to the rancho across the river to begin her new life. She promised she will come back across the river to see us often.

"Now, I have another important announcement on this blessed day.

"Look behind you toward the river. There is a woman and a man on horses from across the river. They are Señora Felicity Two-Feathers and Señor Cedar Jones. They live and work on the rancho across the river with Señor Tree. They tell Pedro and Franco who work on the rancho that they want to be married in our church on the same day as Julia and Tree. So, I ask the village to honor them in this request. They have been waiting for this day as long as Julia and Tree."

The villagers all turned to look at the two visitors sitting on their horses. Felicity with her beautiful black hair and hat was sitting on her horse with a little brown jacket and beautiful red shirt with a black bandanna tied around her neck. Cedar was wearing a black hat and vest and white shirt. He had a new green bandanna tied around his neck.

The priest began speaking again.

"Mi friends, the Apache have never been our friends, even though Dios makes them just like he makes each one of us. They have captured and enslaved the Mexican people for many años. More than any of us have lived.

"This woman, Felicity Two-Feathers, is Lipan Apache. She escaped the white man's school long ago when she was a young girl, I am told. She is not our enemy. Like each of us, she is a child of Dios. Like each of us in this world, she is made in the image of our Dios."

Santiago slowly started walking toward Felicity and Cedar. All of the village looked on in silence.

When he reached them, he looked at them as he smiled and spoke.

"You are welcome in our village and are welcomed to marry in our church by our priest."

He took each of their horse's reins and began to lead them to the church, passing all of the villagers.

When he got to the cobblestone steps, he stopped and turned the horses around to the villagers.

"Mi friends. See what Dios has done today. He brings us the great Tree, who marries our beloved Julia. We hope he allows our Julia and Tree to have little sparrows for the village to love and cherish even though they will live across the river from us. Maybe they will have rojo hair, yes? Now, he brings us the two people from across the river, Señora Felicity and Señor Cedar Jones, the one with the white hair. Pedro and Franco tell me much about both of them. It makes me very happy to let you see them on this blessed day in their lives and our lives. It is my wish that they too, will have little sparrows for us to love and cherish as their two hearts are joined together this day in our church by our priest. Please make them feel welcome."

The village women immediately began to come forward and extend their hands to Felicity, who burst into tears as they helped her off of her horse. The men did the same thing for Cedar as they helped him down. The little children ran toward Felicity and Cedar and began to hold their hands.

The priest tinkled his little bell several times before the villagers began to turn toward him and listen.

"It makes me very happy for our village to give the hand of friendship to our guests of honor from across the river. Who will give the ring to Felicity Two-Feathers today?"

Julia slowly walked toward Felicity. "I will give her this ring from mi madre's hand."

Felicity openly began to cry as Julia placed the ring in her hand.

"And who will give the ring for Señor Cedar Jones?"

Tree slowly let go of Julia's hand and walked toward Cedar.

"I have a little ring. It came off of my saddle. It was all I had. I hope it will fit. The same saddle that was on my horse Bonner when we came off of Mushaway Mountain. One of my fingertips was stuck in it when we got to the bottom, alive. Just like this ring helping to save my life that day as I desperately held on to it with one finger, Cedar Jones saved my life when I was very young when we first met up in the cavalry. He did not just save me from the Comancheros, he saved me from myself. His parents were killed by the Comancheros when he was but a boy. I am proud to say that Cedar Jones is my best friend. Well, maybe my second-best friend, now that I have Julia. Because of Felicity, my friend here is smiling every day, all day long. I am happy to give him this ring from my saddle. We will get him a better one, I promise. It will do for now."

THE MOOD OF THE VILLAGE was buoyant as Cedar and Felicity exchanged their wedding vows. They applauded when Felicity placed the saddle ring on his finger and he and Tree embraced. Then, they began the celebration of the food. The women and men of the village had spent much time in preparation of the food dishes and the corn beer. The young men of the village had spent several days dragging up firewood for the great bonfire that would carry the celebration deep into the night. Tree, Julia, Felicity, and Cedar were greeted by each family in the village and presented with some type of gift.

Santiago and Adelina presented them each with a large blanket.

"This blanket is the biggest one we have to help cover Tree and Julia. May it keep you both warm if the Azul de Norte comes to our village or yours again."

Santiago looked at Julia.

"Mi little bambino that I love and watch grow up. I have a horse for you. She is a good and patient horse, that I train. She will not slip and stumble as she carries you. Her name, it is Mariquita. This is like the ladybug. She is good for luck. Mr. Trujillo, he makes the saddle a long time ago. It is yours, Señora Smith. This is from Adelina and Santiago. We love you."

The guitarra player sat down on a cowhide chair and began to play after the meal. First, villagers just sat and listened to the beautiful music. Then, some began to rise and dance, including the little children. Julia stood up and took Tree's hands. "Come, let us dance."

"Julia, I don't reckon I really know how to dance."

"It is not to worry, señor, I just put my feet on top of your boots, and you just move around a little. No one will be watching us, I promise. Just dance with me and forget everything else. Tonight, I am your wife. Later, we will be happy that we are finally married. But for now, let us dance."

The dancing had gone on for at least an hour when the priest tinkled his little bell. "Everyone, let us gather by the stones. It is time to honor those that have gone before us."

Villagers listened intently as each person that wanted to speak was given the opportunity to do so. Julia held Tree's hand as he listened to the story of each person, relaying the life and death of their loved one as they stood next to their tombstone. Tree's eyes welled up with tears as he listened to the stories of the little babies and children and saw the tiny grave markers. He had never encountered such a group of people in his life. People that truly cared about each other and life. As soon as each person finished speaking, they placed a little dish of the deceased loved one's favorite food next to the grave stone. For the little babies and children, they placed a small skull made of sugar.

Tree turned and looked at Cedar and Felicity. They were completely absorbed in the moment and each other. They had their blanket spread over both of them and were holding hands and talking quietly to each other as they witnessed the celebration.

Finally, everyone in the village had finished speaking. The priest tinkled his little bell.

"Now, before one of our village elder speaks, is there anyone else that has someone to speak about? It is not too late."

Slowly, Ana Martenez made her way to the priest. She motioned Adelina and Santiago to come to her. They both looked at each other and then to Marco in surprise. They walked up to her and she stuck out each of her hands and grasped theirs.

"Mi name, it . . . is . . . Ana Martenez."

The entire village gasped just to hear Nube, the one who never spoke, actually speaking, albeit haltingly.

Marco, sat in silence as his madre spoke. He began to openly weep as she struggled to get the words out.

"I not speak the word for a long time. Comancheros come to our home and kill mi husband and mi little baby. Marco, he hides and they not kill."

Large tears continued welling up in Marco's eyes, now turning to a flood of emotions.

Adelina and Santiago began to cry as she continued.

"Comancheros take me back to Mexico, somewhere in the mountains. I was slave to them. Never talk, just be . . . slave, cook and carry . . . wood for fire. I live there a long time. I leave when they go leave the camp to hunt. I walk many, many days by the river . . . it is very cold. I have a blanket and no food. Then . . . I come here when Azul de Norte come. I see a light in Santiago and Adelina's home. I come to that light, but I am too cold to move anymore."

She turned and looked at Santiago, smiling.

"This man, Santiago, he thinks I am bear sleeping on his porch. But he no shoot at me. They take me into the warm and feed me. Take care of my feet. Now, Señor Tree find my Marco and bring him to Montenegro. I think Dios, he makes sure Señor Tree see my Marco's horse and bring him to me. Marco tells me that mi husband and the little baby, he put them in the ground by a rock on the river where we live when the Comancheros come. One day, he will take me there to be close to them again."

She turned slowly and kissed Adelina and Santiago on the cheeks before slowly walking back to Marco.

The priest, tears in his eyes, looked at the villagers.

"If there is no one else, I have asked Mr. Trujillo, our leather maker, to speak to the village on this day of Día de los Muertos."

Mr. Trujillo was squatted down on one knee and slowly rose to address the crowd.

"It has been a wonderful day, this Día de los Muertos. Would you not agree? The misery that Azul de Norte brought us last winter was not without reward. It also brought us Ana Martenez to our village hoping to get out of its cold embrace. Señora Ana, we use to call Nube. Why Nube? You all know of her love to paint the nube people and the nube animals when Dios sends in the sky as they float by our village. Now, she paints for all families in the village. Her beautiful painting of the Dance of the Sparrows hangs in the church, for all to see and love.

"Then, we see and hear the unspeakable things around Pablo, this Gato Montes. The Santa Biblia says that Dios sends rain on the just and the unjust and that vengeance is his. We do not know why such a man as this is allowed to breathe the air that Dios provides. He brings Señor Tree into our lives. He travels many days to track down this man and his banda to bring them to justice for what they have done. The Comanches, they find them first and then capture Señor Tree. You all see the scar on his face from the Comanches. They make him ride his horse off the mighty Mushaway mountain. He lived. He lived and he find Marco Martenez and bring him to this village where he finds his madre. How wonderful can this be? Then, our Julia finds this man Tree and now she is his wife, on this day. This wonderful day of Día de los Muertos. She goes with him tomorrow to live at the rancho across the river. Maybe one day, Dios will bless them with a little child. If this happens, maybe they bring him back to the arbol viejo to learn to climb, yes? Just like all of the blessed children in this village. They learn to climb the arbol viejo with a few goats that like to get on the low limbs. This Señor Tree, he will be a great and everlasting friend and defender of our village of Montenegro. He stands there, just like the arbol viejo. Then, Dios brings us this day Felicity and Cedar Jones. They sit over there now with the blanket as one.

"So, we are very blessed in our village. We have food to eat and clothes to wear. We have our families and especially the little children. Those here, and those we spoke about this day that have gone before us. It is a very blessed life that we live. There will be days of sunshine and surely days of rain and cold. It is easy to live when the sun is bright and everything is good. It is when the skies turn gray and release their rain and snow that it becomes difficult to keep putting one foot in front of the other. But also, it is during these dark and gray times that we learn the most. So, like Ana Martenez. When the sky is cold and foreboding from all the Azul de Nortes that will come our way. Just hold each other's hands and put one foot in front of the other. In Julia's case, just put your feet on the mighty feet of Señor Tree and he will carry you."

# CHAPTER 33

The villagers gathered on each side of the dirt street as Tree, Julia, Felicity, and Cedar rode out of the village. People smiled and waved to them.

"All of you must come back soon to Montenegro," Marco said. "I will make you some good goat cheese."

Tree touched the brim of his hat as they left.

"I think Tree and some riders are coming in, boys," said DeWitt. "They are four horses and I recognize one to be Mr. Tree as big as he is."

All of the boys were sitting inside the bunkhouse when the four newlyweds came in. Tree and Cedar were each holding their radiant bride's hands as they came in the bunkhouse door.

"Well, life sure takes some fancy turns every so often," said Tree as he looked at all of the men.

"Looks like we have certainly improved the place. Now, we have two women that will grace this ranch with their presence. I just meant to take Marcos Martenez across the river to Montenegro to be with other Mexican people a while back. Said that is what he wanted. He found his mama over there. Kidnapped by the Comancheros a long time ago.

She escaped them in the early winter and made her way somehow to the village. Barely alive when she got there. She recognized Marco as a man even though she had not seen him since he was a little boy.

"This here is my wife Julia. I saw her in the graveyard several times from that little point up there. I did not understand what she and her people were doing in the graveyard, eating and dancing. I do now. They let me be a part of it. I am really proud that they did. It changed my outlook on life, most likely forever. We should all be celebrating each other's lives around here while we are alive." He turned and looked at Julia. "And in death too, I reckon. We aren't just shooting stars, you know. Julia and I were married yesterday. She has come to live on the ranch with me. There is only one problem. Cedar and Felicity came across the river and were married at the village church yesterday as well.

"I told him they can live in the main headquarters house where she has been living. I will stand by that. We are going to build a house right over there next to it. During the meantime, both of these ladies will be able to stay in the main house, and Cedar and I will bunk with you all. I don't want any complaining. Now, all of you need to head out to your jobs. This ranch has got to make a return."

Cedar and Tree took both women to the main house before heading to the barn to unsaddle and feed the horses. Bonner whinnied loudly as Sister approached. She nickered back. Both horses smelled noses over the fence. She playfully laid her ears back and nipped at his neck.

"I believe Old Bonner is glad to see little Miss Sister," said Cedar.

"I think you're right. They are kind of attached at the hip. I believe Ms. Mariquita here will get along fine with both of them. Normally mares will fight. These two don't. Or at least they did not coming over from Montenegro."

"I swear, Tree. Isn't it the craziest thing? These women have all of a sudden come into our lives. Who in the world would could have ever dreamed something up like this? I mean, this woman has changed the way I look at everything. She's even got me pulling my boots off when I come into the house. Who would have ever dreamed of that? And the big thing, I am just happy to pull them off. No whining or nothing. It just makes her happy for me not to be tracking in cow poop on the floor from the bottom of my boots. I really never gave it any thought until she came along."

"Cedar, my woman believes in Dios. Now, I do too. She believes that Dios knew who we were in our mother's wombs and that nothing that happens in our life is happenstance, like me finding Marco just by just barely seeing the tail of his horse before it disappeared, or them Comanches letting me have a chance to live when they killed the others. Just like Felicity riding in here and completely knocking you out of your saddle and interrupted your cattle counting. I suppose Dios knew that in all of our travels, one day our trails would intersect with these two fine women. He probably knew long ago that we needed them far more than they ever needed us. Now, all I can ever think about is Julia and that night on the river, when we felt each other's hearts beat on a big flat rock under the full moon.

"I think she wants to have children. She calls them her little sparrows. The Sparrows of Montenegro. Maybe Dios will grant that wish."

# ABOUT THE AUTHOR

BJ Mayo was born in an oil field town in Texas. He spent the first few years of his life living in a company field camp twenty-five miles from the closest town. His career in the energy industry took him to various points in Texas, New Mexico, Colorado, Utah, Louisiana, Bangladesh, Australia, and Angola West Africa.

He and his wife were high school sweethearts and have been married for forty-seven years with two grown children. They live on a working farm near San Angelo, Texas. He is also the author of *Alfie Carter*. Find out more at bjmayo.com.